THE BRIDAL SUITE

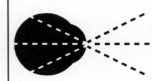

This Large Print Book carries the
Seal of Approval of N.A.V.H.

THE BRIDAL SUITE

ROCHELLE ALERS

THORNDIKE PRESS
A part of Gale, a Cengage Company

GALE
A Cengage Company

LIBRARY OF CONGRESS CIP DATA ON FILE.
CATALOGUING IN PUBLICATION FOR THIS BOOK
IS AVAILABLE FROM THE LIBRARY OF CONGRESS

ISBN-13: 978-1-4328-7524-4 (hardcover alk. paper)

Published in 2020 by arrangement with Dafina Books, an imprint of Kensington Publishing Corp.

Printed in Mexico
Print Number: 01   Print Year: 2020

I dedicate *The Bridal Suite* to my granddaughter, Puerto Rican princess Nadia Gabrielle Gonzalez. Grammie loves your mofongo!

ACKNOWLEDGMENTS

I cannot end this series without acknowledging those responsible for making it so very special for me:

Tara Gavin — editor extraordinaire. You are simply the best.

Kristine Mills — The covers are magnificent. I thank you for your incredible artistic talent.

Nancy Coffey — agent and friend. When we first talked about the sister-girl road trip I don't believe we knew where it would take us.

Steven Zacharius — Kensington CEO. Thank you for leaving the door open so I could come back home.

The entire publishing staff at Kensington Books. You are one of a kind. Stay strong.

Start children off on the way they should go, and even when they are old they will not turn from it.

— Proverbs 22:6

CHAPTER 1

"Miss Santiago. Miss Washington is waiting inside for you."

Nydia opened her eyes. She hadn't realized she had fallen asleep for the second time that morning. The text message from a car service indicated a five a.m. pickup in front of her parents' West Harlem brownstone. The drive to the Westchester regional airport was accomplished quickly, and a sleek private jet was on a runway awaiting her arrival.

She was one of seven passengers on the aircraft scheduled for several stops, with San Diego, California, as the final destination. Once they were airborne, members of the flight crew served a sumptuous breakfast prepared by an onboard chef, and as soon as the cabin lights were dimmed she reclined her seat and slept until the attendant woke her minutes before noon to inform her they were approaching the Louis Armstrong

11

New Orleans International Airport.

Once the jet landed, she was whisked through to baggage claim and found a car service driver awaiting her arrival. She got into the comfortable sedan and promptly fell asleep again.

When they arrived, the chauffeur opened the rear door, and she placed her hand on the man's palm as he assisted her out of the vehicle. "Thank you." Tilting her head, she sniffed the hot, humid air and smiled. There was something about the way New Orleans smelled Nydia found intoxicating.

The hotel's bellhop rushed over to the town car and removed her bags from the trunk. Jasmine's fiancé had made the arrangements for her to stay at the boutique hotel where Cameron rented a suite.

When she'd asked her friend why her fiancé lived at a hotel, Jasmine had revealed his living arrangements were temporary; he had recently purchased a three-story Victorian converted warehouse with a rear courtyard and a garage with enough space for three vehicles. She said they planned to use the first floor for entertaining family, friends, and clients, and the two upper floors for their personal use.

Nydia took a step and bit down on her lower lip to stifle a gasp when she felt a slight twinge in the incision from a recent surgical procedure. It was a reminder that it had only been three days since she was medically cleared to travel. She had ignored what had become chronic pain in her right side for several weeks until it had become so debilitating that she was forced to call her father and plead with him to take her to the emergency room. Forty-five minutes after their arrival, she was wheeled into the operating room for the removal of a ruptured appendix. The surgery could not have come at a worse time, because she had been scheduled to fly down to New Orleans for the wedding.

This was her third trip to the Big Easy in thirteen months. The first was last July when she, Jasmine Washington, Tonya Martin, and Samara, Tonya's daughter, drove from New York to visit their former coworker, Hannah DuPont-Lowell. So many things had happened to Nydia and her friends since they were downsized from an international Wall Street private investment firm.

Nydia, and two dozen other employees, could have never imagined when they walked into Wakefield Hamilton on a warm, sunny morning in May that it was to become their last day of employment. The company had merged with another institution, and although they were given generous severance packages, none were offered the option of staying and commuting to Trenton, New Jersey.

She, Tonya, and Jasmine had returned to New Orleans in October as bridal attendants for Hannah's wedding to her former high school classmate St. John McNair. And Nydia's third trip would have been this past June to witness Tonya's wedding to St. John's cousin, Gage Toussaint, if she hadn't been hospitalized. She was back again to stand as maid of honor for Jasmine's wedding to Cameron Singleton. A wry smile parted her lips. She didn't know what it was about the Crescent City, but it was obvious her friends had been seduced by the food, music, and the men.

Gathering her purse, Nydia slowly followed the bellhop into the Louis LaSalle. The automatic doors opened, and the scene unfolding before her eyes made her feel as if she had stepped back in time. Marble floors, a trio of massive crystal chandeliers, overstuffed brocade-covered chairs and sofas welcomed one to linger a while. Gilt-framed paintings of men and women dressed in their finery from a bygone era hung from the ornately papered walls. An enormous bouquet of fresh flowers overflowing a hand-painted glazed vase set on a large round mahogany table was the lobby's focal point.

"Bienvenido de nuevo a La Gran Fácil."

Nydia turned and smiled. She hadn't noticed Jasmine's approach. The affection she felt for her friend was reflected in her smile as she extended her arms and hugged Jasmine. She was still attempting to wrap her head around the news that her former coworker was pregnant and planning to marry the father of her unborn baby in two weeks.

"I can't believe you're welcoming me back as if you've lived here for years instead of a few months," Nydia teased.

Jasmine returned her smile. "I never thought I'd ever move from the Big Apple, but now that I live here, I've come to love the Big Easy."

Easing back, she studied Jasmine's face. The interior decorator turned human resource specialist's longer, coal-black, wavy hair framed a face that was noticeably fuller than when they were last together. The genes she had inherited from her African-American father and Filipino mother had blended with a gold-brown complexion, slightly slanting eyes, a pert nose, and lush mouth. Nydia could see why Cameron

15

hadn't been able to pull his gaze away from Jasmine at Hannah's wedding reception.

"You're actually glowing."

"Don't you mean growing?"

"Please, Jazz," Nydia drawled. "You don't look pregnant." Her friend had just completed her first trimester.

"It's the dress. I'm already losing my waistline." Jasmine looped an arm through Nydia's. "Come with me. I'll take you to your room." She signaled for the bellhop with Nydia's bags to follow her. "Oh, I forgot to ask. How are you feeling?"

"The incision is still a little tender, but other than that I'm good."

"Good enough to dance salsa at my wedding?"

Nydia met Jasmine's dark eyes. Both had agreed how much they enjoyed dancing to live Latin music. "You hired a band?"

A mysterious smile touched the corners of Jasmine's mouth. "I couldn't get one on such short notice, so I had the DJ compile a playlist with some popular dance numbers."

They rode the elevator to the fourth floor in silence. Jasmine had confided to Nydia that only Hannah, Tonya, and Cameron's family knew she was going to marry him the afternoon following his parents' fiftieth

16

he's quite talented."

"Is he better than Tonya's in-laws?"

Jasmine shook her head again. "Not quite. There's something about the food from Chez Toussaints that's indescribable. That's why I told Cameron I wanted Eustace and Gage to cater our wedding."

"You have to remember that Tonya's no slouch when it comes to throwing down in the kitchen," Nydia reminded Jasmine.

She turned and made her way down a narrow hallway, peering into a half bath before entering the bedroom that also included an ensuite spa-bath. Yards of diaphanous white sheers draped a California-king mahogany four-poster bed and wall-to-wall, floor-to-ceiling windows. A seating area with a brocade cream-colored chaise, a small mahogany round table with two pullup chairs, and a bookcase filled with hardcover and paperback books and magazines provided a space to sit and while away the hours. The heavy, dark furniture was the perfect contrast to the off-white furnishings.

"Coño, mija," Nydia drawled. "You really hooked me up."

"It's the least I could do for *una princesa puertorriqueña.*"

Nydia couldn't stop laughing. She'd occasionally referred to herself as a Puerto

Rican princess. Other than family members, Jasmine was the only one with whom she occasionally spoke Spanish. Her friend had learned the language from her mother and Tagalog from her grandparents whenever she'd visited the Philippines.

Jasmine followed Nydia into the living room and sat on the love seat, while Nydia sat on the sofa. "I knew you would like the bridal suite."

Nydia sobered and gave Jasmine an incredulous stare. "You put me in the bridal suite?"

"Yes. It's one of the nicest ones in the hotel. If you're going to live here for a month, then you should have the best amenities. Other than the connecting suite where Cameron and I stay, all of the others only have minibars and microwaves. And it's the least I could do for my maid of honor. And if you hadn't strong-armed me into going out with Cameron, I never would've been given the chance to become a romance novel heroine and experience a happily ever after."

"I didn't strong-arm you, Jazz. I said you had nothing to lose by having one dinner date with the man."

Jasmine patted her belly over the sundress. "And look what it got me."

20

"It got you what you've always wanted: a baby and a husband who doesn't need your money. Cameron is nothing like that slug you married who not only parked his shoes under another woman's bed and got her pregnant, but subsequently snipped his cheating-ass dick and denied you a child. And on top of that the slimeball tried to pimp you out of a business you'd shed blood, sweat, and tears to make a success. Fastforward a few years and you meet Cameron Singleton, who'd professed he didn't want to marry or father children and boom! He takes one look at Ms. Jasmine Washington and folds up like an accordion." She pressed her first two fingers to her lips, and then pantomimed dropping a mic. "Santiago out."

Jasmine laughed until her sides hurt. "You know you missed your calling. You should've become a stand-up comedienne instead of an accountant."

Nydia shook her head, and a mane of loose, dark-brown curls moved around her small, round face as if taking on a life of their own. "I'd never be able to come up with enough jokes to earn a living, and I'm not about to recreate stories about some of my crazy family members or people I grew up with, because that would be dangerous

21

to my health. They'd know immediately who I was talking about. Some of the dudes in my old neighborhood have street names like Loco Carlos or Diablo Flacito and are walking billboards of ink advertising drugs, murder, and prison."

Jasmine stopped laughing. "Talk about earning a living, have you given any further thought about investing in Hannah's Du-Pont Inn? You know she's expecting you to be her CFO." Nydia had become the last holdout when it came to investing in Hannah's new project to turn her ancestral home into an inn. Although Nydia found the offer quite tempting, she still wasn't certain whether she wanted to relocate. Her family was in New York, and the opportunity to secure a position with a company looking for a certified public accountant with a salary commensurate with her education and experience had kept her from committing to becoming an innkeeper.

"I have thought about it. It is very enticing."

"If that's the case, then what's stopping you, *chica* ? And if you tell me you're seeing Danny again I'm going to go, as you say, ape-shit."

A slight frown marred Nydia's youthful-looking features. She'd recently celebrated her thirty-third birthday, yet she was still mistaken for a college coed and carded whenever she ordered alcohol. And with her recent weight loss of more than ten pounds her petite frame could ill afford to lose, she appeared even younger.

"I told you before, I'm done with Danny. You know I was angry with Wakefield Hamilton because they'd fired us without warning, but now that I look back I know it's the best thing that ever happened to me. If not, I still would've been renting a furnished apartment in my nosy landlady's house and hoping, wishing, and praying for Danny to get his act together. Once Tonya told me I could sublet her apartment and I moved in, I was able to experience what it meant to be in complete control of my life for the first time since moving out on my own, because I don't have someone clocking who's coming and going in and out of the apartment. And one of the many perks in living in the renovated building is the security. Closed-circuit cameras are integrated within the intercom system, which allows me to see who is ringing my bell. So, even if Danny does happen to find out where I live, I don't have to let him in."

"I know you're living out Tonya's renewal lease until next year, but what are you going to do once it expires? Are you going to take it over under your name?"

Nydia exhaled an audible breath. Jasmine was asking a question she'd asked herself over and over the closer it got to the lease's expiration date. "Lately I'm not sure. I know if I had a permanent position with a company I would definitely consider it. I gave Tonya the entire year's rent in advance from my savings, and while I'm doing the books for several restaurateurs, I earn enough to cover nearly three-quarters of the monthly rent, which means with the new lease I'd have to dip into my savings to make up the difference and pay for utilities and buy groceries."

"Have you begun looking for something permanent?" Jasmine asked.

"Not yet. I've decided to wait until after Labor Day to begin a job search. My brother's friend who is an intelligence analyst for the FBI has been urging me to apply to the Bureau as an accounting and finance special agent." Nydia knew she had shocked Jasmine with this disclosure when her jaw dropped.

"Why the FBI?" Jasmine questioned.

"Because I have the qualifications: bachelor's degree in forensic accounting, an MBA and CPA."

"What other qualifications are they asking for?"

"I'm within the age range, and have more than three years' professional experience. Of course I'd have to pass a security clearance background check and a physical."

Jasmine stared at the framed watercolor of a Venetian palazzo overlooking a canal with moored gondolas. "You're an independent woman with options as to where you want to take your future."

Nydia leaned forward. "Why would you say it like that?"

Her dark-brown eyes met a shimmering clear-brown pair with glints of green and gold in a complexion that reminded Jasmine of frothy mocha icing. "All my life I've relied on men to take care of me. First there was my father, and then Gregory Carson, who was my first lover and mentor. Gregory was thirty years my senior and he gave me what I needed to become a much sought-after successful interior decorator. I met Raymond Rios after Gregory died and married him a year later. I probably still would be married to him if I hadn't discovered he'd cheated on me. Now three years later it's Cameron Singleton."

"What's so wrong with that, Jazz? So many women never experience a man's protection. And after what you had to go through with Raymond, you've been given a second chance at love."

Her eyelids fluttered. "I know, but I wanted to wait until after giving birth to marry Cameron."

A rush of color suffused Nydia's complexion, and she clenched her teeth. "Why? So you can become a baby mama? Do you have any idea how many women would love to change places with you? I know girls who've had wonderful relationships with their boyfriends until they mention the B word, and then their men act as if she's come down with bubonic plague. Halfway through our second year my college roommate told me her boyfriend wanted her to have an abortion over the winter break because he claimed he couldn't afford to take care of another child. That's when she found out that he had two other kids and both his baby mamas had taken him to court for child support."

Jasmine smothered a gasp. "Did she have the abortion?"

Nydia nodded. "It was either get rid of the baby or lose the man. A month after she had the procedure he broke up with her. Talk about a hot mess. She had an emotional breakdown and dropped out of school. When I called her parents' home, they told me she'd moved to Arizona to live with her older sister. Now back to you, Miss Soon-to-be Mrs. Cameron Singleton. You probably think Cameron wants to marry you because you're carrying his child, but didn't you tell me he's admitted to being in love with you?"

"He has, and I'm in love with him."

"Then, what's the problem? Has he said anything about you going into business with Hannah?"

"No. He couldn't because I'd given Hannah my word and we'd finalized our business agreement even before I realized I was pregnant."

"The man has allowed you to be an independent woman and control your life, something his father hadn't permitted his mother. So, why are you being a drama queen? I didn't come down here during the hottest month of the freaking year to listen to you talk about marrying Cameron after you push out his baby. I love you like a sister, but, so help me, Jazz, I *will* go apeshit and show my natural ass and end up on the local news if you don't go through with this wedding."

"You wouldn't!" Jasmine whispered.

"Girl, please," Nydia drawled. "There's a

crazy side to Nydia Stephanie Santiago you don't ever want to see." She snapped her fingers. "I can bring the *funk* with the best of them."

"I didn't say anything about not marrying Cameron. I was just saying —"

"Don't say anything else, Jasmine," Nydia interrupted. "Either it's hormones or pre-marital jitters, but I'm going to help you get through this. I remember my sister-in-law's mood swings when she was pregnant with her first child. She drove my brother crazy when she began calling him Nelson rather than Luis, which happens to be his middle name. We later discovered one of her exes was named Luis, and she did not want to relive her past, so to humor her we all started calling him Nelson."

"What did he say to that?" Jasmine asked.

"My brother worships his wife, so she can do or say no wrong. Personally I think he goes along with her just to keep the peace. Being a cop is stressful enough without coming home to bitchin' and moaning. His motto is: happy wife, happy life."

Jasmine noticed Nydia's eyelids drooping as she attempted to stay awake. She pushed to her feet, reached into the pocket of her dress, and placed two key cards on the coffee table. "I'm sitting here running off at the mouth when you need to rest after getting up before dawn. I'm going upstairs to my suite to take a nap before we get together later for dinner. I'll meet you in the lobby at seven."

Nydia stood. "Will Cameron be joining us?"

"I'm not sure. He's scheduled an early dinner meeting with a client, and I'm not certain how long it will last."

"Tell him I really appreciate his taking care of my travel arrangements."

She nodded, smiling. "You can tell him yourself when you see him." Turning, she walked to the door, opened it, and then closed it behind her. She'd wanted to tell Nydia that she *was* experiencing premarital jitters. That she'd committed to marrying a stranger — a man who had gotten her pregnant the first time they'd made love, despite using protection.

Jasmine had vacillated whether she wanted to marry before or after the birth of her child because she wanted Cameron to want her for his wife and not because she was carrying a Singleton. Openly admitting to Nydia that he loved her had helped her to acknowledge she'd made the right decision to marry the father of her unborn child at this time. Nydia said she loved her like a sister, and it was the same with her when it came to the gifted young accountant who'd graduated college with honors and passed the CPA exam on her first attempt; she could always count on her friend not to sugarcoat what she needed to hear. Not only had she asked Nydia to be her maid of honor, but she also planned to ask her to become godmother to her son or daughter.

CHAPTER 2

Nydia punched the elevator button for the lobby. She'd put off taking a nap until after she'd eaten the caprese, chicken salad and mixed greens with a balsamic dressing. She then set the alarm on her cell phone to wake her at five o'clock, which gave her time to unpack and take a bath. Relaxing in the garden tub and luxuriating in the feel of pulsing jets of water on her body for the next half hour had revived her to where she was ready to reconnect with her friends and enjoy the warm camaraderie they'd developed over the past year.

At thirty-three she was the youngest of the quartet, and there was a twenty-plus-year age difference between her, Tonya, and Hannah; however, at no time had she ever thought of them as mother figures. To her they were her older sisters. Nydia still marveled that she was able to hold her own when interacting with them, perhaps because she tended to say exactly what came to mind. Jasmine accused her of having no filter, but the truth was she detested duplicitous people. She preferred folks to speak their mind, even if she didn't agree with them.

The elevator stopped at the lobby, the doors opened, and as soon as she exited the car she saw Tonya, Hannah, and Jasmine standing together near the table with the massive bouquet. Tonya spied her first and approached Nydia. It was apparent marriage had more than agreed with the professional chef. A light-blue sleeveless linen sheath dress flattered Tonya's toned body, while her short, gray-flecked hair flattered a flawless dark complexion radiating good health. Twin dimples dotted her cheeks when she smiled.

"Welcome back, sweetie."

Nydia hugged Tonya. "I'm sorry I missed seeing you marry your *muy*-sexy Papi."

Throwing back her head, Tonya laughed. "When I told Gage you were coming down, he said he couldn't wait to meet you."

Nydia had caught a glimpse of the talented musician for the first time when Hannah had taken them to a jazz club during their initial visit to the city, and she doubted that she was the only woman in the place transfixed by the handsome trumpet player's Creole, Cajun, and African ancestry. Not only was he a gifted musician, but he was also a skilled Parisian-trained chef. Tonya and Gage Toussaint had begun a whirlwind romance once she became an apprentice at his family's local restaurant, Chez Toussaints, and were married eight months later.

Nydia looped her arm through Tonya's. "I'm planning to be here for a month; that is, if the heat doesn't get to me like it did last summer." She, Jasmine, and Tonya had cut their two-week stay short because of record temperatures and humidity.

Tonya shook her head. "After moving down here I realize I'd rather put up with the heat than the cold and snow."

Hannah joined them. The tall blonde had put on a little weight since she'd married St. John, and Nydia had to acknowledge she looked wonderful. "Welcome back," she drawled, smiling.

Nydia's lids fluttered as she forced back the tears filling her eyes. She hugged Hannah, the recognizable scent of Chanel No. 5 wafting to her nose. Everyone was welcoming her back as if she'd left home. She hadn't spent as much time in New Orleans as Tonya or Jasmine, yet there was something about the city that beckoned her to come and stay. It wasn't called the Big Easy for nothing, because she always felt completely relaxed whenever she came for a visit.

"I'm glad to be back. And you're looking good, Mrs. McNair." Hannah was dressed entirely in white: cropped slacks, a man-tailored shirt, and ballet-type flats. Her silver-streaked, chin-length platinum hair was pulled off her face with a black-and-white pinstriped headband.

An attractive blush darkened Hannah's fair complexion. "I feel wonderful."

"Should that be attributed to married life?"

A fringe of pale lashes shadowed her cheekbones when she demurely lowered eyes. "St. John's a wonderful husband." Her green eyes narrowed as she gave Nydia a long, penetrating stare. "You've lost a lot of weight."

Nydia glanced down at the navy-blue stretch capris she'd paired with a white tank top. "Not so much that I lost my booty."

"Stop playing yourself," Jasmine said, as she gave her a *you have to be kidding me* look. "I didn't say anything earlier, but I wanted to tell you that you look a hot mess. And I'm going to make certain as long as you stay here, you'll have regular meals and gain some of that weight you lost."

Nydia wanted to tell her friends that the pain before the appendectomy had been so debilitating she had almost stopped eating altogether. Once she was discharged from the hospital she'd refused to take the prescribed opioid because she feared becoming addicted, so she endured the lingering discomfort as she waited for the incision to heal. However, in recent weeks she had regained three of the fourteen pounds she'd lost.

Tonya dropped an arm over Nydia's shoulders. "I'm with Jasmine. Every day Mama's going to make a special plate for you and have someone bring it over to you."

She felt a warm glow flow through her from her friends' concern about her. After she'd called Jasmine to tell her she was in the hospital, it was apparent she'd informed Hannah and Tonya, because they'd called to check on her condition, while Jasmine had sent her an enormous basket filled with fruit, gourmet confectionaries, cheese, crackers, and nuts from all three.

"Speaking of eating," Jasmine said, "it's time we head to the restaurant because everything has been set up for us."

"Are we going out?" Tonya asked.

Jasmine shook her head. "No. I reserved

35

one of the small private rooms here at the hotel where we can eat at our leisure. I hope y'all don't mind that I ordered for us, because the kitchen gets real busy around this time."

"I don't mind," Hannah said.

"You won't get an argument out of me," Nydia quipped. In addition to her friends, she missed the local dishes. She'd bought a cookbook featuring New Orleans cuisine and attempted to duplicate some of the recipes. It had taken several tries before she was able to perfect her favorite dish of red beans and rice. Even her mother raved about the kidney beans flavored with Cajun seasoning and spicy andouille sausage.

Nydia entered the room with the others, smiling when she saw the round linen-covered table with seating for four set with china, silver, and crystal. Mouthwatering aromas wafted from a number of chafing dishes on the buffet table. There were also bottles of wine, water, soda, and a large bowl of ice.

Jasmine picked up a plate. "Don't be shy, ladies. Let's eat."

"You don't have to tell me twice," Nydia said, smiling. There were trays of fried chicken and catfish, red beans, rice, grilled shrimp, jambalaya, and jalapeño cornbread.

"I hope that's not all you're eating," Tonya said, as she stared at Nydia's plate.

"No. As soon as I finish this, I'm going back for more." She'd selected shrimp, cornbread, and beans and rice.

"Once you're finished with Jasmine's wedding, I'd like you to teach me how to make *pasteles.*"

Nydia nodded. She did promise Tonya to show her how to make the tamales filled with pork, chickpeas, yucca, olives, capers, and other spices. There was never a holiday or celebration in a Puerto Rican home where *pasteles, perñil,* and *arroz con gandules* weren't on the menu. Before Tonya moved to New Orleans, Nydia had taught her to make *mofongo* and *alcapuría.*

"No problem." Every year she joined her mother, sister-in-law, and grandmother to make at least one hundred *pasteles* for the Christmas holidays.

Tonya's dimples deepened when she smiled. "Thanks. I want to put them on the menu for my restaurant's Caribbean night."

Nydia had no doubt that the restaurant Tonya and Gage planned to open once the inn was operational would become a much sought-after dining establishment. Tonya told her they would offer a few of Chez Toussaints's signature dishes, and also a variety of small plates featuring international cuisine.

It appeared as if her former coworkers were busy planning the next phase of their lives, while her future was still in limbo. And she knew she had to make a decision before the end of the year when it came time to renew the lease. Nydia had talked about her ex finding a real job, but now she found herself in the same situation; she had to stop dragging her feet and seriously think about securing permanent employment.

Hannah had asked her to invest in her new business venture, which would give her ten percent ownership in the inn. Even if she did decide to invest, she still would have some money from her severance payout, and if she did move to New Orleans she would live rent-free in her own suite at the DuPont Inn. Whenever she thought about going into business with her former coworkers, the more appealing the notion had become.

She didn't have children or a significant other to consider, and her extended family was only a couple of hours away by plane if she needed to fly up to New York. Nydia had a month to contemplate her next move, and once she returned home she would know whether to accept or reject Hannah's offer to become an innkeeper.

Hannah touched the corners of her mouth with her napkin. "This hotel is where St. John and I reunited for our fortieth high school reunion."

Nydia met her eyes. "It didn't take you long to become reacquainted before you married him."

Hannah smiled and nodded. "Remember, St. John and I were high school classmates, and when you get to my age you don't want or need a long engagement. I knew even before we slept together the first time that I wanted to marry him."

Tonya gave Hannah a side-eye glance. "You didn't act like it when you came back to New York to close up your apartment. When we asked how things were going with St. John you said they weren't, because he'd admitted to cheating on his ex-wife. And if we hadn't threatened to sleep with your man, you would not have married him."

Hannah lowered her eyes. "I'll tell y'all about that later."

Nydia knew Hannah had aroused her curiosity along with the others. She'd known with a single glance that there was something going on between her former coworker and the handsome college professor when he'd come to the DuPont House to take Hannah for their ballroom dance lesson. St. John was the total package: looks, brains, and breeding, and it was obvious the way he'd looked at Hannah that he was as enthralled with her as she was with him.

"How are the renovations going on the inn?" Nydia asked Hannah, deftly changing the topic of conversation.

The former corporate attorney rolled her eyes upward. "Much slower than I'd anticipated." She gave Nydia a direct stare. "The offer's still open if you want to become the CFO."

Suddenly Nydia felt as if Hannah had put her on the spot in front of the others. It was one thing to discuss the business arrangement one-on-one, but with Jasmine and Tonya already onboard she felt vulnerable. She knew her friends wanted her to relocate and join them in their new venture. "I'm still thinking about it."

Tonya patted Nydia's back. "Don't think too long, sweetie. My mother used to say, 'Opportunity is like a baldheaded man. You have to catch him as he's coming toward you. Once your hand slips off it's gone.' "

"Amen to that," Jasmine and Hannah intoned at the same time.

Nydia angled her head as she struggled

40

not to laugh. "Please don't tell me you rehearsed this in advance."

Jasmine shook her head. "There's nothing to rehearse. We all feel that you would be perfect looking after our investments. I was really shocked when Wakefield Hamilton let you go, because the word was you were one of the best accountants they'd ever hired."

Nydia made a sucking sound with her tongue and teeth. "I was one of the newbies, so that meant I was expendable."

"Don't even go there," Jasmine drawled, frowning. "You were ten times brighter than that idiot who headed your unit, and there were rumors that you completed his monthly reports. I'd occasionally sit in on the department head meetings, and when it came time for Hank to give his report he babbled like someone under the influence."

"That's because he was taking meclizine for vertigo. He told me this in confidence, so I never mentioned it to anyone," Nydia said in defense of her former supervisor.

Tonya took a sip of water. "So you covered his ass?"

"It wasn't so much covering."

"What else was it, Nydia?" Jasmine questioned. "You did the man's job, and you'd think he would've recommended you for a promotion." Her mouth twisted in derision.

"I saw more underhanded crap I didn't need to see working in HR."

Hannah emitted an unladylike snort. "It was the same in the legal department, and it wasn't until we were standing on the sidewalk with our banker boxes that I realized that more than half the downsized were female. Not only do we make less than our male counterparts for the same work, but when it comes to handing out pink slips we're the first to be shown the door. Now talking about promotions, Jasmine, you should've been the one to head HR after Brian Harvey left. Instead they brought in that pimply-faced boy who didn't know his ass from his elbow to replace him."

Jasmine raised her goblet of sparkling water. "I agree, but that's because they didn't want me privy to the merger and who they'd planned to lay off."

"Would you have let it slip about the layoffs?" Nydia asked Jasmine.

"No. Even if my name was on the list I wouldn't have said a word to anyone."

"That's because you're ethical," Hannah stated.

Tonya ran a finger down the stem of her wineglass. "I don't know about the rest of y'all, but Wakefield Hamilton did me a favor letting me go."

"If they hadn't let you go, would you have commuted to New Jersey?" Hannah asked.

"I doubt it. I'd have to be on the train at four in the morning to make it down to Trenton in time to set up the kitchen for a breakfast meeting."

"Everything worked out for you," Nydia said, "because you'll open your own restaurant with your *papi.*" Everyone laughed at her description of Gage. Suddenly, she sobered. "I don't know about the other employees, but it appeared as if being downsized has worked well for you guys." Three pairs of eyes were fixed on Nydia as a swollen silence followed her statement. "What's the matter?"

"Why aren't you going to include yourself in that equation?" Tonya questioned. "And please don't tell me you're still messing with that bum who's looking for his big break?"

Nydia's eyes burned with amber fire as she struggled to control her rising temper. "Why can't you believe me when I say I'm through with Danny?"

Jasmine met her eyes. "You may be through with him, but I'm willing to bet that he's not through with you."

Nydia glared at Jasmine. She regretted telling her about Danny seeking out her parents to ask about her whereabouts after

43

she'd sublet Tonya's apartment. "It doesn't matter, because I'd given him too many chances to get his act together. And even if he did secure a record deal, I still wouldn't go back with him. I've learned a lot of things about myself since I'm no longer involved with Danny. I may have been in love with him, but I never allowed my heart to over-rule my head. And more importantly, I'm at a stage in my life where I believe I don't need a man to complete me."

"How old are you now?" Hannah asked.

"Thirty-three."

"Don't you want to marry and have kids?"

Nydia's eyebrows lifted slightly. "I still have a few years before my biological clock starts winding down."

"Just don't wait as long as I did," Jasmine hinted with a broad grin.

Tonya turned to look at Jasmine. "Didn't you tell me you and Cameron didn't plan for this baby?"

Jasmine nodded. "We even used a con-dom."

"Daddy must have nuclear-powered sperm to penetrate latex," Nydia stated, deadpan.

Pinpoints of color dotted Jasmine's gold-brown complexion at the same time Han-nah and Tonya burst into laughter. Seconds later, Nydia joined them; she was laughing so hard at Jasmine's shocked expression that her side hurt.

She pointed to Hannah. "Don't laugh, Hannah, because you may be the next one to announce that she's in the family way."

Hannah blotted the tears running down her cheeks. "That's not going to happen, because I'm finished with menopause, and St. John had a vasectomy when he was still married to his first wife." She exhaled an audible breath. "Remember when I told you that St. John had admitted to cheating on his wife."

"Yes. What happened?" Tonya asked.

Nydia's shocked expression mirrored Jasmine and Tonya's, her mouth gaping, as she intently listened to Hannah explain that St. John's first wife had been sexually abused as a child by her uncle, who'd gotten her pregnant. She hadn't told her aunt that her uncle was the father of her unborn child because he'd threatened to kill her if she revealed their secret liaisons. Her aunt arranged for her to undergo an abortion, and the trauma had scarred her for life so she would not permit her husband to make love to her.

Tonya's eyes were brimming with unshed tears. "How long were they married?"

Hannah bit down on her lip. "More than thirty years." She ignored the gasps coming from the others in the room. "It wasn't until Lorna filed for divorce that she was able to tell St. John about her uncle's abuse. She claimed she was afraid to say anything because she feared what St. John would do to him."

Jasmine shook her head. "So, instead of trusting her husband to protect her from the pedophile, she denied him her body for three decades, which forced him to become an adulterer."

"That's a damn shame," Tonya whispered. "If I found out that some man had abused my daughter I would've sharpened one of my chef knives, cut off his dick, and then cauterized it with a Firestarter and see how long he could piss out of a nub."

"Whoa!"

"Damn!"

"No, you didn't say that!"

Jasmine, Hannah, and Nydia had all spoken at the same time. "Why are y'all looking at me like that?" Tonya asked. "I only said what you'd be thinking if you had a daughter."

The mood lifted when Nydia mentioned Tonya's daughter's surprise engagement. Samara had come to her mother's wedding with her fiancé, and wearing a diamond engagement ring. The recent Spelman College graduate had not told her mother that she had been dating a student from Morehouse School of Medicine, who'd also graduated that spring. Samara, who was pursuing graduate studies, had recently moved into her fiancé's parents' guesthouse until she could rent an apartment.

Ninety minutes after they sat down to eat, while baring their souls, the four women took turns hugging one another. Nydia felt as if time and distance did little to affect the closeness she'd developed with her former coworkers. She'd thought it ironic during the four years she'd been employed at Wakefield Hamilton they'd only gotten together during the bank's sanctioned holiday celebrations, and now fast-forward fifteen months, and they had formed a sisterhood that she was certain would impact the rest of their lives.

Jasmine joined Nydia as she took the elevator to her floor. Jasmine had promised to show her the converted warehouse where she would live with Cameron once the renovations were completed before they visited a local bridal salon to select gowns for the wedding.

The elevator arrived at the fourth floor, and they shared a smile. "Thanks again for getting everyone together to welcome me back."

Jasmine quickly smothered a yawn behind her hand. "There's no need to thank me. It felt good to get the gang back together. I'll meet you in the lobby at ten." She stepped out of the car with Nydia. "I'm going to take another elevator that stops at the fifth floor."

"*Luego, mija.*"

Jasmine wiggled her fingers. "*Buenas noches, chica.*"

Nydia walked to her suite. A wave of fatigue washed over her as soon as she opened the door, despite having taken a nap earlier that afternoon. She usually sat up watching late-night TV, but tonight wouldn't be one of those times. She cleansed her face of the light cover of makeup, brushed her teeth, and then secured her shoulder-length hair in a single braid. She slipped into a cotton nightgown, and within minutes of getting into bed she fell asleep.

CHAPTER 3

Lamar Pierce checked his watch when he heard the sound of an approaching vehicle. He smiled. She was on time. His client's fiancée had called the day before to ask whether he would be available to show her the new construction to the rear of the property she wanted as a loggia for al fresco dining, and he had quickly rearranged his schedule to accommodate her.

When Cameron Singleton introduced Jasmine Washington as an interior decorator and his fiancée, Lamar hadn't been unable to conceal his surprise. It was the latter that had taken him aback, because he was well aware of Cameron's reputation as an eligible bachelor. Subsequent to their meeting, Cameron had contacted him and asked him to save the date for his wedding and not share the news with anyone, because he wanted it to be a surprise. Lamar wanted to tell him it would be more than a surprise to those in the Big Easy. It was certain to shock those who hadn't expected the wealthy, very eligible certified financial planner to marry, and definitely not to a woman of color, because Cameron's taste in women tended to extend to blondes and redheads.

He walked over to the gleaming, late-model pearl-white Honda Odyssey parked along the curb behind the construction crews' vans and pickups. Lamar opened the driver's-side door, extended his hand, and assisted Jasmine out of the vehicle. She looked nothing like the woman he'd met for the first time in the private dining room at the Louis LaSalle hotel. Then, she'd appeared very businesslike in a pantsuit and with her hair styled in a twist off the nape of her neck. He'd commissioned the interior decorator for a personal project and was astounded by her artistic flair and attention to detail. Today she wore a loose-fitting floral-print top with a pair of navy leggings and matching peep-toe booties. A loose ponytail had replaced the chic twist.

Lamar extended his hand. "Good morning."

Jasmine smiled and took his hand. "Good morning. Thank you for making time for me."

"It's . . ." His words trailed off when he

saw the petite woman with a wealth of dark curls floating around her shoulders emerge from the passenger seat of the minivan. His eyes met a pair of hazel ones that were almost an exact match to his. Lamar's mother had drilled into him that it was impolite to stare at someone, but at that moment he completely forgot his home training. If he was staring, then she was also. Lamar didn't know why, but she reminded him of the illustrations of fairy-tale princesses in the books he read to his daughter.

"Lamar, I asked to meet you because I wanted to show Nydia the property before it's completely renovated. Nydia, this is Lamar Pierce. He's project engineer responsible for turning this place into a showplace. Lamar, Nydia Santiago."

Nydia offered Lamar her hand. "It's nice meeting you."

Jasmine's introduction shattered his silent entrancement with the woman with delicate features and a flawless taupe complexion He grasped the small hand, which disappeared into his larger one. "My pleasure, Ms. Santiago."

She smiled. "Please call me Nydia."

His eyebrows flickered slightly. "And I'm Lamar."

It took Herculean strength for Lamar to

pull his eyes away from the slender woman with eyes that reminded him of semi-precious gems and a generous mouth that probably had men fantasizing about kissing her. As soon as the notion entered his head, he chided himself for entertaining licentious thoughts about a woman whom he knew nothing about except her name.

"Please wait here," he said. "I'm going to get some hard hats from my truck." Lamar knew he had to put some distance between him and Nydia if only to deal with his unexpected reaction to her; it had been more than ten years since a woman had enthralled him within seconds of his meeting her, and that woman was one he'd eventually married.

Nydia exchanged a look with Jasmine as Lamar walked down the block and opened the door to a black pickup. "We have the same color eyes."

Jasmine nodded. "That's what I thought when I first met him. However, yours have more green, while his have glints of gold."

"Something about him bothers me."

"How, *chica*?" Jasmine asked.

"Although I'm flattered by his staring, he also made me feel uncomfortable."

A hint of a smile touched the corners of

Jasmine's mouth. "That's because he likes what he sees."

A frown settled into Nydia's features. "Oh hell no, *mija*. What he likes and what he gets are entirely two different things. Did you not see the band on his left hand? The man's married, and I'm not one to entertain another woman's husband. My mantra is if I can't be the entrée, then I'm not going to be the appetizer or the dessert. At least when Cameron couldn't take his eyes off you, some woman didn't have papers on him."

"I think you're being a little too hasty in —"

"Hasty!" Nydia said, cutting her off. "Please, Jazz. I don't want to talk about Lamar Pierce." Once Nydia ended her relationship with her ex she had purposefully put up a shield to keep all men at a distance, and had given herself a year of not dating anyone to assess what she wanted for her future.

A beat passed before Jasmine said, "Okay."

Nydia exhaled an audible sigh of relief as she glanced up at the building, set behind a massive wrought-iron door. "This place is huge."

"It used to be a warehouse where bales of raw cotton were stored before they were loaded onto ships and transported to New England or European cotton mills."

"Why did Cameron decide to buy a warehouse?"

"He said although he finds it convenient living in a hotel, he claims he wanted a place where he could entertain clients, friends, and family without reserving a room at the LaSalle."

"I haven't even seen the inside, but I'm willing to bet it's as large the DuPont Inn."

Jasmine nodded. "It's about the same."

"*Coño, mija.* I can't believe it's only going to be you, Cameron, and that little muffin cooking inside you living in this mansion. After you have your baby, you need to wait for your six-week checkup and start working on another one. A house this big needs the patter of a lot of little feet."

"That's not happening, Nydia. If Cameron and I decide to have more children, then we'll adopt. And speaking of babies, I'd be honored if you'd be godmother to this one."

Nydia stared wide-eyed, unblinking. "Are you sure?"

"Of course I'm sure. I wouldn't be asking if I wasn't sure."

Unexpected tears filled Nydia's eyes, and she was suddenly overcome with a swell of

54

emotion. She had wanted to be godmother to one of her nieces, but when it didn't happen she dismissed it as her sisters-in-law's choice to make. "Thank you, Jasmine. I'm really honored you asked me."

"No more talk about the baby," Jasmine said *sotto voce*. "Lamar's coming back."

Nydia reached into her cross-body purse for a tissue and touched it to the corners of her eyes. She rarely exhibited public displays of emotion, but Jasmine asking her to become godmother to her son or daughter was an honor she would cherish forever. If only a few people knew about Cameron marrying Jasmine, even fewer knew that he was going to be a father.

Lamar handed each a bright yellow hard hat. "Please put these on, and watch where you step once we're inside."

Nydia ignored Lamar's furtive glance as she put on the hat. She had to concede he was extremely attractive, but she found his features rather delicate for a man. She estimated he was at least forty or close to it despite his close-cropped prematurely gray hair, which was a striking contrast to his unlined sable-brown complexion. High cheekbones and a hint of the cleft in his strong chin all made for an arresting face. He was casually dressed in a pair of khakis, a navy-blue golf shirt, and tan work boots.

Lamar put on his own hard hat and un-locked the wrought-iron door leading to a cobblestone walkway that opened out into an expansive courtyard. Several dumpsters and construction equipment took up two corners of the open space that was an emerald jungle with trees, flowering shrubs, and ferns growing in abandon. There was also an enormous fountain in the middle of the enclosure with a marble cherub holding a pitcher from which water would flow if operable.

"Can you imagine holding a cookout here?" Nydia whispered to Jasmine, unaware that Lamar had overheard her. "I thought St. John's backyard was big, but this is incredible."

Jasmine nodded. "If the house had been completely renovated, I would've convinced Cameron to have the ceremony and recep-tion here."

"I saw the video from Tonya's wedding, and the courtyard where they exchanged vows made it look like a fairy-tale wedding."

"I'm sorry you missed it."

Nydia hadn't experienced a lot of disap-pointment in her life, but not being able to attend Tonya's wedding was one. She'd been confined to a hospital bed with pain and antibiotic fluids running through an IV and into her body while her friend was marrying a man with whom she had been given a second chance at love. Nydia knew even if she hadn't delayed seeking medical attention with the onset of pain in her side, she still wouldn't have been cleared to travel in time to attend Tonya and Gage's nuptials. However, she was given the opportunity to attend another wedding two months later as Jasmine married Cameron.

She wasn't able to conceal a gasp of astonishment when Lamar opened another oak door to an enormous street-level space with stone floors and brick walls. The sounds of hammering, sawing, and drilling could be heard over the distinctive voice of Michael Jackson's "Billie Jean."

"Watch your step," Lamar cautioned as he led the way to the rear of the property. Several men nodded to him before going back to concentrate on their tasks.

Nydia pulled her eyes away from a trio of staircases leading to the upper stories. She carefully wended her way through saw-horses, wheelbarrows, stacks of bricks, cinder blocks, coils of wire, and copper piping. When Jasmine had informed her that Cameron had bought a house, she thought it would be similar to the ones featured in the French Quarter with shuttered windows and decorative wrought-iron balconies, and not one where intercoms were essential in order to communicate with one another.

Nydia and Jasmine expelled audible gasps at the same time when they stepped out onto the loggia with the cross-beamed ceiling supported by brick columns and terracotta flooring. It was the perfect place to begin and end the day.

"I hope it meets your specifications," Lamar said to Jasmine.

Her smile mirrored approval. "It's perfect and beyond my expectations." She pressed her palms together. "Thank you again for taking the time to show me what you've done with the loggia. I hope to see you again at my wedding."

Lamar smiled, the expression making him appear rather boyish despite the gray hair. "Of course. I wouldn't miss it."

"By the way, Nydia's going to be my maid of honor."

Lamar angled his head as he gave Nydia a direct stare. "I hope you'll save a dance for me?"

Nydia narrowed her eyes. "I will, but only if Mrs. Pierce doesn't mind you dancing with me."

Throwing back his head, Lamar laughed

loudly. "The only Mrs. Pierce I know is sixty-five and lives in Baton Rouge with my sister and her grandchildren."

Nydia's eyelids fluttered, her breath quickened, and her cheeks became warm from embarrassment; she was angry with herself for assuming Lamar was married. Well, dammit, she thought, he *is* wearing a wedding band.

She curbed the urge to stick out her tongue at him. It was something she'd done as a child when she felt the need to punish someone. "Yes. I will save you a dance."

Lamar's smile was still in place when he inclined his head. "Thank you."

Nydia looped her arm through Jasmine's as they turned to retrace their steps. "I'm going to get you for that," she said under her breath, speaking Spanish. "Why didn't you tell me the man's not married?"

"I tried to tell you," Jasmine replied in the same language, "but you cut me off saying you'll never be a married man's appetizer or dessert, but the main dish. He's a widower," she added.

Nydia rolled her eyes. "Why the heck is he still wearing a wedding ring?" she continued in Spanish.

Jasmine smiled. "You can ask him that when you dance with him at my wedding."

"No entraré en el negocio personal del hombre." Nydia had no intention of getting into the man's personal business. She would dance with him, and leave it at that; it did not matter if she did find Lamar attractive, he would become an acquaintance and nothing more.

Her friends and family members had told her repeatedly to stop dating Danny, and there were occasions when she had. However, that was short-lived, whenever he called begging that he loved and missed her. It had all come to an end when she moved out of her landlady's house, leaving no forwarding address and blocking Danny's number. That day in November she'd made herself a solemn promise not to date anyone for a year. And she'd come to learn a lot about herself over the past nine months. Not only hadn't she needed a man to complete her, but she also liked her own company.

She'd invite her cousins and a few friends she'd grown up with in her old neighborhood over to the apartment where they'd spend hours eating, drinking, laughing, and talking about what was happening in their lives. The get-togethers reminded Nydia of the camaraderie she'd shared with Tonya, Hannah, Samara, and Jasmine when they'd set out on their road trip from New York City to New Orleans. And she continued to marvel at how quickly she had bonded with her coworkers, and what she had to decide before the end of October was whether to renew the lease or give notice that she was vacating the apartment before January 31.

"I like this swagger wagon," Nydia said, as Jasmine maneuvered the minivan into an empty space at the rear of the bridal salon.

Jasmine laughed. "I'm beginning to like it, too. The automatic sliding doors make it hands-free for loading and unloading."

"Do you miss your Denali?"

"Not really."

"Why didn't you call your ex and ask him if he's willing to buy it from you?" Nydia teased.

Jasmine shook her head. "You know you're wrong, *chica.*"

"No I'm not, because you know damn well your leech ex-husband was ready to fight you tooth and nail for that vehicle so he could ride that woman and her tribe of kids around in it."

"Well, he'll never get it, because I transferred the title to my cousin."

"Isn't it funny that aside from a larger share of your design business the two other things he wanted most your cousin has: the condo and the Denali?"

Jasmine went completely still as she stared out the windshield. "When you say you're so over Danny it's the same with me, Nydia. In less than two weeks I'm going to marry a man I never believed I could love. And hopefully before the end of the year we'll move into our new home and then ring in the new year with a child I never thought I'd ever have."

Unbuckling her seat belt, Nydia leaned over and hugged her friend. "You deserve everything coming to you, and some."

Jasmine held onto Nydia's forearm. "What about you, *chica*? Don't you think it's time for you to have a happily ever after?"

"What makes you think I'm not happy? I don't have ex-husbands or children like you, Hannah, or Tonya, but that doesn't mean my life is fraught with angst or filled with bad memories. Danny was my first real serious boyfriend, but at no time did I ever allow my heart to overrule my head."

"What attracted you to him?"

Nydia extricated her arm from Jasmine's and pressed her head to the headrest. "His positive attributes are he's extremely talented and he didn't cheat on me. But it was his refusal to become gainfully employed that was a continual source of contention between us. He earned just enough working as a part-time waiter and singing with a Latin band on the weekends to pay for studio time. I got tired of telling him that all the men in my family worked and supported their families, and I expected the same from him. Even if I had greater earning power I wouldn't have held that over his head."

Jasmine patted Nydia's hand. "Don't beat up on yourself, *chica*. You gave him more chances than he deserved."

"You've got that right. Now before we go in, do you have any idea of what type of gown you want?"

"I told the owner I wanted a gown with an empire waist because it would de-emphasize my waistline."

"You're not showing."

"I'm getting thick in the waist."

"Let's go, *mija*. We need to pick out a gown for you and one for me, along with all of the accessories."

Nydia settled down on the loveseat, picked up the remote device, and flicked on the wall-mounted flat screen. She blew out an audible sigh. It felt good to just sit and relax. Jasmine had extended an invitation for Nydia to join her and Cameron in their suite for the evening meal, but she'd declined and ordered room service.

Earlier that morning it had taken her and Jasmine almost three hours to pick out their gowns. The salon owner and her staff were patient and gracious, offering them water, juice, and freshly prepared fruit and green salads for a light snack during a break.

Unlike Jasmine, who knew exactly what style and color she wanted, it wasn't the same for Nydia, who'd always found herself in a quandary when it came choosing between more than one garment. It wasn't until she'd resorted to the nursery rhyme *eeny, meeny, miny, moe* that she had finally selected her bridesmaid gown. Fittings followed, and the seamstress set a date for them to return several days before the wedding for a final fitting.

Nydia turned the television to a popular entertainment channel and became suddenly alert when she heard the correspondent mention her ex-boyfriend's name. More than two million hits on Danny Ocasio's YouTube video had landed him a record deal with a major recording company. A publicist from the company had predicted Danny was certain to become a Latin crossover artist with the sensuality of

Enrique Iglesias and a voice comparable to Marc Anthony's.

Nydia's cell phone chimed a familiar ringtone; she picked up the phone after the second ring. "I just saw it, Millie," she said to her cousin.

Milagros Baez's distinctive laugh came through the mouthpiece. "Can you believe it? He finally made it!"

"Good for him."

"I know you had your ups and downs with Danny, but you don't sound excited that he's going to be a big star."

Nydia closed her eyes. What did her cousin expect her to say? Danny had worked hard to get a recording contract, even if it meant forfeiting a relationship with her. "I'm happy for him, Millie. He deserves every good thing coming his way."

"Danny called me a couple of days ago to let me know the segment was airing tonight," Milagros continued. "He said he wanted to personally share his good news with you, but you'd blocked his number." A beat passed. "He wanted me to tell you that he still loves you and would like to see you in person. Of course I didn't tell him where you were, but said I would pass along the message."

"You can tell him I'm out of town and I'll

65

contact him once I return to New York after the Labor Day weekend." Nydia didn't tell Millie that she had no intention of reviving her relationship with Danny because emotionally she had moved on.

"I'll let him know. How are you feeling, *prima*?" Milagros asked.

"I'm real good."

A slight twinge on her right side was a reminder of her recent surgical procedure, and Nydia realized it would take time before she healed completely. She muted the television and listened to her cousin, who updated her about the latest love of her life. Nydia smiled as Millie rambled on about the too-good-to-be-true man she'd met on a dating site. She was happy for the woman who'd had her share of heartbreak.

Ten minutes after answering the call, Nydia hung up. She'd planned to stay up and watch a movie but changed her mind. After turning off the television, she adjusted the thermostat, and then walked into the bathroom to shower and brush her teeth. The glowing numbers on the bedside clock displayed 8:01.

I've become my abuela, she thought. Nydia's eighty-five-year-old grandmother had established a routine of going to bed at eight o'clock every night to get what she called her beauty sleep. She had to acknowledge her *abuelita,* who never smoked, rarely drank, except for a glass of coquito during Christmas, could easily pass for a woman at least ten years younger.

Nydia knew the heat and humidity were responsible for her lethargy, and it would take at least a week to acclimate her body to the tropical-like weather.

CHAPTER 4

Nydia helped Jasmine as she stepped into her wedding gown. For the past two weeks she had felt like a hamster on a wheel, running around in endless circles, and since arriving in New Orleans one day had blurred into the next one.

She had tried on several gowns in varying shades of yellow before selecting a sunny-yellow, one-shoulder chiffon gown, nipped at the waist, and flowing around her feet like frothy meringue. Strappy matching satin-and-patent-leather platform sandals added four inches to her five-two height.

And as promised, Tonya prepared and delivered a two weeks' supply of frozen dinner entrées. It had become a struggle not to overindulge on the delicious dishes before the final fitting for her bridesmaid's dress.

She'd also accompanied Jasmine to countless local antique dealers and furniture warehouses and several in Baton Rouge to shop for furnishings for her new home. Tonya had mentioned her husband's mother owned and operated an antique shop in Lafayette, but thankfully Jasmine had decided not to take the over one-hundred-seventy-mile ride until after her wedding.

Cameron had invited her to join him and Jasmine to share dinner with his parents, and Nydia got to see firsthand why Jasmine had agreed to marry him. He was patient, attentive, and affectionate, confirming Nydia's pronouncement that Cameron was willing to go after what he wanted, and it had been apparent from the first time he saw her at Hannah's wedding reception that he wanted Jasmine Washington.

"This has to be some crazy shit!" Nydia spat out as she fastened the tiny buttons of the golden beaded bodice on the back of the empire waist gown of beaded silk crepe and georgette artfully disguising Jasmine's slightly rounded belly. "Most brides take months and even up to a year to plan their wedding, while you're pulling yours off in three weeks. And last night you showed up as Daddy's fiancée and now twenty-four hours later, you're about to become Mrs. Daddy."

Jasmine met Nydia's eyes in the reflection of the full-length mirror. "It wouldn't have been possible if Nathan and Belinda had not celebrated their golden anniversary last night. Cameron and I already had the venue, the invited guests, and the event planner."

"It is a slick move."

Her friend revealed that Cameron, his brothers, and sister had decided to host their parents' fiftieth wedding anniversary on a Friday night at the Louis LaSalle and subsequently informed the invited guests that Cameron was getting married the following day. They did not identify the bride, which only served to pique their curiosity. However, Cameron did inform his college fraternity brothers that he was marrying the woman who'd accompanied him during their reunion yacht party and had hotel management block out a number of rooms for those committed to attend.

Jasmine had attended her future in-laws' soirée for the cocktail hour, then left to spend the night in her suite with Nydia. They'd sat up talking for hours about any and everything until Nydia suggested they go to bed because they had appointments with the hairstylist and the makeup artist Hannah had employed for her wedding.

Nydia glanced at the clock on the table. It was fifteen minutes before six. "You better put your shoes on, because your father said he'll be here at six." Her gaze swung back to Jasmine, who'd opted not to wear a veil; the stylist had styled her hair in a mass of tiny black curls reminiscent of a Grecian goddess. The woman had threaded a narrow gold silk ribbon through the curls, tied it in a bow with streamers flowing down her back and ending at the hem of the gown.

Nydia slipped the groom's rose-gold wedding band with a brushed finish on her thumb and then scooped up Jasmine's bouquet of yellow and white roses tied with several yards of wide white ribbon off the table before picking up her own bouquet of yellow roses, mums, and daisies.

It was the second time in less than a year Nydia would become a bridesmaid for a former coworker. A wry smile flitted over her features when she realized Hannah, Tonya, and now Jasmine were celebrating their second marriages, while she was yet to have her first, and when she married she hoped it would be her last. Her parents had recently celebrated their thirty-sixth wedding anniversary and appeared more in love with each other with every passing year.

Jasmine smiled at Nydia. "I need to give you something for standing up as my maid of honor."

71

Nydia shook her head. "No, Jazz," she said in protest. "I'm just honored you asked me." She and the interior decorator had become best friends, and there wasn't anything she wouldn't do for her. Jasmine had become the sister she'd always wanted. She gasped when Jasmine handed her a bangle bracelet with princess-cut diamonds.

"It's the least I could do for your encouragement and support, because without it I never would've answered Cameron's text asking me to have dinner with him. I had the inside inscribed with the date and love from me and Cameron."

Nydia slipped the bangle on her wrist and secured the safety clasp. Judging from the weight of the metal she knew it was platinum. "I'll treasure it always."

Jasmine hugged her. "And I treasure our friendship."

There came a knock on the door. "Ten minutes."

"Okay, Daddy," Jasmine called out. "I just have to put on shoes and get my engagement ring."

Nydia raised her left hand. "I have Cameron's band."

Jasmine slipped her feet into her shoes, chuckling softly under her breath. "I've never seen you look so tall."

Nydia patted the curly hair brushed off her face and secured on the top of her head with jeweled hairpins. "With four inches of heels and another three of hair, I can now make the height to become a supermodel."

There came another knock on the door. "We're ready out here."

"Coming," Nydia and Jasmine chorused.

Nydia opened the door to find Jasmine's father dressed in tuxedo finery. She followed Jasmine and Richard Washington down the hallway to the elevator. A hotel employee waited for them to enter the car and punched the button for the first floor. When it reached the lobby level, he escorted them to the ballroom where Philip Baxter, Cameron's college roommate and best man, waited for them.

"Hell, doll," Philip crooned, grinning like a Cheshire cat, while offering Nydia his left arm.

Nydia was more than prepared for the overly flirtatious man. Jasmine had told her about the number of times he'd been married, and that he was currently engaged to a woman half his age, and she cautioned her to ignore his not-so-subtle advances. Nydia curbed the urge to roll her eyes at the man with thinning red hair, as she affected what passed for a smile.

"Hello, Philip." His grin faded quickly when he registered the neutral tone in her greeting. She had no intention of sending the man a signal that she was even remotely interested in him even if he hadn't been engaged.

The doors to the ballroom opened, and a string quartet continued to play as she went into the room on Philip's arm. She bit back a smile as necks craned to see who the bride could possibly be. The music changed as the familiar strains of the "Wedding March" filled the ballroom, and Nydia chuckled as a loud gasp went up from the assembly amid applause from the Singletons.

She'd grown up hearing people say the only way two people could keep a secret was if the other was dead. Well, that wasn't the case with Cameron and his fiancée. It was apparent, with the exception of Cameron's family members, close friends, and his fraternity brothers, that the truth behind his relationship with Jasmine had been a successful closely held Big Easy secret.

Lamar hadn't realized he had been holding his breath until the constriction in his chest forced him to exhale as he stared at Nydia on the arm of Cameron's best man. She had gone from an ingénue in cropped jeans, running shoes, and a tank top to an ethereal vision in a frothy yellow gown that looked like buttercream frosting against her mocha-hued complexion. A moment before she took her place opposite the best man, he met her eyes and he smiled when she lowered hers demurely. The gesture was so unabashedly virtuous he wondered if she truly was as innocent as she appeared.

"Did you know Cameron was marrying this girl?"

Lamar glanced at the hand on the sleeve of his suit jacket. The enormous golden South Sea pearl surrounded by a triple halo of brilliant diamonds resembled a bird's nest. Mrs. Abigail Attenborough currently headed her family's charity, and as an Attenborough her name was on the city's social calendar for every philanthropic fundraiser and society wedding. The tiny widow with bright-blue eyes and snow-white, stylishly cut short hair that was an almost match for her alabaster complexion was still recovering from hip surgery. However, it was apparent the Singletons hadn't informed her about the woman Cameron planned to marry. He debated whether to be truthful or evasive and decided on the latter.

"Not really."

Lamar's association with Cameron was personal *and* business. He'd married a colleague of Cameron's sister Evangeline, who had been maid of honor at their wedding. Evangeline had taken Valerie's death hard because they'd made a pact that their daughters would grow up to be fast friends like their mothers. His late wife's friend had held up her end of their pledge when his daughter was invited to sleepovers with Evangeline's twin daughters.

Earlier in the year Cameron had contacted his engineering firm to check the viability of converting the warehouse into a personal residence. After inspecting the property, Lamar completed a report with a recommendation that since the building was structurally sound, Cameron should purchase the building.

"It took him long enough to pick a wife," Mrs. Attenborough whispered. "I'd heard talk that maybe he was using women as a cover because he really liked men."

Lamar wasn't about to dignify the wealthy widow's supposition with a response. In all of the years he had come to know Cameron, there had never been a time when he suspected the man preferred a same-sex liaison.

"But I have to say that he certainly picked a beauty."

"That she is," Lamar confirmed. He wanted to tell the chatty woman that he didn't want to engage in gossip but concentrate on the ceremony as Jasmine's father placed her hand on Cameron's extended left.

The minister motioned for everyone to take their seats. A pregnant silence fell over the ballroom as the officiant peered over his half-glasses. "We are gathered here for a simple ceremony. Today we will celebrate the wedding of Jasmine Esperanza to Cameron Averill and we will also celebrate the symbolism of the rings. Some say the ring is a sign of ownership, but I believe it is a symbol of a union that has no beginning and no end."

Lamar stared straight ahead, his mind drifting to another time and place. He mentally recalled exchanging vows with a woman with whom he'd prayed he would be together long enough to celebrate countless anniversaries. He and Valerie had talked about having children, becoming grandparents, retirement, and the many countries they planned to visit during their lifetime.

He forced his attention back to the exchange of vows and rings. Cameron had placed a band on Jasmine's hand as he promised to honor and cherish her and be her devoted husband as long as they both shall live. Jasmine repeated her vow and slipped a band on her husband's finger.

The minister smiled for the first time. "Cameron and Jasmine, with these rings of gold, you have taken a vow to love and cherish each other for the rest of your mortal lives. In the presence of God and these witnesses, this day, I pronounce you husband and wife, legally and lawfully married for as long as you both shall live. Cameron, you may kiss your wife."

Cameron lowered his head and pressed his mouth to Jasmine's for a prolonged kiss that elicited a smattering of laughter. "Ladies and gentlemen, I'm honored to introduce you to Mr. and Mrs. Cameron Averill Singleton." Whistling and applause followed the announcement as Cameron's fraternity brothers, all wearing black-and-red-striped ties, broke into their fraternity hymn.

Lamar waited for the wedding party to leave the ballroom and then followed the other wedding guests into an adjoining ballroom for the cocktail hour. The space had been set up nightclub style with low tables positioned in front of loveseats and banquettes. There were also bar tables and stools. The guests were lining up at the open bars, at opposite ends of the ballroom, for liquid refreshment.

He offered Mrs. Attenborough his arm as she leaned heavily on her cane for support. He'd replied to the invitation that he was attending unaccompanied. There was a woman he would have considered bringing as his plus-one but then changed his mind, because their relationship was solely physical and not romantic in nature. As the widowed father of a ten-year-old girl he refused to expose his daughter to those with whom he occasionally slept. And he made certain they lived far enough away from New Orleans so they wouldn't encounter one another.

"Something smells good," Mrs. Attenborough said, smiling.

He nodded and smiled. "If Chez Toussaints is catering, then I'm certain everything is going to be delicious." The waitstaff was busy circulating with trays of hot and cold hors d'oeuvres and flutes of champagne, Bellinis, and kir royale. He assisted Mrs. Attenborough as she folded her body down on a loveseat. "Is there anything you'd like to drink?"

The woman waved her bejeweled hand. "No. Now go and enjoy yourself. I'm just going to sit here and people-watch."

Lamar accepted a flute of champagne and

a mesquite-smoked brisket slider from passing waiters. The chipotle-rubbed melt-in-the-mouth beef topped with coleslaw was one of more than three dozen dishes available to more than one hundred invitees. Red-jacketed servers standing behind long banquet tables were offering small plates of shrimp etouffée, fried catfish, and chicken fingers, with accompanying dipping sauces, okra and corn fritters, red beans and rice, spicy smothered shrimp, and Creole crab dip with pita chips. He ate sparingly, because he wanted to save his appetite for the sit-down dinner that was to follow.

The event planner and her staff ushered everyone into another ballroom where banquet-style tabletops were dressed with white satin showcasing votives and vases filled with orange orchids atop mirrors. Lamar returned to Mrs. Attenborough and assumed his role as her escort.

She leaned against his side. "You should be hanging out with some of these young, single girls and not a woman old enough to be your grandmother."

Lamar patted the hand tucked into the bend of his elbow with his free one. "I happen to like hanging out with you." He didn't tell the octogenarian there was only one hopefully single girl he was interested in who'd promised to dance with him.

Once everyone was seated, the planner nodded to the DJ, who lightly tapped the microphone. "Ladies and gentlemen, Mr. and Mrs. Cameron Singleton."

Lamar stood and clapped with the others as Cameron escorted Jasmine across the marble floor to the bridal table set on a raised dais. Nydia followed with the best man. He retook his seat, silently applauding his good luck to be seated opposite the wedding party.

Nydia knew once Tonya and Gage opened their restaurant at DuPont Inn it would become an instant success. The Toussaints chefs had prepared an exquisite sit-down gourmet dinner beginning with white asparagus soup topped with sturgeon caviar, Meyer lemon-avocado puree, and asparagus tempura, and followed the soup with a bite-size Caesar salad with shards of parmesan, shaved romaine, and creamy Caesar dressing.

Champagne and wine flowed to accompany dishes of wild-caught prawns with watermelon, Serrano ham, and watercress. Those requesting meat and chicken dishes were offered Moroccan rubbed double-chop rack of lamb, cowboy steaks with smoked shallot butter, and honey-glazed game hens.

Each course was more stunning and delicious than the previous one: ravioli of wild salmon carpaccio and avocado topped with caviar and roasted beets, chilled marinated lobster with fresh lychee and green papaya, and the main course of Thai-style lobster with grilled mussels, lime-coconut milk infusion, fried Thai basil, bok choy, and baby carrots.

When jasmine told Nydia the Singletons were hosting back-to-back soirées at the same venue she had insisted the Taussaints vary the menus. They'd planned to offer their signature Cajun and Creole dishes for the cocktail hour and Asian and international cuisine for the sit-down dinner. She had convinced Cameron to forego many wedding rituals like champagne toasts with announcements from the best man and maid of honor, their first dance together as husband and wife, father-daughter dance, tossing the garter, bouquet, and the symbolic cake cutting, because she did not want a repeat of the traditions of her first wedding. And in lieu of gifts, they'd urged their guests to donate to their favorite charities.

Nydia raised her water goblet to her mouth and stared at Lamar over the rim. She didn't know if it had been arranged beforehand, but they had an unobstructed view of each other. She hadn't thought about the engineer asking her to dance with him at the wedding until she noticed him sitting in the row behind Cameron's family members. He looked incredibly handsome in a midnight-blue tailored suit, white shirt, and silver silk tie. A hint of a smile parted Nydia's lips when Lamar raised his own glass in a silent salute and inclined his head, acknowledging their recognition of each other. She lowered her eyes, her smile still in place. It was obvious Lamar was flirting with her, and she liked it.

Since her final break with Danny, Nydia had consciously thwarted the advances of any man who appeared even remotely interested in her. The owner of one of the restaurants whose books she maintained had asked to take her out, and she was forthright when she told him she never mixed business with her social life. What she didn't tell him was even if she didn't work for him, he wasn't someone whom she would consider dating.

And she had been truthful when she told Millie that she was happy for Danny, but there was no way she wanted to revive her relationship with him. Fame was certain to change him; she refused to compete with his homeboys and other women for his attention, and she was certain he would cheat on her because it would be hard for him to resist all of the panties thrown his way. Nydia had attended a number of social events where Danny had performed with the house band, and she'd overheard women talk about wanting "to do" the lead singer. One even went as far to say: "The minute he drops that *puta* I'd be on him like stink on shit." She'd dropped him months ago, and they were welcome to him.

"I don't think I can eat another morsel," she whispered to Jasmine, as the waitstaff cleared away the remains of dinner; at the same time dessert tables were set up on the far side of the ballroom.

"I'm going to wait for dessert," Jasmine said. "I want to see what . . ." Her words trailed off when the DJ lowered the volume on the soft jazz that had played throughout the dinner and his sonorous voice echoed throughout the ballroom's hidden speakers.

"Ladies and gentlemen, the bride and groom decided they wanted more dancing than talking and toasting, so it's time for you to get up and move. And since this is a celebration I'm going to start you out with a Kool and the Gang anthem."

Nydia smiled when "Celebration" blared

from the powerful PA system. Many of the guests were up on their feet as they sang along with the classic tune. She did not have time to react when Philip stood up and extended his hand.

"May I have this dance?"

She met his bright blue eyes, smiling, and placed her hand on his outstretched palm. "Yes, you may."

Nydia did not lack for partners as she danced with Jasmine's father, Cameron's father, brothers, and brother-in-law, and Jasmine's uncle Keith. Keith and Danita Moore had closed their Long Island bed-and-breakfast for the weekend to attend their niece's wedding.

She'd just returned to her table when she saw Lamar approach, knowing he had come to claim his promised dance. Not only did he look good, but he also smelled wonderful. His cologne was a tantalizing combination of sandalwood and musk. Even with four-inch heels and her stylized hair atop her head, he still towered over her by at least four inches. And seeing him this close also made her aware, despite the cropped gray hair, he was younger than at first glance.

"I suppose you've come to claim your dance," she said, smiling.

Lamar smiled. *"Sí, señorita."*

Nydia did not have time to react to his speaking Spanish when he led her out onto the dance floor and spun her around and around to Marc Anthony's "Nadie Como Ella." She knew Jasmine had added that particular song to the playlist because it was one of her favorites sung by the salsa Grammy winner.

Within seconds of Lamar resting his hands at her waist, she lost herself in the man and in the music as he led her across the dance floor, easily following his fluid movements as if they'd choreographed it. Her hips had taken on a life of their own as she dipped and swayed to Marc singing "No One Like Her." Lamar wasn't just a good dancer, he was excellent, twirling her around and around on her toes before dipping her low to the thunderous applause reverberating throughout the ballroom.

The song ended, her head inches above the floor, Lamar's warm breath sweeping over her mouth. "Please let me up." Her heart beat a double-time rhythm as she struggled to catch her breath. And sharp pain from the incision on her right side was a reminder that she was still healing.

Lamar flashed a wide grin, his perfectly aligned teeth showing whitely in his face. *"Gracias por el baile."*

86

"Where did you learn to speak Spanish?"

"I'll tell you if you agree to another dance."

Her right side was throbbing from the exertion. Nydia shook her head. "Only if it's a slow number." As if on cue, the lights dimmed and the DJ announced he was going give everyone a chance to catch their breath with some slow jams.

Lamar tightened his hold around Nydia's waist. "The DJ must have read your mind."

She laughed. "Lucky me."

"No. Lucky us."

Nydia rested her left hand on Lamar's shoulder. "Where did you learn to salsa?"

Easing back, he stared down at her. "I thought you wanted to know how I learned to speak Spanish."

"That, too."

A beat passed. "I learned it from one of my college classmates who was from East Harlem."

Nydia stopped in mid-step and would have lost her balance if Lamar hadn't steadied her. "I live in East Harlem."

He blinked once. "You're kidding."

She shook her head, smiling. "No I'm not. Talk about a small world."

Lamar dropped his arm but did not let go of her hand. "Come with me. We need to

87

find a place where we can talk without having to shout over the music."

She held back. "Wait here. I want to tell Jasmine where I'm going if she needs me for anything."

Lamar nodded. "I'll be outside." Turning, he walked out of the ballroom.

Nydia found Jasmine dancing with her husband. "Excuse me, Cameron. I need to talk to your *wife* for a minute."

Cameron smiled. "No problem." He walked away to give them some privacy.

Looping her arm through Jasmine's, Nydia whispered in her ear. "I'm going to the hotel lounge to talk with Lamar. And by the way, he speaks Spanish."

Jasmine's eyes grew wide. "Say what?"

Pinpoints of heat pricked Nydia's face as she recalled what she'd said to Jasmine about becoming involved with a married man before she was told Lamar was a widower. "He learned it from a friend, and that means he probably overheard me telling you that I'll never become a married man's appetizer or dessert, but his main dish."

"Do you intend to apologize to him for the remark?"

"No! I meant every word I said."

Jasmine gave her a long, penetrating stare.

88

"You like him, don't you?"

"I don't know enough about him to like him." Nydia realized she sounded defensive, but it was the truth. "I find him intriguing."

"Cuidadoso, chica," Jasmine teased, "or you'll find yourself packing your bags and moving to Nawlins to hook up with your new man."

"That's not happening. If I move down here it will be to become the accountant for the DuPont Inn, and not because of a man." Nydia released Jasmine's arm. "I'll catch you up later about Lamar, because your husband is giving me the stink-eye for monopolizing his wife."

Jasmine smiled. *"Buena suerte, chica."*

Nydia waved her hand at the same time she shook her head. There was no need for Jasmine to wish her luck. After tonight, she doubted whether she would ever see Lamar again.

CHAPTER 5

Lamar led Nydia out of the ballroom, through the hotel lobby, and into the lounge. Wedding guests and a number of Cameron's frat brothers and their significant others had claimed every seat at the bar and seating area.

He gave her fingers a gentle squeeze. "We're going to have to find another place."

"Come with me," Nydia said. "There's somewhat of a secret alcove between the private dining rooms. Let's hope no one else has discovered it."

"How do know about this little hideaway?"

Nydia smiled at him over her shoulder. "I'm staying here."

"How long will you be here?"

"I plan to be here through the Labor Day weekend."

Lamar quickly calculated the number of days in his head. "And what do you plan to do for the next two and a half weeks?"

"Hang out with my friends and hopefully soak up some of the Big Easy nightlife. Here we are." Tucked in between two doors with signs indicating private dining was a padded bench seat with enough room for two. Nydia sat, patting the cushion beside her. "Sit down. I promise not to take advantage of you."

Chuckling, Lamar sat down beside her. There was something about Nydia that made him feel completely relaxed when around her. It was if she didn't have a pretentious bone in her body. What you see is what you get. He stretched out his legs, crossed his feet at the ankles, and folded his arms over his chest.

"Before I tell about my adventures in East Harlem, why don't you tell me a little bit about Nydia Santiago."

"What do you want to know?"

He turned his head and stared at her delicate profile. "What do you do that allows you a month's vacation?"

Nydia adjusted the flowing skirt of her gown. "Right now I'm my own boss."

His eyebrows lifted at this disclosure. "What is it you do?"

"I'm an accountant."

"So, the pretty lady likes numbers."

"I love numbers. They don't talk back like

91

people."

Lamar laughed. "I never thought of numbers like that."

Nydia folded her hands in her lap. "You're an engineer, so you're more than familiar with math."

He sobered quickly. "You're right about that." One of the reasons he'd decided to become an engineer was because he'd excelled in math and science. "How did you meet Jasmine?"

Nydia exhaled an audible sigh. "We used to work together. That is before we were unceremoniously let go last May. We worked for a private Wall Street investment bank that merged with another institution, and one day we walked into the building and were told it was our last day. An hour later twenty-eight of us stood on the corner with banker's boxes filled with our personal belongings."

"Well, damn!"

"We said words that were a lot more colorful than that, but there wasn't anything any of us could do about. We were given generous severance packages and paid health insurance for a year." She paused. "Do you know Hannah DuPont?"

Lamar nodded. Most long-time residents of New Orleans were familiar with the Du-

Pont name. "She's now Hannah McNair."

"At that time she was DuPont, and worked in the legal department. She had an apartment within walking distance of the bank, so Jasmine, and Tonya Martin, who is now Tonya Toussaint, and I went to Hannah's place to commiserate over mimosas and Bellinis. It had become a strange bonding of women who never socialized outside the workplace. We all decided to take the summer off before seeking future employment, and that's when Hannah invited us to come down here and hang out for a few weeks.

"She also told us about converting her home into a business and offered us a percentage if we decided to invest in her new venture. Tonya was the first to take her up on her offer. Once the renovations to the guesthouses are completed, she and Gage will open their restaurant on the property."

He angled his head, taking a furtive glance at Nydia, because he didn't want to be caught staring at her again. "What about Jasmine?"

"She's also in."

Lamar found himself holding onto every word Nydia was saying. "Cameron told me he met Jasmine at Hannah's wedding."

Nydia nodded. "He took one look at her and he lost his natural-born mind. He's become her genie and grants her every wish."

Lamar had to agree with Nydia. When Cameron met with him and the architect, he'd informed them to revise the plans to the house to give Jasmine exactly what she wanted. "What about you, Nydia?"

"What about me?" she asked, answering his question with one of her own.

"Have you decided to invest in Hannah's venture?"

It was a full thirty seconds before Nydia answered his query. "Not yet. There are still a few things I have to work out *if* I decide to commit."

"Does your ambivalence have anything to do with the man in your life?"

Nydia met his eyes, her stare unwavering. "Why would you think my decision would be centered on a man?"

Lamar realized he'd made a serious faux pas when he registered the cold edge in her voice. "I'm sorry I asked that." He extended his hand as a peace offering. "And I apologize for being presumptuous."

She stared at his hand as if it were a venomous reptile. It seemed to be an eternity before she took it. "Apology accepted. And for your information, I don't have a man in my life."

He knew it was time to change the conversation; he didn't want to say something that would further insult Nydia. Talking about his facility with Spanish was a much more benign topic. "I'd taken Spanish courses in high school, and although I could read and write it, I still had a problem when it came to speaking it. That all changed when I went to college and met Ignacio Gonzalez. We became study partners after sharing some of the same classes. One year when I decided to spend the winter in New York rather than return to New Orleans, he invited me to stay with him and his extended family."

"In East Harlem?"

"Yes. Iggy's grandmother only spoke Spanish, so when she spoke to me and I replied in English, she would tap the back of my hand and insist, *'Dilo en español.'* "

"Did you?"

Lines fanned out around Lamar's eyes when he smiled. "It was difficult at first because I would search my head for the words, but after a while they came easier. She made Iggy promise to bring me back every weekend so I could practice with her. Not only did I learn to speak fluent Spanish, but I was also introduced to food and flavors I hadn't known existed. I'd wait all week to eat *maduros, tostones, mofongo,* and of course *perñil.* A few times we would hit the clubs, and that's when I learn to dance salsa."

"Wepa!"

Lamar threw back his head and let out a hearty laugh. It had been years since he'd heard the expression, which translated into: *All right! Oh yeah! Cool!* Other than his marriage to Valerie and the birth of their daughter, the years he'd spent living in New York City were incredibly memorable for him. He'd bonded with Iggy when it hadn't been with his roommates, and the bond surpassed friendship to the point that he thought of his former classmate as the brother he never had.

"Where were you living?" Nydia asked, breaking into his musings.

"I shared an apartment in Brooklyn with two other students."

"Where did you go to college?" Nydia asked.

"New York University Tandon School of Engineering. I'd enrolled in the Brooklyn Tech Center."

"How long has it been since you've been to Brooklyn?"

"It's been about fifteen years."

"And East Harlem?" Nydia had asked him

96

yet another question.

"It's been the same time. After we graduated Iggy got a position with an overseas company putting up homes, office buildings, and hotels in Dubai, Bahrain, the United Arab Emirates. He fell in love with a woman from Bahrain, converted to Islam, and married her. They have three beautiful children who speak English, Spanish, and Arabic. And before you ask me, the answer is no, I've never been to Bahrain. However, it is on my bucket list of countries to visit. We keep in touch using email and Skype."

"Thank goodness for social media."

Lamar nodded. "It can be a blessing and a curse."

"Why would you say that?"

"I have a ten-year-old daughter who's addicted to social media. Lately I've put parental controls on her computer and phone, which limits her to how many hours she can access them. I've warned her over and over that she will lose her phone privileges if she doesn't keep up her grades."

"Did it work?" Nydia asked.

A wistful expression flitted over Lamar's features as he stared at the toes of his polished slip-ons. "Yes and no. She passed all of her classes, but her attitude sucks. My mother convinced me to let her come to

Baton Rouge for the summer to spend time with her aunt and cousins. I'm sorry, Nydia. I shouldn't be unloading on you about my daughter."

"It's all right. Every once in a while Titi Nydia has to run interference between my nieces and sister-in-law." She pushed off the bench, Lamar rising with her. "I think it's time we headed back."

Lamar tucked Nydia's hand in the bend of his elbow. She wanted to go back and he didn't. If possible, he wanted to spend the next hour talking to her about any and everything. There was something about her outgoing personality that reminded him of Valerie, although she looked nothing like his late wife.

"What's on your calendar during the rest of your stay?"

"I'm going to visit with my friends. Why?"

"I'd like you to have dinner with me before you go back so we can continue our conversation."

A cold shiver eddied its way down Nydia's back, and it had nothing to do with the frigid air flowing from air-conditioning vents. Lamar asking her to share dinner with him mirrored Cameron making the same request of Jasmine at Hannah's wedding reception. However, Cameron had had to wait five months to reunite with Jasmine, while Nydia did not have the excuse she was scheduled to return to New York the following day.

"I'll give you the number to my cell and we'll take it from there," she stated. Although she'd enjoyed talking with him, Nydia wasn't ready to commit to seeing Lamar again.

"Give me your number."

"I'll write it down for you once we get back to the ballroom."

"You don't have to write it down. Just tell me."

Nydia stared at him and recited the number. "Are you certain you're going to remember it?"

"Very certain," he said confidently. "I have what's known as eidetic memory."

It was the first time Nydia had met someone who'd admitted having a photographic memory. "Your IQ must be off the charts."

"No comment."

She smiled. "I like a man who's not ashamed to exhibit a modicum of modesty."

"I can assure you that I'm not that modest."

Lamar's modesty wasn't the only thing Nydia liked about him. He projected a confidence she rarely found in the men with whom she had been involved. She'd only had two romantic relationships: one as a graduate student and the last one with Danny, and the two men were as different as day and night. She'd made the drastic mistake of sleeping with her taxation professor, who'd conveniently neglected to tell her that he was married and that his wife was living in California caring for her elderly, invalid parents. In that relationship not only was she his appetizer, side dish, but also the deceitful man's dessert.

She knew very little about Lamar other than what he'd shown her. He was a father who wanted the best for his daughter and had made education a priority for her. Nydia had asked him many questions, despite telling Jasmine she didn't want to get into the man's business, because she enjoyed listening to his speech pattern validating he was truly a New Orleanian.

The frivolity was still in effect when they returned to the ballroom. The DJ was spinning upbeat tunes, the dance floor was crowded, bartenders were busy pouring and mixing drinks, and there were lines two deep at the dessert stations. Nydia scanned the crowd for Jasmine but failed to see her.

She eased her hand from Lamar's elbow. "I'm going to see if I can find Jasmine." The corners of her mouth lifted as she smiled. "Thank you for the dance, and I really enjoyed talking with you."

Lamar's lids lowered, hiding his innermost feelings from her. "Can I count on a repeat?"

"Dancing or talking?" she teased.

He suddenly appeared startled by her suggestion, but then recovered quickly when he said, "Talking. And if that goes well, then I wouldn't mind dancing with you again."

"Call me and if our schedules don't clash, then perhaps we can work something out."

Liar, liar, pants on fire, the voice in her head taunted her as soon as the words rolled off her tongue. She'd told herself that she doubted whether she would ever see Lamar Pierce again, yet in a moment of madness she had not only given him her phone number but also permission for him to call her.

Lamar inclined his head. "Thank you."

Nydia smiled up at him through a fringe of lashes. "You're welcome. And I bet you'll forget my number." She turned her back on him, not seeing his startled expression with her unexpected departure. She had said all she wanted and needed to say to the single father who apparently hadn't let go of his dead wife, because he continued to wear his wedding ring. Lamar was someone she would think of as a friend, but nothing beyond that.

Her life was still too unsettled to even consider dating. Nydia realized she had until the end of October to decide whether she would take over the lease in Tonya's apartment, which meant she wouldn't be able to invest in Hannah's DuPont Inn. She also needed to secure employment with a salary and benefits package commensurate with her education and work experience. Even after she secured permanent employment, she would continue to maintain the books of the three restaurateurs. The money she earned from the part-time gig she planned to invest in her retirement fund.

During her convalescence she'd had her father drive her to each of the restaurants to meet with the owners to set up a computer program where they would electronically input the work hours on each of their employees for her to generate computerized paychecks. Nydia had also recommended a system where payroll checks would be directly deposited into the workers' bank accounts. However, much to her disappointment, too many of the employees did not have checking accounts but relied on check cashing companies that charged them what she considered excessive fees.

She found Cameron laughing and talking with his frat brothers. She managed to get his attention, and he excused himself. He'd shed his tie, tuxedo jacket, and undone several buttons on the dress shirt. His deeply tanned face was flushed with high color, which made his blue-gray eyes appear lighter than usual. Prisms of light from an overhead chandelier reflected off the silver in his light-brown hair.

"I'm sorry to pull you away from your friends, but I'm looking for Jasmine."

"Jasmine left and went upstairs a few minutes ago. She said she's exhausted. And please don't apologize, Nydia. I've never said this, but I have to you to thank for this day."

A slight frown appeared between her eyes. "What are you talking about?"

"Jasmine told me if you hadn't encouraged her to go out with me when I sent her that text, this night would've never happened. I knew she was special when I first laid eyes on her, but I didn't get to know how special until our first date. Jasmine and I have decided if we have a girl we're going to name her Nydia."

Nydia shook her head. "You don't have to do that. Becoming godmother to your son

103

or daughter is an honor I'll cherish for the rest of my life."

Lowering his head, Cameron pressed his mouth to her hair. "Thank you."

"It has been a long day for Jasmine, and I know you guys are flying to Cabo San Lucas in the morning, so tell her I'll see her when you come back. Congratulations again. I'm also going to turn in. *Buenas noches.*"

Cameron had surprised Jasmine several days ago when he announced he had planned a weeklong honeymoon at the Mexican resort. He'd confided to Nydia, and she agreed that Jasmine needed to slow down and not concern herself with looking for items to decorate their new home once the extensive renovations were completed.

Cameron winked at her. *"Bonne nuit."*

Nydia didn't realize how tired she was until she entered the suite and kicked off her shoes. Exhaustion swept over her like a powerful wave as she walked into the bathroom. She removed her makeup, brushed her teeth, and took a quick shower. Twenty minutes later, an audible sigh slipped past her parted lips when she crawled into bed and pulled the sheet and lightweight blanket up over her limp body. Within seconds of turning off the bedside lamp, Nydia sank into the comforting arms of Morpheus.

Lamar waited three days before he called Nydia's cell phone. He'd synched his phone with his car's Bluetooth feature. It rang three times before he heard her greeting.

"Hola."

His whole face spread into a smile. "Hello. What do I win for not forgetting your number?"

"Did we wager anything?"

"No, but you did say 'I bet you'll forget my number.' And knowing I was going to win I should've had you put up a wager."

"It's looks as if I was wrong about you."

"Are you saying that I won?" he asked.

There was a pause before Nydia's voice came through the speaker again. "Yes."

Lamar stared through the windshield at the slow-moving traffic leading to the exit for Baton Rouge. "Do you mind if I select the prize?"

There came another pause. "No, I don't mind."

"I'd like to take you to one of my favorite clubs."

"I'm game as long as it's not a strip club."

His chuckles echoed throughout the interior of the vehicle. "I don't do strip clubs."

"I'm just checking, because there *are* different types of clubs."

"True. But I was referring to a jazz club. The one I'd like to take you to offers wonderful food and music."

"Are you talking about Jazzes?"

"You've been to Jazzes?"

"Yes. Hannah took us there last summer."

"The place I'm talking about is nothing like Jazzes. It's what you'd call rustic."

"It sounds interesting."

Lamar held his breath for a few seconds. "So, you're willing to go with me?"

"Sure."

He curbed the urge to pump his fist in victory. "Are you busy Thursday night?"

"Yes. I'm teaching Tonya how to make *pasteles.*"

"You're kidding!"

"No, I'm not."

"The last time I had *pasteles* is when I celebrated Christmas with Iggy's family." The first time he had the tamales, he couldn't stop eating them. Iggy's grandmother packed up a dozen for him, and over the following two weeks he'd eaten one each day along with his dinner.

"I'll be certain to save a few for you."

"Which night are you free?"

"Friday."

He smiled. Friday fit perfectly into his plans, because he was scheduled to pick up his daughter Sunday afternoon and bring her back to New Orleans for the first day of the new school year. Lamar didn't want to remind Nydia that Friday was date night. "Friday it is. I'll meet you in the lobby at seven."

"Luego."

"Later," Lamar replied in English. He disconnected the Bluetooth and thought about what had just occurred. He'd asked a woman out on a date — something he hadn't done in nearly a decade. And he had to ask himself, why Nydia? Why a woman who lived nearly thirteen hundred miles away, and one he doubted he would see again once she returned to New York.

When Lamar really thought about it, he realized Nydia was safe; she was passing through and despite being attracted to her beautiful face, intelligence, and wit, there wasn't the possibility of his becoming *that* involved with her. He had two responsibilities: his daughter and his company.

Lamar maneuvered onto the road leading to his sister's house and pulled into the driveway to the house with the architectural style that reflected South Carolina's Low

Country. Petra's dream home's classic design was updated with all the provisions for modern-day living. His sister had met her politician husband when she clerked for his father, who'd been appointed to the state's appellate court. She'd moved to D.C. during the first year of her marriage, but once she discovered she was pregnant, she informed U.S. Congressman Jonathan Reynolds she wanted their children to be raised in their home state.

Lamar shut off the engine and waved to his mother as she came down off the porch. Gloria Pierce had sold the house she'd shared with her husband and where she raised her two children after he passed away in his sleep, and moved in with her daughter and son-in-law, who'd had a two-bedroom guesthouse built on the property for her. Once his mother volunteered to babysit her granddaughters, Petra went to work for a prestigious Baton Rouge firm specializing in litigation.

Gloria had been her deceased orthodontist husband's dental assistant, and now at sixty-five she volunteered every other weekend at a local hospital. Jonathan always returned to Louisiana whenever Congress was in recess, and during that time Gloria and a few of her friends who'd referred to themselves as the Globetrotting Grannies took off for foreign and exotic locales.

Lamar got out of the vehicle and met his mother as she came down off the last step. She'd cut her silver hair again, the cropped strands hugging her head like a cap. His parents' genes had compromised when he inherited his father's height and complexion and his mother's eye color and prematurely gray hair.

"Hi, beautiful," he crooned, kissing her cheek. The scent of lily-of-the-valley wafted to his nostrils. He couldn't remember when his mother had not worn that fragrance.

An attractive blush darkened Gloria's tawny-brown face with the compliment. "You definitely are your father's son. He was always the silver-tongued devil."

Lamar put his arm around his mother's shoulders and led her up the porch steps and into the house with large folding doors that had replaced a traditional front entry to completely open the central hallway. "Dad knew what he was getting when he married Grambling State's homecoming queen, who not only was blessed with beauty but also brains."

"That's enough sweet talk, Lamar. That's something you should save for Petra's coworker who has been asking about you."

A slight frown furrowed Lamar's forehead. "Who are you talking about?"

"Don't you remember that cute intern with the dimples who came to the Memorial Day cookout?"

"There's no way I could forget her, Mom. She flirted with every man who came within three feet of her, and it didn't matter whether they were married or single. So, no thank you."

Lamar had told his mother a number of times after becoming a widower that he did not want to be set up with a woman. He'd given himself another eight years before he could even consider remarrying. By that time Kendra would be eighteen and off to college. And any woman with whom he would find himself involved would have to accept his daughter as her own because they were a package deal. It would be the same if he met a woman with children.

He glanced around the central hallway's highly polished heart of pine floors and matching ceiling. The blades from an overhead fan circulated cooling air above a round mahogany table with four oyster-white slipcovered chairs. "Where's everyone?"

"Jonathan and Petra took the girls shopping for school clothes and supplies. Kendra has grown so much over the summer that I doubt she'll be able to fit into last year's school uniform."

"I wish you would've told me before I left New Orleans."

Gloria patted Lamar's shoulder. "I didn't know what their plans were until about ten minutes ago. Then it would've been too late because you were already on the road."

Lamar rested his hand over the one on his shoulder. "No harm done. I can hang out with you until they get back."

"That may not be for a while. You know how Jonathan likes to take the girls out to eat."

He gave his mother's fingers a gentle squeeze. "That's not a problem, because I don't get to see you enough."

Gloria nodded. "It's the same with me. Talking on the phone isn't the same as seeing each other in person. Did you plan to take Kendra back with you today?"

"No. I just came up to take her shopping for school clothes and supplies."

"I've been running off the mouth so much that I forgot to ask you if you had breakfast."

"Ramona prepared something for me."

Lamar's live-in housekeeper's duties included cooking and looking after Kendra whenever he was away from the house. Ramona Griffin had become an integral part of his household even before Valerie's passing. His late wife had hired the professional nanny to care for Kendra after a two-year leave from her career as a flight attendant.

"You need to learn how to cook for yourself, Lamar."

"I can cook, Mom."

"You put meat on a grill. That's called grilling, not cooking. Even Jonathan has learned to put together a passable breakfast now that he's been taking lessons."

Lamar did not want to remind his mother that his brother-in-law worked an average of one hundred thirty days a year, so he had time to become another Martha Stewart. "Good for him."

"Do I detect a hint of jealousy?"

"Never." He didn't always see eye-to-eye with Jonathan when it came to politics, and the result was he refused to get into a debate with him.

"Come with me to the kitchen. I was just getting ready to make a pitcher of lemonade. Then we can sit on the porch, and you can tell me all about Cameron Singleton's wedding."

Lamar smiled when his mother mentioned Cameron's wedding. It had been a night filled with surprises. The bride and groom had deviated from the tradition of speeches, toasts, cutting the cake, and tossing the bouquet and garter. The reception had been still in full swing, ongoing revelry that continued beyond his midnight departure.

The gathering had become even more memorable when he shared a couple of dances with Nydia Santiago, spent time talking with her, and now he looked forward to taking her out for a date that he hoped wouldn't be the last time before she returned home.

CHAPTER 6

Nydia felt her pulse quicken when she spied Lamar walking into the Louis LaSalle lobby. It had been almost a week since their last encounter and images of him would creep into her mind when she least expected it. He wasn't the type of man she'd found herself drawn to in the past — but then she hadn't chosen very wisely in the past.

Those she'd encountered when she worked for the investment bank, who were attracted to her, tried too hard to impress. They were braggarts, egoists, and a few egomaniacs. They turned her off, while Danny had become a refreshing change from the well-heeled men earning six and seven figures. She'd told her ex over and over his salary did not have to match or exceed her annual income, but he needed to secure a permanent job where he could become an independent adult.

Lamar wasn't a braggart or egoist, but

intelligent and modest. He was an engineer, widowed, and a single father with a ten-year-old daughter. The fact that he spoke Spanish and was familiar with Puerto Rican food were assets and not liabilities. *Hey now,* she mused as he came closer, *Papi's got a little swagger in his walk.* He was casually dressed in a pair of dark slacks, an untucked pale-blue shirt, and Italian slip-ons.

It had taken her a while before Nydia selected what she'd planned to wear to a place Lamar deemed rustic. And she interpreted rustic as a dive, greasy spoon or juke joint. Her bed was filled with discarded garments until she decided on a pair of black stretch pants, paired with an off-the-shoulder black-and-white striped stretched top, and four-inch animal-print sandals. At five-two, and she estimated Lamar was at least six foot, she needed a little assistance in the height department.

She stared up at Lamar through her lashes, unaware of how seductive it appeared. "Hello again."

Lamar angled his head and kissed Nydia's cheek. "Same here," he said. When he saw Nydia standing near the table in the middle of the lobby he felt as if someone had punched him in the gut. The gown she'd worn at Cameron and Jasmine's wedding had concealed a petite body with curves in all the right places. "You look wonderful." She looked *and* smelled wonderful.

"Thank you." She held her hands out at her sides. "I hope what I'm wearing is okay."

"It's perfect."

Lamar wanted to tell her she would look okay wearing a burlap sack. Her subtly applied makeup accentuated her hazel eyes and lush mouth. The hair that had been styled atop her head was brushed off her face and fashioned into a bun on the nape of her neck. He marveled that she could appear so refreshingly young and womanly and sophisticated at the same time. He tucked her hand into the bend of his elbow and slowed his stride to accommodate Nydia's shorter legs as he led her through the lobby and out of the hotel to the parking lot.

Lamar noticed men taking furtive glances at Nydia as he escorted her to where he'd parked his vehicle. He opened the passenger-side door to the Volvo and helped her up onto the leather seat, and then circled the SUV and took his position behind the wheel.

Nydia sniffed the air as she buckled her

seat belt. "Your car still has a new-car smell."

"That's because it's new. I bought it a couple of months ago. My old Volvo had more than one hundred thousand miles, and even though it was still running I decided it was time to buy another with updated safety features." He punched the start-engine button and backed out of the space. "How did your *pasteles* turn out?"

Nydia shifted on her seat and met his eyes when he glanced at her. "They were delicious. I saved a few for you. I'll give them to you after we come back."

"Thank you so much! Who taught you to make them?"

"My grandmother. The year I turned ten, Abuelita said it was time I learned to cook. Making *pasteles* was always a family affair that included my mother and aunts. Initially I was given the task of going to the supermarket and buying the onions, peppers, garlic, cilantro, culantro, *ajices dulces,* and tomatoes for the sofrito. Abuelita wanted me to recognize all of the ingredients that went into making it.

"Once she trusted me enough to use a knife without losing a finger, I chopped everything and put it into a food processor. Then she would grade me after spooning a

117

tiny portion into the palm of her hand and tasting it. It took a couple of attempts before she gave me her approval.

"When I graduated to peeling *yautia* and *calabaza* I was ready to literally throw in the towel because the skins are so hard to remove. However, in the end, all of the labor-intensive work was worth it, because the *pasteles* were delicious."

"How many did you make, and how long did it take to teach your friend?"

"She caught on easily because she's a professional chef. But it took nearly four hours to make about one hundred."

"Why so many?"

"Tonya plans to offer them on her Caribbean night menu once she opens her restaurant at the DuPont Inn. If they become a hit with their customers, then she and Gage will make them regular items."

Lamar tapped a button on the steering wheel and tuned the satellite radio to a station featuring soft jazz as he left the central business district and drove in a northerly direction along Canal Street to Canal Boulevard. "Where did you grow up in New York?" he asked Nydia after a comfortable silence.

"I lived in East Harlem for the first five years of my life, until my parents bought a brownstone in West Harlem. My father, who was a police officer, applied to HUD's Good Neighbor Next Door program and bought an abandoned three-story brownstone. He was eligible for a low-cost loan through the program to make renovations. Mami and Papi had the contractors divide the spaces on the second and third story into two apartments, each with three bedrooms. They rented out the apartments on the second and third story, and we lived on the first. There was enough room for me, my brothers, parents, and my grandmother whenever she came for an extended visit. We finally convinced her to move out of her apartment into the mother-in-law suite at my brother's house in White Plains."

Lamar listened intently to Nydia as she talked about leaving home for the first time when she attended college on Long Island. Living on campus had allowed her a modicum of independence from her overprotective father.

"I moved back with my parents while I got my MBA, then left for good after passing the CPA exam and securing permanent employment. I'd rented a furnished apartment in a three-family house in the Bronx, but my landlady was so nosy she should've been a covert agent for the CIA. I got a reprieve last year when I sublet Tonya's East Harlem apartment. Now I can come and go without being surveilled."

Lamar laughed. "Good for you."

"If you ever want to show your daughter where you used to hang out in *el barrio,* then let me know and I'll have my parents put you up in their place now that my brothers are married and live elsewhere. My eighty-five-year-old grandmother will probably talk your ear off if she knows you speak Spanish. She complains that her family members, her great-grandchildren in particular, have become so American that they never speak Spanish anymore, while my mother constantly reminds her that as a Puerto Rican she is also an American and fluent in English."

Momentarily shocked by Nydia's invitation, Lamar stared straight ahead. There were a number of times, whenever Kendra asked him what he'd seen or done as a student, when he'd considered revisiting New York City and showing her where he'd attended college. His daughter knew he expected her to attend college, because she was bright and had the ability to become an exceptional student if she was able to remain focused.

"I'm certain Kendra would love that.

Whenever I talk about New York City she pleads with me to take her there on vacation."

"Why haven't you, Lamar?"

He lifted his shoulders. "I must confess that I really don't have an excuse. Maybe if I can convince my two partners to close the office for the week between Christmas and New Year's, then we can spend the holiday in New York."

"You own your company?"

"Yes."

"You don't have an excuse if you run your own company with two other partners."

"I know and don't remind me."

"Someone should remind you that all work —"

"Makes for a dull boy," he interrupted.

"I was going to say something else, but I'll keep it to myself."

Lamar's eyebrows lifted slightly. "You're not one to bite your tongue, so spit it out."

Nydia laughed. "Oh, so you noticed."

He stopped for a red light, stared at Nydia, and then burst into laughter. "Of course I noticed. Has anyone ever told you that you don't have a filter?"

"Plenty of folks," she said proudly. "I've never been one to sugarcoat a situation or predicament. What you see is what you get

121

when it comes to Nydia Stephanie Santiago."

"I happen to like what I see, Miss Santiago, because at thirty-eight I'm much too old to play head games."

Nydia wanted to tell Lamar that at thirty-three she also was too old to play head games. She had become an adult at eighteen, but it was only over the past year that she'd actually felt as if she had reached the full potential of the responsibilities of being an adult. She stared out the side window at the passing landscape. There were abandoned properties interspersed with one-story structures with young barefoot children playing in the yard.

"Thank you for offering your folks' place, but I can't impose on them."

"It wouldn't be an imposition, Lamar. They love entertaining company. Whenever my cousins come up from Puerto Rico, they prefer staying with Mami and Papi."

"I'm not going to promise anything except that I'll think about it."

Nydia knew if Lamar and his daughter decided to celebrate Christmas with her family it would become an event they would not only enjoy but remember for a while. This year her brother Nelson had offered to open his house for the festivities.

"Were you affected by Hurricane Katrina?" she asked Lamar as he drove along a one-lane unpaved road.

"No, but many folks were not so fortunate. The area was flooded, and the homes built on the ground sustained a lot of water damage. Some folks were able to rebuild while others were forced to relocate. I try to patronize the businesses here rather than in the French Quarter because they're still struggling to survive."

"Do you ever take your dates to places in the French Quarter?"

Lamar's hands tightened noticeably on the steering wheel. "No. I don't date."

Nydia went completely still. She hadn't missed the iciness in Lamar's voice. And she knew what she was about to ask him would either make him turn the car around or continue to the restaurant as planned.

"Are you celibate?"

Lamar's stone-faced expression changed like a snake shedding its skin when the corners of his mouth lifted before his lips parted in a smile. "Well, damn, woman. You truly aren't subtle about saying what comes to your mind."

She smiled. It was apparent he wasn't angry. Just taken aback. "Weren't you the one who said you're too old to play head games? Well, it's the same with me, Mr. Pierce." She winked at him. "I'm a thirty-three-year-old accountant who in the past year discovered exactly who she is and what she wants for her future."

"And that is?" Lamar asked, slowing to less than ten miles per hour.

"I'm in control of my own destiny. That I do what is good and best for me."

"That sounds a little selfish."

She blinked slowly. "Why would you say that?"

"Because it sounds as if there's no room in your life for other people. What if you fall in love and marry or have children? Then it can't be all about you."

"I wasn't talking about marriage or children. Of course my life would change if I had a husband or a child. Now, back to my question. Is your daughter the reason you don't date or sleep with women?"

"I never said I don't sleep with women."

A flash of humor swept over Nydia's features. "So, you're not celibate." Leaning to her right, she peered closely at Lamar. "Are you blushing?"

His mouth tightened. "I don't blush."

"Yeah," she drawled, "and I have a bridge in Brooklyn I want to sell."

Lamar signaled and then pulled into a

parking area behind a one-story clapboard building that needed a coat of fresh white paint. The lot was filled with old and new vehicles ranging from pickups to SUVs, minivans to sedans. There were even a few motorcycles. He shut off the engine and rested his arm over the back of Nydia's seat, his expression a mask of stone.

"When my daughter lost her mother I made myself a promise that I wouldn't do anything that would have her believe she isn't the most important thing in my life. And that's why I'm not involved with a woman, because I don't want her to think I'm replacing her."

Nydia silently applauded the sacrifice and loyalty Lamar afforded his daughter. He had deprived himself of female companionship for the sake and emotional well-being of his child, who probably was still grieving the loss of her mother.

"You are an incredible father."

Lamar shook his head. "No, I'm not. I'm just a father who happens to love his daughter."

"A lot of men love their daughters, but that doesn't mean they would be willing to give up having a woman or women in their lives."

"It depends on the circumstances, Nydia.

If Kendra's mother and I had been divorced, then it would be different. And that's not to say I would expose my daughter to the woman I was seeing unless it was serious enough for me to consider marrying her. Kendra's ten, and it won't be long before she'll start talking about some boy she likes and wants to go out with and that's —"

"— when Daddy meets him at the door and threatens to rip his head off if he touches his daughter inappropriately," Nydia said, cutting him off.

Attractive lines fanned out around Lamar's luminous eyes when he laughed. "You must have been reading my mind. How did you know?"

"That's because my father and brothers did the same thing to me. And knowing Papi was a cop had a lot of boys in the neighborhood afraid to even talk to me."

Lamar unbuckled his seat belt. "Fathers want to protect their daughters because they know what they've done to the daughters of other men." He held up both hands. "I plead the Fifth." He reached over and caught Nydia's left hand. "Don't move. I'll help you down. I don't want you to turn your ankle in those stilts."

She raised her right foot and wiggled her blood red painted toes. "These aren't even

126

my highest pair."

Nydia waited for Lamar to get out and come around to help her down. His hands spanned her waist, she holding on to his neck to maintain her balance as he effortlessly lifted her until her feet touched the ground.

He laced their fingers together. "Are you ready to get your eat on?"

She smiled up at him. "Lead on."

Lamar had mentioned the place where they were going to eat was rustic, and Nydia realized it wasn't an over exaggeration. The sign over the front door identified the restaurant as Ruby's, and the establishment had roughly hewn log walls that matched long tables and benches. Tree stumps doubled as smaller tables and chairs. It was dimly lit in contrast to the raised stage where the spotlight shone on a scantily clad, plump, middle-aged woman who was bellowing out a tune about a cheating husband and what she'd planned for him when he came home. The rhinestone-covered black bustier, tutu, and matching thigh-high patent leather boots were better suited to a much younger woman. Several televisions were tuned and muted to news and sports channels.

Nydia knew Lamar was a regular customer

when he was greeted by a number of men and women seated at the bar and tables. She hadn't missed the curious stares and whispers when they saw her with him.

"Hey, Pierce," the bartender called out. "Where have you been hiding her?"

Lamar waved to the man as he led Nydia to a round table for two and helped seat her. "What do you feel like eating?"

Nydia met his eyes across the table. The bartender questioning Lamar about seeing him with her confirmed his declaration that he did not date. He'd claimed he wasn't dating, but did that also extend to her? That tonight she wasn't a date to him?

She moved the lighted oil candle to the middle of the table. "Is there a menu?"

Lamar pointed to a far wall. "The menu is on the whiteboard."

She studied the handwritten selections. "What is the mess?"

"A little bit of this and that."

"Please explain this and that."

"Fried chicken, catfish, crab, shrimp, oysters, okra, and grilled corn."

Nydia scrunched up her nose. "It sounds like a lot of food."

Lamar chuckled. "What it sounds like is goodness."

"You've had it?" He nodded.

"Okay. I'll have the mess."

Lamar signaled a passing waiter heading for the kitchen. "We'll have the mess for two." He returned his attention to Nydia. "All meals come with a complimentary pitcher of beer, but if you want something stronger then I'll order it from the bar."

Nydia recalled the two times she'd overindulged during her visits to New Orleans. She'd sampled her first hurricane and felt the effects almost immediately. And she'd overindulged on champagne at Hannah's wedding reception, which left her lethargic and slightly hung over the next day.

"Beer is okay."

"You don't drink much." Lamar's query came out as a statement.

"It all depends on what I'm drinking. I have a two-glass limit when it comes to wine and champagne, while I'm barely able to finish a hurricane or Sazerac."

"Did you ever do shots as a college student?"

Nydia shook her head. "I never drank until I was twenty-one."

"How old were you when you graduated college?"

"Twenty-one. I took AP courses in high school and graduated college in four years with a BA and MBA."

129

"So, you were a nerd."

"It takes one to know one," Nydia countered with a wide grin. "And don't deny you weren't a nerd, Lamar."

"There's no shame in my game."

Nydia's response was preempted when their server returned with a pitcher of beer and two frosted mugs and set them on the table. "Your mess is coming right up."

Lamar filled one mug and gave it to her before filling the other with the sudsy brew. He raised his glass in a toast. *"Salud."*

"To health," Nydia said in English.

Within minutes of their toast the table was filled with a heaping platter of crispy fried food, plates, place settings, and napkins. Lamar mentioning goodness had not even come close to describing the items that made up the mess. Nydia found her taste buds bombarded with a plethora of flavors. The spicy and crispy Cajun-brined chicken was deep-fried perfection. The shrimp and oysters literally melted on her tongue. She ate slowly, savoring every morsel she put into her mouth.

"This food is like crack," she whispered. "One bite and I'm hooked."

Lamar gave her a questioning look. "What do you know about crack?"

She made a sucking sound with her tongue

and teeth. "I've seen enough crackheads to know once they get on the stuff they crave it over and over. And no, I've never done drugs."

Lamar held a forkful of catfish inches from his mouth. "Did I insinuate that you did?"

"No, but your expression spoke volumes."

He set down the fork. "What did it say?"

"That maybe I had some experience with substance abuse."

Reaching over the table, Lamar took her hand, increasing the pressure on her fingers when she attempted to pull away. "The thought never entered my mind. If you say you didn't drink until the legal drinking age, then I figured you didn't do drugs. It had nothing to do with your father being a cop, because I've known kids whose parents were in law enforcement and it was only their intervention that kept them out of either jail or prison."

Nydia felt properly chastised as she stared at their hands. "I'm sorry about what I said, and will you please let go of my hand? I want more of this mess," she added with a forced smile. The mention of drugs served to change the mood from easygoing to tense as they finished their meal in complete silence.

The only information Nydia knew about

Lamar was what he'd revealed to her, and it was apparent she had misjudged him. There were times when her quick tongue had gotten her into situations from which she had to work hard to extricate herself, and she didn't want to have to repeat the action with Lamar. Spontaneity had come into play when she invited him to come to New York and stay with her parents; once the words were out she wasn't able to retract them.

She remembered her grandmother's warning over and over whenever she'd gotten into a verbal confrontation with her mother: *"Piensa antes de hablar."* It had taken years, and after being grounded over and over she made certain to think before talking back to Isabel Santiago.

Lamar settled the bill and escorted her out of Ruby's. There was no exchange of conversation during the drive back to the city, and if it hadn't been for the radio, the car would have been as silent as a tomb. Lamar found a spot in the lot for hotel guests and parked.

Nydia now knew the drill. She'd wait for him to open the passenger-side door and help her out. He held her hand as they made their way to the entrance to the hotel. The daytime heat had only slightly abated with the setting sun, but not the humidity, and she had come to recognize the smell of the Mississippi River, which was within walking distance from the Louis LaSalle. The lobby was crowded with guests in formal dress filing into one of the ballrooms. It was only a week ago the Singletons had taken over the entire hotel for an anniversary and wedding celebration.

"What floor are you on?" Lamar asked Nydia when the doors to the elevator opened.

"Fifth." He punched the button for the designated floor. The doors closed, and the car rose swiftly.

Nydia removed her key card from her wristlet and swiped it. The light turned green, and she pushed open the door. "Please come in. I have to get the *pasteles* out of the freezer."

Lamar walked into a suite that was nearly twice as large as the two-bedroom Brooklyn walk-up he'd shared with two engineering students. The apartment had contained a galley kitchen, a minuscule eating area, a tiny bathroom with a commode and shower, and every third week someone would sleep on the living room's convertible sofa. He dreaded those weeks, because the mattress was so thin the springs left an imprint on his body. After a while he bought a roll-away cot; although smaller than the sofa, it was a lot more comfortable.

He stared at Nydia when she took off her heels and left them on a mat near the door. He smiled. Even her feet were tiny and delicate. She smiled at him over her shoulder. "Would you like some coffee?"

Lamar nodded. "Only if you're having some."

"I'm going to make *café con leche,* or as you folks call it down here, café au lait."

"There's nothing better than café au lait and beignets in the morning. That's what I call powdered crack."

Nydia gave him a long, penetrating look. "Please. No more crack jokes."

He pantomimed zipping his lips. "Done." Lamar stared the laptop, printer, and stack of folders on the desk in a corner near the wall-to-wall windows. It was obvious Nydia had brought work with her. "Do you always work while on vacation?"

Nydia waited until after she'd ground coffee beans to answer his question. "Yes, but only because I'm handling the payroll and taxes for three neighborhood restaurateurs. The owners input the hours for their employees, and I compute the withholding and generate electronic payroll checks. I also electronically file quarterly and year-end taxes, reconcile bank statements, and oversee accounts payable and receivable."

"Wouldn't you do the same if you become the accountant for Hannah's business?"

She nodded. "Yes. The difference is Hannah doesn't want me to maintain her books remotely. Once I invest in her venture it would be best for me to live here. Hannah is hands-on when it comes to her business. This is not to say she will micromanage what we do, because she's perceptive enough to recognize her partners' expertise."

Lamar wanted to ask Nydia why she hadn't accepted Hannah offer to invest in the inn. She'd claimed she wasn't involved with a man, so he wondered what else was going on in her life that would prevent her from relocating. There were so many questions he wanted to ask her, yet he did not want to pry all the more into her personal life.

Pushing back his chair, he rose and walked over to the windows. Nightfall was complete, and he could barely make out the slow-moving waters of the Mississippi River. The river, the sights and smells, the distinctive speech cadence of locals, the food, music, architecture, the city's ethnic mix and colorful history served as aphrodisiacs that Lamar was helpless to resist. He'd flown to different countries and islands in the Caribbean for vacation and over long holiday weekends during his first year of marriage because of the benefits afforded him through his flight attendant wife. However, anytime he spent more than a week away from his city of birth he would experience a restlessness that made him crave home. What he found ironic was that he hadn't felt that way when attending college in New York City, perhaps because there were parts of the city that reminded him of the Big Easy: the ethnic mix of different neighborhoods, the offbeat Bohemian funkiness of Greenwich Village, the many international restaurants, jazz clubs, and the nonstop excitement of a city that never went to sleep.

When Nydia had invited him and his daughter to come to New York to visit with her family during Christmas, initially he'd believed she was throwing out the idea to see his reaction, but then he realized she was serious. There was something about Nydia that reminded him of Iggy, who'd invited Lamar to share his family with him. Interacting with the Gonzalez family had assuaged his homesickness.

"The coffee is ready."

Lamar turned from the window and returned to the dining area. Nydia had set two mugs of steaming coffee on woven placemats. He pulled out a chair and seated her, unaware he'd lingered a bit too long over her for propriety, as he inhaled the coconut scent on the strands of her shiny dark-brown hair. He recalled Nydia saying that Cameron was Jasmine's genie who sought to grant her every wish. He didn't know why, but he wanted to become Nydia's genie and grant at least one of her wishes. And as unguarded as she presented, he felt there was another side of her personality she would never reveal. Only those closest to her would be privy to her innermost secrets.

He rounded the table and took his own seat. "Do you like our French roast and chicory blend better than Bustelo?" Lamar recalled drinking the robust coffee that was brewed in espresso coffeemakers.

Nydia stared at him over the rim of her mug. "It's a tossup. I prefer café au lait with beignets because the bitterness of the chicory offsets the sweetness of the powdered sugar, while Bustelo can be drunk as espresso or blended with warm milk and sugar for *café con leche.*"

"You sound very diplomatic."

"There's no way I'm going to utter a bad word about your local foods, because it's truly off the chain."

Lamar winked at her. "At least we can agree on something."

Nydia's eyelids fluttered wildly. "Why would you say that? It's not as if we've been arguing about nonsensical things."

Suddenly Lamar felt as if he'd come down with another case of foot-in-mouth. "You're right. I must confess we have gotten on rather well for strangers."

Nydia smiled. "I agree."

Lamar continued to stare at Nydia as he drank his coffee. He had to acknowledge that she brewed an excellent café au lait. He drained the mug and stood up. "It's time I head out."

"Don't leave until I give you the *pasteles*." Nydia rose, walked into the kitchen, and opened the freezer to the French door refrigerator. She returned with a decorative shopping bag and a plastic container filled with tamales wrapped in parchment and tied with butcher twine. She placed the *pasteles* in the bag and handed it to Lamar. *"Buen provecho."*

He took the bag from her outstretched hand and then leaned over and kissed her cheek. "Thank you." There was no need for her to wish good appetite; he knew it was going to be a struggle not to devour them in a few days.

Nydia walked him to the door. "Thank *you* for a most enjoyable evening."

His eyes lingered on her delicate features as if committing them to memory. "It's been my pleasure."

She opened the door. "Get home safe."

Lamar forced a smile. "I will." He walked out of the suite and down the hallway to the elevator.

During the drive home he thought about the three hours he'd spent with a woman whom he'd wanted to get to know better, yet he hadn't been able to bring himself to ask her if he could see her again before she returned to New York.

He had only a few more days before his vacation would come to an end. And he was scheduled to return to Baton Rouge on Sunday to pick up Kendra and bring her back to New Orleans for the start of the new school year. Monday would signal a return to life as he knew it: work and caring for his daughter. Interacting with Nydia was a pleasant and temporary distraction — something he hadn't anticipated when Jasmine had called to ask him if he could show her friend the renovations on the house.

And Jasmine's friend and maid of honor was someone who had reminded him of how routine his life had become. If the employees and regulars at Ruby's were shocked to see him bring a woman to the restaurant, then he'd surprised himself when he'd asked Nydia to accompany him. The venue had always been a favorite of his, but he had never been able to convince Valerie to go with him because she refused to visit what she'd called a juke joint.

When he first met Valerie he'd found himself drawn to her sunny, outgoing personality, a trait perfect for a flight attendant whose duties included tending to the needs of her passengers. Once they began dating she exhibited a wicked sense of humor and a passion that had him waiting for her to return from her assignments.

Valerie had been a wonderful wife, a devoted mother, and when she died a part of him had also died with her. She may have been gone, but her image lived on in her daughter. Kendra's resemblance to her mother was uncanny, and the only thing Lamar regretted was that his daughter's personality had changed dramatically after Valerie's death. The once happy child became sullen, refusing to talk, and preferred spending hours in her bedroom texting on her phone. Lamar had enrolled her in counseling to deal with the loss of her mother, but sessions yielded not much more than he'd suspected. She was angry with Valerie for dying and leaving her when her cousins and friends still had their mothers.

He'd allowed Kendra to spend the summer with her cousins, and whenever he went to visit her in Baton Rouge he'd found her changed. She appeared more carefree, laughing and playing with his sister's daughters, while saying she would talk to him later. For Lamar, later meant her coming home, and he wanted her to feel comfortable enough to talk openly with him about any and everything.

He entered the Upper French Quarter and drove down the dead end street to the last house on the block. He slowed and maneuvered through the *porte cochère* and into the courtyard. Light shone through the windows of his housekeeper's bedroom. It was apparent Ramona had returned from her two-week vacation.

He parked the Volvo in the two-car garage next to her Mini Cooper and scooped the shopping bag off the passenger seat. Lamar got out and disarmed the security system outside the door leading directly into the kitchen. He opened the freezer and placed the container with the *pasteles* on the shelf with vacuum-wrapped, labeled, and dated meat packages.

Lamar felt as if he'd hit a grand slam when he'd asked Nydia to save him a dance at Jasmine's wedding. Not only was she feminine, sophisticated, and smart, but she was also refreshingly witty. Whenever she opened her mouth he could not imagine what she would say. She'd kept him off-balance, which meant he was forced to step up his game to keep up with her. A slight smile tilted the corners of his mouth as he left the kitchen and headed for the back staircase. He liked Nydia and thoroughly enjoyed the time he'd spent with her. Four months. That's how long it would be before he would see her again.

He decided not to say anything to Kendra about taking her to New York during her school's Christmas break. A change of scene during that time of year would benefit both of them. Valerie had lost her life two days before Christmas.

CHAPTER 7

Nydia's departure was a repeat of her arrival: dinner with Jasmine, Hannah, and Tonya in the hotel's private dining room. Her gaze lingered on each of her friends, and she felt their loss even before leaving them.

Her month-long stay had sped by quickly. She'd become accustomed to ordering beignets and café au lait for breakfast, but she knew when she returned to New York, it would be a bagel with cream cheese and coffee light and sweet. And she had also gotten used to the sweltering summer temperatures and oppressive humidity.

The first time she'd set out on foot to explore the central business district she'd discovered the Outlet Collection at the Riverwalk. Nydia felt like a kid in a candy shop when she strolled through the mall with more than 120 stores. It had become the perfect place for her to shop for Christmas gifts. It had taken several days for her to cross off all the items on the list she wanted to give her parents, grandmother, brothers, sisters-in-law, and nieces. She also took advantage of the hotel's business office services when she wrapped and shipped her purchases to her parents' brownstone for safekeeping until it came time for the family's Christmas Eve tradition of exchanging gifts.

Jasmine and Cameron had returned from their honeymoon tanned and seemingly more in love with each other, and the new bride had enlisted her support when she admitted she had to shop for clothes to accommodate her thickening waistline.

Tonya and Gage were featured in the entertainment section of the local newspaper after a renowned food critic had interviewed them about the impending launch of their new supper club in the Garden District. He'd been assigned to critique the Singletons' anniversary soirée and their son's wedding, and the columnist had given the professional chefs rave reviews and had highly recommended reservations once Toussaints opened to the public.

Her gaze lingered on Hannah, who'd talked incessantly about seeing the light at the end of the tunnel with the ongoing

144

renovations to her ancestral home. She claimed she was eager to begin her new career as an innkeeper.

Hannah met her eyes. "I know you're tired of me beating my gums, but this is the last time I'm going to ask you whether you want to be the DuPont Inn's CFO."

Nydia felt all eyes on her as she gave the lawyer a direct stare. "I'm still not sure."

"What aren't you sure about?" Tonya asked.

"Whether I want to move from New York."

"What's keeping you there?" Hannah questioned. "Didn't you tell us you're no longer seeing your deadbeat boyfriend?"

"I broke up with Danny almost a year ago." Nydia didn't know why, but she felt as if she were being interrogated about a crime she did not commit.

Tonya glared at her. "So, there's really nothing in New York to keep you from relocating."

"What about my family?" Nydia said defensively.

"That's the same excuse I used," Jasmine added. "I didn't want to leave my parents because I'm an only child. Meanwhile I had no idea they'd planned to leave New York and move to North Carolina."

Nydia blinked slowly. "Your circumstances

were different. Your parents were leaving New York, and you're pregnant with Cameron's baby."

"That's bullshit, *chica*, and you know it! I had no idea I was carrying Cameron's baby when I came down for Tonya's wedding. And even if I wasn't pregnant, I'd still already committed to investing in the inn."

Tonya dabbed the corners of her mouth with her napkin. "Maybe you should find a local man like the rest of us and give up the Big Apple for the Big Easy."

"She already has," Jasmine confirmed. "She went out with Lamar Pierce. When I first met him I thought he looked like the CNN journalist Don Lemon. That was when Cameron told me Don Lemon is also a native Louisianian."

Nydia rounded on Jasmine. "Since when did you become a snitch?" She did not want to believe her best friend had revealed what she'd told her was a secret.

"Are you talking about Lamar Pierce who lost his wife in a drunken driving accident?" Hannah questioned.

Jasmine nodded. "Yes."

Nydia sat, stunned, when Hannah related the details of Lamar losing his wife. "Everyone said they were the perfect couple. Valerie was a flight attendant, and she was on her way to the airport when a drunk driver hit the taxi in which she was a passenger and it burst into flames, instantly killing her and the driver."

Nydia folded her hands in her lap. "How long ago did it happen?"

Hannah crossed her arms under her breasts. "It will be four years this Christmas. I remember the incident because I'd come back home to celebrate the holiday with Paige and LeAnn. Her death had become front page news because the driver of the other car was the grandson of a wealthy local oilman."

Tonya leaned forward. "What happened to him?" she asked Hannah.

"He was arrested and his family hired a high-priced attorney, who got the judge to agree to an exorbitant bail and the forfeiture of his passport. The lawyer claimed he wasn't drunk, but had neglected to take his bipolar medication. The lawyer also asked for a change of venue because he knew his client could never get a fair trial in New Orleans. The spoiled little shit had been involved in several DUIs."

"What happened to him?" It was Nydia's turn to repeat Tonya's query.

"He OD'd on heroin a month before he was scheduled to stand trial. I don't know whether it's true, but I'd heard through the legal grapevine that Lamar sued the family's estate for the wrongful death of his wife and the mother of his daughter. The case was settled out of court and all documents relating to it sealed."

Nydia rested a hand over her throat. She'd invited Lamar and his daughter to celebrate Christmas with her and her family not knowing of the tragedy that had torn his family apart during the most festive holiday season of the year.

Hannah lowered her arms and took a sip of wine. "When you went out with him, he didn't tell you about losing his wife?"

"No."

"How many times did you see him?"

"Just once."

"Maybe they didn't talk but decided to do other things that were much more pleasurable than talking," Tonya teased with a dimpled grin. "Look what happened to Jasmine when Cameron asked her out for what should've been one date."

"I knew I shouldn't have told you about that," Jasmine mumbled under her breath.

Nydia pointed at Jasmine. "See how it feels when someone snitches on you."

Hannah threw up a hand. "Stop it! We're all grown-ass women who shouldn't be ashamed to talk about what we do with our men."

"Like St. John going commando and you giving him a lap dance in the backyard?" Tonya said, deadpan.

"Damn!"

"Coño!"

Jasmine and Nydia had spoken at the same time. "You didn't tell us that," Jasmine said accusingly.

A flash of humor crossed Hannah's face. "That's because what goes on in the family stays in the family."

"And what are we, Hannah? Chopped liver? Just because you and Tonya are married to cousins, does that make me and Nydia outsiders?"

A noticeable blush appeared on Hannah's cheeks with Jasmine's sharp retort. "I'm sorry I made you feel like an outsider. I never thought I'd say it, but you, Nydia, and Tonya are the sisters I wish I'd had. You women have always had my back and for that I'll be eternally grateful, and that means I trust y'all with my life."

Nydia felt tears prick the back of her eyelids with Hannah's passionate entreaty. Even though she did not have a sister, she felt as close to the three women as if they were related by blood. "Dial it down, Hannah, or you'll have all of us crying and soupin' snot."

Hannah touched a napkin to the corners of her green eyes. "I know I can get a little emotional at times but —" She didn't get to finish her statement because the other three women at the table tossed cocktail napkins in her direction. Throwing back her head, she laughed until tears rolled down her cheeks.

Nydia pressed her palms together. "I'm not going to promise anything definitive at this time, but I'll let you know once I get back to New York and tie up a few loose ends when I'm going to join you all as an innkeeper." She knew her pronouncement had shocked those sitting at the table when they stared at her. "Isn't that what you wanted to hear?"

They recovered enough to flash wide grins. It had taken months of uncertainty, but now that Nydia had committed to becoming an innkeeper she felt as if a weight had been lifted off her. Not only had she missed her friends but she also had come to love New Orleans enough to make it her home. She'd talked about leaving her family when they were only a phone call away. And with FaceTime, she could see them anytime she wished.

"Why are y'all sitting there like bumps on a log?" She raised her wineglass. "It's time we toast my new beginning."

Tonya winked at Nydia. "Now you sound like a real Southerner when you say 'y'all' for 'you all.' "

"Does this mean I can call y'all heifers instead of *putas*?"

Jasmine landed a soft punch on her shoulder. "You're incorrigible."

"And you love me for it, don't you?"

Jasmine rested her head against Nydia's. "You bet I do. I wouldn't have you any other way." She reached for her clutch on the table beside her plate and opened it. "I wanted to wait until tonight to give you guys something to show my appreciation for supporting me when I needed it most. Hannah, I thank you for helping me get what I deserved during my divorce. Tonya, I can't thank you and the Toussaints enough for the incredible dishes you created for my wedding. And Nydia, *chica,* I'll always love you for encouraging me to go out with Cameron, because I had no idea I could be this happy."

She handed each of them a velvet drawstring bag. "I know y'all saw *Girls Trip,* where four best friends come to New Orleans wearing necklaces with 'FP' for 'Flossy

151

Posse.' We're not the Flossy Posse but from now on we'll be known as 'The Innkeepers.' "

Nydia opened the bag, and a pendant suspended from a white gold chain shimmered on her palm. The letters TI were at least an inch-long drop and covered with a shimmering display of blue-white diamonds. Her gasp echoed Tonya's and Hannah's. Jasmine had given her a diamond bangle as a gift for being her maid of honor and now the pendant.

"You didn't have to do this, *mija,*" she said.

"Yes, I did, *chica.* We all have hit bumps in the road we call life and have overcome. That's not to say that there won't be other bumps, and if there are, then I want y'all to be there for me. We may all come from different mamas, but if I had to choose my sisters, then it would be the women seated at this table." Pushing back her chair, Jasmine stood up, gathered her clutch, and walked out of the room, leaving them staring at her back.

"Let her go," Nydia said, when Hannah stood up to follow Jasmine. "She gets even more upset when people see her cry."

"It has to be hormones," Tonya stated.

Hannah retook her chair. "I just don't

want Cameron to believe that we've upset his wife. The man is like a rabid pit bull when it comes to Jasmine. Say one wrong thing about her, he's coming for your throat."

"That's because he's been afflicted with a condition called love," Tonya said. "The man waits until he's ready to join AARP to fall in love, marry, and become a first-time father."

"Don't knock it, Tonya," Hannah countered. "There are times when I can't believe how much I love St. John. It's not to say I didn't love my first husband, but this time it's different, because I trust St. John. And to me, trust in a marriage supersedes love."

"Don't forget the fact that Daddy is taking care of you the way you deserve to be taken care of. Didn't you say that St. John takes care of business in bed?" Nydia teased. Hannah nodded. "I rest my case, counselor." She gave Tonya a sidelong glance. "And I know your papi is laying pipe right."

Tonya covered her eyes as she burst into laughter. "What are we going to do with that mouth?"

"Nothing, but accept the truth, Mrs. Toussaint. I saw that hickey on your neck you tried to cover with a bandana the night of the Singletons' anniversary dinner. It was apparent Gage was sampling more than the dishes he'd prepared."

Hannah lifted pale eyebrows. "You seem very glib when it comes to love, and I'm willing to bet that one of these days you'll meet a man who will turn your life upside down and for the good."

"I doubt if that's going to happen," Nydia countered. "And besides, I'm not ready to deal with a man at this time in my life."

"What about Lamar?" Hannah asked.

Nydia shook her head. "Especially not Lamar. I don't think I have the temperament to get involved with a man with a teenage daughter. We would clash and combust like tossing a match on gasoline." She stood up and rounded the table and hugged Tonya, and then Hannah. "I'm going to turn in because I have to be up early for my flight."

Hannah kissed her cheek. "When are you coming back?"

"I'll call and let you know." She blew a kiss to Tonya. "Love you."

Nydia walked out of the dining room and headed for the elevators. She never liked goodbyes, especially if there would be distance between her and the ones from which she departed. During the ride to her suite she recalled what Hannah had said about Lamar losing his wife, and there was no way she could imagine his grief when he'd been told the mother of his child had died in a fiery crash. And the fact that he was still wearing his wedding ring indicated he hadn't stopped grieving for her.

She liked Lamar, enjoyed spending time with him, but she drew the line when it came to becoming romantically involved with him, because there was no way she would be able to compete with a dead woman for his love. She'd been in a relationship where unknowingly she had become the other woman, and she vowed it would never happen again.

Reaching into the pocket of her jeans she took out the key card and the velvet bag with the pendant Jasmine had given her. Her friend had had a jeweler design the pendants in advance of her agreeing to become an innkeeper. And Nydia wondered if Jasmine knew her better than she knew herself. Well, she had given Hannah her word that she would invest in the DuPont Inn, and anyone who knew Nydia Stephanie Santiago knew she never went back on her word.

Nydia waited a week after returning to New

York to unblock Danny's number and call him. His phone rang three times before he picked up.

"*Hola, muñeca.*"

She frowned. Nydia hated when he used her father's endearment for her. "Hello, Danny."

"I guess you got my message."

"Yes. Millie said you wanted me to call you."

"Did she tell you I got a recording contract?"

"Yes," she half lied. She'd viewed the television segment minutes before her cousin's call. "Congratulations! It's well deserved."

"Thank you. It is possible for me to see you?"

"For what, Danny?"

"I thought we'd get together and celebrate over dinner."

Nydia shook her head although he couldn't see her. "I don't think that's a good idea."

"Look, Nydia, I know what we had didn't end well, but I've been getting together with everyone who has been supportive to me during my journey to secure a record deal. And you're the last on the list of those I need to thank in person."

156

Shifting into a more comfortable position on the bed, Nydia adjusted the pillows cradling her back and shoulders. She wanted to reject his offer to meet, yet she registered something in his voice that wouldn't permit her to tell him no. What, she thought, could it hurt to see him one more time? And it wasn't as if they would reconcile, because she'd agreed to become an innkeeper in New Orleans.

"Okay, Danny. Where do you want to meet?"

"How about El Rincon?"

Nydia smiled. Danny knew that was her favorite restaurant. "I'm okay with El Rincon."

"Are you busy tomorrow night?"

Monday night fit into her plans because she'd promised her mother she would come by and spend the day with her. She owed it to Isabel to tell her in person that she was planning to move to New Orleans. "Tomorrow night works well for me. What time do you want to meet?"

"I'll pick you up at six."

Did he really believe she was that gullible? There was no way she wanted him to know where she lived. "I'm not going to be home. What if I meet you at the restaurant at six?" she countered.

A pregnant silence ensued before Danny said, "Okay. I'll meet you there at six." There came another pause. "Thank you, Nydia."

"You're welcome, Danny."

She tapped the screen, disconnecting the call, and set the phone on the bedside table. Seeing her ex again would not only close a chapter on what they'd had, but also the book. Danny had sacrificed a relationship with her to make his dream a reality, and she was truly happy for him.

Nydia unlocked the door leading to the first story in her parents' brownstone. It was apparent her father had replaced the runner along the hallway and the carpeting on the staircase, which had begun to show signs of wear.

Luis Santiago had prided himself on being an excellent landlord. Since his retirement from the NYPD he'd taken over some of the maintenance responsibility from the elderly longtime building superintendent. Her father now shoveled snow and mowed the small patch of lawn at the rear of the property. He'd also parceled off a section of the backyard for his wife, who'd planted an herb garden along with tomatoes and peppers.

She rang the bell to the apartment even though she had a key.

"It's open," Isabel shouted from somewhere inside.

Nydia pushed open the door and entered the expansive entryway with its exquisite parquet floor in a herringbone pattern. It had taken years for her parents to restore the property to its original magnificence. She walked through the living and dining rooms to the kitchen, where she found her mother and grandmother sitting at the table watching the television that rested on the countertop.

"No digas nada," Ana Medina whispered without taking her eyes off the television when her granddaughter kissed her.

Nydia swallowed a groan. She should have known better than to come when *Maury* was on. It was rare that her grandmother missed the *Maury* and *Jerry Springer* shows. And because Isabel closed her salon on Mondays, the older woman had recruited her daughter to watch them with her. She sat through two segments of "You *are* and you're *not* the father!" before garnering her mother's attention and signaling she wanted to talk to her.

Nydia looped her arm through Isabel's and led her out of the kitchen and into the family room. The obvious gray in her mother's short, wavy, dark hair indicated she'd stopped dyeing it. And those who saw them together were astounded by their resemblance. It was as if Nydia were Isabel's younger clone.

"Thank you for rescuing me," Isabel whispered. She sat on the love seat, and Nydia dropped down next to her.

Nydia gave her mother a sidelong glance. "I thought you liked *Maury.*"

"It was entertaining when I first started watching it, but after a while there's a limit to the theatrics."

"It's too ratchet for me," Nydia admitted. "And you know I'm not into sitcoms or reality TV." She'd grown up watching nighttime dramas with her mother. "Where's Papi?"

"He went fishing with a few of his retired buddies. I didn't tell you, but they pooled their money and bought a twenty-foot boat. They moor it off City Island, and a couple of times a week they go fishing."

"You're kidding."

"I wish I was. At first I thought they used the boat just to hang out and drink beer, but when Luis came home with an ice chest filled with almost a dozen fish I was really impressed."

"Good for him." It was nice that her father had found a new hobby other than tinkering around the house. "I came over to tell you that I've decided to accept Hannah's offer to invest in her inn."

It had only become a reality for Nydia when she'd downloaded and printed out Hannah's partnership agreement. She'd read it over twice and then forwarded it to her attorney sister-in-law for her approval. Twenty-four hours later she received an email with a thumbs-up emoji. It was only when she'd electronically signed the contract and authorized her bank to wire a check to Hannah that she'd felt compelled to tell her family about her future plans.

Isabel's expression spoke volumes as a smile spread across her face. "Oh, I'm so happy for you. When you first told me about your friend's offer to make you a partner in her business I kept waiting for you to say you'd do it."

"But why didn't you say something, Mami?"

Isabel's lids lowered over her dark green eyes. "Because I didn't want you to think I was trying to run your life. I heard that enough when you were younger."

Nydia laced her fingers through her mother's. "That's because I thought I knew everything."

Isabel smiled. "A hard head makes for a soft behind."

"Now that I look back I would've preferred you spank my behind rather than be grounded for half my childhood."

"I had good reasons for grounding you. I can put up with a lot of things, but not my children talking back when I tell them to do something. Your brothers were quick learners, but it seemed as if you had a problem with your hearing, because everything I'd say would go in one ear and out the other."

Nydia nodded. "And I remember you wishing when I have a daughter she'll be just like me. Then I'll know what you had to go through."

Isabel shook her head. "Now that I look back I wouldn't wish that on anyone. Not even you. It was as if you couldn't stop challenging me."

"Papi said I was just exercising my independence."

"As far as your father was, and still is, concerned you can do no wrong."

"I didn't turn out too badly, did I?"

"You turned out wonderfully." Isabel kissed her hair. "And I'm even more proud of you now that you're going into business for yourself." Isabel paused. "And whatever time I have left on this earth I don't ever want you to call me again and say that you were fired without cause."

Nydia rested her head on her mother's shoulder. "I hope it never happens again, too." She knew if she were to secure a position with another company, bank, or investment firm there was no guarantee she wouldn't experience what she had with Wakefield Hamilton.

"When are you leaving?"

"I don't know, Mami. Renovations are still ongoing. Hannah is hoping they'll be completed before the end of October."

"That's next month, Nydia."

"True. I've given Tonya money to pay rent on her apartment through the end of the year. And when she notifies building management she's not going to renew the lease, then they'll have to return her security, which she has promised to give to me."

"And that means what?" Isabel asked.

"I'll probably move sometime around the end of December or the first week in January."

Isabel shifted, looking directly at Nydia. "Do you still plan to celebrate Christmas with the family?"

"Of course. And speaking of Christmas I invited someone I met in New Orleans to join us for Christmas Eve."

"Is that someone a man?"

"Don't give me that look, Mami. Yes, it's a man, and if he comes then, he's bringing his daughter."

"How old is the child?"

"Ten."

"What about her mother?"

Nydia exhaled an audible sigh. "She died four years ago just before Christmas."

Isabel emitted a soft gasp. "It must have been devastating for that child to lose her mother at that age."

"I'm sure it was and still is."

"Have you heard the news about Danny Ocasio getting a record deal?" Isabel asked, deftly changing the topic of conversation.

"Yes. Millie called and told me he wanted to talk to me."

"Did you?"

"Yes. We spoke yesterday, and I'm going to meet him tonight at El Rincon. It will probably be the last night we'll ever see each other. There's no doubt he's going to be a superstar recording artist, and I'm moving to New Orleans."

"Are you certain you don't want to reconcile with him now that he's signed a lucrative contract?"

Nydia closed her eyes for several seconds.

"I'm very certain. There were issues other than money that impacted our relationship." She would never reveal to her mother that Danny had told his friends he didn't need to hold down a steady job because his girlfriend earned enough to support him until he broke into the music business. And once he became a star he could have any woman he wanted.

She didn't want to discuss Danny. "I'm going back to sit with Abuelita. She always complains that she doesn't see me enough."

Isabel pushed to her feet. "I'm coming with you."

CHAPTER 8

Nydia leaned closer to the partition separating her from the taxi driver. "You can put me out at the next corner." They were three blocks from El Rincon, and she decided to walk the rest of the way. She shoved a bill through the slot and got out of the cab. The wailing of sirens and flashing lights, along with bumper-to-bumper traffic along Second Avenue, was an indication she would not make it to the restaurant to meet Danny on time. And being tardy was one of her pet peeves.

The sidewalks were teeming with people entering and leaving stores and those standing on corners waiting for the lights to change. Nydia shouldered her way through a group of young girls wearing their school's uniform. They were talking over one another, their voices escalating as they attempted to make their point.

She smiled. There had been a time when

she was one of those girls, talking louder and faster to make herself heard. Nydia estimated they were around fifteen or sixteen, and she wondered if she'd been that loud or obnoxious at that age. Her mother had made her teenage years a living nightmare, when she punished her for talking back while Nydia thought of it as speaking her mind. It had taken a while for her to understand it wasn't what she'd said, but how she'd said it. Once she tempered her tone, Isabel appeared more open to her opinions and requests.

Nydia held out her hand to signal a driver to stop turning the corner as she stepped into the intersection. As an adolescent she would have screamed at the driver that the pedestrian had the right of way, or if she was feeling particularly hostile, flip them the bird. Thankfully those incidents were behind her, and navigating crowded streets and sidewalks on her way to work would become a thing of the past once she moved to New Orleans and into her suite in the Garden District mansion.

As the CFO for the DuPont Inn, she would live rent-free on the premises; and her meals at the café Martine and the supper club Toussaints were also gratis. Food and lodging were the most important and significant components in any household budget — two factors that would no longer exist for her.

However, Nydia knew she would have to either buy or lease a car to get around her new city. Her father had taught her to drive, but owning a car in Manhattan had become prohibitive because of the dearth of available parking. She hadn't wanted to get up every other morning to move her vehicle from one side of the street to the other for opposite side of the street parking, or drive around aimlessly to find a space blocks from her home. And there was no way she wanted to spend hundreds of dollar a month for a space in an indoor garage.

She made it to the restaurant with minutes to spare. There were a number of empty seats and booths in the popular eating establishment. If it had been the weekend Nydia knew she would have had to wait to be seated. She spotted Danny at a booth for two located close to the kitchen. He'd put on sunglasses and a baseball cap, probably in an attempt to conceal his identity.

He stood up with her approach. "Thanks for meeting me, doll," he whispered in her ear. "Please change places with me, because I want to sit with my back to the door."

She complied, sat, and slipped off the

strap of her cross-body bag and placed the small purse on the seat beside her. "How are you dealing with the fame?"

Danny Ocasio lowered his eyes. Long, dark lashes touched a pair of high cheekbones in a sculptured face that reminded Nydia of the Greek statues she'd seen in museums during her school's field trips. His thick black hair fashioned into a man bun, swarthy complexion, large, seemingly laughing dark eyes and balanced features had most women giving him a second and occasionally a third glance. Danny was the epitome of self-confidence when it came to his artistic talent and looks, but there was an exception few were aware of: height. Standing five-seven in bare feet had become his Achilles' heel, and he had made it a practice always to date girls who were shorter than he.

"It comes and goes," he said in a quiet voice. He looked up, his eyes boring into Nydia's. "It's like winning the lottery, and everyone you know wants a piece of your prize."

"That's where you're wrong, Danny. I want nothing from you."

He nodded. "I knew you would be the exception." A waitress came over and left menus on the table. "Please give us a few minutes," he said when she lingered at the table.

"Okay, *mi amor,*" she drawled, and then winked at him.

Nydia lifted her eyebrows. "Before it was Danny, and now you're *mi amor?*" she teased.

A flash of humor crossed his face. "What did I say about wanting a piece of the prize?"

She knew he was right. Any time news floated around the neighborhood about someone winning Lotto or money from a legal settlement, relatives they never knew surfaced. "When do you start recording your album?" she asked in an attempt not to talk about money — the very subject that had become the source of her refusal to commit to a future with him.

"Next month. I'll be going to LA with my manager and publicist."

"You already have a manager and publicist." Her query came out as a statement.

Danny nodded. "Once I got more than two million hits on the song I uploaded to YouTube, this dude contacted me and said he could get me a recording contract if he signed on as my manager. I had nothing to lose and everything to gain, so I signed on the dotted line. Three weeks later the head of new talent called and asked me how many songs I'd written. When I told him over thirty, he said he would contact my manager and discuss what they were willing to offer."

He paused and smiled as if hiding a secret. "I have to confess that my manager is as lethal as a piranha when it comes to negotiating. I got a very lucrative signing bonus and a lot of other perks usually afforded gold record artists."

Resting her elbow on the table, Nydia supported her chin on her fist. "They did it because they recognize your talent."

"But do you?"

She blinked slowly. "What are you talking about?"

"Did you really believe I'd never make it, Nydia?"

Nydia lowered her arm. "It was never about your talent, Danny. It was all about you accepting responsibility for taking care of yourself that was a problem in our relationship. And it wasn't about my making more money than you."

"Then what was it about?"

She counted slowly to ten to compose herself; otherwise her tongue would get the best of her. And she'd promised herself after her final break with Danny that she never wanted to spew expletives at another man as long she lived. If they disagreed about something she would state her opinion and then walk away to avoid an acerbic verbal confrontation. She'd had enough arguments with Danny Ocasio to last her several lifetimes.

"It was about my not wanting to be used by you. Word got back to me about you telling your so-called homeboys that I would take care of you until you got your big break, then after that you could have all of the . . . let me get this right. All of the bitches you'd ever want." Danny stared at her as if she'd suddenly grown a third eye in the middle of her forehead. "Are you going to deny you said it?"

Danny closed his eyes and shook his head. "No. I only said it because my boys were on me about having a girlfriend who was making crazy money."

Nydia leaned forward. "It was *my* money, Danny. Not yours or theirs. I gave up a social life in college because I had to study practically around the clock because I didn't want to lose my scholarships. I sacrificed again to get a graduate degree and then study for the CPA exam. I was paid well because I'd put in the work, and all I'd asked was that you get a job where you earned enough so you wouldn't have to depend on your relatives to put a roof over your head or food in your belly."

"Get real, Nydia. You know how much rents are in Manhattan."

"Of course I know, because I'm renting an apartment in Manhattan, and before that a furnished apartment in the Bronx, which if you'd had a job rather than playing gigs on the weekend you could've afforded. You had options, Danny. What's wrong with working in any of the brand name stores along 125th Street? Sixteen dollars an hour for an eight-hour workday, Monday through Friday, adds up to more than twenty-five hundred a month before taxes. You'd earn enough to pay rent, and with your weekend gig you could've used that money to buy studio time."

Smiling, Danny slowly shook his head. "I'm still amazed that you can compute numbers in your head." His expression changed as his smile faded. "I guess I couldn't see it then. I was so fixated on singing that everything else was secondary. And what I regret most is losing you. But if you give me another chance I'd like to make it up to you."

Nydia went completely still, her breath catching in her chest as she stared numbly

173

at Danny when he slid off the booth and went down on one knee. He reached into the pocket of his jeans and opened a ring box. The size and brilliance of the center stone rendered her mute. She could not believe he was proposing marriage. Then, without warning, someone emerged from the kitchen and pushed a microphone close to her face while the flash from a camera temporarily blinded her. It only took seconds for Nydia to reach for her bag and push through the crowd that had gathered to watch the spectacle.

"Are you going to marry him?" a woman called at her departing back.

Nydia shook her head. She raced out of the restaurant as several people followed her retreat. She didn't want to believe Danny had chosen a public place to blindside her with a marriage proposal. It had been nearly a year since their breakup, and he was mistaken if he thought she was so desperate that she would become his wife because he was a celeb.

"Miss Santiago, are you going to turn down Danny Ocasio's proposal?"

She turned to find a man with a microphone standing only a few feet away. There was another next to the curb filming her. She clamped her teeth tightly to keep from saying what she really wanted to say. This was one time she wanted to let loose with every vulgarity she'd ever known.

"No comment," she said, flashing a tight smile. "I wish Danny all the success he deserves," she added diplomatically.

That said, she turned and walked down the block to hail a taxi. One skidded up to the curb and she got in, and she gave the driver her address. Nydia covered her face with her hands and struggled not to cry. Never in her life had she been so publicly humiliated. The old Nydia would have cursed Danny in English and in Spanish and behaved so badly she would have brought shame on her family. But she had turned a corner in her life, and she never wanted to resurrect the old Nydia.

She waited until she was back in her apartment before she called her cousin. *"No puedo creer que él me hiciera eso,"* she blurted out in Spanish once she heard Milagros's greeting.

"What don't you believe? Who did what?"

"Danny." She quickly revealed her meeting with her ex and his impromptu proposal.

"Coño, prima," Milagros drawled. "He should've known better than to spring something like that on you. Has he forgotten that you broke up with him last year?"

175

"I don't know, but he has to be living in an alternative universe if he believes we can take up where we left off as if nothing happened. Now that he has money he can have all of the *putas,* bitches, hoes, or whatever derogatory names men call women."

"And you know girls are going to be on him like stink on shit once the word gets out that Nydia Santiago turned down his proposal. They'll be throwing panties, thongs, and G-strings at him to get his attention."

"I don't care what they do, Millie, but I'm through with him."

"How big was the ring?"

Nydia smiled in spite of herself. "Let's say it was too big for my hand."

"Damn! Was it Kardashian big?"

"I'm no expert when it comes to judging the size of a diamond, but I'd wager it was at least six or maybe seven gaudy-ass carats." She recalled Jasmine's three-carat engagement ring, and the one Danny had shown her was twice as large. "What he should've done was save his money."

Milagros's snort came through the earpiece. "I would've taken the ring and after a few months break the engagement and then sell the bad boy. You put up with more crap from him than I would have."

"That's because I told myself that I loved him."

"You may have loved Danny but I never heard you say you were in love with him. There is a difference."

"I know that now." Nydia had only admitted to Jasmine that she'd stayed with Danny because of sex. But after a while even sex wasn't enough to keep them together.

"You said there were media people at the restaurant, so do you think footage of his proposal will end up on television?"

"It probably will. Danny said he now has a publicist, so I'm certain everything was staged in advance. I'm not going to worry about it because I'm leaving New York by the end of the year."

Milagros gasped. "So, you're really moving to New Orleans?"

"Yes." Nydia had told her cousin about Hannah's offer but at the time hadn't reached a decision as to whether she wanted to invest or leave New York.

"I've always wanted to go to New Orleans for Mardi Gras, but whenever I tried to get a hotel room near the action my travel agent confirmed they were all booked up."

"You won't have to worry about that next year, because I'll save a room for you at the inn. Or you can share my suite."

"Thanks, Nydia. Once next year's vacation schedule at my job becomes available, I'm going to take off and come down to Nawlins to hang out with my favorite cousin."

Nydia chatted with Milagros about her future plans before ending the call. She still did not want to believe that Danny had set up the entire scenario where he would be recorded proposing marriage to a woman he'd purported to love. Not only was he devious and duplicitous but also so overconfident that she would take him back because he had made it.

Even if she had thought about a possible reconciliation, she couldn't, because she didn't trust him. She remembered Hannah saying trust in a marriage supersedes love. And if Nydia ever fell in love and married, then she would have to trust the man even more than she loved him.

Nydia's worst nightmare was manifested three days later when she walked out of her apartment building and was accosted by a reporter recording her on a cell phone. The woman wanted details behind her relationship with Danny, whose single had become the most downloaded song for the past three weeks.

"No comment." It had become her pat response. Turning, she walked up the steps and back into the building. There were more than a million people living in Manhattan, and someone from the media had found her address. What she found odd was her name wasn't even listed on the building's lease. Perhaps she was being paranoid, but she suspected the taxi driver who had been conveniently double-parked outside of the restaurant had also been a plant.

Nydia knew if she were now face-to-face with Danny, she would tell him exactly what she thought of him. That she wouldn't allow him to use her for salacious gossip just to enhance his newfound image. It wasn't happening, because she refused to become a pawn in a scheme concocted by his publicist who wanted to project a good-guy image for his client by urging him to propose marriage to his longtime girlfriend. So many male celebrities were seen with a merry-go-round of women, while others were content becoming baby daddies, so it was obvious the publicist was playing a new angle.

Danny had made the grievous mistake of not taking the time to really know who she was when they were dating, because then he would have known she didn't need a man to define her.

■ ■ ■ ■

Nydia waited two days before attempting to leave her apartment again, only to encounter this time a man who'd been sitting in a car across the street from her building. He was a lot more persistent, but when she threatened to call the police and charge him with stalking, he got back into his car and drove away. Then she did something she'd promised herself she wouldn't do again: she called Danny and left a voice mail message that she was going to sue him for harassment if he didn't stop the press from invading her privacy.

He didn't call back later that night, and she knew why. Footage of their meeting in El Rincon, and the subsequent encounter with the reporter waiting for her when she'd left her building, were featured on *TMZ*.

Her cell phone had rung constantly throughout the afternoon when friends and relatives revealed they'd viewed the segment with her and Danny. She literally had to talk her police sergeant brother off the ledge when he threatened to tune up Danny for shaming his sister.

"No, Nelson. I don't want you to lose your job with the NYPD because of that clown."

180

"I wouldn't do it myself."

"I don't care. He's not worth it. Now, promise me you won't do anything to him. Nelson?" she asked, when encountering silence.

"Okay, sis. Only because you asked me. Pops is so mad that Mami threatened to leave him if he went looking for Danny."

Nydia did not want to believe the men in her family were ready to end Danny's professional singing career before it had begun. "I'll call Papi later once he's calmer."

"Are you sure you're going to be all right, because I can have some of my men drive by your place to make certain you're not being harassed."

"They'll probably leave me alone now that the videotape is out."

"I hope that's true."

Nydia didn't feel as confident as she sounded, but hoped she was right.

Lamar was sitting in the family room watching television, while Kendra sat on a window seat talking on her cell phone, when the image of Nydia and the man she assumed was her ex appeared on the screen. He was transfixed seeing her expression of shock and distress once she realized she was being filmed by a popular syndicated entertain-

181

ment and gossip news program. He'd tuned the television to the station because Kendra told him she wanted to write a report to compare different entertainment news programs for her English class. He took a furtive glance at his daughter. It was apparent she was more interested in talking to her classmate than focusing on the television screen.

The segment was over when Kendra sat beside him. "That was Casey. Her mother said she can't do a report on supermarket tabloids because they print lies, so I told her to buy the entertainment magazines instead."

Lamar smiled and placed an around her shoulders. "What did she say?"

Kendra returned his smile. She'd been recently fitted for braces, and it taken time for her to get used to them. She always carried a small cosmetic case with a toothbrush and paste to brush her teeth after every meal to prevent food from sticking to the brackets.

"She said her mother was okay with the magazines."

Lowering his head, he pressed a kiss to her neatly braided hair. Not having his daughter for the summer had changed both of them. It appeared as if she'd grown several inches and appeared less childish, and the older she'd become, the more she resembled her mother.

"How many segments of *TMZ* do you have to see before you're familiar enough with their format to make a comparison between *Access Hollywood, Extra, Inside Edition,* and *Entertainment Tonight?*" he asked.

"No more than three each. Remember there are four of us in each group, so we're going to pool our research and decide on what we want to present to the class."

Originally Lamar had thought the subject too mature for sixth graders, but when the English teacher sent home a permission slip with explicit details of the project, he gave his approval for Kendra to participate. She had a choice between radio, print, and television with topics covering music, sports, entertainment, and news programming.

Picking up her pen and pad, Kendra listened intently to what the different journalists were reporting and their delivery. "Maybe I should DVR the shows and then play them back on a night when I don't have school. Now that I'm in the sixth grade I have so much more homework."

Lamar turned his head so his daughter wouldn't see his smirk. It was the same thing he'd said to her when she'd begun the project. "That sounds like a good idea."

Kendra kissed his cheek. "I'm going to my room to finish my math and science."

"I'll set the DVR to record your shows."

She came to her feet. "Thanks, Daddy."

"Don't stay up too late."

"I won't."

Kendra had promised him she would turn off her phone when doing homework and would leave it off until the next day. Lamar knew he had to trust her not to go back on her pledge.

Lamar waited until Kendra had retreated to her bedroom before he called Nydia. "Are you all right?" he asked when she picked up. He'd promised Kendra to DVR the shows, but he planned to delete the footage with Nydia. He didn't want his daughter to connect the woman whose life was flashed across the screen with a scandal not of her choosing.

"Yes."

"I saw the *TMZ* segment."

"You and probably millions of other people."

He ignored her acerbic tone. "Are you all right?" he asked for the second time.

"I will be once all of the nonsense dies down."

"Are you certain it will?"

There was a pregnant pause. "I don't know, Lamar."

Extending his legs, he slumped lower on the love seat. "Talk to me, Nydia."

He heard the pain and frustration in Nydia's voice when she told him she was being hounded by the press and slandered in social media because she didn't want to marry Danny Ocasio. She also admitted to being a prisoner in her own home since there was always someone lurking outside her apartment building hoping she would give them an interview.

"I know his publicist is behind the scheme because he wants to market Danny as this up-and-coming heartthrob who is a tortured soul because his muse and the love of his life has broken his heart. I may have been his girlfriend, but never his muse."

"It sounds good because it sells copy. Give me your address?"

"Why?"

"I want to mail something to you."

"What?"

He smiled. "It's a surprise."

"Aren't you going to give me a hint?"

"No. Then it wouldn't be a surprise." Lamar mentally stored her address, including her apartment number, into his memory.

185

"Look for it to arrive this weekend."

"I'll be here. And thank you, Lamar."

"For what?"

"For lending your shoulder."

"Anytime you need a shoulder, I'm here for you."

"Thanks. Good night."

"Good night."

Lamar hung up and retreated to his home office to go online to search for flights to New York. He hadn't told Nydia his surprise was to run interference between her and the press so, hopefully, they would leave her alone. He found several flights for the weekend and booked a red-eye into La-Guardia for early Saturday morning and reserved a return flight for Sunday evening. His next task was to arrange for a car service to pick him up to take him to the airport.

Lamar knew he had to tell his daughter and housekeeper he would be away for the weekend. He found Ramona in the kitchen peeling potatoes while listening to the radio. When he first hired her, whenever he referred to her as Miss Griffin she'd correct him and say to call her Ramona. Although divorced, she hadn't dropped her ex-husband's surname. She always prepared the next day's dinner the night before, which allowed her to relax once she finished her housework. He regarded the tiny, dark-skinned woman with a coronet of salt-and-pepper braids as a part of his extended family. She claimed it was her calling to take care of other people's children because she could never have any of her own. Her husband of fifteen years had left her for another woman, and she claimed it was the best thing that had happened in their marriage. She had grown tired of his cheating.

"Ramona."

Her head popped up. "Yes."

"I'm flying up to New York this weekend, and I want to know if you're willing to look after Kendra. If not, then I'll drop her off at my sister's Friday afternoon and pick her up Sunday night."

"I don't mind looking after her. We'll get along just fine."

Lamar gave the fifty-something woman a long, penetrating stare. "And I don't want her to invite Evangeline's twins or the Kelly girls for a sleepover. I haven't told her that I'm leaving, but I'm going to warn her that she's to stay home while I'm gone."

Ramona Griffin blinked slowly, her large eyes unwavering. "What about her having company over?"

Lamar ran a hand over his head. It was as if his daughter and housekeeper were cocon-

187

spirators. "Yes, she can have company. But no sleepovers."

Ramona smiled. "I like when the house is filled with children's voices."

"Yeah, I know." One time she had crossed the line between employer and employee and asked if he was ever going to marry again and have more children. He had given her a withering stare, and she immediately apologized. Lamar made it a practice not to discuss his personal life with his house-keeper.

It wasn't that he didn't want to fall in love again and marry, but his daughter came first. She would turn eleven in November, and that meant he had another seven years before she went off to college. By that time, he would be forty-five, unencumbered, and free to engage in a relationship which could possibly lead to marriage.

"Thank you, Ramona." She nodded and went back to peeling potatoes.

Lamar went up the staircase to the second story and knocked on the door to Kendra's bedroom. "May I come in?"

"Give me a sec, Daddy." The door opened slightly and Kendra smiled at him. "Yes?"

He peered over her head. "May I come in?"

She opened the door wider. "Of course.

I'm not on the phone," Kendra said quickly. "You can check if you want."

Lamar tugged at a braid falling over her shoulder. "There's no need for me to check. I came to tell you that I have to go away this weekend. I told Miss Ramona that you can have company, but no sleepovers."

The girl's eyes lit up like someone turning on a light. "Really, Daddy?"

"Yes. And company means no boys."

A rush of color darkened Kendra's cheeks. "I'm not into boys. They act so stupid."

Not yet, Lamar thought. He knew there would come a time when she would be into them. "Not all boys are stupid," he said in defense of his gender. "I'm leaving Friday night and I'll be back on Sunday."

"Where are you going?"

"New York."

She pushed out her lips. "You promised me you were going to take me to New York."

"And I intend to keep that promise this year. I have a friend who invited us to spend Christmas in New York with her and her family."

Kendra caught his arm. "Who is she?"

"Someone you'll meet once we get there."

She let out a piercing scream that threatened to deafen him. "Whoa, baby girl. What are you trying to do? Make your old man

189

hard of hearing?"

Kendra went on tiptoe and kissed his cheek. "You're not old, Daddy. A lot of my friends' fathers have gray hair."

Lamar wanted to tell his daughter her friends' fathers were in their late forties and early fifties and were on their second and some even third marriages. "I don't want you or your friends to give Miss Ramona a hard time or —"

"I know," Kendra interrupted. "I won't be able to have company for a long time."

"Or I won't let you go and visit your friends."

She nodded. "I know, Daddy."

"I'll let you get back to your homework. Don't stay up too late."

"I won't. Good night."

He smiled. "Good night, sweets."

Lamar closed the door, walked across the hall, and entered his bedroom. It took less than twenty minutes to pack a carry-on with what he needed for the weekend. It was only when he put a toiletry case in the bag that he questioned what he was about to embark upon. He was planning to fly up to New York to provide comfort to a woman he'd met three times. The first was when he'd stared at her like he'd been shocked with an electric current and unable to move. The second was Cameron's wedding, when they danced together. And the last was when he'd taken her to Ruby's.

And with each encounter he'd found himself becoming more and more enthralled with Nydia Santiago. He'd made the decision to go to New York because he felt compelled to be there for her, but the underlying reason was to discover why she'd crept into his thoughts when he least expected. As CM, or construction manager, for his company, he was responsible for the oversight of all new and ongoing projects. Their company had been awarded several contracts to build commercial office buildings and military substructures. He'd accepted the offer to oversee the renovations on Cameron's future home because it was personal. Once the former warehouse was converted and decorated for family living, he knew it would become an award-winning showplace.

Lamar returned to his home office and sent an email to his partners informing them he would be away over the weekend; he was scheduled to be out of the office for the next two days inspecting the construction of a medical building in Abita Springs and the restoration of an antebellum mansion on the Great River Road.

He spent the next two hours reviewing the plans for both projects, and when he finally climbed the staircase to ready himself for bed he noticed there was no light under Kendra's door. She'd gone to bed without his telling her.

He'd found Kendra different after spending the summer with his sister's family. It was as if she'd stopped challenging him, and he wondered if she needed to be around more children her age. And it wasn't for the first time that he regretted not giving Kendra a sister or brother. He and Valerie had talked about having more children, but she wanted to wait until Kendra was two. By that time Valerie complained she wanted to go back to work.

He'd broached the subject of increasing their family once Kendra celebrated her fourth birthday, and it wasn't what Valerie said but what she did not say: she preferred her career to motherhood. After a while, Lamar dropped the subject, and he thought he was fortunate to have been blessed with one child.

It wasn't quite ten o'clock when Lamar climbed into bed after showering and brushing his teeth. He had to be up early and on the road to meet with the construction foreman before his crew began their eight a.m.

shift. His last thought before he surrendered to sleep was the expression of shock on Nydia's face when a reporter shoved a microphone at her. There was no doubt she needed a friend other than her family and those who were familiar with her and her deceitful ex, and he hoped when he returned to New Orleans she would no longer be harassed by the newshounds and paparazzi.

CHAPTER 9

Nydia was startled when the buzzing of the intercom echoed through the apartment. She glanced at the clock on the microwave. It was almost eight-thirty. Lowering her feet, she stood up and walked to the door. The intercom rang several times a day since the fiasco at El Rincon, and whenever she activated the video feature she saw a face that was totally unfamiliar to her and suspected it was a reporter.

Pressing the button on the panel, she gasped when Lamar's face appeared on the video intercom. He'd said he was sending her a surprise, and Nydia never would have guessed that he would deliver it in person. She pressed another button and disengaged the lock on the door leading into the building's vestibule.

Nydia still did not want to believe all that had happened in the span of five days: she'd been blindsided with a shocking marriage proposal; stalked by reporters and paparazzi looking for gossip about her and Danny Ocasio; and footage of her as his runaway fiancée had appeared on prime-time and cable entertainment news stations. Now she was reluctant to leave her apartment because she didn't know who was waiting to snap her picture or ask for an interview.

Her parents wanted her to come and stay with them, but she'd refused their offer. Her stubborn streak had surfaced when she told her mother she wasn't going into hiding. She would remain at her apartment until all of the hoopla died down.

Hannah and Tonya had also called to offer their support, while Jasmine asked if she wanted Cameron to reserve a private charter to fly her to New Orleans. She thanked her friends and reassured them she was counting down the days to when the entire incident would become old news.

Nydia opened the door and smiled. Lamar had stopped halfway up the stairs, seemingly trying to catch his breath. Her heart rate quickened when his head popped up. She couldn't see his eyes behind a pair of sunglasses, and he'd covered his head with a black New Orleans Pelicans' cap. He hadn't shaved, and the stubble appeared more gold than gray against his rich mahogany-brown face. And she liked seeing him casually dressed in a pair of black jeans, matching pullover and running shoes. His black attire made him appear taller and slimmer.

"Come on. You can make it," she teased, as he slowly made his way up the staircase to the fifth-floor landing.

Lamar shook his head. "I can't believe you do this every day."

"I must confess it took me more than a month before I was able to come up without stopping on the third floor to catch my breath. Please come in and sit down before you fall down."

Lamar dropped his carry-on and sat on the padded bench seat in the entryway and slipped out of his running shoes. He stood, removed his cap and glasses, and then lowered his head and kissed Nydia's cheek. "Thank you."

Her eyes lingered on the slight cleft in his chin. He was more handsome than she'd remembered. "You should've told me that you were my surprise."

"Are you disappointed?"

"Oh, no," Nydia said much too quickly. She grasped his free hand. "I'm glad you came, because I could use someone impartial other than my family to talk to. They're

196

like rabid dogs chomping at the bit to take Danny apart."

"I'm not *that* impartial, Nydia. I'm certain if I would've been with you when that buffoon blindsided you I would've clotheslined him where he'd never sing again. Who proposes to a woman with whom you haven't had a relationship in a year?"

Nydia laughed freely for the first time since Monday night. "I never thought you would resort to violence."

He winked at her. "Nerds can get gangsta, too."

She was still attempting to deal with Lamar flying up from New Orleans to be with her during what had become a stressful time in her life, and she was also amazed at the thrill she had felt when seeing his image on the video intercom.

Looping her arm through Lamar's, she steered him in the direction of the kitchen. "I'm glad you're here. How long are you staying?"

"I'm flying back tomorrow night."

"I know they didn't feed you on your flight, so I'm going to make breakfast for both of us."

"I need to wash up first."

Nydia released his arm. "I'll take you to the bathroom." She led him through the living room and dining area and down a hall. "Take your time. By the way, how do you like your eggs?"

"Over easy."

Lamar entered the bathroom and closed the door. The instant he noticed the dark circles under Nydia's large hazel eyes he knew she hadn't been sleeping well. Even before boarding the flight departing New Orleans, Lamar had asked himself several times whether he was doing the right thing flying to New York. After all, Nydia had friends and family to support her, so was showing up at her place unannounced an exercise in futility? But seeing her smile when she opened the door had defused his apprehension.

He glanced around the bathroom as he washed his hands in the pedestal sink. There was a claw-foot tub, shower stall, and commode. The colors of seafoam green and pale yellow, along with potted plants on the window ledge, gave the space a tropical appearance. The shelf below a low table held a collection of towels in tropical colors of pink, green, yellow, and pale blue. Candles in the corresponding colors crowded the top of the table.

Lamar dried his hands, walked out, and

peered into the bedroom only a few feet away from the bathroom. The entire space was decorated in white with varying shades of blue ranging from cornflower to robin's egg, from the pale walls with a border embossed with tiny blue flower buds to the blue-and-white-striped linens and quilt. His gaze lingered on the off-white queen-size iron bed, double dresser, and matching bedside tables, and he wondered if Nydia's ex had shared the bed with her.

He shook his head to rid it of the image of Nydia sleeping with a man. She'd openly admitted she wasn't in a relationship, and he wondered what her ex had done for her to stop seeing him. Lamar had come to see Nydia to lend her emotional support, and also to get to know her better. He wanted to uncover why he was drawn to her when it hadn't been that way since he had become a widower. He liked women — a lot — although he wasn't drawn to a particular type.

Some men preferred women with a particular hair color or texture; others a certain height, weight, and body type. But when it came to a woman Lamar was a blind sculptor who couldn't see, but could smell, touch, and hear. For him it was her feminine scent, the silkiness of her skin, and the timbre of her voice and laugh. Nydia Santiago had scored high where others had struck out, and when he factored in her intelligence, she was a perfect ten.

He reversed his steps and lingered in the living/dining area. The furnishings were reminiscent of an African hunting lodge. A zebra-print rug covered the glossy parquet floor and the off-white sofa and matching love seat cradled throw pillows covered in colorful animal prints. Nydia's apartment was immaculate and meticulously decorated.

He stood at the entrance to the eat-in kitchen watching Nydia as she filled a saucepan with water. She appeared delicate, almost fragile, in a pair of black leggings, oversize tee, and black ankle socks. The hair flowing around her face and ending at her shoulders reminded him of long chocolate Twizzlers.

"Do you need my help?"

She looked up and smiled. "Do you cook?"

"Not very well," he admitted sheepishly. "But I can set the table."

Nydia pointed to an overhead cabinet. "The cups and plates are in there. And the silverware is in a drawer under the countertop."

Lamar opened the cabinet door. "What's on the menu?"

"I thought we'd have a Southern breakfast with grits, eggs, biscuits, and sausage gravy."

He froze. "What do you know about a Southern breakfast?"

She rolled her eyes at him. "This Boricua knows how to cook more than just Latin food. I shared this apartment a couple of months before Tonya moved to New Orleans, and she taught me how to prepare Southern food, while in turn I did the same with Spanish dishes."

"The *pasteles* you gave me didn't last a week."

Nydia stared at him, complete surprise freezing her features. "You ate a dozen *pasteles* in a week?"

Lamar laughed as he removed plates and cups from the cabinet. "No. I had help. I gave my daughter and housekeeper a little piece to see if they liked it, and that was all she wrote. Then I had to boil a couple for them. Three days later, there were none. I've eaten a lot of *pasteles,* but yours were the best I've ever had."

"I'll definitely tell Abuelita that she has another fan. Whenever we used to tell Abuelita that she made the best *pasteles* in the whole wide world, she would give us a

201

sly smile and then say, *'Yo sé.'* My mother would try to get her to say thank you instead of 'I know,' but Abuelita knows her *pasteles* are the bomb."

"They are definitely going to be a hit with the locals when Tonya adds them to her menu," Lamar stated.

"Everything she and Gage prepare will be a hit."

Lamar had to agree with Nydia. Chez Toussaints was renowned when it came to serving Cajun and Creole dishes to diehard customers, but with professional chefs Gage and Tonya Toussaint opening their own restaurant in the Garden District and offering an eclectic international menu, the family's reputation was certain to soar beyond the environs of the Big Easy.

"Are we eating in the kitchen?"

"No. You can set the table in the dining area."

Lamar busied himself setting plates, glasses, cups and saucers, serving pieces, and napkins on the table with seating for four. He hadn't learned to cook well, but he did know how to set a table for formal or informal dining. His mother had given up on him when he refused to grasp the steps that went into preparing a meal, so she assigned him the task of setting the table.

He returned to the kitchen as the distinctive aroma of sausage wafted to his nostrils. "That smells delicious."

Nydia smiled at him over her shoulder. "Tonya turned me on to a local butcher who makes his own sausage. My favorites are country sage and cheese and garlic."

Leaning against the entrance, Lamar crossed his arms over his chest. "You and Tonya were roommates?"

Nydia gave him a quick glance. "Only for two months. We were like college students sharing a dorm. We stayed up late, and slept even later the next morning. We'd go down to Washington Square farmers' market or to the Hunts Point produce market in the Bronx to shop for ingredients we couldn't find locally. Last Christmas when my grandmother wanted to make *pasteles* I told her I would shop for the ingredients. I called the butcher and placed an order for Boston butt and pork bones for the stock, and Abuelita raved about how much better they tasted. I've volunteered to buy everything she needs to make them this year. When you and your daughter come up for Christmas, I want you to be prepared not to get much sleep. The house will be loud and noisy with Nelson and Joaquin's kids underfoot. The women will do most of the cooking, while the men hang out together in Nelson's man cave watching and talking sports all day and half the night."

"I'm really looking forward to it. I told Kendra we were coming up here for Christmas, and she nearly blew out my eardrum when she screamed."

"How long do you plan to stay?" Nydia asked him.

"How long do you want us to stay?"

"Christmas is on a Tuesday this year, so why don't you come up either late Friday or Saturday. We always have a Christmas Eve banquet and at the stroke of midnight we open gifts. Christmas Day is for sleeping in late and eating what is left over. I'd like to plan a few outings for the girls for that week before you and Kendra return home."

"I'm willing to pay for the outings."

Nydia shot him a withering glance. "That's not happening."

He held up his hands in surrender. "Sorry about that." It was apparent he'd put his foot in his mouth without thinking of the consequences. Nydia hadn't mentioned money. Lamar recalled Nydia telling him she was subletting Tonya's apartment, and he wondered for how long she planned to live here. "When does the lease expire?" he asked, verbalizing his thoughts.

"January thirty-first."

"Are you going to renew it?"

Nydia concentrated on breaking up the sausage meat into little pieces with a wooden spoon. "No."

He stood straight. "Where will you live?"

She turned and gave him a direct stare. "I'm moving to New Orleans. I've decided to invest in Hannah's inn, so we'll probably get to see each other in our travels about the city."

Lamar stared at Nydia, speechless for what seemed an eternity when in reality it was seconds. When she told him about her former coworkers investing in the DuPont Inn he'd wanted to encourage her to join them, because there was no doubt they would be formidable partners in a city with too few women owning and running their own businesses. And he also had a selfish reason for wanting her to relocate: it meant he could see her again.

His outward calm belied his inner excitement knowing he and Nydia would live in the same city. "I'm certain we'll run into each other. When do you plan to move?"

"I'm going to wait until after Christmas, that is if Tonya's daughter doesn't need the furniture in the apartment before that time. Samara was planning to move into a new

205

apartment complex while attending grad school, but there was a delay in the construction. Right now she's staying with her future in-laws. If I'd decided to stay here, I was going to rent furniture. Jasmine had promised to decorate for me, but that was before she got involved with Cameron." She lowered the flame and placed a lid on the frying pan. "Do you know what I find strange?"

"What, Nydia?"

"Last May Jasmine, Tonya, and I decided to take the summer off after we were downsized. Hannah already had plans to return to New Orleans for her fortieth high school reunion. Meanwhile, months before, she'd begun the process of converting her ancestral home from a residence to a business, so the impact of her not having employment differed from the rest of us. We all came down for a visit in July, and during that time Tonya committed to opening a café and supper club in one of the guesthouses on the property. And that meant she was leaving the crew. Then Jasmine meets Cameron at Hannah's wedding, and the rest is history. I was the last holdout, and even if I hadn't committed to invest before the debacle with Danny, it would have been the straw that broke the camel's back."

"What do they say about best-laid plans?"

She smiled. "It's apparent they were made to be broken."

Lamar walked into the kitchen and put his arms around Nydia's waist and eased her closer. "It's karma. Or as some say it was predestined. People come and go into and out of our lives for a reason."

Tilting her head, she stared up at him. "Are you saying that crazy shit between me and Danny was destined?"

Lamar nodded. "Yes. If it hadn't happened then I wouldn't be standing here with you. I would've had to wait for Christmas to see you again."

She lowered her eyes. "Why *did* you come?"

"Once I saw your face when that reporter came out of nowhere, and after talking to you and hearing the pain in your voice, I knew I couldn't stay away."

"Why, Lamar?"

"For a very bright woman you have to ask me why?"

Her arms circled his waist, and she rested her head on his shoulder. "I asked because I'd like an answer."

"Remember you telling me that Cameron took one look at Jasmine and he lost his natural-born mind? Well, it was the same with me. The day Jasmine brought you to the worksite to show you the loggia, I felt as if I'd lost more than my mind." Lowering his head, he whispered in her ear the effect she'd had on him.

Nydia started to laugh and couldn't stop as she sagged weakly against his chest. "I'm sorry," she apologized. "But I didn't expect you to disclose that."

Lamar frowned. "It's not that funny, because I was in pain."

She covered her mouth with her hand as she continued to laugh. "I had no idea you rushed off to get hard hats because you didn't want us to see your hard-on."

His expression was impassive. "At least I'm man enough to admit just looking at you was a turn-on."

Nydia sobered. "And I am woman enough to say that although I was flattered when you stared at me, you also made me feel uncomfortable."

"How so?" he asked.

"Because I'd never had a man look at me the way you did. I didn't feel it was lust, but more like curiosity."

Tightening his hold on her waist, Lamar molded her body to his. "It'll never be about sex between us, because that's something you can get from any man."

"What is it you want from me?" she whispered against his sweater.

"Just you, Nydia, because you make me feel things I'd forgotten existed. It's been a long time since I've enjoyed a woman's company."

"Are you saying you haven't dated since losing your wife?"

"Not in the traditional sense."

"Which means you sleep with women?" Nydia asked.

"Yes."

"Have you slept with one since meeting me?"

"No." He hadn't sought out nor had he thought about another woman since Jasmine introduced him to Nydia.

"Thank you for being honest with me."

"I will never lie to you."

"Or I to you," she admitted. Pushing against his chest, Nydia extricated herself from his embrace. "I have to make the biscuits."

Lamar felt her loss immediately. He'd enjoyed the warmth of her body seeping into his and inhaling the scent of coconut on her hair. He sat on a stool and watched as she moved comfortably around the kitchen, checking on the grits and sausage.

He noticed the single-serve coffeemaker

on the counter. "Do you mind if I brew a cup of coffee?"

Nydia smiled at him. "Of course not. It's not the chicory blend you're used to."

Lamar slipped off the stool and plucked a coffee pod from the carousel. "I only drink café au lait when I eat beignets."

"I told my mother I'm going to have to trade in my bagel with cream cheese and light and sweet coffee for beignets and café au lait once I move to New Orleans."

"How did your parents take the news you'll be leaving the Big Apple for the Big Easy?"

"My mother was always very supportive, because she's an advocate of female-owned businesses. She's operated her own hair salon for twenty-five years. My father was against me moving until this craziness with Danny and his people. Now he thinks it is better I leave. Papi is really laid back, but if anyone messes with his *pequeña muñeca,* or little doll, as he used to call me, then he's not so easygoing. History has repeated itself with my brother and his daughters. Nelson is currently a sergeant with the NYPD, and he's like a live grenade. He went ballistic when he heard about the *TMZ* tape, but I managed to calm him down."

Lamar gave Nydia a sidelong glance as he

waited for the coffeemaker to warm up. "How are you doing with the craziness?"

She sprinkled a wooden board with flour and kneaded a ball of biscuit dough. "I'm coping."

"You shouldn't have to cope, Nydia. And you also shouldn't have to be a prisoner in your own home."

"This, too, shall pass," she said under her breath.

"I know," Lamar countered. "After we eat, we're going out for a walk. And to return the favor of you making breakfast I want to take you out to dinner. Don't look at me like that," he warned, "because I intend to run interference if anyone comes at you."

"What are you going to do? Go gangsta on them?"

"Gangsta or not, you can count on me to protect you whenever we're together."

Nydia recalled Jasmine talking about men protecting her. First her father, then her much older lover, and now Cameron. Her friend did not realize how lucky she was, because there were women who went through their entire lives without a man's protection. Other than her father and brothers, she had never been involved with a man willing to protect her. The man in her first

211

serious liaison failed to tell her he was married until confronted by the man's wife; and she didn't want to think of what she'd had with Danny, who'd used her and had planned to use her again with a public bombshell proposal.

She pondered what type of connection she could look forward to having with Lamar. He'd claimed he didn't need her for sex, unlike her married professor who'd claimed she was the best woman he'd ever slept with. And he didn't need her to support him financially, unlike Danny, who'd refused to get a job while waiting for his big break. But more important for her, Nydia had no intention of becoming a replacement for his dead wife. She was willing to offer friendship and not much more, because she now had two strikes in the romance department.

"Are you sure you want to be seen with me?"

Lamar gave her an incredulous look. "What's wrong with being seen with you?"

"New Orleans may be thirteen hundred miles away from New York City, but it could be thirteen when livestreamed on the internet. I've closed my Facebook, Messenger, and Twitter accounts, and set up a new email because of nasty threats from people who don't even know Danny and even less about me. Why should it matter to them if I reject a man's marriage proposal? I'll answer that question for you," she said, not giving Lamar time to reply. "Because Danny's publicist is hyping him up even before his first album drops. Danny admitted the man's a piranha and with this so-called media blitz he's achieved his objective: catapult his client into the spotlight as a spurned heartthrob, while the woman who rejected his undying love is a heartless skank."

"Do you really care what people think of you, Nydia?"

She halted rolling out the dough. "No. What I do care about is dragging my family and friends into the fray. Think about your reputation. Do you want your photo splashed over the pages of some tawdry tabloid for your friends and family to start asking questions about me?"

"I've never put much stock into what people think of me. I live my life by a certain rubric and anything or anyone that doesn't fit within those guidelines I reject."

"That sounds very rigid."

"Is it, because I am," Lamar admitted. "I see things as either black or white."

She cut out a half dozen biscuits, placing them on a greased baking sheet, and then brushed the tops with melted butter. Nydia wanted to ask Lamar, if they disagreed on something, would it be his way or the highway? He'd admitted to being rigid, while she was more adaptable and willing to compromise.

"Where are we going for dinner?" she asked as she placed the biscuits into the preheated oven.

"I rented a car at the airport because I'd like to take you to City Island."

Resting her hip against the countertop, Nydia flashed a knowing smile. "Should I assume my offering to prepare breakfast has nothing to do with you returning the favor, because you'd already planned to take me to dinner?"

Lamar lowered his eyes and flashed a sheepish grin. "Guilty as charged."

"I'm willing to bet that you added a dose of confidence to your Froot Loops for breakfast."

His grin faded, replaced by an expression of astonishment. "How do you know I eat Froot Loops?"

"I have nieces and nephews around your daughter's age, and oatmeal is not at the top of the list if selecting their favorite breakfast cereal."

"I do eat it occasionally when Kendra

decides to take over the breakfast duties from Miss Ramona. The breakfast menu is always Froot Loops, toast with peanut butter and bananas, and orange juice. Talk about sugar overload."

"It's the gesture that counts, Lamar."

He nodded. "I know. How come you don't have any kids?"

"Hel-lo," Nydia drawled. "I'm not married."

"Being married shouldn't be a prerequisite for motherhood."

"For me it is."

"And what if you never marry?"

"Then I won't have any. It's not that I don't have what you'd called maternal instincts, because I love hanging out with my nieces and nephews. It's just that I'd rather be married, because I grew up in a stable household with both parents. I'm certain Papi and Mami had their disagreements, but they were careful not to let us see them at each other's throat. I've been around friends and some family members when they were engaged in knock-down, drag-out, full-blown baby mama and baby daddy dramas. Their kids were crying and pleading with their parents to stop fighting, and I knew that was something I never wanted to experience for myself or my children."

"Maybe that's because the parents think only of themselves and not how their negative behavior is affecting their children's emotional well-being."

"You're preaching to the choir, Lamar."

Nydia had had the same conversation with her mother whenever Isabel asked if she was ever going to have more grandchildren. Nelson's wife had two girls and Joaquin and his partner had adopted two boys, but that still wasn't enough for Isabel. Well, her mother would just have to wait for another grandchild until Nydia met the man with whom she would fall in love, marry, and together plan for a family.

Although she had spent more years with Danny than she should have, Nydia never deluded herself in believing they were even close to considering marriage.

She returned her attention to finishing up breakfast as she made a roux from the sausage drippings and flour. Milk thickened the roux, as she seasoned it with a pinch of salt and freshly ground pepper before adding bits of sausage to the gravy.

Twenty minutes later, Nydia placed golden brown piping-hot biscuits on a platter and handed it to Lamar. He returned to the kitchen to set a serving bowl with grits on the dining area table. She ladled perfectly turned over-easy eggs onto a heated plate, walked out of the kitchen, and joined Lamar as he stood behind a chair, waiting to seat her.

"Thank you," she said, as he pushed in her chair.

Lamar rounded the table and sat opposite her. "You really can throw down in the kitchen."

"I do okay."

"Now who's being modest," he teased.

"You better start eating before everything gets cold."

He picked up a napkin and spread it over his lap. "You don't have to tell me twice."

Nydia picked up a serving spoon and filled her plate with grits, eggs, gravy, and a biscuit. She bowed her head and said grace, knowing Tonya would be pleased that her student had successfully prepared an authentic Southern breakfast.

CHAPTER 10

Lamar blew out a breath, at the same time patting his flat belly over his sweater. "Everything was delicious. If I eat like this every day I'd weigh well over two hundred pounds."

"You wouldn't if you had to walk five flights of stairs several times a day," Nydia said, smiling. "By the way, how much do you weigh?"

"One eighty," he admitted.

"That's not much for your height."

"It's enough for someone who's six foot."

"I thought you were taller than that."

Lamar winked at her. "That's because you're a little bitty thing. What are you, five-one?"

She managed to look insulted. "Not! I'm five foot two."

"Five-two is still petite. My daughter is ten, and she's already five-four."

Nydia leaned back in her chair. "How tall

was her mother?"

"Valerie was five foot six."

"There you go, Lamar. Your daughter will be at least her height or taller. I know she's only ten, but does she know what she wants to be when she grows up?"

Lamar folded his napkin and placed it beside his empty plate. He'd eaten one biscuit, then another, and before long he'd devoured four of the buttery, incredibly melt-in-the mouth quick breads. He wanted to tell Nydia that she was every normal man's dream. She had looks, brains, and she could cook!

"Kendra claims she wanted to be a fighter jet pilot."

Nydia leaned forward. "You're kidding."

Lamar shook his head. "No, I'm not. She loves to fly, and I guess she got that from her mother. Valerie was a flight attendant."

"That would mean a career in the military. If she can get into the Air Force or Naval Academy, then she can write her ticket, because times have changed where women are now piloting military jets."

Lamar spayed his fingers on the table. "That's only a possibility if she keeps her grades up. Fortunately, she's a whiz kid when it comes to math and science."

"I suppose she gets that from Daddy."

"I did okay."

Nydia pointed at him. "There you go again being self-effacing."

"I thought I was modest," Lamar countered, reminding Nydia of what she'd said the night of Cameron's wedding.

"That, too." She stood and began clearing the table. "What type of engineering was your major?"

Lamar rose and gathered plates and flatware. "Construction engineering."

"What's the difference between a construction engineer and a civil engineer?"

He followed Nydia into the kitchen, scraped and rinsed the dishes before handing them to her to stack in the dishwasher. "Construction engineering is a professional sub-practice area of civil or architectural engineering."

"I still don't understand the difference."

"As a construction engineer I deal with designing, planning, construction, and management of infrastructure such as tunnels, roads, bridges, railroads, dams, and other projects. Civil engineers concentrate primarily on the design work, which is more analytical. My partners are civil engineers and I'm the CM, or construction manager. I focus on construction procedures, methods, schedules, costs, and personnel management. My primary concern is to deliver a project on time, within budget, and of course with the desired quality."

"Do you have cost overruns?"

"Spoken like a true accountant," he said, smiling. "Yes. A few times, but that's something we strive to avoid."

Lamar enjoyed the easygoing shared domesticity as he and Nydia cleaned up the kitchen. It was a task he hadn't performed since becoming a widower. Valerie would prepare dinner and he'd always volunteered to clean up afterward. It was their time to talk about what had occurred during the day or what she'd experienced when returning home for a few days or a week of jetting to different cities. Other than sharing a bed it was the only time when they were able to spend quality time together.

"Did you enjoy working for Wakefield Hamilton?" he asked Nydia.

He'd asked because he wanted to know if Nydia used the excuse she didn't want children because she preferred career to motherhood. It was only after Valerie gave birth to Kendra and took a two-year maternity leave that she'd admitted that if she'd had a choice she wouldn't have become a mother, because she loved being a flight attendant. His late wife was always restless

221

and sometimes short-tempered when she wasn't in the air.

"I loved working for them," Nydia admitted. "Firstly, they paid off my student loans, and offered me a phenomenal starting salary with incredible perks and benefits, and secondly I was assigned the responsibility of scrutinizing the accounts of our foreign clients."

"Did you ever uncover any shady transactions?" he asked.

Nydia took a saucer from him and stacked it on the lower shelf. "Once, but I was never given the chance to expand my investigation."

"What happened?"

"When I alerted my supervisor of my suspicion the customer was using the bank to launder money using one of our depositor's real estate properties, he assigned it to another accountant who he claimed had more experience investigating fraud. It was BS. They hired me because I have a bachelor's degree in forensic accounting and an MBA with a concentration in taxation."

"So, you're like that little dude that sharpened his pencil and took down Al Capone for income tax evasion."

Nydia bumped him with her hip. "Don't knock us pencil pushers. We're the ones who find the evidence to indict crooks for embezzlement, corruption, and other financial crimes."

"Have you ever considered working for the feds?"

"I've thought about applying to the FBI as an accounting and finance special agent."

Lamar stared at Nydia out of the corner of his eye. "What made you change your mind?"

She smiled. "My family doesn't need another cop. My father retired from the NYPD as a sergeant, and my brother is also a sergeant who just passed the test to become a lieutenant."

"That's a lot of shields and automatic handguns."

"Word," she drawled, smiling.

"After dinner I'm going to drop you off here and then check into a hotel near the Thruway."

"You don't have to do that. I have a spare bedroom where you can spend the night. Go and open the door opposite the bathroom. It used to be Tonya's daughter's room. She decorated it like a studio apartment, but I use it as an in-home office. The convertible sofa has a firm, full-sized mattress that's a dream to sleep on."

Lamar dried his hands on a terrycloth

towel. He had planned to check into a hotel in the Bronx rather than at the airport because he planned to spend more time with Nydia before his return flight.

He opened the door and smiled. Nydia was right. The bedroom was more welcoming than a hotel with the off-white sofa covered with Haitian cotton that converted into a bed. A desktop computer and printer sat on a computer table. Bookcases packed with books and magazines spanned one wall, while another was decorated with framed movie posters and photos of movie and recording artists. A drop-leaf table held a flat-screen television and audio equipment. His gaze lingered on a large white area alpaca rug covering the gleaming waxed parquet floor. It was a space that beckoned him to come in to sleep, study, or relax. After walking across the room, he opened a closet door to find shelves and a rod to hang and store clothing.

He returned to the kitchen to find Nydia cleaning the stovetop. "I'll take it."

She smiled at him over her shoulder. "Good. As soon as I'm finished here I'm going to change and we can go for our walk."

"While you're changing I'm going to unpack my carry-on."

Lamar didn't want to congratulate himself — not just yet. He'd taken a risk flying up to New York on an impulse, not knowing whether Nydia would appreciate his abrupt intrusion into her life. However, he'd been truthful when he told her how much seeing the distress on her face and hearing the pain in her voice when he'd called her tugged at his heart. And if he were truly honest with himself he would acknowledge that he wanted her the way a man wanted a woman.

He knew he'd shocked her when he'd admitted he'd been sexually aroused seeing her for the first time. That hadn't happened to him since the onset of puberty, when his body would betray him at the most inopportune times, and he had to either conceal the bulge in his groin with his hands or sit and wait for his erection to go down. Lamar could have never imagined that at thirty-eight just a single glance directed at an unknown woman had caused him to lose control of his body. He'd wanted to blame Nydia for returning the long, penetrating stare, which he interpreted as meaning she was just as enthralled with him as he'd been with her. It was as if his ego had gone into overdrive.

Even now that she had invited him to stay over at her place, he found it difficult to get a read on her. Lamar didn't find Nydia uptight or tense with him, and for that he was grateful. She had been through enough with her jackass of an ex-boyfriend so he knew it would take time for her to trust a man again.

He emptied the bag of several changes of underwear, a pair of charcoal-gray slacks, a light blue dress shirt, and a silk and wool-blend gray jacket, leather toiletry bag, and a pair of black loafers in a drawstring shoe bag. Lamar had gotten used to traveling light, a practice that had come from visits to construction sites that required an overnight stay.

The cooler fall weather in New York City had come as welcome respite for Lamar from the unrelenting heat in his hometown. The past two summers were unusually hot, and scientists were blaming it on global warming, and Lamar had begun to agree with them. The daytime temperatures coupled with the humidity made it dangerous to remain outdoors for any appreciable length of time. Tourists and locals alike were carrying umbrellas to shade themselves from the blistering rays of the sun or sought shelter indoors until the daytime heat abated. The nighttime temperatures were in the mid-eighties, and the only saving grace was the absence of sun.

Lamar put away his clothes and then brushed his teeth, a ritual he'd developed from childhood at the insistence of his father. Dr. Abraham Pierce had become the local go-to orthodontist for children needing braces.

Nydia came out of her bedroom at the same time he exited the bathroom. She'd brushed her hair and pulled it off her face into a ponytail. She'd also changed into a pair of jeans, a gray St. Joseph's College sweatshirt, and pair of pink-and-gray running shoes. She held a small leather wristlet in one hand and a pair of sunglasses in the other.

"Ready!" she announced, smiling.

Lamar returned her smile with one of his own. It was obvious she was ready to leave the apartment that had become her sanctuary. "As soon as I get my hat and glasses we can leave. I want to show you the building where Iggy and his family used to live. It's not that far from here."

Going down five flights of stairs was much more enjoyable than climbing them. Lamar opened the doors leading to the street, then grasped Nydia's left hand in his right. They hadn't made it to the corner of the tree-lined street when a woman with a micro-phone appeared between two park cars.

"Miss Santiago, may I have a word with you?"

Nydia lowered her head. "No comment."

She shoved the annoying mic at Lamar. "Sir, can you tell us your connection to Miss Santiago? We saw you going into her apartment building earlier this morning. Were you on your way home?"

He stopped, turned to face Nydia, and cradled her face with his free hand. The sun glinted off the gold band on his third finger, and he deepened the kiss when he spied a man filming them. "Thank you, darling," Lamar said, loud enough to be overhead by the two stalkers when he ended the kiss.

"Is she your wife? Focus on his left hand!" the reporter shouted at the photographer balancing a video camera on his shoulder. "Are you the reason she couldn't marry Danny Ocasio, because she's married to you?" the reporter screamed at Lamar and Nydia as they strolled to the end of the block and turned the corner.

Lamar saw Nydia's shoulders shaking, and at first he thought she was crying, but then she covered her mouth with her right hand to stifle the erupting laughter. "What's wrong with these people? I can't believe the lengths they go to to get a scoop."

Nydia smiled up at him. "I think it's over now."

A frown settled between Lamar's eyes behind the dark lenses. "What are you talking about?" It had taken Herculean self-control not to snatch the reporter's and the photographer's equipment and hurl it to the ground.

She lowered her hand. "They saw your wedding band and because you kissed me they assumed we're married, and that's why I couldn't accept Danny's proposal.

Lamar's laughter floated up from his throat and mingled with Nydia's when she laughed again. They'd only seen his left hand and not Nydia's because he was holding it close to his side. "I believe you're right, sweets." He brought her hand to his mouth and dropped a kiss on her fingers. He'd enjoyed kissing her, even if it was for show. It was something he'd wanted to do when they'd danced together, shared nearly an hour sitting in an alcove at the hotel, and especially after their date at Ruby's.

There were more times than he could count when he'd contemplated taking off his wedding band, but hadn't because he still wasn't ready to let Valerie go. He knew she was gone, and he would never look for her to walk through the door of the home they made together and where they'd made memories that would stay with him for the rest of his life. And Lamar did not delude himself to say he had the perfect marriage, because there were a few rough patches they'd had to smooth over, but he could honestly say he'd enjoyed being a husband and father.

"It's a good thing you don't live here, or you'd become their next stalking victim," Nydia said.

Lamar shook his head. "I don't think so. Danny's folks got what they came for, and now it's time for their client to write a love song about losing the love of his life to another man."

"Now that I look back, I don't think I would've married Danny even if he was a recording star at the time we were dating."

"Why not?"

"I loved Danny, but I wasn't in love with him."

Lamar's shielded Nydia's body with his when a man who appeared to be high on something nearly collided with them. "Is there a difference?"

"Of course there is. I can say I love horror movies or a particular dessert. This means I can give them up at any time if they prove injurious or detrimental to my health or emotional well-being. It's the same with people. There were things I liked and disliked about my relationship with Danny, and in the end I knew it was time to let him go because nothing was going to change."

Lamar waited at the corner for the light to change. "Is it too personal to tell me about it?"

Nydia shook her head. "Not at all."

He hung on her every word, when Nydia revealed her ex's reluctance to look for steady work and his bragging to his friends about her making enough money to support him until he made it big. "Did you tell him how you earned it?"

"No, because it was none of his business. One day I left him in my apartment to run to the store, and when I got back I'd discovered he'd gone through a drawer where I had my pay stubs, and when I questioned him he said he was looking for something to write with. I knew he'd lied when my cousin who was dating one of his friends told me Danny said he was going to hang onto me until he made it big because I made lots of money, then after he was a star, he could have all the bitches he'd ever want. That's when I knew I had to leave. I wasn't his bitch, and whenever we went out I never opened my wallet for anything."

"How did he get money?"

"He was the lead singer in a Latin band. They were booked at different clubs for weddings and other celebrations. He spent most of his money buying studio time."

"Did he live with you?"

She shook her head again. "No way. He lived with his sister. The one time we talked about moving in together I told him he would have to come up with half of whatever the rent was. When he told me that wasn't possible, it gave me another reason to stop seeing him. Now when word gets back to him that I was seen with another man, maybe he and his circus will bring down the big tent sooner rather than later and leave town."

Lamar wondered if her ex really knew whom he'd been involved with. Not only was Nydia a feisty, educated, independent woman, but she lived by a certain set of standards, and she wasn't going to lower them just because she'd dated him.

He gave Nydia's fingers a gentle squeeze. "And just to mess with him, I should download Smokey Robinson's 'Tracks of My Tears' and 'Tears of a Clown' and post them on his Instagram."

Nydia slipped her hand out of his and put

232

an arm around his waist. "That's cyberbullying."

"What he needs is a good thumping. What he's put you through is humiliating and reprehensible, and he's lucky your brother didn't jack his ass up."

"I don't want to talk about Danny anymore."

"What do you want to talk about?"

"Us, Lamar."

"What about us, Nydia?"

Nydia did not want to think Lamar kissing her was for any other reason than what it was: to prove to the reporter she'd rejected Danny's proposal because she was involved with another man who could possibly be her husband. And if the scenario had been different, Nydia knew she would have kissed him back.

"I doubt if anyone's going to recognize you in a cap and sunglasses, but what if they do and identify you as the one who kissed me while we were being filmed? What are you going to say to them? I told you before I don't want to involve other people in this . . . this . . ."

"Crazy shit," Lamar said, completing her sentence.

Nydia couldn't stop fingers of heat stealing across her face. "I have to stop saying that," she whispered.

"What? Crazy shit?"

"Yes."

"Well, sometimes shit can get crazy, and we nerds are entitled to let loose every once in a while."

"Yes, we are," she said, smiling.

He's good for you. Her silent voice confirmed what she was beginning to feel about Lamar. He was the first man she'd met with whom she felt comfortable enough to be herself. With him she did not have to censor whatever came to mind or out of her mouth. Outspokenness and sincerity had become the bedrock for her friendship with Tonya, Hannah, and Jasmine. They did not bite their tongues when they told her to get rid of Danny, because she could do a lot better than dating a man who wasn't able to come to the table and pull his own weight in an adult relationship.

She'd heard *Did you kick his ass to the curb?* so often that it had become a catchphrase each time they'd asked her about Danny. Even when she confirmed she was no longer seeing him, Jasmine would look at her sideways as if she didn't believe her. Nydia was only able to confirm the breakup once she moved out of the furnished Bronx apartment and in with Tonya. It was then her friends realized the separation was final. It had taken her a while, and despite what she'd gone through with Danny, she'd learned from the experience and vowed not to repeat it with another man.

Cultivating a relationship was not a priority at this time in her life. Her focus was on becoming an innkeeper. The instant she downloaded the signed contract with Hannah she knew she had been given a second chance to start over.

"Did you say something?" she asked Lamar as he led her down a side street.

"I asked if you're all right, because you seemed to zone out for a few minutes."

"I was thinking how my life is going to change once I move to New Orleans."

"Do you think the change will be that dramatic?"

"Not as dramatic as different." Nydia glanced up at Lamar staring down at her. "I won't get to visit with my family as often as I'd like, and I don't have to take public transportation to my job, because I'll live onsite."

"You'll be living at the inn?" Lamar asked.

"Yes. Hannah set aside six suites for personal use and twelve for her guests."

"I had no idea her home had that many rooms."

"There are eighteen rooms and two guest-houses on the property."

Lamar slowed his pace, stopping in front of a five-floor walkup. "The size of some of the homes in the Garden District is outrageous, but I suppose the original owners felt the need to flaunt their wealth."

"Do you begrudge people who have a lot of money?"

He shook his head. "Not in the least. If you work hard and manage to accumulate wealth, then more power to you. Did you really believe I'm that shallow?"

A shiver of annoyance snaked its way up Nydia's back at his chastising tone. "I don't know you well enough to say whether you are or not." She knew she'd struck a nerve when a muscle quivered at his jaw. One thing she had come to know was that Lamar had a short fuse on his temper. If she said something that ticked him off, he wasn't reticent in letting her know.

"Maybe one of these days you'll get to know exactly who I am, and then you won't be so quick to judge me."

Anger, frustration, and the enduring helplessness to control her life over the past week surfaced, and Nydia opened her

236

mouth to tell Lamar exactly what she thought of his overblown ego, but the words died on her tongue when he angled his head and kissed her. It wasn't just a joining of mouths but a deep, passionate kiss that made her weak in the knees and forced her to hold onto him to keep her balance. The delight of his tongue in her mouth elicited a rush of moisture between her legs. It was the second time within minutes that he'd kissed her, but this time it wasn't a mere brush of mouths, but a deep, passionate joining that left her knees shaking uncontrollably and forced her to lean against Lamar to keep her balance as she waited for her body's traitorous sensations to subside.

"Get a room!" a booming voice shouted from across the street.

Nydia closed her eyes and buried her face against the soft fibers of Lamar's sweater. She was certain he could detect the runaway beating of her heart against his chest. If the kiss hadn't been so pleasurable she would have told him in English and in Spanish about publicly embarrassing her. She'd had enough humiliation in a week to last her a lifetime.

Hot tears pricked the backs of her eyelids. "Why did you do that?" she asked, unable to keep her voice from quivering.

Lamar removed his sunglasses and cradled her face in his hands. "I knew what you were about to do, and it's the first thing I thought of to stop you."

"Stop what?"

"Stop you from cussing me out."

She sobered quickly. "How did you know?"

Lamar smiled, showing off perfectly aligned white teeth. "You have a habit of biting your lower lip before you explode. I first noticed it when we went out to dinner and you got into a huff when I asked you about crack."

"I didn't cuss you out, Lamar. I simply told you I've seen crackheads."

"It's not what you said, but how you said it, sweets."

"Oh, now I'm sweets?"

He kissed her hair. "Of course you are."

She blinked slowly. "Do you call all women 'sweets'?"

"No. Just the ones I like." His expression stilled and grew serious. "If I didn't like you, Nydia, I never would've come here to stage an intervention for you."

It was the second time Lamar made her feel as if she'd been chastised. Did he do it because as a father he'd had to reprimand his daughter, or did he see her as someone who was immature and impulsive?

There was only a five-year difference in their ages, yet there was something about Lamar that made him seem older, worldlier. Nydia wasn't willing to change who she was, but if she and Lamar were going to remain friends, then he had to accept her as she was.

"I do appreciate you coming to my defense. And I also trust you."

His eyebrows lifted slightly. "Do you really?"

"Of course I do. Otherwise I never would've invited you to spend the night in my home." She flashed a saucy smile. "You may look benign and profess to be a nerd, yet you still could be someone that will befriend a woman and then keep her prisoner in their basement for years, using and abusing her at will."

Throwing back his head, Lamar let out a full-throated laugh. "Something tells me you've watched one too many horror movies. And for your information homes in New Orleans don't have basements because it is the only American city below sea level."

"I do like some horror movies," Nydia admitted sheepishly.

"The one with sexy vampires?"

Her smile was dazzling. "How did you know?"

"Lucky guess." He put back on his sunglasses and pointed across the street. "Iggy's folks lived over there on the second floor before they moved back to Puerto Rico. It's the apartment with the plants in the window."

Nydia looped her arm through Lamar's. Their tense moment had passed as if it had never occurred. "So that's where you became an adopted *Puertorriqueño?*"

"*Sí, cariña.*"

"Showoff. I like being called sweet in Spanish. It's more musical."

"Then *cariña* it is. Do you feel like walking some more, or do you want to go back to the apartment?"

"Let's walk."

Nydia felt more confident to venture outside now that she was with Lamar. He made her feel what she'd been unable to experience with any other man who was not family: protected.

CHAPTER 11

Nydia sat on the bench seat next to Lamar as he tied the laces on his running shoes. His stay had been cut short when a text from his airline informed him all Sunday evening flights into Atlanta were canceled because of the National Weather Service's prediction of severe thunderstorms in the area. He'd called the airline and changed his reservation to a late Saturday night flight.

"How long is your layover in Atlanta?" she asked.

"Ninety minutes. I'll probably get home a little after sunrise."

Their post-breakfast Saturday stroll turned into an extended walking tour of East and West Harlem before they returned to the apartment and spent the afternoon eating popcorn and laughing hysterically at Tyler Perry's *Boo! A Madea Halloween.* The text appeared on Lamar's phone just as the credits were rolling across the screen, preempting their planned dinner on City Island.

"Call or text me once you touch down."

Lamar stood, bringing Nydia up with him. "Of course. I'm sorry about our dinner, but I promise to make it up to you."

Nydia held on to his hand. "Don't apologize, Lamar. There will be other times when we'll go to City Island." He'd made reservations at the Lobster Box, which was one of her favorite restaurants on the quaint fishing enclave at the tip of the Bronx. "Perhaps we'll be able squeeze it in when you come up for Christmas. I hope I'm not getting ahead of myself."

"Why would you say that?"

"I'm assuming because the kids have that week off from school that you'll be able to take time off from your job."

A hint of a smile tilted the corners of Lamar's firm mouth at the same time he winked at her. "Not to worry, *cariña.* Every year we close the office on Christmas Eve and don't reopen until the day after New Year's. The partners rotate being on call in the event of an emergency, so I'm available this year."

Her eyes lingered on his chin before moving up slowly to meet eyes that reminded her of cat's-eye marbles. They were so oddly beautiful in a mahogany-brown face with undertones of copper and rosewood. "If that's the case, then I'll put together an itinerary for the kids and ask for your input before I finalize anything."

"Just what are you hatching in that beautiful head of yours?"

Nydia lowered her eyes. Men had called her pretty and *linda pequeña mama,* cute little mama, but never beautiful. And with Lamar she did feel beautiful whenever he stared at her, and more importantly, she felt protected. She'd dated Danny for three years and never during that time had he ever defended her when his friends or family members made comments about her, nor did he make her feel safe. Nydia wasn't looking forward to becoming intimately involved with Lamar; she was forming an easygoing friendship. He could be someone she could call and ask to accompany her to soirées as her plus-one once she moved to New Orleans.

"I'm still thinking."

"About what?"

"Whether to take the girls ice skating at Rockefeller Center. My nieces have their own skates, but then there's your daughter."

"Don't worry about Kendra. I'll make

243

certain she has a pair of skates, even though she won't have much use for them in New Orleans."

"I wasn't talking about skates because we can rent them, but whether she'll be able to stay up on the ice."

"Kendra will hold her own with your nieces. She may fall down a few times, but she'll get up and try again until she's skating along with the others."

"What about her daddy?"

"I'll sit and observe."

Nydia's eyebrows lifted questioningly. "You don't skate?"

"I *can* skate, but I'd rather play chaperone and eat roasted chestnuts."

She smiled. "If that's the case, then you have a co-chaperone. I'd also like to buy tickets to a Broadway matinee. I want it to be a girls'-only outing. We'll see the show, and then go out for dinner."

"Which shows are you thinking about?" Lamar asked.

"I was thinking about *School of Rock, Aladdin,* or *The Lion King*. Personally I'm partial to *The Lion King* because of the music, costumes, choreography, and stunning sets."

"Have you seen it?"

"No, and neither have my nieces. So I

want it to be a surprise."

"I'm going to ask one thing of you."

Nydia's expression changed, and she held her breath for several seconds. She didn't know why, but she felt Lamar was going to say something that would set her on edge. "What is it?"

"Please let me pay for the theater tickets."

She remembered him saying he was willing to pay for the girls' outings and she'd figuratively bitten his head off. Nydia realized she had to compromise or she would end up debating every decision with Lamar. She nodded. "Okay."

Lamar blew out an audible breath. "Thank you. Send me the details once you select the date, time, and seats and I'll order the tickets."

Nydia let go of his hand. "I've been running off at the mouth when you have to pick up your rental and drop it off at the airport." Going on tiptoe, she brushed her mouth over his. "I can't thank you enough for running interference for me."

Wrapping an arm around her waist, Lamar pulled her close. "I'll do it again anytime you need rescuing."

"Let's hope this is the last time I'll need you to rescue me from something that resembles a scripted reality show."

Lamar stared at her from under lowered lids. "You're right about that." He angled his head and pressed his lips against hers in a surprisingly gentle kiss. "Try and stay out of trouble until we see each other again."

She nodded and took a backward step. "Go before you miss your flight or you'll be forced to check back into my humble bed-and-breakfast."

He laughed as he picked up his carry-on. "I do recall the management offering chicken and red velvet waffles along with mimosas for Sunday brunch, so the next time I check in I hope they'll still be on the menu."

"Of course," Nydia said, as she unlocked the door and opened it. "Goodbye, Lamar."

He shook his head. "It's not goodbye, but later."

Nydia knew he was right. She'd planned to return to New Orleans the first week in October to set up the protocol for managing the finances for the inn, and she was looking forward to seeing Lamar again before returning to New York.

"Luego."

Lamar winked at her. "That's better."

Nydia watched him as he made his way down the staircase and disappeared from view. She had spent a little more than twelve

246

hours with Lamar, yet it felt longer because they'd shared breakfast, toured the rapidly gentrifying Harlem neighborhoods, and laughed until their sides hurt when watching a comedy in which some scenes were definitely over the top.

And aside from an unexpected misunderstanding, Nydia felt they were temperamentally suited to each other. She'd always found herself the outspoken one in a conversation, but it was obvious she had met her match with Lamar Pierce. He might not have been as volatile as she could be, but he also wasn't restrained when it came to saying what he thought and felt.

She closed and locked the door. *I like him,* Nydia whispered. She liked Lamar enough to count down the time when she would see him again.

"Why can't they let it go!?" Nydia shouted at the television as footage of Lamar kissing her filled the screen. It had been three days since she and Lamar were waylaid by the reporter and her cameraman.

The reporter stared directly at the camera. "I suppose we now have our answer why Nydia Santiago won't marry singing sensation Danny Ocasio, because it appears she's already taken. Danny's rep says he's totally devastated to know he'd dated a married woman for three years and not once during that time had she given him a hint that she was married. I suppose Danny can now close the chapter in this book featuring his former muse. This is Renata Joplin, reporting from —"

Nydia picked up the remote and turned off the television. She did not want to believe Danny's people were garnering more than their fifteen minutes of fame. Her cell phone chimed a programmed ringtone. "I know why you're calling me, *mija*."

"Why they still messing with you, *chica*?" Jasmine asked.

Pulling her legs up under her body, Nydia shifted into a more comfortable position on the sofa. "I keep telling myself that I won't get upset, but every time I see or hear something about me and Danny, I'm ready to go to his sister's apartment, call him out, and pound on him with a baseball bat. I thought he was better than this, Jasmine. We weren't the perfect couple but —"

"What couple is?" Jasmine interrupted.

"You and Cameron," Nydia stated emphatically.

"We have our days when we can't see eye to eye on anything."

"It's the hormones, *mija*. After you push

out your little son or daughter everything will be easy like Sunday morning."

Jasmine's laugh came through the earpiece. "Is that still your favorite song by the Commodores?"

"You know it is."

"Now, back to you and what the press is calling your mystery man. Do they know it's Lamar Pierce?"

Nydia's body stiffened in shock as she stared at the darkened TV screen. She hadn't told anyone, not even her mother, about the man who'd come to New York to run interference between her and the newshounds.

"How did you know?" she asked Jasmine, once she'd recovered her voice.

"*Chica,* I've seen Lamar enough to recognize him even with a cap and sunglasses. It was when I saw his wedding band I knew for certain it was him. It's rather unique because it's made with tri-color."

Nydia agreed with Jasmine about Lamar's ring. The band was designed in white, yellow, and rose gold. "I had no idea he was coming to see me," she admitted. She told Jasmine about Lamar's phone call, his promise to surprise her, and the fact he'd become her surprise.

"It looks as if you've found your knight in

shining armor," Jasmine teased.

"What I found is a good male friend."

"I think he's more than a friend, Nydia. The man looked as if he'd been shocked by a surge of electricity when he first saw you. And I've been on the receiving end of men staring at me like that. Next month will be a year since I met Cameron at Hannah's wedding, and you were the one who talked about him liking what he saw. And you were also the one who encouraged me to go out with him, and now I'm his wife *and* carrying his baby."

"You're definitely getting ahead of yourself, Jazz."

"Am I, Nydia? I'm willing to wager every penny I have in the bank that you're going to get involved with Lamar, marry him, and give his daughter a little brother or sister."

Nydia laughed. "You've never said you're a *bruja,* and that means you're going to lose that bet because I'm not going to marry a man who isn't willing to let go of his past."

"Why should he, *chica*? His daughter is a constant reminder of his late wife, and it would be selfish of you to try and pretend she hadn't been in Lamar's life."

Nydia closed her eyes and then exhaled an audible breath. Jasmine had misinterpreted what she meant about Lamar's past.

"Do you really think I'm that insensitive? I wasn't talking about his late wife, but his wedding band. And I'd never have the audacity to ask him to forget the woman he loved enough to marry and have a child with."

There came a beat where Jasmine remained silent. "I'm sorry, Nydia. I shouldn't have said that."

"Forget it, *mija.* I know I can be a little too outspoken for some people, but I know when not to say something."

"Have you asked Lamar why he still wears his ring?"

"No, and I won't ask. He's mentioned his daughter, but is mute when it comes to his late wife. I'll listen if he wants to tell me about her, but I won't add to the commentary."

"Does he know about you and Danny?"

Nydia grunted under her breath. "Yes, he does. He asked, and I told him everything."

"What did he say?"

"He did say if he had been there when I was blindsided he would've gone gangsta and clotheslined Danny so he'd never sing again."

"*Co-ño,*" Jasmine drawled, drawing the word out in two distinctive syllables.

"That calls for *dos coños,*" Nydia said,

251

laughing.

"It's always the quiet ones you have to watch because they usually don't let you know when they're coming for you."

"I don't want anyone to come for Danny. He'll get his for using me to enhance his newfound superstar image. I wouldn't be so pissed off with him if he'd told me what his publicist had planned."

"Would you have gone along with a fake engagement?"

Nydia shook her head, and then realized Jasmine couldn't see her. "Hell no! However, I wouldn't have been opposed to granting an interview about how much Danny had sacrificed to realize his dream. I would've poured it on real thick about how he was a wonderful boyfriend and I never had to concern myself with him cheating on me. I'd end it with while he was concentrating on his singing career, mine was going in a different direction so I had to make an adjustment in my life that did not include Danny."

"All of that is true, but the reality is during your three-year relationship you'd stopped seeing him because he refused to get a nine-to-five."

"I'm certain word will eventually get out why I broke up with him. East Harlem isn't

252

that big, and everybody knows something about somebody."

"Speaking of gossiping, now that you told me Lamar's fluent in Spanish we can't whisper about him in Spanish if he's around."

"The way we sometimes do with Cameron."

"Cameron seems oblivious when I speak to my mother in Spanish or Tagalog."

"Do you plan to talk to your baby in Spanish or Tagalog in addition to English?" Nydia asked Jasmine.

"I plan to have Titi Nydia teach him or her Spanish, while I'll assume the responsibility to speak to them in their maternal grandmother's native tongue. It's an asset nowadays to speak more than one language."

Nydia smiled. "That means whenever I babysit my godson or daughter I will speak Spanish to them." She paused. "I know you don't want to know the sex of your baby beforehand, but what do *you* want — girl or boy?"

"I really want a girl, because then I can share girly things with her."

"Like shopping until you drop?" Whenever she and Jasmine got together it was invariably to have dinner and shop, whether for

253

shoes, beauty products, or a small item to enhance the beauty of their bed or bathrooms.

"Bingo!"

Nydia heard a beep indicating she had another call. "Jazz, it's my mother on the other line. I know she's calling about my so-called mystery man."

"Before I hang up, you have to tell me if Lamar is a good kisser."

"Yes. Bye, *mija.*" She tapped the phone icon. "*Sí,* Mami?"

"This has to stop, Nydia! People are blowing up my phone here at the shop talking about seeing you on television kissing some man in the street."

"I know, Mami. It's not what you think. I'll explain everything when I see you."

"*Cuando* is *eso?*"

Nydia knew her mother was upset whenever she mixed English with Spanish. Isabel wanted to know when she would see her. "Later. I'll come by after you close."

She ended the call and buried her face in her hands. Her mother wanted it to stop, while Nydia wanted to know when it was going to end. Hopefully this would be the last time she would have to talk about Danny to anyone. He was her past, and even if he were the last man on the face of the earth, she wouldn't have anything to do with him. He had caused her enough pain and suffering, and they weren't even married.

Nydia lowered her hands, got up, and walked into the bathroom. She turned on the water in the tub, adjusted the temperature, and added a generous capful of lavender bath crystals; she lit several of the candles lining the top of the vanity, stripped off her clothes, and then stepped into the tub. Soft moans escaped her parted lips when she lowered herself into the steaming bubbles. Beads of moisture quickly dotted her face.

She'd planned to fly down to New Orleans in two weeks, but this was the first time in her life that Nydia could recall wanting to escape her hometown. As she lay in the tub, eyes closed, she wondered how much longer she had to put up with being portrayed as the duplicitous woman who had taken advantage of a man who'd given her all of himself.

Nydia opened her eyes when the water cooled, and the bubbles disappeared. Reaching for a bath sponge, she washed her body and then stepped out on a thick absorbent mat. After drying off, she wrapped the towel around herself and walked on bare feet to the bedroom and went through the ritual of slathering a scented cream over her body before slipping into underwear, a long-sleeved black polo and jeans. She opened a drawer in the double dresser and retrieved the sheet of paper with her flight information.

In that instant she decided to protect her family and take back control of her life. Unconsciously she had surrendered her will to Danny the first time he'd asked to take her out, but it would end now. It took twenty minutes to book an earlier flight and pay the fee for changing the ticket.

Retrieving her cell phone, she tapped Jasmine's name for a text message:

Please reserve a room for me. I'm coming in Friday night. I made arrangements for ground transportation. Will ring you when I arrive at the hotel.

She didn't have to wait for Jasmine's response.

Jasmine: Is everything all right?

Nydia: Everything's good. I just decided to check out of this insane asylum earlier than planned because I need a change of scene.

Jasmine: Good for you! I'm going to tell Hannah and Tonya you're coming in. I'll have Cameron reserve a suite.

Nydia: Luego, mija.

Jasmine: Luego chica.

Nydia didn't know why, but she felt as if she had been reborn. Now she knew how Tonya felt once she'd decided to break up with her on-again, off-again boyfriend and move to New Orleans to operate her own restaurant: completely free.

Nydia rang the bell to Isabella's Tresses and waited for her mother to unlock the front door. Once the footage of Lamar kissing her aired, her cell phone mailbox filled up with calls from family members asking who the mystery man was. The blinds moved slightly and then the door opened.

Isabel pulled her in and quickly locked the door. "Come in before anyone notices that I'm still here. I keep telling my customers that I don't work beyond closing time, but some of them just don't get it. If I don't draw the blinds and turn out most of the lights, they keep ringing the doggone bell."

Nydia took the broom from her mother's hand. "Let me sweep up for you." She slipped her cross-body bag off her shoulder and placed it behind the receptionist's station. She'd come after closing to avoid encountering her mother's regular customers, who were so nosy that nothing was verboten.

"Thanks, *mija*. It's been nonstop since I

opened. Two of my stylists called in sick."

"Sit down, Mami, and I'll finish putting everything away. By the way, what happened to the woman you hired to clean up after you close?"

"I fired her today."

Nydia stared at Isabel. "What happened?"

"I caught her stealing supplies, so I had to let her go."

"I can't believe she begged you to give her a job so she could have a little extra money to buy Christmas gifts for her kids, and she repays you by stealing."

"What can I say, *mija*? You just can't help some folks. Luis has promised to come by every night to help."

"If you want I can clean up for you tomorrow." She had yet to tell her mother she was leaving in a couple of days.

Isabel waved a hand. "That's okay. Luis isn't so busy he can't help me."

Nydia pushed the broom under each station and swept up clumps of hair. "How's he doing with his fishing outings?"

"He and his buddies are still going out on their boat a couple of times a week. It's become their man cave on the water."

"That's going to end soon, because football season starts next week," Nydia reminded her mother. She had learned from a very early age that football was the most important thing in her father's life, second only to his wife and children.

"It's a good thing it's not the type of boat where they can install a television, or they'd be out on the water in below-freezing weather with their frozen eyeballs glued to the screen. Enough talk about your father and football. Now, what's up with you and this so-called mystery man everyone is calling me about?"

Nydia rested the broom against a wall and sat facing her mother. She told her why Lamar had come up from New Orleans and why he'd decided to kiss her. "I was just as shocked as the reporter, but apparently his ruse was successful because she assumed we were married when she spotted his wedding ring."

Isabel's jaw dropped slightly. "You're involved with a married man?"

"No, Mami. Lamar is a widower."

"If his wife is dead, then why is he still wearing his ring?"

"That I don't know."

"He hasn't told you?"

"No, because I haven't asked. Lamar and I are just friends." Isabel's expression spoke volumes. She didn't believe her. "What's the matter?"

259

Isabel held up both hands. "Maybe I'm missing something. You're telling me this man — who just happens to be your friend — flies up from New Orleans to stage, as you say, an intervention."

Nydia scrunched up her nose. "I'd like to think of it as interference."

"Okay, he decides to pretend that he's your boyfriend and/or your husband so that the reporter can tell viewers that you rejected Danny's proposal because you're involved with another man. And he agreed to do this because he's your friend?"

"No, Mami. He didn't agree to do anything." Nydia knew she had to spell out everything for her mother or she would question her ad nauseam. Once she was finished explaining, Isabel appeared satisfied with her explanation.

"That was very nice of him."

"That's because he's very nice."

"What does he do for a living?"

"He's an engineer."

"Nice," Isabel said softly. "At least he has a lot more going for him than that *pendejo* you wasted your time with."

"Danny isn't stupid, Mami. He did whatever he had to do or not do to get over. I told you last year it was over between us, and now it's his time to move on — without

260

me. This past week has been a horror, so I decided to change my travel plans."

"When are you leaving?"

"Friday."

"Is the bed-and-breakfast open for business?" Isabel questioned.

Nydia shook her head. "No. Hannah had planned for a late-October or early-November grand opening, but things are going a lot slower than anticipated."

Isabel stared at her reflection in the wall of mirrors facing the half dozen stylists' chairs. "You know I've always wanted the best for you, *mija,* and even though I've never interfered in your life once you became an adult, this is one time I can't remain silent."

Nydia sucked in a lungful of air, held it, and then exhaled an inaudible breath. When living at home she had acquiesced to her mother's authority and their role as mother and daughter, but once she moved out they'd become more like good friends.

"What do you want to tell me?"

Isabel met her eyes. "It's not what I want to tell you, but what you should know."

"I'm listening, Mami."

"I've watched you grow up, and for some reason you always felt as if you had to be tough and in control of everything. I don't

261

know if it comes from having two older brothers and you wanted to keep up and compete with them. Joaquin and Nelson have settled down with their partners and children, and for some reason you just can't get it right when it comes to choosing someone to share not only your life but also a future. You have so much going for you, yet you get involved with men who aren't worthy. And I'm not talking about education.

"You came to me devastated when you'd discovered the professor you were dating was married. And when I tried to tell you the signs were obvious that he had someone in his life, you accused me of not wanting you to be happy. When a man puts off answering his voice mail until he's alone, that's a clear indication that he doesn't want you to hear him talking to a woman. And when you found a woman's underwear in one of the dresser drawers, you believed him when he said they belonged to his sister. It was only when his wife showed up unexpectedly that it became a reality for you."

"Please don't remind me, Mami," Nydia whispered. It was a scene branded into her memory like a permanent tattoo. Three people were not only surprised but shocked that early Sunday morning when her lover's wife walked in to find her husband and a much younger woman in bed together.

"I guess you could say I was young and stupid."

"No, Nydia. You were young and impressionable. He was older and more experienced than you, which you found exciting. You wait years before dating again only to go out with someone who is the complete opposite of your professor when it comes to intellect. I kept asking myself what was your attraction to Danny Ocasio other than his looks and talent. After a while I realized you'd stayed with him because you controlled the relationship. You had your own apartment while he lived with his sister. And remember you had two college degrees and you were a CPA, compared to his high school diploma, and that afforded you greater earning power, and Danny resented this."

"How do you know this?" Nydia asked.

"I could see the resentment in his eyes whenever you and your brothers talked about something that went completely over his head. I don't have to be a *bruja* to predict that he would've proposed marriage, paraded you on his arm for a while before photos of him with some half-naked *putas* were splashed over the pages of supermarket tabloids. Of course you'd break the engagement and he would be free to screw any woman willing to open her legs for him."

"You're right, Mami," Nydia admitted, and then told her mother what Milagros had told her about what her ex overheard: Danny bragging about her taking care of him until his big break, and then he could have all of the bitches he'd ever want. "That's when I knew we could never have a future together."

Isabel smiled. "Good for you." She sobered. "Now that you're going to move to another state, I hope you are going to be a lot more discriminating when dating again."

"You don't have to worry about that. It hasn't been a year since I broke up with Danny, and I have a rule to wait at least a year before dipping my toe back into the dating scene. Remember I have to adjust to a different climate, and I'll be busy setting up an accounting program for the inn, along with continuing to do the payroll for the three restaurants. The owners have convinced their employees to let me prepare their tax returns next year. Of course I'll charge them half of what they would pay other accountants."

"You have a lot on your plate."

Nydia nodded. "I know. But I like being busy."

"Make certain you don't become a workaholic like your mother."

"I won't. How many more years do you intend to stand on your feet cutting and blowing hair?"

"Three. I'll turn fifty-seven in November, and before I celebrate my big six-oh I'm selling this place to the first person who comes close to my asking price. You mentioned cutting hair. Do you want me to trim yours before you leave?"

Nydia released her hair from the elastic band and combed her fingers through the thick, loose curls. Since she'd been downsized she had let her hair grow until it was only inches above her shoulders. "Cut it, Mami."

Isabel lifted her eyebrows. "How short do you want it?"

"I'll leave that up to you." She trusted her mother to give her a style that required minimal upkeep.

"Don't get up. I have to get my comb and scissors."

Minutes later Nydia stared at her reflection in the mirror while her mother wet her hair with water from a spray bottle and then sectioned her hair. Isabel wielded a pair of scissors like the pro she was as strands of dark brown curls fell on the cape covering her clothes.

If she was going to have a new job in a new city, then she wanted a new look. Nydia had told herself she wasn't running away but starting over. It had taken her thirty-three years to finally get her professional and personal life in synch. She smiled at her reflection in the mirror.

It was now mid-September, and she planned to return to New York to join her family for Thanksgiving, which gave her two months to adjust to not waking up to the sounds of vehicle traffic and the wail of sirens from first responders. Once she vacated the apartment she would not have to concern herself with venturing out in sleet, snow, and below-freezing temperatures. The exception was visiting her family during the Christmas season.

Her smile grew wider. She never could have imagined the day she was downsized from Wakefield Hamilton that she would become an innkeeper.

CHAPTER 12

Lamar activated the telephone's speaker feature on the phone and then placed the receiver on the handset. He had spent the past five minutes trying to convince his partners not to put in a bid for a construction project to build a new shopping center in Lafayette. Resting his feet on the corner of the desk in his home office, he stared at the toes of the worn leather moccasins that had seen better days, but he was loath to throw them away before getting another pair to replace them.

"We're stretched thin as it is, and to take on a project a hundred fifty miles away from home base is something we need to discuss in depth."

"What is there to talk about it, Pierce? It's only a strip mall," Omar countered.

Lamar swore to himself. If he hadn't put the two men on speaker, he would have placed the call on hold and really let loose.

It was a rare occasion that he, Kirk Wallace, and Omar Robinson did not agree on whether to accept a project, and for Lamar this was one of those times. As the company's construction manager he was responsible for traveling to construction sites to take care of any problems. He didn't mind driving if it could be accomplished in one day; however, he had made it a practice to be home during the week whenever school was in session because it was his time to eat breakfast with his daughter.

"Whether large or small, it's still a construction project that is geographically undesirable."

"For who?" Kirk questioned.

"For me," Lamar said. "Have you forgotten that I'm the one overseeing the sites and I'm also a single father?" His partners were married with children.

"What's the problem, Pierce?" Omar asked. "You have a live-in housekeeper."

"And you dudes have stay-at-home wives who get to see your kids off before they head out to school. In case you're not aware of it, I have made it a practice to eat breakfast with my daughter and tell her that I love her before she walks out the door to get on the bus."

There was a pregnant silence until Omar's

voice came through the speaker. "Man, I'm sorry. There are times when I forget Valerie's gone."

Lamar wanted to tell the man that he was so focused on making money that it had become a priority for him. There came a knock on the door, and he glanced up to find Kendra in the doorway. He picked up the telephone receiver, covered the mouthpiece with one hand, and beckoned her in. "What is it, sweets?"

"I didn't know you were on the phone. I'll come back later."

"Stay." He removed his hand from the mouthpiece. "Can we talk about this in the office tomorrow?"

"No problem."

"Sure."

Omar and Kirk had spoken at the same time.

Lamar hung up and rose to his feet. "What do you need?" he asked Kendra.

She smiled. "I finished my robotic project and I want you to be the first one to see it."

He came from around the desk. "Oh, now I can see it?"

"Daddy, you know why I didn't show it to you before it was finished."

He dropped an arm around his daughter's shoulders as they walked upstairs to her bedroom. "I don't know why. Perhaps you can enlighten me, Miss Pierce."

"Because you'll critique it like you did when I made the model of an Aztec village."

"But, sweetie, it wasn't Aztec but Incan. There is a difference." Lamar recalled Kendra bursting into tears after she'd spent countless hours recreating a replica of Machu Picchu, when it should've been Teotihuacan.

"I know that now, Daddy. But instead of making me take it apart I could have told my teacher that I decided to pick Peru instead of Mexico as my country for International Week."

"And that would have been dishonest, Kendra. If you make a mistake, then you have to own it."

"Do you know how long it took me to mold a clay model of the Aztec calendar?"

"It took you long enough to get you an A."

A slow smile flitted over Kendra's delicate features. "It did turn out okay."

"It was more than okay, Kendra. It was perfect."

Kendra put an arm around Lamar's waist. "You say that because I'm your daughter."

He dropped a kiss on her braids. "I'd say

it was perfect even if you weren't my daughter."

Lamar followed Kendra into her bedroom and pretended he didn't see the pile of clothes on the floor in a corner. Despite having an en suite bath with a hamper Kendra preferred leaving clothes on the floor. He had only two rules for her to follow: do well in school and keep her room clean.

"I know, Daddy. I'm going to put the clothes away before I go to bed."

Lamar smiled. "Did I say anything?"

Kendra gave him a sidelong glance. "No, but I know what you're thinking."

"I didn't know my daughter was a mind reader."

"I'm not, but I saw you look over there."

She reached for his hand, directing him to a cherrywood-topped, off-white worktable that matched an L-shaped desk. Once Lamar discovered Cameron's fiancée was an interior decorator, he'd commissioned her to decorate Kendra's bedroom. He told Jasmine his daughter was spending the summer in Baton Rouge and he wanted to surprise her with new furniture and accessories conducive for studying and total relaxation.

Lamar's chest swelled with pride when he saw a trio of robotic catapults Kendra had constructed for her science project. He leaned closer. "These are incredible."

"Move back, Daddy. I'm going to show you how they work."

He took a backward step and watched Kendra place a small Styrofoam ball in the basket. She picked up a remote control device linked to her tablet and tapped the screen. The robotic arm moved up and the ball sailed across the room and bounced off the area rug.

Lamar applauded. "It's a direct hit! What made you decide to design a catapult?"

Kendra repeated the action with the second robot. "I saw a movie where soldiers filled the baskets of several catapults with hot tar and launched it at the invading army using a battering ram to destroy the walls of the castle."

Lamar picked up the ball and handed it to Kendra. "You know you're a genius." Kendra lowered her eyes. It was obvious he'd embarrassed her. "You're very smart, Kendra, and it's time you accept it."

Her head popped up and she met his eyes. "Smart girls aren't popular."

He went completely still. "Popular with who?"

"Everyone, Daddy. Boys always believe they're smarter than girls, and some girls don't like me because they think I'm trying to show them up."

Taking her hands, Lamar led her over to the bench at the foot of her bed and sat. "Sit down, Kendra." He waited for her to sit beside him and laced their fingers together. "There will always be boys and girls who won't like you for reasons that are completely asinine. It could be they're jealous because they feel you're prettier, smarter, or they're jealous of the way you dress."

"It can't be clothes, because everyone in school wears the same uniform."

"Okay, we'll cross clothes off the list," Lamar conceded. "For now."

Kendra rested her head on her father's shoulder. "Why for now?"

"You won't wear a uniform when you go out on a date."

Kendra sat straight. "That's not going to be for a long time. Didn't you say I couldn't date until I was seventeen?"

"Yes, I did."

"All my friends' parents say they can start dating at sixteen."

"I'm not your friends' parents, Kendra."

"What if I'm super grown-up at sixteen?"

Lamar tugged on one of the thick plaits falling over Kendra's shoulder. "You won't

273

be super grown-up at sixteen. It's not until you're an adult and accept all of the responsibilities that go along with it that you'll become what you say is super grown-up."

"What responsibilities?"

"Securing employment to earn enough money to pay rent or a mortgage so you don't join the ranks of homeless people living on the street. You'll also have to buy or lease a car so you don't have to depend on public transportation to get around. Then, there's food and clothes. And what if you have a family? Your kids are going to need new shoes every six months, and what if you have teenage boys who will eat and drink you out of house and home?"

"That's not going to happen, Daddy."

"Because you say so?"

"Yes, because by that time my husband will help me."

"I want you to finish college and establish a career before you think about getting married."

"But I'll be too old," Kendra whined.

"Sweetie, you won't be too old. If you graduate college at twenty-one or -two, and then get a job and work for three or four years to get established, you won't be too old."

"How old were you when you married Mom?"

"Twenty-six. And speaking of husbands and marriage, what happened to boys are stupid?"

"By the time they are as old as you they won't be so stupid."

"Thank you for the compliment."

"I'm serious, Daddy. I know you want the best for me, and I'm trying. But you have to understand that I'm just a kid and —"

"I know that," Lamar said, cutting her off. "I know sometimes I put a lot of pressure on you to get good grades —"

"Sometimes, Daddy?" Kendra interrupted. "You do it all the time. And just because you do, I deliberately mark the wrong answers on tests."

Lamar did not want to believe what he was hearing. His daughter had decided to rebel knowing how he felt about her doing well in school. Why hadn't she come to him before she'd barely passed two of her classes?

"What is it you want, Kendra?"

"I want you to stop threatening to ground me if I don't make the honor roll."

Lamar was momentarily speechless, his mind in tumult. He hadn't realized the pressure he'd put on his daughter to succeed.

His parents had impressed upon him at an early age the importance of getting an education, and he'd continued the practice with Kendra. Learning had come easy for him because everything he read he retained, so his parents hadn't had to issue threats of reprisals.

"I'm sorry, baby girl. Starting tonight, I promise no more threats." He held out his little finger. "Pinky swears?"

Smiling, Kendra looped her finger with his. "Pinky swears."

"Do you know where we haven't gone in a long time?"

"Where, Daddy?"

"Mamma's Place for Sunday brunch."

Kendra let out a scream and quickly covered her mouth. "Sorry about that. I love their chicken and waffles. Daddy, can I invite Morgan and Taylor to go with us?"

"You can if you ask their mother."

Kendra jumped up. "Wait here, Daddy, while I call them."

Stretching out his legs, Lamar crossed his feet at the ankles. Kendra's revelation that he'd put too much pressure on her was definitely a wake-up call to let her be a kid. He knew there would come a time in her life when she would be faced with more pressures than making her school's honor roll.

"Daddy, Miss Evangeline would like to talk to you. I'll put you on speaker." Kendra handed him her cell phone.

"Hi, Evie. I'm taking Kendra to Mamma's Place for Sunday brunch, and she would like to know if Taylor and Morgan can join us."

"Of course they can. There are no classes this Monday because it's professional development day for teachers, so would you mind if Kendra spends Sunday and Monday with the girls? I'll drop them off at school on Tuesday."

"Please, please, please, Daddy," Kendra whispered.

"Yes, Evie, she can stay over." Kendra dropped to her knees, pressed her hands together in a prayerful gesture, and mouthed a thank-you.

"What time do you want me to drop off the twins?"

When he'd asked Evangeline why she had given her twin girls names usually attributed to boys, she said she didn't want her daughters to face gender discrimination based on their names. "Aren't you going to join us?"

"Don't tell me you need me to help you chaperone three giggly preteen girls?"

277

Lamar winked at his daughter. "Yes, I do."

"Then, you're on. What time do you want to meet?"

"Twelve. Does that work for you?" he asked Evangeline.

"Twelve is okay."

"I'll call and make a reservation for five."

"Thanks for the invite, Lamar. See you Sunday."

"Good. I'm giving the phone back to Kendra."

Lamar left his daughter's room and took the back staircase down to the family room. He folded his body down into his favorite chair and turned on the wall-mounted television, tuning to encore footage of a baseball game. He needed to watch mindless television so he wouldn't think about what he would face when confronting Kirk and Omar. Whenever there was a quandary between them, they usually put it to a vote. And this time Lamar felt he was going to lose because he was the odd man out when it came to putting in a bid for a new construction project.

Although he didn't always agree with his partners, he still liked and respected most of their decisions. They all worked for one of the largest engineering firms in the state, and during a moment of madness they got together and decided to tender their resignations and start up their own company.

The first year had become a test for survival when they lost a number of bids to other well-established companies for new construction following the destructive aftermath of Hurricane Katrina. Things changed when they did come in as the lowest bid for a medical office building and completed the project three months before the proposed opening date without incurring cost overruns.

This was followed by the construction of small private hospital in a Shreveport suburb. The company had established its reputation for completing a project on time, while saving the developers money. However, victory for Lamar wasn't as sweet. He had been 350 miles away when his wife had gone into labor eight weeks before her due date. When he'd finally returned to New Orleans it was to find Valerie in a hospital, weakened from blood loss, and heavily sedated after a Cesarean section. Their barely four-pound baby girl had survived, but would spend the next month in the neonatal unit.

Fast forward six years. Kendra was a first-grader when she lost her mother, and Lamar made his daughter a solemn vow that they would always eat breakfast together on days on which she had classes. That was four years ago, and to date he had kept the vow.

Nydia's connecting flight touched down on time at the Louis Armstrong New Orleans International Airport in Kenner, Louisiana. The local temperature was in the mid-seventies with near 100 percent humidity. Jasmine had sent her a text informing her it had been raining steadily for two days.

She deplaned and made her way to baggage claim, where she found her driver holding a sign with her name waiting for her. "I'm Miss Santiago," she said, introducing herself to the dark-suited man.

"Welcome, Miss Santiago. I'll get your bags for you."

Nydia stood behind the driver, waiting and watching for bags coming onto the conveyer belt. She pointed to a Pullman with a bright red ribbon attached to the handle. "That one is mine. There's another one just like this, but smaller."

She'd packed enough clothes to last at least three weeks, even though she'd planned to stay longer. Utilizing the hotel laundry was definitely more convenient than her schlepping bags of dirty clothes down five flights of stairs to a nearby laundromat.

Nydia followed the driver, pulling both bags, out of the terminal to curbside, and waited for him to retrieve his car from the parking lot. The humidity wrapped around her like a lead-weighted blanket as fingers of mist feathered over her exposed skin. She shifted the carry-on with her laptop from one shoulder to the other. After spending hours in the airport waiting to board, then deplaning, and boarding again after a ninety-minute layover, she craved a shower and a firm bed.

The driver finally maneuvered up to the curb and got out to open the rear door for her. Nydia managed a smile mirroring exhaustion as she literally collapsed on the rear seat. She wasn't as physically tired as she was mentally. Her normal uneventful existence was now on display for public consumption and she was being unfairly judged as some type of femme fatale. A friend from college had called her to say there was chatter on Facebook that she'd seduced Danny Ocasio, hiding from him the fact that she was married, and once he proposed marriage she rejected him to avoid being labeled a bigamist. And the words *cheater* and *adulteress* had become commonplace when linked to her name.

Her father had come to her apartment earlier in the afternoon to drive her to the airport. Luis Santiago was unusually quiet during the ride, and she knew he was conflicted about her moving to New Orleans. He knew he could not forbid her to go, yet he had not been reticent when voicing his opposition to losing his little doll. Her father had all but accused her of running away and said that as a Santiago she should fight back, because they had never run and never would.

Nydia did not have to be a professional therapist to understand Luis's motivation as an attempt to convince her not to relocate. She was his only daughter, and he had doted on her all of her life, and he wanted for her what he had with his wife: that when she left her father's house it would be to move into one with her husband.

She wasn't relocating — not yet — but visiting New Orleans for an extended working vacation. Nydia wanted to take the next four or five days to unwind before meeting with Hannah, Tonya, and Jasmine to establish budgets and projections for the lodgings, café, supper club, and personnel. It was imperative she maintain separate accounts for each component of the inn for the three of them to recoup their initial investments.

There was something about numbers that held her enthralled whenever she worked on three-, six-, nine-, and twelve-month projections, profit and loss statements, and balance sheets; and she made a mental note to set aside time to read the city's and state's tax codes.

In between work Nydia planned to have some fun. A smile parted her lips when she thought about Lamar. She decided to wait for a couple of days before letting him know she was going to be in his hometown for a while. She knew their reunion was certain to be vastly different from when he'd surprised her in New York, because they no longer had to concern themselves with newshounds jumping out from between parked cars.

Nydia stared out the side window. The driver had decelerated to less than ten miles per hour in the bumper-to-bumper traffic heading toward New Orleans. The thick fog shrouding the region reminded her of movies depicting London when Jack the Ripper prowled the streets and alleys hunting his next unsuspecting victim. She'd become captivated with anything resembling Victorian England after first reading Arthur Conan Doyle's *The Hound of the Basker-*

283

villes. While in high school, she had devoted an entire summer to reading Doyle, Jane Austen, Charles Dickens, and Emily and Charlotte Brontë. She'd only left her bedroom to shower and eat. Brontë's *Jane Eyre* and Austen's *Mansfield Park* were favorites she reread every five years.

"It's slow going tonight because of the fog, miss."

The driver's voice shattered her musings. "It's okay. I just want to get there in one piece." Nydia had given Jasmine her flight information, so she knew when to expect her. Reaching for her carry-on, she took out her cell phone and tapped Jasmine's number. It rang twice before she heard a man's voice.

"Cameron?"

"Yes," he whispered. "I'm answering Jasmine's phone because she's in bed and I knew she was expecting your call."

Nydia's pulse quickened. "Is she okay?"

"If you were to ask her she would say yes. The truth is she's exhausted. She's still running around like a chicken without a head looking for stuff to decorate the house. I keep telling her the place won't be move-in ready till around early November."

"Is she taking naps?"

"I don't know. There's no way I can monitor her because I have to go into the office now that my father's is semi-retired. Whenever she calls me and I ask her where she is, she says she's in her car. I need you to do me a favor."

"What's that, Cameron?"

"I know I don't have a right to ask you this, but try and get her to slow down. Convince her to take a siesta like they do in certain European countries."

Nydia realized Cameron was concerned about his wife's health, but she wanted to tell him Jasmine was an adult and, unlike a child, she couldn't be relegated to a time-out. "I'll do what I can, although I can't promise she'll listen to me."

"I'll be eternally grateful for whatever you do. I didn't wait until I'm almost fifty to marry and look forward to becoming a father to lose the two most precious things in my life."

Nydia heard the pain *and* the passion in Cameron's voice. She didn't know the certified wealth manager well, but what she'd observed was an attractive, middle-aged, wealthy man from a prominent New Orleans family in total control of his life and his career. However, after spending several days with her friend, the serial dater and one of the city's most eligible bachelors had been ready to turn in his dating card for a wedding band.

"I'll slow her down even if I have to threaten not to become the godmother for your baby," Nydia teased, smiling.

Cameron's low chuckle caressed her ear. "I believe that will work, because that's all she talks about now that you'll be moving here."

Nydia's smile faded. "I know I haven't told you this, but thank you for giving Jasmine what she needs." Her friend had been through enough with a cheating husband who'd denied her a child, while attempting to pimp her out of everything she'd worked so hard for.

A beat passed. "There's no need to thank me, Nydia. I love Jasmine, and there isn't anything I wouldn't do to make her happy because I feel as if I'm the luckiest man in the world to have her in my life."

Nydia was temporarily mute from Cameron's unexpected and fervent confession. This was another side of the overly confident and at times arrogant man whom she discovered was a master when it came to hiding his emotions. When he'd stared at Jasmine during Hannah's wedding reception she'd believed him rude, interpreting his staring as predatory. He saw something

286

he wanted and would not stop until he captured it. And he had.

It was the same stare she'd encountered when meeting Lamar for the first time. She'd found it flattering and frightening at the same time, and that was something she'd admitted to him. However, for Lamar it was purely physical, because he hadn't been able to control his body's reaction to seeing her.

Nydia knew she had to be a certified dimwit not to know that Lamar's entrancement with her was physical. He'd openly admitted that to her. And it was not to say she wasn't attracted to him. However, her attraction did not necessarily translate into sleeping with him. When Jasmine had asked if she'd enjoyed his kiss, she'd confessed she had. What she'd enjoyed more than Lamar kissing her was his easygoing personality and feeling so comfortable with him that she could extend an invitation for him to sleep in her spare bedroom.

"Don't worry, Cameron," she said after a pregnant silence. "I'll do whatever I can to keep Jasmine safe."

"Thank you, Nydia. The key to your suite is at the front desk. Unfortunately I couldn't get you into the bridal suite because it's booked solid until the end of the year."

She smiled. "That's all right. Bridal suites should be for brides and grooms." *And I'm definitely not a bride,* she thought. "Tell Jasmine to call me tomorrow morning. I plan to stay in for most of the day."

"Will do."

Nydia ended the call and closed her eyes. She had made it a practice not to get involved with couples, whether married or not, when they confided to her about what was going on between them and their partners, because of an incident between her first cousin, Milagros Baez, and her then boyfriend when both were teenagers. She'd overheard rumors that Millie's boyfriend was cheating on her with another girl and told her cousin. The confrontation that ensued led to threats of violence between Millie and the other girl and had to be defused by adults who were reluctant to become involved in adolescent squabbles. She'd been taught a hard lesson about repeating gossip, and her mantra was: see no evil; hear no evil; speak no evil.

"Finally," she whispered under her breath when the driver parked in front of the hotel.

Gathering her carry-on, she was out of the town car before the driver could come around and open the door for her. A bellhop appeared and removed her luggage from the trunk. Nydia thanked the driver and slipped him a generous tip.

It took her less than fifteen minutes to check in and take the elevator to her room. She waited until the bellhop set the Pullman onto a luggage rack; she tipped the young man and closed the door behind him. The space was smaller than the bridal suite but just as inviting. The bedroom contained two full-size, four-poster beds with piles of vintage lace-trimmed pillows, bed skirts, and contemporary down quilts. It was a quiet retreat to sleep and/or while away the hours reading or watching television.

Nydia opted for a quick shower rather than a leisurely soak in the garden tub. She plugged her cell phone into the charger, activated the Do Not Disturb feature on the hotel phone, slipped under crisp white sheets and fell asleep within minutes after her head touched the pillow.

CHAPTER 13

"Isn't that your sister-in-law?" Nydia asked Jasmine as they walked across the parking lot to the restaurant for Sunday brunch. She pointed to the tall, slender brunette with two young girls.

Jasmine had called her Saturday morning asking if she would accompany her to look at china patterns. Nydia, remembering her promise to Cameron, asked for a rain check because she was still fatigued from traveling. She'd suggested they order room service and once it arrived they spent hours talking about their futures as innkeepers, Jasmine's plans for decorating the rooms in her new home, and for the first time Nydia revealed the intimate details behind the relationship with her college professor and how she'd felt betrayed.

She knew she had shocked Jasmine with the admission and then confessed that she had been too ashamed to tell her; that she had been so naïve she refused to see what had been so obvious.

It had become a time of reveals as Jasmine told her about the connection with Lamar and the Singletons. Lamar and Cameron's sister, Evangeline, had attended the same high school.

They reunited at a fellow student's political fund-raiser where she introduced Lamar to her flight attendant coworker. Valerie and Evangeline were bridal attendants at each other's weddings and delivered their babies two weeks apart.

"Yes. It's Evie and her twin girls, Taylor and Morgan," Jasmine said, smiling.

Nydia had met Cameron's two brothers, sister, and their spouses, days before his wedding and found the Singletons rather standoffish until the patriarch welcomed her like a missing family member. It was as if they'd suddenly been given permission to interact with her. However, she saw a more uninhibited side of their personalities at the wedding when they laughed, danced, and drank with abandon. She had to give it to the Singletons because they certainly knew how to throw a party while enjoying it themselves.

Jasmine called out to get Evangeline's attention. Evangeline McDonald turned in their direction. Arms outstretched, she hugged Jasmine, her dark blue eyes sparkling like polished sapphires.

"If you'd called to tell me you were coming, I would've picked you up." She glanced around the lot. "Where's Cameron?"

Jasmine returned the hug. "He had to drop something off for your father to look over. He said he'll join us later. Evie, you do remember my best friend and maid of honor?"

"Of course I do." She laughed and hugged Nydia. "Who could forget the woman everyone couldn't stop talking about when she danced salsa with Lamar? Speaking of Lamar, I'm meeting him here with his daughter. Maybe we all can sit together."

Nydia's breath caught in her lungs when Evangeline mentioned Lamar. She'd wanted to wait to contact him when she returned to New Orleans, but apparently she no longer had to text him because they would soon come face-to-face.

"It's nice seeing you again," she said to Cameron's sister. "And who are these two beauties?" It was obvious the girls were identical twins. Both had dark red, curly hair, light blue eyes, a liberal sprinkling of freckles over their cheeks, and pert, upturned noses. Nydia estimated they were between nine and eleven, the same age as her nieces.

"I'm Morgan."

"I'm Taylor."

Nydia smiled. They'd spoken at the same time, and she wondered if, like a lot of twins, they each knew what the other was feeling or thinking. She extended her hand. "I'm Nydia, and it's nice meeting you." The girls looked at their mother, who nodded. Each took Nydia's hand and mumbled the proper greeting.

"We need to get inside," Evangeline said, steering her daughters to the entrance of Momma's Place. "We have a reservation for noon." She glanced over at Nydia. "Who cut your hair? It looks absolutely fabulous. I've been thinking about cutting mine, but I still can't decide on a style. Pulling it back in a ponytail or in a bun is not very sophisticated for a thirty-eight-year-old mother of ten-year-old girls."

Nydia shared a glance with Jasmine. "My mother is a hairstylist."

Evangeline patted her hair. "Do you think she could work wonders with this mop?"

Nydia nodded. "My mother's reputation has preceded her. She's known in the neighborhood as *la reina del cabello,* and that translates to the queen of hair."

"Please don't tell me I have to go to New York to get a good cut?" Evangeline teased as she pushed open the door at the rear of the restaurant. It had stopped raining and had cooled down enough for diners to eat alfresco under a large white awning.

Nydia was preempted from answering when she saw Lamar standing off to the side of the hostess station. When his jaw dropped there was no doubt he was shocked to see her. The young girl, she assumed it was his daughter, did not see her father's reaction to her as she and Evangeline's girls hugged one another, all talking at the same time.

A smile tugged at the corners of his mouth when he met her eyes. "I didn't expect to see you again this soon."

Wow! she mused. How had she forgotten how sexy he sounded? His voice was deep, smooth, and velvety. And the cadence was slow enough for her to hang onto his every word. "I didn't expect to come down this soon," she replied.

"Mr. Pierce, your table is ready." The hostess's voice shattered the man's warm spell that had pulled Nydia in and refused to let her go.

Lamar turned to the woman. "We're going to need a larger table. I made a reservation for five, but now there are seven of us."

"Make that eight," Jasmine added. "Cameron's going to join us."

The hostess studied the seating chart on the podium. "If you can wait a few minutes I will have a server set the banquette for you."

Lamar approached Nydia, his gaze lingering on her coiffed hair. The chic style was perfect for her small, round face. She'd applied only a hint of makeup to her eyes and mouth, a mouth he'd kissed and longed to kiss again. He'd returned to New Orleans, unable to clear his head of everything he'd shared with Nydia. It was the first time in his life that he cursed having total recall.

Lamar thought of Nydia as a chameleon. There were times when she looked like a fresh-faced college coed, but could easily transition into a stylish, well turned-out young sophisticate, and she was the latter today with her chic hairstyle and white silk blouse and tailored cropped black slacks and Tory Burch flats. The designer's shoes had been a favorite of his late wife's.

"When did you get in?" he asked quietly.

"Friday night."

Lamar's brow unconsciously furrowed. "You flew in during the fog?" It had rained for a couple of days and once it ended a heavy mist had blanketed the city, lowering visibility to one-tenth of a mile.

Nydia nodded. "Yes. Once we touched down it seemed like an eternity before my driver arrived at the hotel."

"You're staying at the LaSalle?" She nodded again. "How long are you staying?"

"Mr. Pierce, your table is ready."

The hostess preempted Nydia's reply. "Thank you." He beckoned to Kendra and the twins. "Come on, girls. Let's sit down." Cupping Nydia's elbow, he escorted her to the banquette in a corner of the crowded, popular restaurant, Evangeline and Jasmine following.

He waited until everyone was seated on the U-shaped upholstered bench before sitting next to Nydia. The three girls sat together, giggling uncontrollably. The two sisters-in-law whispered to each other, laughing softly as if sharing a secret.

Lamar leaned over and tapped his daughter's shoulder. "Kendra, this is Miss Nydia. She's the one who made the *pasteles.* Nydia, I'd like you to meet my daughter, Kendra."

Kendra clapped a hand over her mouth. "You really made them?" she asked through her fingers.

Nydia smiled. "Yes. I made them with my friend."

"What are past-tell-is?" Evangeline asked.

Jasmine placed a hand on Evangeline's arm. "They're tamales filled with meat and root veggies. Puerto Ricans usually serve them around Christmas or when they have a large celebration. Talk about delicious."

Kendra moaned audibly. "They were the bomb! Miss Ramona and me ate more than Daddy."

"If they were that good, then you should bring them to the school's International Week dinner," Taylor said.

"Last year I had an empanada for the first time, and I was mad I didn't take more than one because all the boys were dogging them," Morgan stated, frowning.

"What foods do they serve for the dinner?" Nydia asked.

The three girls began talking at the same time until Evangeline put up a hand. "Girls, please. One at a time."

"I'll go first," Taylor volunteered. "Every student has to pick a country and write a report and create a model, painting, or diorama of that country's famous buildings or monuments. At the end of the week we have a dinner, and students, parents, and teachers bring in foods from around the world."

"We ate food from Vietnam, France, Italy, Mexico, India, and even some African countries," Kendra continued.

"I got to eat a lot of foods I never tasted before," Morgan offered, "but there were some that tasted nasty."

"Morgan!" Evangeline scolded softly. "I've told you time and time again that if you don't like something you don't say it's nasty, because it may taste good to someone else." Morgan and her mother engaged in a stare-down until the waitress approached the table and handed each of them a menu.

"Miss Nydia? Can you teach me how to make *pasteles*?" Kendra said, catching everyone at the table off-guard with her query. "That way I can bring them to this year's International Week dinner."

"Can you teach us, too?" the twins asked in unison.

Lamar rested his hand at the small of Nydia's back. "Think before you answer," he said, warning her just above a whisper. "Because this trio can be very manipulative," he continued in Spanish.

Nydia paused, staring at Kendra and then the twin girls. "I can't commit until I speak to your parents. If they agree and I decide

298

to give you cooking lessons, I'll start with Kendra because there are a lot of steps and it takes hours to make *pasteles*. Once Kendra shows me she knows what's she's doing, then she can assist with Morgan and Taylor."

"Please, Mama," the twins chorused.

Kendra rose slightly and leaned forward and flashed a look Lamar interpreted as her woe-is-me face. "Daddy?"

"Girls! We'll talk about this later." There was a hint of finality in Evangeline's voice.

Seconds later Taylor, Kendra, and Morgan pretended interest in their menus.

Lamar picked up his menu. "You could've said no," he said under his breath.

Nydia gave him a sidelong glance, her eyes appearing more green than gold under a sweep of long dark lashes. Staring at her, Lamar realized why her ex hadn't wanted to let Nydia go. She'd been blessed with a natural beauty and intelligence she did not flaunt, and a sensuality that had him fantasizing about making love with her.

Nydia held him captive in a longing that was so foreign that it frightened him. Lamar had never professed to be a choirboy when it came to interacting with women; he'd sown his wild oats before settling down to become a husband and father.

Lamar had had his first sexual encounter at sixteen with an older woman who'd taught him how to please her, and she in turn made him cognizant of his body and how best to use it to bring himself ultimate pleasure and satisfaction. At that age he was very discriminating and refused to sleep with any of the girls at their school. Too many were into kissing and telling, and he wanted to avoid the pitfalls of some of his male classmates, whose girlfriends told them they were pregnant and keeping the baby. It was never an option for him to father a child out of wedlock, and he always took the precaution to use protection. Once he'd begun dating Valerie he never looked at another woman. He had remained a loyal and faithful husband throughout their marriage.

Nydia leaned against his shoulder. "I wasn't prepared to say no because I remember myself at their age. I'd come home after school, change my clothes, and then go into the kitchen to do homework and watch my mother or grandmother prepare dinner. I'd always ask what's for dinner. And if they were making my favorites I'd tell them I wanted to learn to make it. Mami and Abuelita were the best teachers a girl could have, and by the time I was sixteen I was able to put a full meal on the table. And that included soup, salad, bread, and entrées. When I lived on campus I had a dorm with a kitchen. I became quite the saleswoman when I cooked and sold dinners to other students."

Lamar pressed a fist to his mouth to suppress a laugh. "You were selling dinners like folks do when hosting house-rent parties."

"What do you know about house-rent parties?"

"Come on, *cariña*. Black folks have been selling dinners for generations to get money to pay their rent. And I'm certain people in your neighborhood still do, because it wasn't that long ago that Iggy and I bought fish dinners on Fridays from one of his neighbors."

Nydia laughed softly. "You're right. When the word went out around the campus that Santiago was cooking, students came through with the ducats. I made enough money to pay for my books and then have some left over."

"So, you'd become a hustler."

"Correction, Lamar. I was the *unmitigated* hustler. I'd grown up watching dudes in my neighborhood hustling everything from clothes to meat that would conveniently fall off a truck. They never sold anything to my mother because they knew my father was a cop."

"Did he ever arrest them?"

"No. He didn't work out of our neighborhood precinct."

"Tell me about your hustle."

"I'd buy large bags of rice, packages of dried beans, yellow and green plantains, and whatever meat, chicken, or fish was on sale. Every once in a while I'd roast a pork shoulder and the entire building was filled with mouth-watering aroma of *pernil.* A few of the students would complain about the smell of garlic, oregano, and cumin and wanted to report me to management, but they were intimidated by my regular customers. I gave them more food on a five-dollar plate than what they'd get in the cafeteria, snack bar, or nearby fast food joints. If you want, I'll teach Kendra to cook a few traditional Spanish dishes, and I promise not to tell her about my days as a college foodie hustler."

Lamar offered his hand. "You've got yourself a deal, as long as it doesn't interfere with her schoolwork."

Nydia shook his hand. "Deal. I'll be meeting with Hannah, Tonya, and Jasmine on business while I'm here, so I'll let you know when I'm free so we can coordinate our schedules."

"I'll tell once I get her home. By the way, how long do you intend to be here?"

"I have a ticket to return to New York the Monday before Thanksgiving."

Lamar quickly calculated the weeks and smiled. Nydia offering to teach Kendra to cook meant he would get to see her at least once or twice a week. And the more he saw Nydia, the more he wanted to be with her. She was a free spirit he found exciting and intoxicating.

Their server returned, pad in hand. "I notice you have an empty place setting. Are you waiting for someone else?"

"Yes," Jasmine said. "I'm not certain when he's going to arrive, so you can take our orders."

The young woman glanced around the table. "Would anyone like to order a beverage? Today's brunch includes unlimited pop, fruit drinks, mimosas, Bellinis, and Bloody Marys."

Evangeline pointed to the three girls. "The kids will have whatever fruit drinks you have available, while I'll have a Bloody Mary."

"I'll have a virgin Bloody Mary," Jasmine said. "Please make certain the bartender doesn't put gin or vodka in it."

The waitress nodded. "I'll be sure to let

him know." Her gaze shifted to Nydia. "What can I get you?"

"I'll take a mimosa."

"And you, sir?"

Lamar paused, debating whether he wanted a cocktail with tomato juice, and quickly changed his mind. "I'll also have a mimosa."

Cameron finally joined them, taking turns kissing his sister, nieces, Kendra, and Nydia, before shaking hands with Lamar. The food and energy from those at the table offered Nydia a glimpse into why Jasmine had so easily adjusted to life in New Orleans. She watched the interaction between her best friend and Jasmine's sister-in-law as they laughed with each other. At first Nydia thought the Singletons had welcomed Jasmine into the family because she was carrying Cameron's child, but she dismissed that notion when the twins addressed Jasmine as Aunt Jazz.

The bond between Kendra, Taylor, and Morgan had been cemented when Evangeline had become godmother to Valerie's daughter, and Valerie returned the honor when becoming godmother to Evangeline's twin girls.

And once she moved to New Orleans Nydia knew she would also be drawn into the orbit of the Singleton family and friends when she became godmother to Cameron and Jasmine's son or daughter. She found it strange and fascinating at the same time that sixteen months ago she, Jasmine, Tonya, and Hannah were coworkers who barely acknowledged one another when passing throughout the office building, yet now they were inextricably connected by a unique friendship and a new business venture.

"How are your eggs Benedict?" Lamar asked Nydia.

She touched her napkin to the corners of her mouth. "They're delicious." She had ordered the poached eggs atop English muffins with thick slices of Canadian bacon and covered with a warm Hollandaise sauce, with a side dish of crispy tater tots. "The sauce has a touch of heat from what I think is cayenne."

Lamar smiled, drawing her gaze to linger on the attractive cleft in his strong chin. "If your palate is not ready for a little hot spice, then you've moved to the wrong city. Spicy is what we do best."

"Do you want to join Kendra when I teach her to cook?"

"No."

"Why not?"

"Because there's no need for me to cook when I pay someone to prepare my meals. And when Ramona is on vacation or takes a few days off, I eat out."

"Why are you so opposed to learning to cook?" Nydia insisted. "You claim you have total recall, so it should be easy for you to remember exactly what to do." She narrowed her eyes and gave him a long, penetrating stare. "Are you a throwback to men who believe a woman's place is in the kitchen?"

Lamar gave her an incredulous look. "How can you ask me that when I have a daughter?"

"Having a daughter doesn't change anything. No one is more macho than my father, and when he married my mother he couldn't boil water to make a cup of tea. She taught him to cook and now he's better than she is, and Mami is no slouch in the kitchen. You'll see that for yourself when you join us for Christmas."

"Why is it so important that I learn to cook, Nydia?"

"So your daughter can be proud of her father other than because he makes money to take care of her."

"Damn woman! Are you trying to run a

guilt trip on me?"

Nydia's expression feigned innocence. "Of course not. As a single metrosexual, if you add the ability to cook to your personal profile it definitely would enhance your image."

A frown furrowed his forehead. "I don't do dating sites."

"I'm not saying you do, but perhaps in the future you will when Kendra is older and in college and you want to start dating again."

"I'll cross that bridge when I come to it."

Nydia saw the quivering muscle in his jaw and knew he was annoyed with her. "Look, Lamar, I'm not trying to run your life but hopefully make it better. Young girls see their fathers as superheroes, and cooking with Kendra can only strengthen the bond you have with her."

Lamar's frown was replaced by a knowing smile that lit up his gold-flecked eyes. "You know you missed your calling."

Her eyebrows lifted questioningly. "Why would you say that?"

"You should've become a therapist because you're able to get into people's heads."

"That was never a thought. I liked numbers too well. They don't talk or fight back."

"What happens when you can't get a balance sheet to add up?"

She smiled. "I put it aside for a few hours or sometimes even days, and when I look at it again it's like starting over."

"Are you a good accountant, Nydia?"

Nydia was slightly taken aback with his question. Was he testing her? And if he was, then for what reason? "My accounts believe I am."

"That's good."

"Why did you ask? Is your company looking for an accountant?"

"Not at this time. The one we have is semi-retired, and there's going to come a time when we'll have to replace him."

Nydia shook her head. "I doubt if I'll be able to help you out, because I'm going to have my hands full with the DuPont Inn, my mother's salon, and three New York City restaurants. There's no way I'm going to spread myself that thin just because someone offers me more money."

"What happened to your hustling spirit?" he teased.

"I stopped hustling once I graduated. At the time it was a means to an end. I've continued to do the books for the restaurants because sometimes accountants don't devote the same time to small businesses that they would to larger companies. I've seen too many mom-and-pop stores close because their accountants or bookkeepers embezzled from them."

"So, you've become the champion of the underdog?"

"There's no need to sound so cynical, Lamar," she countered sarcastically. "I gave a renowned international bank my blood, sweat, and sometimes tears, and they rewarded me with a pink slip and a banker's box. And they sought to assuage their deceit with severance pay and paid health insurance for a year, but that still didn't diminish the angst of attempting to secure future employment with commensurate salary and benefits. It's taken me more than a year to come to the conclusion that it is more satisfying to work for myself than for someone else's company."

"Are you an equal partner with your friends?" Lamar lowered his head and his voice.

"Not in terms of ownership, but we all have an equal say when it comes to which direction we want to take the inn." Nydia paused, wondering if Lamar was experiencing problems with his partners. "Do you and your partners share equally in your firm?"

"Yes, but there are times when we don't see eye-to-eye on certain projects."

"That's to be expected, Lamar, because no one is the same."

"True," he agreed, "but my personal life sets me apart from them."

"Do you want to talk about it?"

"Not here."

Nydia saw the others at the table staring at her and Lamar. They were probably curious that they'd been so engaged in talking to each other that they had totally ignored everyone else. *"Luego,"* she said under her breath.

"Kendra is going home with Evie, so we'll talk later."

She patted his hand under the table. "Okay."

"What were you two whispering about?" Evangeline asked.

"Work," Nydia replied.

Evangeline's lashes fluttered, and she appeared as if she was going to cry. "Talk about work, I truly miss flying."

Cameron stared at his sister. "Don't start, Evie. You know you promised Daniel you would give up your career as a flight attendant once you had your kids."

"A woman shouldn't have to give up her career just because she's married with

310

children," Nydia said matter-of-factly. As if rehearsed in advance, Jasmine and Evangeline rose slightly and gave Nydia high-fives.

"Preach, my sister," Jasmine said, ignoring the scowl on her husband's face.

Nydia realized she'd made a serious faux pas mentioning mothers working outside the home when she saw Cameron's thunderous expression. She knew he was conflicted because Jasmine intended to assist Hannah managing the inn once it opened for business, *and* after she returned from an extended maternity leave. Jasmine confided to Nydia that LeAnn and Paige DuPont, Hannah's first cousins, had volunteered to help out until Jasmine's six months' leave ended. An uncomfortable silence settled over the banquette that even the children noticed.

"Mom, we're finished eating," Taylor announced. "Can we leave now?"

Evangeline smiled. "Of course, darling."

Lamar signaled for the check, but Cameron had removed his credit card from a small leather case and handed it to their server. "Hold up, Lamar. It's my turn to pay for brunch."

Nydia wondered how often the Pierces and Singletons got together for Sunday brunch. The girls had ordered chicken and waffles, Lamar and Cameron steak and eggs, and Jasmine a grilled skirt steak with creamed spinach, mashed potatoes, and crispy onion straws, and Evangeline ordered a Cobb salad.

After settling the bill, Cameron assisted Jasmine, who'd admitted eating too much, with standing. Nydia knew not only had she eaten too much, but she also should not have had the second mimosa before she was feeling the effects of the champagne. The bubbly wine always left her feeling slightly lightheaded and very sleepy.

"Are you all right, partner?" Lamar said in her ear as he helped her to her feet.

"I'll let you know once I start to walk. Champagne usually does a number on me." She'd only taken a few sips at Jasmine and Cameron's wedding before setting aside the flute.

Lamar cradled her elbow. "Don't worry; I'll catch you before you fall."

Nydia rolled her eyes at him. She was just a little tipsy, not falling-down drunk. She had never been much of a drinker, and once she took her first drink at twenty-one she knew instinctively that she had a two-drink limit. The first and last time she'd known what it was to be hung over was after Hannah and St. John's wedding, and that was something she never wanted to experience again. After her first glass of the premium bubbly wine she discovered it tasted nothing like the ones she'd had before. She hadn't felt tipsy and continued to indulge until she lost count of the number of glasses she'd drunk, and paid for overindulging the next day when she woke up with a dry mouth and a pounding headache.

She didn't protest when Lamar took her hand and escorted her out of the restaurant to the parking lot. He didn't release her fingers until they stood at the rear of his vehicle. He slid his foot under the back of the Volvo, and the lift gate opened automatically. He handed Kendra a Vera Bradley quilted floral-print tote and then kissed her hair.

"I'll see you Tuesday night, sweetie."

"Bye, Daddy." Kendra took the tote and raced over to where Evangeline had parked her SUV.

"I'll take Nydia back to the hotel," he said to Jasmine as she slipped on a pair of sunglasses.

"Are you sure? I have plenty of room in my swagger wagon. Cameron came in his sports car, and now that I'm pregnant I find it so low he has to help me in and out of it."

Lamar nodded. "I'm very sure and promise to bring her back safe and sound."

Jasmine leaned in and kissed Nydia. "I'll see you tomorrow. Cameron and I have decided to stay in tonight."

Nydia pressed her cheek to Jasmine's. "Get some rest, *mija.*" The interior decorator now sported a slight baby bump. She waited for Cameron to help Jasmine into her minivan before he slipped behind the wheel of the two-seater Porsche and followed Jasmine's vehicle, and then she turned to find Lamar staring at her.

"What's on this afternoon's agenda?"

Lamar angled his head. "It all depends on what you want to do."

Nydia glanced down at Lamar's loafers. The soft leather looked very comfortable. "Would you mind if we go on a walking tour? When I came down last summer it was too hot to stay outdoors for any length of time without coming down with heatstroke."

He took her arm and led her around to the passenger side. "We'll walk *and* talk."

CHAPTER 14

"What do you want to see?" Lamar asked Nydia as he left the CBD and drove along St. Charles Avenue in the direction of Canal Street.

Nydia shifted on her seat and stared at Lamar. There was never a time when she hadn't found him impeccably groomed. Not a strand of his cropped gray hair was out of place, and whether clean-shaven or electing to sport a stubble, Lamar was the epitome of a metrosexual. His long, slender fingers with clean, square-cut nails indicated he was mindful of his overall appearance.

Nydia did not want to believe she was that superficial to be attracted to a man because of the way he looked, as it had been with Danny, but she knew deep down inside Lamar was as different from her ex as night and day. Danny refused to take responsibility for himself, preferring to depend on his sister to house and feed him. Lamar, although widowed, had elected to remain single because his daughter had become his priority. He had admitted to sleeping with women before meeting Nydia, but hadn't disclosed whether he'd introduced any of them to Kendra.

"The French Quarter," she replied, "Bourbon, Ramparts, Basin and Burgundy Streets, and the Farmers' Market."

Lamar gave her a quick glance. "Hold up, beautiful. You want to see a lot in just a few hours."

Nydia rested her left hand on his right one, which cradled the gearshift. "If you don't mind being my guide, then I'm willing to space out the tour over several weekends. That is, if you don't work weekends," she added.

"I try not to work weekends, because I want to plan things to do with Kendra."

"But you came up to New York to see me on the weekend," she reminded Lamar.

"That was the exception. It was apparent you needed my help."

She removed her hand. "You're right, and for that I'll be eternally grateful."

"It's not about gratitude, Nydia. You'll learn soon enough that folks down here look out for one another."

"I haven't officially become a New Orleanian."

"That doesn't matter, because you will." Lamar rested his arm over the back of her seat when he stopped for a red light. "Now that you've twisted my arm and got me to agree to learn to cook, what are you going to start out with?"

"I'll show you how to put together a salad and a sandwich."

He chuckled. "That sounds easy."

Her smile was dazzling. "Aren't you overly confident?"

"How difficult can it be to make a salad, *cariña*? All you need is lettuce, tomatoes, and maybe cucumber. And a sandwich is meat between two slices of bread."

"Salads aren't always made with greens, sweetie. There's caprese made with tomatoes and mozzarella cheese and basil leaves; salad niçoise. There's also Greek, tabbouleh, potato, and Cobb salads. Please tell me if a Cuban sandwich is just meat between two slices of bread?"

"No way," Lamar countered. His fingers combed through the hair on her nape before his hand returned to the gearshift.

Nydia inclined her head. "I rest my case."

"I find Cuban sandwiches addictive," he admitted.

317

"They can be if made with the right ingredients. I won't be able to show you how to make them until we have pernil."

Lamar noticed Nydia had said *we* as if they were a couple. And he had to ask himself whether he wanted them to be a couple, and the answer was a resounding yes. He wanted to spend as much time with her as he could, given his work schedule and looking after Kendra.

Gloria Pierce had nagged him for years to learn to cook, and he knew she would be shocked to know her son had agreed to take lessons from a little slip of a woman who unknowingly ensnared him in a sensual trap from which he did not want to escape.

"Do you think Kendra is going to resent me being around you?"

Lamar's foot hit the brake, bringing the vehicle to an abrupt stop. He glanced up at the rearview mirror and exhaled an audible breath that there wasn't a car behind his to rear-end the Volvo. He stared at Nydia as if she were a stranger. "Why would you ask me something like that?"

"You're holding up traffic, Lamar," Nydia said amid a cacophony of blaring horns.

Returning his attention to the road, Lamar drove through the intersection. "You didn't answer my question."

"I didn't answer because you didn't answer mine."

"No, I don't think she'll resent you."

"Am I the first woman outside your housekeeper and family members she's seen you with?" She had asked him yet another question.

"Yes, but what does that have to do with anything?"

"I saw her watching us at the restaurant."

"That's where you're mistaken. Kendra was too involved with her friends to pay any attention to us."

"That's where *you are* wrong," Nydia argued softly. "Every once in a while I saw her glance at us when she thought we weren't looking."

When Nydia mentioned Kendra staring at her, Lamar knew it wasn't because she had recognized her from the television footage he'd taped. He'd spent hours fast-forwarding the tapes and deleting the coverage with Nydia and her ex. "Why do think she was looking at us?"

"I think it's because she's curious. Call it a girl thing, but she probably wants to know how we met, and if I'm going to be someone she will have to share her father with."

"And what do you intend to tell her if she

asks?" Lamar questioned.

"The truth, and that her father and I are friends just like Morgan and Taylor are her friends."

Lamar nodded as he pondered Nydia's proposed explanation if Kendra did ask about their association. He and Nydia were friends, but then he had to ask himself if he wanted more than friendship, and at this time he didn't have an answer.

"And I'll also tell her the truth because I've never lied to my daughter. That you and I are friends."

"Make certain to reassure her that she will not have to share you with me."

Lamar signaled and turned down the blocks leading to Bourbon Street. "That's something I'm not going to do, and that is allow my daughter to control or monitor my life. I'm the adult and responsible for her and will be until she's emancipated. The only promise I hold to is the tradition of eating breakfast with Kendra on days she has classes. It was something I promised her after her mother died, and so far I've been able to keep it." He maneuvered into a parking space, shut off the engine, and released his seat belt. Shifting on his seat, Lamar met Nydia's eyes. "I'd like your opinion on a predicament I need to resolve with my partners tomorrow."

Nydia unbuckled her seat belt and leaned closer. "I'm all ears."

Lamar told her about the discussion he'd had with his partners about submitting a bid for the strip mall in Lafayette. "There's no guarantee we'll secure the project, but if we come in as the lowest bid, then I would have to oversee the construction, and that would take me nearly two hundred miles from home. And that is something I oppose, because I don't want to leave Kendra alone for days at a time."

"But is she going to be alone, Lamar? Don't you have a live-in housekeeper?"

"Yes, and Kendra doesn't mind being home with Miss Ramona on the weekends, but it's the weekdays and more importantly school days that can be upsetting for her. She'd just entered the first grade when she got up one morning looking for her mother, who was on her way to the airport. Valerie had gotten a call early one morning asking her to fill in for another flight attendant who had come down with the flu. Kendra was upset because her mother had promised to make pancakes for breakfast. She liked her mother's pancakes because she would surprise her when she made them using molds with different shapes. Valerie never made it to the airport because a drunk driver hit the taxi in which she was a passenger. It burst into flames, instantly killing her and the driver. It took a while for Kendra to realize her mother wasn't coming back because I'd opted for a graveside service in lieu of a funeral mass. That's when I promised her that we would always eat breakfast together before she left for school."

"Have you spoken to Kendra about the possibility that you may be away from home for work?"

"No."

"Well, you should, Lamar. A ten-year-old isn't the same as a six-year-old. Kendra has friends who now play an important part in her life. And she seemed more than happy to stay with them over the weekend. And her telling you she'll see you Tuesday means she's not going to be around to eat breakfast with you on a school day. Why are you so sure Kendra will be upset? Are you experiencing guilt because of your promise to her?"

Lamar massaged his forehead with his fingertips. Perhaps Nydia was right. When he'd left her in Baton Rouge to spend the summer with his mother and sister, his daughter barely acknowledged him whenever he drove up to see her. "She is growing up."

Nydia patted his shoulder. "And she's going to grow up even faster over the next few years. I assume right now she's not into boys, but in a couple of years she'll be whispering on the phone or texting her girlfriends about a boy she likes. And once she begins dating, then Daddy will no longer be the most important male in her life."

Lamar grimaced. "Please don't bring that up."

"My father used to say having a girl is karma's payback for what he's done to other men's daughters."

"Amen," Lamar whispered. He smiled. "Thanks for helping me see this from another perspective. I'll call and talk to Kendra tonight and get her opinion before I approach my partners tomorrow."

"I don't know how close you are to Evangeline, but if you know you're going to be away for more than one day, then perhaps you can have Kendra stay over with her."

"I'm godfather to her daughters, and she and her husband are Kendra's godparents."

"There you go. Why were you making a mountain out of a molehill?"

"I don't know, sweets. There are times

when I tend to overthink a situation, and I suppose this is one." Lamar held Nydia's hand and kissed the back of it. He'd kissed her hand when it was her mouth he wanted to taste, but he reminded himself that he was much too old to make out in a car with a woman. She stared up at him through her lashes, unaware of how seductive she was. It was as if she was silently beckoning him to kiss her.

"Thank you again."

Nydia smiled. "There's no need to thank me. As friends we do what we can to help each other out."

Lamar applied the slightest pressure on her fingers. "Is that what you want, Nydia?

"What are you talking about?"

"Do you just want to be friends, or could we possibly become more?"

Nydia carefully pondered her response. She, who usually blurted out whatever came to mind, knew whatever she said would change her and her association with Lamar. He was someone who'd managed to penetrate the wall she'd erected so she would not become involved in a romantic relationship. She was now in what she thought of as her business mode. Doing the payroll for the three restaurateurs was time-consuming, and she was also singly focused on becoming an innkeeper in a new state where she would be more than a thousand miles away from her family. She now thought of Tonya, Hannah, and Jasmine as her older sisters in her newly formed family. And she had to ask herself if she was ready to become involved with a man with a ready-made family, because she had never envisioned herself as a stepmother — and especially to a preteen girl with all of the angst that went along with maturing into a woman.

She knew the instant she'd seen Lamar's image in the video intercom that he hadn't been that altruistic in coming to her rescue, but had an ulterior motive — and that was he was interested in her the way a man was in a woman. Nydia was grateful, flattered, and most of all deeply affected by his coming to her rescue. She'd had two relationships, and once they ended she took a long, hard look at herself and what she had given up in order to make them work.

Tough-girl, fast-talking Nydia Stephanie Santiago had permitted men to use her for their own selfish needs; she knew and refused to acknowledge it until it was too late. And if Jasmine, and expressly Tonya, who regarded her as a daughter, hadn't told her get rid of Danny, she probably would have continued to see him.

She saw something in the eyes of the man who had shown her nothing but confidence since their initial meeting and wondered if he was going through what she felt — indecision and perhaps a hint of fear. A hint of a smile played at the corners of her mouth as she winked at him. Lamar was everything she'd want in a man with whom to have a relationship, and she did not want to pass up the opportunity to date someone who was honest and mature enough to say what he felt and wanted.

"We can become *mucho más que amigos*," she said, mixing English and Spanish.

Lamar kissed her fingers again. "We'd better get out of this car before I do something that would ruin both our reputations."

Nydia pressed her forehead to his. "And what's that?" she teased. Lamar put his mouth to her ear and whispered what he would like to do to her. She gasped. "That is so kinky!"

He pulled back. "You think nerds can't get kinky?"

She laughed until tears filled her eyes, turning them into pools of green and gold. Nydia was still laughing when Lamar got out and came around to help her out of the SUV. And for the first time in a very long time she felt as if she did not have a care in the world as they walked, holding hands, along Bourbon Street, passing strings of bars offering lethal concoctions with names that made her afraid to take a sip. Blues, rock, and jazz could be heard from open doorways as locals and tourists jockeyed for space along the crowded street.

Lamar pointed to the lacy balconies on the buildings above the sidewalks. "They're usually so crowded from the weight of drinking revelers during Mardi Gas that it's a miracle they haven't collapsed to the streets below."

"Do you attend Mardi Gras?" she asked him.

"Not anymore. There was a time when I wouldn't miss it."

"Did you go every year?"

"I did until I left for college. I went the first time when I was sixteen and drank myself into a stupor. When I got home my father raised so much hell that I swore I'd never drink again until I was legal."

"Did you keep that vow?"

Lamar nodded. "My father was very easygoing, but if you riled him up he was like a tiger ready to pounce. He knew I wanted to go away to college and said if he even suspected I was drinking then I would have to live at home and attend a local school. And as long as I lived under his roof I'd do whatever he said or get out."

She grimaced. "Ouch!"

"Dad was once a drill sergeant in the Corps, so he saw himself as a badass with everyone except my mother and sister. After he put in for his discharge he used his military benefits to attend college and became an orthodontist."

"So that's why you have such beautiful teeth."

Lamar pulled Nydia to his chest when a man came toward them weaving unsteadily as he tried drinking from a go-cup. "The first time my braces were removed I refused to wear the retainer so they shifted, so I had to endure them a second time. That's when I learned to wear the retainer every night for almost two years."

"I noticed Kendra has braces."

"She has teeth like mine. My dad died two years before Kendra was born, so she never got to meet her grandfather."

"What about her maternal grandparents?"

"That's a long story, Nydia."

"Is it something too personal to disclose?"

"No. Valerie's mother was a runaway who'd had her at fifteen. She delivered her in the hospital, and two days later walked out and left a newborn baby girl with a positive toxicology for heroin. The baby spent several weeks in the hospital detoxing. She should've been quickly adopted by couples waiting for a newborn, but her medical history made her a risk for future mental and physical manifestations. She went into the foster care system and was shuttled from one family to another until she was eight.

"An elderly couple finally adopted her. They became the parents she always wished she had. Both passed away a year after she graduated high school, and once again she was orphaned. Evie and I had gone to the same high school, and she introduced me to Valerie when both were flight attendants. We dated for a year and then married. A year later we had Kendra. She was overjoyed at being a mother, but after two years she complained that she missed flying. She interviewed a few nannies, and after hiring Ramona, Valerie went back to work. I really beat up on myself because as much as I'd tried, I couldn't convince her not to go to work that morning. If she'd stayed home she would still be here."

"Do you really think you could've avoided what was destined, Lamar?" Nydia asked him. "We all have an expiration date, and it's a good thing we don't know when it is because we would stop living to prepare for the inevitable. There are bumps and obstacles in the road we call life, and it's up to us to learn to navigate them to reach our goals."

Lamar stopped, pulled her close to his body, and rested his chin on the top of her head. "I said it before and I'll say it again, you missed your calling, *querida*. You should've become a therapist rather than an accountant, because you're so easy to open up to."

Nydia buried her face against his warm throat and inhaled the sensual fragrance of the cologne that blended so well with his body's natural scent. Everything about Lamar was so overwhelmingly masculine that she wanted to stay in his embrace for more than a few minutes as she delighted in the muscles in his back and chest. "Maybe it's because you feel comfortable enough to confide in me." She eased back and smiled up at him. "I have a practice not to date for a year after a breakup, but I've decided to change my mind."

"When will it be a year?" Lamar asked.

"November."

"That's only six weeks away."

"Six weeks to find out if we really like each other," Nydia said teasingly.

"I liked you the first time I saw you."

330

"That's because you liked what you saw." Nydia did not want to remind him that he'd confessed to getting an erection when they first met.

"No shit!" Lamar drawled. "I'm sorry; I shouldn't have said that."

A shadow of annoyance settled between Nydia's eyes. "Don't ever apologize for what you say, Lamar. Because what comes out of your mouth comes from your heart. I appreciate honesty, even if it's something I don't agree with. I've had enough deceit from men with whom I've been involved to last me a lifetime, and I don't want to have that with you."

"You really don't bite your tongue, do you, Nydia?"

"No and never. What you see is what you get."

Attractive lines fanned out around Lamar's eyes when he smiled. "And you know I like what I see."

Her hand moved from his chest to his waistband. "Just make sure a certain part of your body doesn't decide to make an unscheduled appearance."

Throwing back his head, Lamar laughed loudly. "You're so naughty."

Nydia scrunched up her nose. "Only sometimes, and you like it, don't you?

Haven't you heard that naughty girls are a lot more fun than the goody two-shoes?"

"Hell yeah!" Lamar kissed her hair.

A couple bumped into them, and Nydia knew they were impeding pedestrian traffic. "How far is the French Market from here?"

"It's about ten blocks. Do you want to go there?"

Nydia nodded. "Yes." She wanted to see what produce was available for her potential cooking projects.

"I'm going to take you back to pick up the car. After you visit the market I want to take you to my home, which is also in the Upper French Quarter."

Lamar's offer to take her to his house had caught Nydia completely off-guard, but she recovered quickly. She should not have been surprised, because she and Lamar had agreed she would give him and Kendra cooking lessons.

"Let's go, McDuff."

Lamar placed his arm over her shoulders. "You like the bard?"

"I love the bard. I definitely would've become an English lit teacher if I hadn't majored in accounting."

"Should I assume you like British drama?"

Nydia held onto the hand resting on her shoulder. "I love, love, love them!"

Lamar pulled her closer to his side. "I think I would enjoy them more if I could understand what they were saying, because they talk funny."

She stopped mid-stride and would have tripped if Lamar hadn't steadied her. "Talk funny? You're got to be kidding me, Lamar. You folks down here talk funny."

"So do New Yorkers, when they say *earl* for *oil,* and *turdy-turd* for *thirty-third.* I didn't know what the heck this dude was saying when he talked about an *earl burner.*"

"That's Brooklyn. They speak differently from people in Manhattan."

"All New Yorkers talk funny, even those upstate."

"Please don't diss my state, because it's all I know and love."

"For now, sweetie. Once you move down here you'll become a bona fide Louisianan. After a while *y'all* will roll off your tongue and you'll cut the ending off your words. It'll no longer be good morning, but mornin'."

"I ain't giving up the Apple that easily."

"You will when the Easy puts a spell on you that you won't be able to get rid of. Look at Jasmine."

"What about her?"

"She's adapted well to the South."

"That's because her father is a South-erner, and as a kid she used to spend her summers in North Carolina, while I spent my summers in Nueva York and only went to Puerto Rico for a relative's wedding or funeral."

During the return walk to the parking lot, Lamar decided to test her by rattling off a series of Southern colloquialisms, and she was unable to translate fewer than half. It didn't take her long to conclude she would never be bored spending time with him, because he made her laugh, and that was something she hadn't done enough over the past few months. Chronic pain before and after surgery from her ruptured appendix had left her out of sorts, and knowing she wouldn't be able to attend Tonya and Gage's wedding had exacerbated her de-pression. Her dark mood finally lifted with Jasmine's wedding, but descended again with her ex's asinine stunt.

Her skies had brightened once again with her return to the Crescent City. This time she was given eight weeks to acquaint herself with what would become her new city and begin the process of becoming an innkeeper.

Nydia knew she had misjudged Lamar when

he parked his car under a porte cochère. She stared through the windshield at an expansive open courtyard. It was a Garden of Eden with towering oak trees draped in Spanish moss, with ferns, rose bushes, and enormous banana-type leaves growing in well-ordered abandon. A large marble fountain with the sculpted figure of a cherub holding a water jug had become the courtyard's focal point. A number of tables were positioned near a large fire pit. Lamar's house was similar to other traditional nineteenth-century Creole residences with beautiful second-story cast-iron balconies like she'd seen in the older sections of the city. She did not know why, but she would have thought he'd have preferred a more contemporary home.

Lamar assisted her out of the vehicle, and she walked ahead of him, her eyes taking in everything around her. She felt the heat from his body as he rested his hands on her shoulders.

"What are you thinking about?" he said in her ear.

"This courtyard is magnificent. Weather permitting, it is the perfect place to begin watching the sun rise and end the day under the stars."

"It is," Lamar agreed. "Whenever Kendra

invites the twins and the two Kelly girls, who live next door, for a sleepover, they pretend they're princesses and use the courtyard as their castle."

Nydia glanced up at Lamar over her shoulder. "You must have the patience of a saint to put up with five girls sleeping under one roof."

"I'm used to it. Do you want to see inside?"

"Yes." She felt the courtyard was large enough to hold an intimate dinner party or a buffet with at least fifty or sixty people.

"The garage used to be a carriage house," Lamar explained as he led to a door at the far end of the courtyard.

"How many bedrooms do you have?"

"There's four on the second story and three on the first. I've converted one on the first floor into an office, and Ramona has her own suite, and the extra one is now a laundry room."

Nydia flashed a knowing smile when Lamar unlocked the door to reveal an ultramodern open floor plan with the family, living, and dining rooms flowing into a kitchen with top-of-the-line appliances. Shades of brown, blue, and off-white were tasteful and inviting.

"Nice." She also noticed working fire-

336

places in the family and living rooms.

"I can't take credit for anything you see here. Valerie hired an interior decorator once the renovations were completed."

She wondered if Lamar had changed anything in the house since his wife's death, or had left it intact because he wanted to preserve her memory. Nydia walked into the gourmet kitchen with Viking appliances. "You can do some serious cooking in this kitchen," she said, smiling and meeting Lamar's amused expression.

"The only time I come in here is to get some water or brew a cup of coffee, otherwise it's Ramona's domain."

"Do you think she's going to mind me invading her domain?"

"Not in the least. She doesn't seem to mind it when Kendra prepares her somewhat unorthodox breakfasts and leaves a mess."

Nydia wanted to tell Lamar that he paid the woman to keep his house in order and/or clean up messes, but she held her tongue, while at the same time applauding herself for exercising restraint. She knew there were times to open her mouth and other times to keep it closed. And this was one of those times. She'd promised herself not to interfere in Lamar's personal life unless he asked for her opinion. Then she would not withhold it if they were going to have a friendship based on honesty.

"Do you mind if I check out the cookware? I need to know what I'm working with before we begin the cooking lessons."

Lamar walked over to a wall of off-white cabinets and opened one. "Ramona keeps her pots and pans in here."

A number of shelves were filled with blue Le Creuset cookware. There were Dutch ovens, skillets and fry pans, stock and saucepans. There was even a matching teakettle. She also noted a cast iron skillet, blender, and food processor, so essential to a well-stocked kitchen. She bent down to search through the lower shelves.

"What are you looking for?" Lamar asked.

Nydia stood straight. "A panini press."

He shook his head. "I doubt if we have one, but I'll call Ramona later on tonight and ask her. If we don't, then I'll pick up one during the week."

"It doesn't have to be too big or fancy. You'll probably only use it for grilled cheese and Cuban sandwiches." She'd said that because it was obvious Lamar had spared no expense when purchasing gourmet cookware for the kitchen. She closed the cabinet door. "Once you learn to cook, you're going to have a good time putting meals together."

Lamar rolled his eyes upward. "If you say so," he drawled.

"I do say so. I'm ready to see the rest of the house."

Nydia peered into the laundry room with a late-model washer and dryer and enough room for portable drying racks. An ironing board was set up in front of a countertop with stacks of neatly folded sheets and towels. She followed Lamar past a family room with a number of leather reclining chairs, facing a wide, wall-mounted television, and into his office. There was an L-shaped desk with a desktop computer and printer, a drafting table, and another table covered with bound reports. Nydia stared at two tall stainless steel containers filled with what appeared to be dozens of tubes of plans.

"How long have you been in business with your partners?"

"It will be twelve years this coming February."

She sat on a stool at the drafting table. "How did you meet?"

Lamar sat on the edge of the mahogany desk. "We met in graduate school and eventually went to work for the same engineering firm. Even before graduating we'd planned to set up our own company. However, the decision was where. Omar came from Oakland and Kirk from Los Angeles. We knew setting up in California was not going to be easy, so I suggested New Orleans, not only because I live here but the city was just beginning to recover from the destruction of Hurricane Katrina. Soon after we incorporated we applied to the federal and local governments for bids geared to minority-owned companies."

"Are your partners African Americans?"

"Omar is, and Kirk is black and Vietnamese. His father fought in Vietnam and married a local woman. He arranged for her to come to the States, and even before she became an American citizen she had Kirk and his sister, who is a neurosurgeon."

Grinning, Nydia made a fist. "All power to the people."

Smiling, Lamar walked over to Nydia and pulled into her an embrace. "What am I going to do with you?"

She returned his smile. "Keep me around so I can make you laugh."

He stared at her under lowered lids. "You're right. There are times when I'm much too serious."

"Don't you take time out to have fun?"

"Not enough," Lamar admitted.

"Before Jasmine and Tonya moved down here we used to meet a couple of times a month for dinner. We'd alternate eating at different restaurants or at one another's apartments. It was our time to laugh and unwind."

He angled his head. "Are you saying we should get together to eat, laugh, and unwind?"

"No, I'm not. It is just a suggestion. After all, you do have a daughter to look after."

"What about our cooking together?" Lamar asked.

Nydia anchored her arms under his shoulders. "That doesn't count."

"What does count, Nydia?"

"It's not all about me, Lamar. What about your partners? I know you interact with them in the office, but how about socially? Do you take time to go out for drinks at the end of the week, or get together for family gatherings to celebrate a birthday or after you're awarded a new construction project?"

"Not too often. But that will probably change once we begin dating."

Nydia was totally confused with his statement. What did she have to do with his dearth of social life? "Why would you say that?"

"Because every time I get together with

Kirk or Omar they invite a woman they want me to meet. It becomes very awkward, at least for me, because usually who they choose isn't someone I'd want to go out with."

"So you think if you take me as your date they'll stop trying to hook you up with someone?"

"I know they will."

She thought about his inference. Lamar had a point. If she did attend a social event with him, then perhaps his partners would believe that he was involved with a woman. "You helped me out, and now I'm going to return the favor. The next time they invite you to something I'd be happy to go along."

"What if I hold something here?"

Nydia went completely still. "You mean you want to host a gathering here?"

Lamar's face lit up like a child on Christmas morning. "Yes. It's been a while since I've had folks over. The last time was a surprise birthday party for my mother's sixty-fifth birthday."

"When was that?"

"Last June."

"You're talking about a couple of months ago."

"I know," he admitted under his breath. "We held it here because my mother lives

342

with my sister, and Petra said it was impossible to plan a surprise event without Mom getting wind of it, so I volunteered to have it here." Lamar paused seemingly deep in thought. "Kendra's birthday is at the end of October, and she hasn't had a birthday party in years. What do you think of a birthday/Halloween theme party?"

Nydia thought of Halloween and how her parents forbade her to go treat-or-treating or accept candy or fruit from anyone because of stories about children finding needles and other dangerous objects. She did not know about Halloween traditions in New Orleans, but celebrating at home in a controlled environment was preferable to roaming the streets.

"I think it's a good idea. Do you want it to be a surprise?"

"No. I'll ask her who she wants to invite and have her give the invitations to her friends. Their parents will have to call me to confirm whether their children will attend. Halloween is on a Saturday this year, and I'm thinking about inviting some grown folks, too. The kids can party inside and the adults outside. What do you think?"

Nydia angled her head as she met Lamar's eyes. They were filled with excitement. "I like the idea. Are you going to cater it or cook?" she teased.

"Believe it or not, I can grill steaks, burgers, and links." There was a hint of pride in his voice.

"So you do cook."

"I grill, Nydia."

"Grilling *is* cooking, Lamar. Do you realize how difficult it is to grill the perfect medium-rare steak or a well-done burger? I don't know how many times I've requested a well-done burger and get what looks like a charred hockey puck. So don't be so self-deprecating, because you do cook."

Lamar kissed her forehead. "Now that I've accepted that I can cook, I'm going to buy a smoker to go along with the gas grill."

Nydia shook her head. "I think validating you as a cook has made you a little too cocky," she said as she teased him again. "First you deny you can cook and now you want to become a pit master." She eased out of his arms. "I'll help you plan Kendra's party; now please show me the rest of the house."

She entered Lamar's bedroom, and her first impression was it was wholly masculine. There wasn't a hint of femininity. The colors of off-white and dark gray predominated. The room was spacious enough for a California king bed, triple dresser, chest-on-chest, and armoire, and she wondered if Lamar had had the room redecorated after losing his wife so not to remind him that she had been there.

A slight gasp slipped past her parted lips when she walked into Kendra's bedroom. A queen-size, honey-toned, hand-painted sleigh bed caught her immediate attention. Delicate vintage white cotton, linen, and lace bed dressings were the epitome of girlishness. The gossamer bed skirt matched the floor-to-ceiling embroidered window drapes. Varying shades of white and green and the furnishings could easily transition from childhood to adulthood. A corner with a desk, laptop, printer, worktable, and bookcases served as Kendra's bedroom-office. She noticed several photographs on the desk of Kendra at different ages and with a young beautiful woman Nydia knew had to be the girl's mother. Dark and pale green pillows crowded a built-in window seat. She ran her fingers over the green-and-white checkered seat cushion.

"It's a twin with a trundle that converts in a full bed," Lamar said as he stood in the doorway.

"This bedroom should appear on the pages of a decorating magazine."

Lamar nodded. "That's what I told Jasmine."

Nydia blinked slowly. "Are we talking about the same Jasmine?"

"Yes. When Cameron introduced her to me as an interior decorator and she said how she wanted to decorate the loggia, I asked her whether she would be willing to come and look at my daughter's bedroom, which definitely needed to be updated from one for a little girl to a young adult. Everything was done while Kendra spent the summer with her mother and sister in Baton Rouge, and when she came back and saw her new bedroom she screamed, cried, spun around like a whirling dervish, and then screamed some more."

"She had a right to scream and cry tears of joy because this bedroom is definitely a showpiece." Nydia had witnessed firsthand Jasmine's artistic gift for decorating when she first visited her friend's condo. She knew once the renovations on the converted warehouse were completed and Jasmine decorated the interiors, it would be worthy of a layout in an architectural magazine.

"Evie's twins and the Kelly girls take turns sleeping over."

Nydia wanted to tell Lamar his daughter was very lucky to have him as her father.

He'd denied himself an open relationship with a woman and had made her emotional well-being a priority. She hoped the young girl appreciated his sacrifice.

The tour of his house ended after she viewed the two guest bedrooms and he drove her back to the hotel. He escorted her to her suite, waited until she opened the door, and then brushed a light kiss over her mouth before turning to walk back to the elevator.

There were no parting words or promise to contact each other. It was unnecessary. Both had agreed to keep an open mind as to where they wanted to take their friendship. Nydia was willing to date Lamar, while she still wasn't ready to acknowledge that she wanted to sleep with him. Sharing a bed with Lamar would change not only their relationship, but her. And for her it meant a commitment that could possibly lead to something more. And more important, she did not want to get in so deep that she would bond with Kendra, and if she and Lamar broke up then the girl would experience the loss of someone she could possibly view as her stepmother.

Nydia closed the door and stared at the pattern on the carpet. And there was the opposite view; she had to decide whether she was cut out to take on the responsibility of dealing with a pubescent girl who might be opposed to sharing her father with any woman.

CHAPTER 15

Nydia sat in the McNair sunroom with Hannah, Jasmine, and Tonya and outlined the projected financial schematic for the inn. It had taken three attempts before Tonya was able to commit to attend the meeting. Not only was she working full-time at Chez Toussaints, but she was also assisting her husband and brother-in-law with catering orders.

Nydia opened the laptop and inserted a thumb drive into a port. "Tonya, I'm going to begin with you."

The bond that had developed between her and Tonya during the six weeks she'd shared Tonya's apartment was like mother and daughter rather than former coworkers. A failed marriage and a subsequent relationship had made the professional chef wary of men until she met fellow chef Gage Toussaint, who'd experienced a similar past. Both were divorced with twenty-something children.

Tonya smiled, flashing deep dimples in her flawless brown cheeks as recessed light shimmered off her short salt-and-pepper curls. "Thank you."

Nydia had set up a file with the café Tonya had named Martine's, and Toussaints for the supper club. "I decided to keep the budgets for the café and supper club separate because revenue and expenditures streams will vary greatly." She glanced at Hannah sitting on a cushioned love seat. "Initially, until Tonya is able to recoup her investment, you will have to be responsible for the cost of purchasing the food for the inn's guests, who will be offered a buffet breakfast. You will have to determine how much you are going to charge a guest for a daily rate, and a portion of that will have to go to providing breakfasts."

Hannah exchanged a glance with Tonya. "I told Tonya I would be willing to cover the cost for the breakfasts."

Nydia was slightly taken aback with this disclosure. "Is there a time limit?" she asked Hannah.

The blonde shook her head. "No. It's for perpetuity. I will factor the cost of the breakfast in with the daily rate."

Nydia nodded. "Okay. Have you thought

about how much Tonya will be paid for preparing buffet breakfasts seven days a week?"

Silence descended on the space like a shroud as the four women exchanged glances. "I didn't think of that," Hannah said after an uncomfortable pause.

"I don't mean to sound nasty, but you can't expect her to cook and not be paid," Nydia said in a quiet voice.

Pinpoints of color dotted Hannah's pale cheeks. "You're right, Nydia. I thought paying her for running the supper club would take care of that."

Nydia shook her head. "That can't happen. I've broken down every unit it takes to run the inn, and that includes everything it takes to make it operational. Lodging will have a separate budget, which will include housekeeping, repairs, and utilities. Tonya will be totally responsible for the supper club, and, Jasmine, you will oversee all employee benefits, design, recruitment, training, and development. If Tonya is having a problem with one of her kitchen help or waitstaff, then Jasmine will become the go-to person to resolve it so that she and Gage can concentrate on preparing meals for their customers. Hannah and I have agreed to open a business account that will require both our signatures for expenditures. I will closely monitor the revenue coming in from the inn's guests and the supper club. As the inn's accountant, I will be responsible for dispensing paychecks and reporting taxes to the appropriate local, state, and federal departments. Each of you will receive a yearly budget along with three-, six-, nine-, and twelve-month projections. I'd like for us to get together at the end of each quarter to review your budgets to ascertain whether you're experiencing over-runs or if I have to adjust a particular budget line. I know I'm sounding a little hard-nosed, but I have the responsibility for keeping the inn solvent so we all can earn back our initial investments and share in potential profits."

"Don't apologize, Nydia," Tonya said. "You have to do what you need to do to make us successful innkeepers."

"I agree," Hannah added.

"Amen," Jasmine intoned.

Hannah leaned forward in her chair. "I forgot to tell y'all that once the inn is up and running, LeAnn and Paige have volunteered to step in for Jasmine when she goes on maternity leave. They'll alternate checking in and checking out guests and will fill in wherever necessary."

"Are they tired of globetrotting?" Tonya said teasingly.

Nydia laughed along with the others. Hannah's first cousins, retired schoolteachers, had spent more than two years traveling to six of the seven continents. Their last trip was an African safari. "They're probably trying to catch their breath before they take off again."

Hannah shook her head. "I doubt that. LeAnn got sick in Kenya and was afraid she'd picked up malaria even though she'd been inoculated, so it's going to be a while before she leaves the country again. I'm just grateful they've offered to help out."

"And I'm just a phone call away in the event of a HR problem," Jasmine stated.

Nydia managed to redirect everyone's attention back to her schematic. She was able to get estimates from Tonya for the start-up costs for her supper club. Tonya said she and her husband were going to forego a salary for the first year to maximize profits.

Tonya gathered her tote and stood up. "I'm sorry to cut out so early, but I'm usually in bed by ten because I need to get to the restaurant at six to prepare for the lunch crowd. Gage and I have decided to host a small gathering at the house a week from this Sunday. It will be our first time entertaining friends and family as a married couple."

"What time Sunday?" Hannah asked.

"Any time after one."

"Do you want us to bring anything?" Nydia questioned.

Tonya nodded. "Yes. You can bring your new man. And he can also bring his daughter, because Gage's sisters are bringing their kids. The same goes for you, Jasmine. You can invite your in-laws because the more the merrier. I must say catering the Singletons' anniversary and yours and Cameron's wedding proved to be priceless. The food critic from one of the dailies who attended both events came to the restaurant to interview us. He went on and on about the dishes we prepared, and I indulged in a little shameless bragging when I told him about the DuPont Inn and our plans to serve a buffet breakfast to the inn's guests, and that Toussaints will be open to the public."

Hannah gave Nydia a long, penetrating stare. "You and Lamar are a couple?"

Nydia lowered her eyes. "Yes and no."

"Please enlighten me."

She glared at the attorney, because she didn't like being put on the spot in front of the others. Nydia wasn't bothered discussing her love life, or lack thereof, one-on-one with Jasmine or Tonya, but she drew the line when she had an audience.

"We've agreed to see each other."

Hannah smiled, and lines fanned out around her brilliant green eyes. "Good for him. St. John told me women were lining up to get Lamar's attention once they found out he was single, but he didn't seem the least interested in them. And good for you, Nydia, because you deserve someone decent after that parasite you were dealing with."

Nydia held up her hand. "From this moment on I want all of us to swear that we will never mention Danny Ocasio again." The three women held up their hands in agreement. She inclined her head. "Thank you, ladies." She didn't know why, but Nydia felt a sense of relief that she could reveal that she was involved with Lamar.

She did not have any expectation of anything beyond their seeing each other, and she planned to enjoy the time they would spend together. He'd openly embraced seeing himself as a nerd, but he wasn't anything like the nerds she'd encountered in college who'd preferred hanging out together discussing their courses rather than attend a campus social mixer. Although a serious student, Nydia did take time to socialize with fellow students.

She spent the next forty-five minutes going over Hannah's budget and projections. The former corporate attorney gave her a conservative number of employees needed to keep the inn operational. Nydia had recommended a rotating staff of part-timers to avoid paying overtime. She also suggested Hannah cross-train her employees in the case of terminations or absences. Kitchen help should be familiar doing laundry or cleaning suites.

"That's really a good idea," Hannah agreed.

"I'm glad you like it. If I had to make beds, clean bathrooms, and vacuum every day I'd find myself just going through the motions. But if I could be assigned to the laundry room every other week, or assist in the kitchen, it would break up the monotony of coming to work."

Jasmine took a sip of water, peering at Nydia over the rim of the glass. "If Hannah is going to agree to cross-training her employees, then I'll definitely keep that in mind when I interview applicants. Someone may be willing to do laundry, but may object to working in the kitchen."

"Do you plan to institute a probationary period before we put them on the payroll as permanent employees?" Hannah asked Jasmine.

Jasmine nodded. "Yes. Three months is long enough to ascertain whether to keep them or let them go. I also intend to do a criminal background investigation on everyone before they're hired, because we can't have guests accusing us of theft if something goes missing."

"I know someone who can do the background checks," Hannah said. "We went to law school together before he went on to work for the FBI as an investigative analyst."

"Hannah, I know you don't want to set up cameras in the suites because it would violate your guests' privacy," Nydia said, "but do you intend to install safes for them to secure their valuables?"

"Definitely," Hannah replied. "I've already ordered them."

Nydia entered all of the information she needed to complete the budget for the inn.

Jasmine was next, and she told Nydia what she needed to become the human resources specialist and co-manager for the inn.

It took less than three hours to complete the interviews, and she'd gleaned most of what she needed to begin putting together a draft of preliminary budgets. She would revise and update them closer to the date of the inn's grand opening.

Nydia hugged Hannah. "I'm going to take a few days to go over everyone's projected budget before we meet again to finalize them."

"When do you need me to transfer the funds into the account?"

"Not until the contractor gives you a proposed completion date for the renovations. I estimate opening the business account a month before you plan to open for business."

Hannah closed her eyes and ran both hands over her hair. "I've waited so long that I've given up predicting a grand opening. I've cried, wrung my hands, and spent so many a sleepless night that St. John refuses to listen to me anymore when I bring it up."

"You've got to stop stressing over something over which you have no control, Hannah. The inn will open when it's time."

"Now you sound like St. John."

"That's because your husband is right," Nydia said in a conciliatory tone. "Most construction projects are not completed on time. Whenever I pass a new construction site the signs will usually project the season of a particular year, because engineers try to factor in problems that may arise."

Hannah lowered her hands. A hint of a smile tilted the corners of her mouth. "Look at you. Hanging around Lamar has rubbed off on you."

Nydia wanted to tell Hannah she was wrong. With the exception of telling her about his not wanting to bid on a project that would take him away from his daughter for days at a time, she and Lamar did not talk about his work. He'd spoken to Kendra about his inability to share breakfast with her when he had to go out of town on business, and he was mildly surprised when his daughter said she wasn't a baby and wasn't going to cry if he left her with Miss Ramona for a few days. He'd thanked her over and over for her advice to approach his daughter, and then said he still had a lot to learn about raising a girl.

"It happens," she said instead.

"I was sincere when I said I'm glad you found someone who will treat you with the respect you deserve."

"Thank you, Hannah."

"There's no need to thank me, Nydia. You should know better than any of us that we don't bite our tongues when it comes to issuing advice or telling one another what we probably don't want to hear. But, in the end, it's always the truth."

"Why do you feel the need to get maudlin, Hannah?"

"I know sometimes I can get emotional, but this too will pass as soon as the inn opens."

"And once it opens you'll forget about all of the setbacks," Jasmine said. "Meanwhile you need something to take your mind off the inn."

Hannah exhaled an audible breath. "You're probably right. Paige and LeAnn have tried to get me to join them in a bowling league with a group of retirees."

"Why haven't you?" Nydia questioned.

"They need one more person to make a foursome for their team."

"I might join you," Nydia volunteered.

With wide eyes, Hannah stared at her. "Are you serious?"

Nydia smiled. "I'm very serious. How long, what day, and when does it begin?" she asked Hannah.

"It's for six weeks, and they meet for the first time next Wednesday night."

"Hold on, I need to call my father." She picked up her cell phone to call her father. She didn't have to wait for him to answer. "Papi, I need you to overnight me my bowling bag." She paused. "Yes, send it to me at the hotel. Mami has the address. Thanks,

Papi. *Y te amo.*"

"Well, I'll be damned," Hannah swore. "You bowl like that?"

Nydia nodded. "When I was in high school I bowled with a league that met at an alley in the Bronx. I must say, we were awesome!"

"What was your highest game?" Jasmine asked.

"I average around two-forty, but I did bowl a perfect game twice."

Hannah pumped her fist. "Yes!"

Nydia powered down her laptop. Once she'd begun bowling seriously she decided she needed her own ball, because most times she wasn't able to find one that fit her fingers or one she could lift easily without injuring her wrist. "Don't forget to text me the address."

"I'll pick you up at six-fifteen. We begin bowling at seven." Hannah shifted her attention to Jasmine. "Do you want to join us?"

"I'm not going to bowl," Jasmine said, "but I'm willing to keep score. Don't bother picking Nydia up. We'll come together."

Nydia and Jasmine hugged Hannah before taking their leave.

Nydia stared through the windshield listening to the slip-slap of tires on the roadway as Jasmine left Marigny and headed for the CBD. She felt her first financial meeting with her fellow innkeepers had gone well. It would take time to develop preliminary budgets before she requested another meeting. She knew Hannah was frustrated with the slow pace of the renovations in the centuries-old mansion, but Nydia knew once they were completed and the inn was open for business, her angst would dissipate like a drop of water on a heated griddle.

Jasmine gave Nydia a quick glance before returning her eyes to the road in front of the Honda. "I can't believe you never told me you bowled."

"It's been a long time since I last picked up a ball, and I hope I haven't lost my edge."

"I've tried bowling a few times but gave it up when I always threw gutter balls."

Nydia stared at the brake lights on the car in front of them when traffic stopped for a red light. "It took me more than six months before I was able to bowl above ninety."

Jasmine laughed softly. "You know folks on the other teams are going to think you're a ringer, especially since you're too young to be a retiree."

"They can think whatever they want. What they can't do is show prejudice because of my age."

"True. I'm glad I'm going to be there to witness their reactions when you show up with Hannah and her cousins."

Although she hadn't bowled in years, Nydia knew it was like riding a bike. She was certain once she put on her shoes and held her custom-made ball the skills she'd acquired over the years would resurface.

"*Chica,* I need your opinion."

Nydia registered concern in Jasmine's voice. "Talk to me, *mija.*"

"Cameron wants to take a week off and drive over to Galveston Island to look at vacation properties."

"That sounds like a wonderful plan. What's the problem, Jasmine?"

"We are still living in a hotel while our home is undergoing extensive renovations, and now he wants to go and buy more property."

Nydia stared at Jasmine as if she'd taken leave of her senses. "Why are you complaining about how he wants to spend his money? Have you forgotten you had one husband who would've left you with nothing if you hadn't asked Hannah for legal advice to hang onto what you'd worked so hard for?"

"I know, but I don't think we need another house."

Nydia took a deep breath, held it, and then let out slowly. "Don't be a fool, Jazz. If the man wants to buy a vacation home on the beach where you both can kick back and relax, then don't fight with him about it. All of us have been given a second chance, *mija,*" she continued, this time in a softer, more conciliatory tone. "Hannah lived with a man who'd cheated on her for more years than she could count and she stayed with him because she honored her marriage vows until his cheating ass died. Then, there's Tonya, who was married to a man who attempted to control her life so much that he didn't want her to succeed, and her only way of getting away from him with her daughter was to escape like someone on the FBI's most wanted list. And thanks to you, Tonya, and Hannah preaching to me to get rid of the bum and kick his sorry ass to the curb, I was finally came to my senses to look out for Nydia Stephanie Santiago. You have a good man, Jasmine. A man who loves you and that baby you're carrying, and I don't want you to blow it because all of a sudden you woke up to the realization that you're a strong, independent woman who doesn't need a man to take care of you or give you what you need."

Jasmine's eyelids fluttered. "I know Cameron loves me, and I love him but —"

"This is the last I'm going to have a discussion with you about Cameron," Nydia said, interrupting her.

"I thought you were my friend, Nydia, so why are you taking his side?"

"I'm not only your friend but your sister, *mija.*" Nydia combed her fingers through her hair, trying to find the words to say to Jasmine as not to upset her more than she was. "What do you want, Jazz? I mean really want."

Jasmine turned into the hotel's parking lot and maneuvered into her reserved spot, and shut off the engine. She stared straight ahead, appearing as if carved out of stone. Only the rising and falling of her chest indicated she was still breathing.

"I want to give birth to a healthy baby," she said after a noticeable pause.

"And that is all we should be talking about. Not about Cameron buying a beach house, or whether you'll be able decorate your home here in New Orleans. And while you're complaining about living in a hotel there are thousands of people who live on the street, sleep under bridges and in alleys every single day in every big city in the country. When did you become such an elitist?"

Jasmine closed her eyes. "Why are you so angry? I know Danny did you wrong, but there's no need to take it out on me."

Nydia bit her lip and counted slowly to ten. She had to control her temper or say something that could possibly end her friendship with the one woman she had come to think of as her sister. She'd confided things to Jasmine she hadn't with some of her family members.

"I am not angry." She had enunciated each word. "Danny didn't do anything to me that I didn't permit him to do. And it was the same with my college instructor. What I refused to do is internalize things where they fester and negatively impact my life. The day I moved in with Tonya was the day I changed. The day my father carried me into the ER because I was in so much pain that I believed I was dying, my life changed completely. And when I woke up after surgery and my mother told me the doctor said I would've died if I'd waited one more day because the infection had spread throughout my body. That's when I was reborn. I don't give a damn about a man or a job, because they come and go. It's the same with where I live. There was a time when I believed owning property was the next rung on the ladder of success for a young thirty-something professional woman. Now, the only thing that matters to me is staying healthy. Everything else is irrelevant!"

With wide eyes, Jasmine's expression mirrored shock and another emotion Nydia could not identify. She didn't know what she had to do or say to convince her former coworkers that she was not the same person who'd commiserated with them in Hannah's apartment that warm, sunny May morning. Okay, she'd concede that she did break up and reconcile with Danny a few times, but once she moved and left no forwarding address and blocked his number, Nydia knew she had left her past behind.

"I'm sorry," Jasmine apologized as tears filled her eyes. "I don't know what's wrong with me," she said, sniffling as she struggled not to cry. "I don't know if it is hormones or that I feel as if my life is spinning out of control. I'm married to a man who I still think of as a stranger, and even though I always wanted a baby I wanted to plan for it."

Unbuckling her seat belt, Nydia leaned over and hugged Jasmine. She had no idea her friend was experiencing so much uncertainty. She'd believed Jasmine had found her prince and they were going to live happily ever after.

"Weren't you the one who told me even though you were married to Raymond for twelve years you still didn't know him?"

Jasmine blinked back tears before they fell. "Did I?"

"Don't play yourself, *mija*. You know right well you said it. Look at Hannah. She was married to her first husband for almost thirty years, and she had no idea he was sleeping around until he had a heart attack and felt the need to confess his sins."

Shaking her head, Jasmine emitted an unladylike snort. "That's when she should've smothered the cheating bastard with a pillow!"

Taken aback by Jasmine's outburst, Nydia gave her a long, penetrating stare. "Now, who's angry?"

"I'm not angry, but bored as hell. I'm not used to *not* working. That's why I took that part-time position with the social services program last year. And I'm jealous of you because you manage to keep busy doing the books for your restaurateurs, and now you're working up the financial records for the inn. And don't forget you've offered to teach Lamar's daughter to make *pasteles*. Right now I've hit a brick wall with shopping for things for the new house because

368

I'm not certain what paint colors I want or the final dimensions of some of the rooms."

Now Nydia understood Jasmine's frustration. She wasn't one to sit around and do nothing. As a creative person she had to keep busy. "I saw a needlecraft shop along a side street in the Upper French Quarter, and it reminded me that you knit and crochet. Why don't you take it up again and make a few pieces for the baby?"

"What were you doing in the Upper Quarter?"

Nydia smiled. "After Lamar and I left Momma's Place we went for a walk because I wanted to see the French Market. Then we went back to his house, and I saw how you'd decorated his daughter's room."

Jasmine's expression brightened. "I loved redecorating her room. Even though I'm a resource specialist, decorating is still my passion."

"Well, you'll have your work cut out for you once you move into your new home. You can strap man-man or little mama on your back like the women in Africa and do your thing."

"You're right. I do have something to look forward to."

Nydia angled her head. "Are we finished with this pity party or you do want to hang around for the after-party?"

"I'm done," Jasmine stated firmly. "I'm going inside to tell my man that I'm ready to look at vacation homes, and I want it big enough so we can invite friends and family for one humongous sleepover."

"That's my girl." Nydia got out of the minivan and walked with Jasmine into the hotel.

"Tell Lamar I said hello when you see him," Jasmine as she headed for the elevator that would take her to her suite.

"Catch you later, *mija*."

"Luego, chica."

Nydia made it to her suite and set the leather tote with the laptop on a chair in the dining area. Spending several hours with her fellow innkeepers was definitely an eye-opener. Hannah and Jasmine were upset because they'd believed renovations on their properties were going much too slowly. She could understand Hannah's frustration, because the projected grand opening had been pushed back a number of times, pending approval of permits and the malfunctioning of the massive wrought-iron gates protecting DuPont Inn. The workmen were currently installing the elevator in the main house and working on converting the guesthouses into the café and supper club.

It wasn't as if Hannah and Jasmine didn't have somewhere to live. Hannah lived with her husband in a large house in Marigny, and Jasmine in an adjoining luxurious suite at the Louis LaSalle.

And Nydia had not lied to Jasmine about not concerning herself with anyone or anything but her health, because she had not realized how close she was to dying until she was informed she would have to spend days in the hospital and be given massive doses of antibiotics to offset the sepsis.

All three future innkeepers had married men who loved and protected them, and that was what Nydia wanted if or when she fell in love and married.

CHAPTER 16

Lamar was waiting on the street in front of his house when the taxi pulled up. Nydia had sent him a text informing him she would arrive around ten that morning. The last time he spoke to her he'd volunteered to pick her up, but she rejected his offer because she had someone who would drop her off. He'd thought that someone would be Jasmine and not a taxi driver.

He opened the rear door and picked up a large covered wicker picnic basket off the seat, and then extended his hand to help Nydia out. She held a large bouquet of flowers wrapped in colored cellophane in her left hand. Leaning down, he kissed her cheek. Lamar had stored everything about Nydia's face in his indelible memory, and he found her equally beautiful with or without makeup. She'd brushed her hair and held it off her face with a wide white headband. With her bare face, long-sleeved black polo, jeans, and black ballet-type shoes she looked like a fresh-faced college coed.

"Hola."

"Hello yourself," she said, smiling. "Wait, I have to pay the driver."

Lamar rested his free hand at the small of her back. "Don't worry. I'll pay him." He waited for her to walk through the porte cochère to set the basket on the ground and reach into the pocket of his jeans for a money clip. He paid the man and then followed Nydia, opened the door, and stepped aside to let her enter.

"What on earth is in this basket? Rocks?"

Nydia gave him a mysterious smile. "It's filled with goodness."

Reaching for her free hand, he led her across the living and dining rooms and into the kitchen. "Kendra will be down in a few minutes."

"There's no need for her to rush. I have to empty the basket and wash everything before we begin prepping."

Lamar set the basket on a stool at the cooking island. "Do you need me to help with anything?"

Nydia handed him the flowers. "These are for Miss Ramona."

His eyebrows lifted slightly. "She's not

here. When I don't have anything planned for the weekend, she always stays with her sister in Metairie. I have a vase but I know nothing about arranging flowers."

"If you get the vase I'll arrange them."

Lamar knew if Ramona had been there she would have been overjoyed with the flowers. Working in the courtyard garden had become her passion when she'd first come to work for him. She told him he didn't need a landscaper because her father had been one and that she'd learned to identify different trees, ferns, and flowers at a very early age. And taking her advice he didn't re-sign with the landscaper and let her take over his duties. The result was a riot of floral cornucopia growing in precise abandon rivaling award-winning gardens on grand estates.

By the time he returned with the vase, Nydia had emptied the basket. Plastic bags with vegetables he couldn't identify and some he was familiar with littered the countertop. A smile spread over his features. It was apparent she had gone to a butcher when he saw the pork shoulders.

"Please tell me you're going to make *pernil*."

Nydia's head popped up. "Yes. I'm going to marinate the larger one overnight for

374

Sunday dinner and use the smaller one for the *pasteles.* I also plan to make *arroz con gandules,* and *tostones.* I thought it was time to introduce your daughter to foods she'll eat when you guys come up for Christmas."

Lamar rubbed his hands together in anticipation of sitting down to a traditional Puerto Rican dinner with roast pork, fried plantains, and rice and with pigeon peas. When he'd asked Nydia if she was busy Sunday and she said no, he'd invited her to join him and Kendra at an award-winning local restaurant; she'd thanked him and then offered to make Sunday dinner, because she preferred cooking for herself to eating in restaurants.

"I'm certain she's going to love eating Spanish food as much as her father." Walking over to a cabinet, he opened it and tapped a button for the audio component. "What type of music do you want to listen to?"

"It doesn't matter."

Lamar tuned the radio to a station featuring hip-hop and R&B, adjusted the volume, and programmed the speakers for the kitchen only. He'd concealed speakers in every room in the house and could regulate the volume with a remote device. He smiled

375

when Rihanna singing "We Found Love" filled the space. "I love her music." Lamar knew that if Kendra hadn't been in the house he would have asked Nydia to dance with him.

Nydia nodded. "Me, too," she agreed. "I have thirty of her greatest hits on my phone's playlist. I was in grad school when this song dropped, and I remember going to a party and they played the extended version over and over. I danced so much that I couldn't get out of the bed the next day."

Lamar took a step, bringing them only inches apart. "One of these days we're going to have our own private dance party when Kendra spends the weekend with some of her friends."

She stared up at him through her lashes. "Is that when you plan to seduce me?"

Lowering his head, he pressed his mouth to her ear. "I hadn't planned to seduce you, but now that you've mentioned it, perhaps I will."

Going on tiptoe, Nydia leaned into him. "What if I am not ready?"

A chuckle rumbled in his chest. "Then I'll wait until you're ready."

She placed a hand over his heart. "You should back it up, cowboy, before your daughter sees you in a somewhat compromising situation."

Lamar took a backward step. "Is that far enough?"

Nydia scrunched up her nose. "Take another step. And another one," she said when he'd barely moved.

"All right," he said, as he walked around the cooking island and rested his arms on the quartz countertop. "Is this far enough?"

"Sí, mi amor."

Lamar went completely still while at the same time he held his breath. The endearment had rolled off Nydia's tongue as if it was something she said without thinking. "Am I?"

She gave him a direct stare. All traces of gold had disappeared, leaving them rich verdant green. "Are you what?"

"Am I your love?"

Nydia shrugged her shoulders. "It's just a figure of speech. Like you calling me sweets."

His eyebrows shot up. "Oh, I see."

"Oh, I forgot to tell you. Tonya and Gage Toussaint invited us to their home next Sunday for brunch. You can bring Kendra, because Eustace's grandchildren are also coming."

"What's the occasion?"

"There's no special occasion. Tonya said

it will be the first time they're going to host a gathering as a married couple."

"Are you aware that they live a couple of blocks from here?"

Nydia's mouth opened, but nothing came out. "You're kidding," she said when recovering her voice.

"No. You didn't know?"

She shook her head. "She held her wedding at Gage's house and the reception in St. John's garden, and I missed both because I was in the hospital."

"You're still experiencing discomfort, aren't you?"

"How did you know?"

"I see you wincing and gritting your teeth every once in a while."

Nydia peered into the basket. "I had to undergo an emergency appendectomy in June and I'm still healing."

"How long were you in the hospital?"

"Four days."

A slight frown furrowed Lamar's smooth forehead. "Why so long?"

"I'd ignored the pain for almost a week, and by the time I went to the hospital the sepsis had spread throughout my body. They put me on massive doses of antibiotics to counter the infection."

"You should've known something was wrong when you were in pain for that long."

Nydia met his eyes. "At first I thought I'd pulled a muscle from either twisting my body the wrong way or lifting something that was too heavy. But when it became too intense I called my father and asked him to take me to the hospital. The entire ordeal taught me a valuable lesson: do not ignore pain, because there is definitely something wrong."

Lamar ran a finger down the length of her nose. "My mother used to say a hard head makes for a soft behind."

"Amen to that."

He noticed Nydia looking at something over his shoulder and turned to find his daughter heading in their direction.

Nydia had just removed two aprons from the basket when Kendra entered the kitchen. "Are you ready for your first lesson?" she asked the tall, slender young girl who had covered her braided hair with a colorful bandana stamped with flags from different countries.

A shy smile parted Kendra's lips as she met Nydia's eyes. "Yes, ma'am."

Nydia winced. Kendra calling her "ma'am" made her feel much older than she was. "You may call me Nydia."

Kendra nodded. "Okay, Miss Nydia."

Suddenly it dawned on Nydia that some young people in the South addressed their elders as Miss or Mister. She handed Kendra an apron. "If you're going to become a serious cook, then you need to wear an apron."

Kendra opened the package and clapped a hand over her mouth when she unfolded the bright yellow bibbed apron with a spatula and whisk and *Chef-in-Training* stamped on the front. "I need to get my phone and take a picture of this to send to Morgan and Taylor."

"You can send it later," Lamar said, smiling. "Miss Nydia has a lot to go over with you, so the sooner you start, the more you'll learn."

Kendra slipped the apron over her head and secured the ties around her waist. "But can you videotape some of it so I can show it to my friends?"

Lamar paused, and then said, "If it's okay with Miss Nydia, then I'll do it."

Nydia smiled at Kendra. "I don't mind." If the girl was serious about learning to cook, then she was willing to help document her progress. She waited for Lamar to leave the kitchen before reaching into the basket again. Nydia reached into the basket and removed a gaily wrapped package with a profusion of curling ribbons. "This is also for you, but you can open it later." She'd given the girl a perfumed gift set of body gel, cream, and matching cologne. Nydia's mother had presented her with a similar gift set the year she turned eleven to keep her from sneaking into her bedroom to spray herself with her expensive perfume.

Kendra's reaction was totally unexpected when her eyes filled with tears. Her chin trembled as she tried composing herself. "Thank you, Miss Nydia." Seconds later she launched herself at Nydia and hugged her so tightly that she was unable to draw a normal breath.

Nydia kissed the girl's cheek. "You're welcome. Now, you're going to have to let me go so we can begin."

Kendra managed a sheepish grin. "Sorry about that."

She winked at her. "That's okay. The first thing we're going to do is wash the vegetables to get off any dirt or preservatives." She handed Kendra several pairs of disposable latex gloves. "We'll use the gloves when it comes time to work with the raw meat." Nydia didn't want to say that touching raw meat was her pet peeve. "The recipe I'm going to use will make about two dozen *pasteles.*"

Lamar had returned with a small camcorder. He crossed his arms over his chest. "Is that all you're making?"

Nydia gave him a direct stare. "Once I go back to New York I'll be up to my eyeballs making more than one hundred for family and friends, so to answer your question: yes, two dozen is enough."

"Daddy, please," Kendra pleaded. "Miss Nydia and I need to start our lesson."

He held up his hands in supplication. "Okay. I'm going to sit here and watch. Let me know what you want me to record."

"Kendra and I are going to begin making *sofrito,* which is a recipe that is essential to flavor Latin dishes. It's easy to make and can be frozen."

Lamar nodded. "Let me know when I should start recording."

Over the next two hours Nydia showed Kendra how to make *sofrito,* which Lamar recorded from beginning to end, the pork stock, and pork filling, and the root vegetable batter.

They took a break to eat a bowl of gumbo the housekeeper had prepared, and after Lamar retreated to his office, Nydia and Kendra concentrated on spooning the batter and pork filling, and topping it with olives and pieces of red pepper from *alcaparrado* — a mixture of olives, pimentos, and capers — on pieces of parchment paper, wrapping it tightly before securing the tamales with kitchen twine.

"Some people wrap the *pasteles* in parchment in banana leaves, but my grandmother never used them when she made hers."

Kendra washed her hands in the double sink with an automatic faucet. "We made more than two dozen."

Nydia nodded. "You're right. It is more like three. We can have them for dinner with a salad." The built-in refrigerator/freezer was stocked with dairy, fresh fruit, and produce.

"What kind of salad, Miss Nydia?"

"Miss Ramona has feta cheese, so we can make a Greek salad."

"I like cooking," Kendra said as she dried her hands on a cotton towel. "Can we do this again?"

"I'm coming back tomorrow to prepare Sunday dinner, and I'm going to need an assistant when I make *perñil,* rice with pigeon peas, and fried green bananas. Usually I'll marinate the pork for two to three days, this time it will be overnight."

Kendra's dark eyes shimmered with excitement. "What kind of marinade are we

383

going to use?"

"I like a wet rub that's known as adobo mojito made with peeled garlic, and either sea or kosher salt, black peppercorns, dried oregano, olive oil, and white vinegar. I noticed Miss Ramona doesn't have a mortar and pestle, so I'm going to use the bottom of a cast iron skillet to pound the garlic cloves and salt into a paste, before incorporating the peppercorns and oregano into the paste. After that we'll add the oil and vinegar. While I'm making the rub I want you to take a sharp knife and make slits in the pork shoulder to fill them with the wet rub."

Kendra's eyebrows flickered a little. "How do you remember what to do without looking at a recipe book?"

"I've had a lot of years of practice. When I was a little girl I used to go to my grandmother's house and sit on a stool to watch her cook. By the time I was your age she let me help her. I hated having to go to the supermarket with her to pick out what she needed for a particular dish. She'd tell me, *Tráeme un poco de culantro,*' which translates as 'bring me some culantro' in English. When I'd bring her cilantro she would lecture me sternly that culantro is not the same as cilantro. She liked it because its

384

flavor is more intense than cilantro."

"But, Miss Nydia, we made the *sofrito* with only cilantro,"

Nydia smiled. It was apparent her student was very astute. "That's because I couldn't find any when I went to the market."

Kendra rested her elbows on the countertop. "Who taught you to speak Spanish?"

"My grandmother."

"Do your parents speak Spanish?"

"Yes. Even though they were born in New York they learned the language from their parents and grandparents. But, like a lot of New York Puerto Ricans, when they talk they tend to mix both languages. It's known as Spanglish."

"Give me an example."

"Instead of saying I'm going to the park, they'll say, 'I'm going to the *parque.*' Or 'bring me un container of leche' for a container of milk."

"Next year I'll go into the seventh grade and I have to select a foreign language. I've decided to choose Spanish because my dad speaks it."

Nydia wondered if Kendra had overheard her father speaking the language or if he'd told her. "The easiest way to learn a language is to speak it. Once you become familiar with certain words you should practice with him."

"Morgan and Taylor said they are taking Mandarin, while the Kelly girls are taking French." Kendra paused, seemingly deep in thought. "Tell me how it was to grow up in New York."

Lamar returned to the kitchen in time to hear Nydia answer his daughter's questions about her life as a child in New York City. Nydia was the first woman he'd introduced to his daughter since becoming a widower, and he couldn't believe his good fortune, because she seemed to get along well with Kendra. She was patient as she demonstrated how Kendra should slice something, and was effusive in her praise when she accomplished it.

He was still uncertain emotionally when it came time for him to assess his feelings for Nydia. Everything about her screamed an unadulterated sexiness he'd found missing in many of the women he'd met, whether socially or professionally. And there were times when he could not understand her need to play down her sexiness. When he'd strolled through the Lower Quarter with her he'd noticed men giving her furtive glances, which only served to bolster his male pride in having her on his arm. The chic hairstyle, her flawless gold-brown complexion, and brilliant jewel-like eyes, pert nose, lush mouth, and curvy, compact, petite body definitely garnered a second or third glance. Although she was shorter and less endowed than the women to whom he'd found himself attracted, there was something about Nydia that had him mesmerized.

And what he really appreciated was her frankness. She wasn't afraid to speak her mind; that was something that had irked him with Valerie. His wife would occasionally shut down rather than discuss things that she deemed important to her. He'd believed she was experiencing postpartum depression after Kendra was born. It was he who got up in the middle of the night to walk the floor in an attempt to comfort the crying infant, and he also learned to feed, bathe, and change his daughter whenever Valerie took to her bed and refused to leave.

Making love with his wife had become a thing of the past, and when he suggested she see a doctor to talk about what he believed was depression, she turned on him like an agitated mother bird protecting her young and said there was nothing wrong with her. The impasse continued until Kendra celebrated her second birthday, and that was when Valerie talked about hiring a live-in housekeeper because she was going back to work.

Lamar would have agreed to anything if only to get back the woman he had fallen in love with and married. Once Valerie received the okay to go back to work she was like a colorful butterfly emerging from a cocoon to spread its wings. Each time she returned home from a flight the house was filled with laughter and a gaiety he had come to anticipate. As long as Valerie was flying off to different cities she was like a kid in a candy shop. It took a long time for him to believe she wasn't coming home, and he knew he had to be both mother and father to a young girl who would grow up without her mother. He had put Kendra in counseling, but he knew it was difficult for a six-year-old to understand and accept the inevitability of death; she'd asked about her mother for more than three months before she appeared to accept that her mother wasn't coming back.

Lamar wasn't looking a mother for his daughter, but if asked, he definitely would have considered someone like Nydia. And watching her interact with Kendra filled him with conflicting emotions as to whether he wanted her in his and Kendra's life. There was no doubt she would be a positive role model for Kendra, who needed to look up to a strong, educated, and independent woman who was not afraid to speak her mind.

"When's dinner?" Nydia and Kendra turned around at the same time.

"Daddy, we just ate lunch."

He entered the kitchen and sat on a stool. "That was just a snack." Lamar peered at the clock on the microwave. "That was nearly three hours ago. Right now I'm feenin' for *pasteles.*"

"There's no such word as *feening,*" Kendra countered.

"Yes there is. You tell her, Nydia," Lamar insisted.

"Well, it's really not a word, but people use it when they say they're craving something."

"Well, that's what you should have said, Daddy. You always tell me to use the right word, and now you're not."

Lamar managed to look contrite. His daughter was right, because he constantly corrected her when she said something that didn't remotely resemble the English language. "You're right, and I apologize."

She inclined her head, laughing. "I accept your apology."

Nydia also laughed and said, "You're going to have to *crave* them a bit longer because it's going to take at least an hour for them to cook. Meanwhile, I can make you a fruit salad."

"Hold off on the fruit salad. I'll get a beer instead to tide me over while I watch the game."

Kendra leaned in close to Nydia's ear and whispered, "Daddy loves sports. He watches baseball, football, and basketball. And sometimes he goes to football games."

"I heard that," Lamar called out as he opened the door to the refrigerator.

"There's nothing wrong with being into sports," Nydia said to Kendra. "In fact I've been to Yankee Stadium to watch the Yankees and Citi Field for the Mets. The executives at the company where I used to work would purchase season tickets to all of the local professional sports teams for their elite clients and would sometimes give them away as perks for their employees."

"How about football games?" Lamar asked.

Nydia shook her head. "I'm not really into football or hockey. I like baseball and then basketball."

Lamar removed the cap from the beer and took a long swallow. "I occasionally get

390

tickets to the Pelicans basketball games. Would you ladies be willing to go with me?"

"Can I go, too?" Kendra asked. A frown had settled between her eyes.

"I did say 'ladies.' "

"I'm not a lady, Daddy. I'm still a girl."

"Of course you're a girl, but you are also a young lady."

Kendra's expression brightened. "I like that. And yes, I would like to go to a basketball game."

Lamar winked at Nydia smirking at him. "When I get the tickets I'll let you know the date and time."

He knew attending sporting and social events with Nydia would start tongues wagging about his relationship with her. The Pierces had deep roots in New Orleans going back at least four generations, and his father had established a reputation as the go-to orthodontist. When he was growing up, people who knew Lamar rarely called him by his name. He and his sister were known as Dr. Pierce's girl and boy.

Lamar curved an arm around Nydia's waist as he escorted her into the elevator. The two days when she'd come to his house to cook had sped by much too quickly, and he wasn't certain who enjoyed her company

391

more: he or Kendra. He had uploaded the videotaped segments of them cooking together on Saturday and Sunday to Kendra's phone for her to share with her friends. And he had to agree with Kendra that the dishes Nydia prepared were exceptional.

Ramona had returned from Metairie Sunday afternoon in time to share dinner with them, and she, too, raved about the roast pork, rice, and pigeon peas, and the thin crisp slices of fried green bananas; they had the option of eating them plain or topping them with mojito — a garlic dipping sauce. His housekeeper plied Nydia with countless questions about what she used to season the pork, the ingredients for *sofrito* and mojito. Kendra proudly announced she knew how to make *sofrito* and offered to create another batch once they used the containers stored in the freezer. Lamar had sampled Nydia's Southern and Latin dishes and found her equally proficient with both.

"You know Kendra's going to talk my ear off about you when I get home."

"You're very lucky, and she's a joy to be around."

Lamar loved his daughter unconditionally; however, there were times when she tested his patience. He'd learned early on that she was strong-willed, and he was careful not to break her spirit, because he wanted to her grow up to become a strong, independent woman who did not have to depend on a man to take care of her. "I think I'll keep her," he teased.

Nydia smiled. "If you don't want her, I'd be more than willing to take her off your hands."

Lamar didn't know whether Nydia was teasing or serious, that if their relationship became permanent, she would be willing to be a stepmother to his daughter. "And the first time you experience one of her funky attitudes you'll send her back without further ado."

The car arrived at the designated floor, and Nydia stepped out. "What you have to understand is that she's a young girl whose hormones are in flux, and that may be responsible for her mood swings. She'll soon be eleven, and some girls her age are already menstruating, so I advise you to buckle up and take the ride with her. One day she'll be that adorable little girl you used to hold in your arms and rock her to sleep, and the next day she may slam doors and scream that you're ruining her life."

"Is that what happened to you?" Lamar asked as he walked Nydia to her suite.

She swiped her key card. "The only thing

I'm going to attest to is that I spent a lot of time being grounded."

Reaching over her head, he pushed open the door and entered the suite before her. Late afternoon shadows filled the space where Nydia hadn't drawn the drapes. Lamar closed the door and took her in his arms and buried his face in the thickness of her hair. "Do you know that you drive me crazy?"

Nydia wound her arms around Lamar's waist. She had fought her feelings for the man who had not only become her protector but also had helped her heal enough to trust getting involved again. She was more than aware of the restraint both had exercised because of his daughter's presence. The few times Lamar touched her hand or his body brushed against hers she struggled not to react to the sensations coursing through her. And she knew if Kendra hadn't been there the fragile wall she'd built to dam up sexual desire would have snapped, and she might have begged him to make love to her.

She enjoyed making love with a man. It had been that way with her two former lovers, and it had taken Herculean strength to forfeit that phase in her life. Even weeks after she'd ended her relationships the urge for physical gratification was slow to wane. Now it was back — with a vengeance. Nydia did not know what it was about Lamar that had rekindled the need to make love with him. Perhaps it had something to do with his revealing that within seconds of meeting her for the first time her presence had triggered an erection, which had planted a seed of curiosity in her mind.

Easing back, she tried to make out his expression in the muted light. "We both agreed we're too old to play head games, so I need to tell you something."

"Is it something that's going to ruin what we've shared the past two days?"

Nydia rested a hand along his jaw, and her fingertips grazed the emerging stubble. "Oh, ye of little faith," she teased, smiling. "I want you to know that I like you, Lamar."

His dark eyebrows shot up. "Really?"

"Yes, really," she countered.

"You know how I feel about you, so what are we going to do about it?"

"That's what I was going to ask you. After all, you're the one who is a single dad."

"That's no longer relevant, because Kendra really likes you. She told me that last night after you'd left, and wanted to know if I was going to go out with you."

"What did you say?"

Lamar smiled. "I told her I was thinking about it. That's when she told me not to think too long because she did not want some other man to — I think the phrase she used was 'scoop you up.'"

Going on tiptoe, Nydia kissed his warm throat. "Tell her not to worry because I'm not looking for a man to scoop me up. I like her father too much for that."

Lamar lifted her effortlessly off her feet as his demanding lips caressed hers in a kiss that left her struggling to breath, and Nydia kissed him with a hunger that shouted to be assuaged. Never in her life had she wanted a man as much as she did at that moment. But she didn't want Lamar to make love to her and then get up to go back home. If or when they did sleep together she wanted them to spend hours together and wake up the next day in each other's arms.

It was with great reluctance that she ended the kiss. "To be continued," she whispered.

Lamar was breathing as heavily as she was. "Right place, wrong time," he intoned.

She inclined her head. "I agree. *Buenas noches, mi amor.*"

Cradling her face in his hands, Lamar pressed a kiss to her forehead. "Good night, my love."

Nydia waited until she'd closed the door

behind Lamar's departing figure and then sank to the floor. "What have I committed to?" she asked aloud. She had agreed to become involved with a single father with a tween daughter who wanted him to date her, but hadn't said anything about wanting her father to possibly have a future with her. And for Nydia dating did not necessarily translate into marriage.

She had to ask herself about the intent of her involvement with Lamar Pierce and his daughter. She knew Kendra liked her because she wanted to learn to cook to show up her peers, and she wondered if that was the only ulterior motive for her wanting Lamar to continue to see her.

There were times when Nydia realized she would overthink a situation, and this was one of them. It was something she needed to discuss with Jasmine when she saw her before they went to the bowling alley.

She pushed off the floor and walked into her bedroom. First she would take a shower and get into bed and reread a Jane Austen novel she knew almost verbatim. All of her heroines in her favorite author's novel were only concerned with falling in love and finding a suitor with means to marry. Well, at thirty-three she would never be a Jane Austen heroine because she was too old to be considered for marriage. The only exception was if she were a wealthy widow.

Nydia chided herself for getting ahead of herself. She would date Lamar, enjoy her times with him, and if or when it ended she would have wonderful memories to look back on.

CHAPTER 17

"So you're really ready to date a man with a ready-made family?"

Nydia gave Jasmine an incredulous stare as she drove into the parking lot behind the bowling alley. "What's wrong with dating a single father?"

Jasmine shifted into park and turned to look at her. "There's nothing wrong with dating a single father, *chica*. I only asked because I want you to think of the possibility that you could be a stepmother."

"Time out, *chica*. Lamar and I have had exactly one date and you already have us married."

"Would that be so terrible?" Jasmine questioned.

Nydia shook her head. "I haven't thought that far ahead. At this point we haven't even slept together."

Jasmine lifted her shoulders. "It will come. At least you know he can make babies."

"Stop it, *mija*! I haven't even slept with the man and you're already talking about him swelling me up."

Jasmine rested a hand over the bump under her loose-fitting blouse. "This little boy or girl will need someone to play with, and the sooner the better."

"Hannah would have a bitch fit if we both ended up pregnant within months of each other." The owner of DuPont Inn had promised an extended maternity leave for her partners. Instead of six weeks she had offered six months because she knew how important it was for a mother to bond with her newborn.

"It would be different for you, Nydia, because you can always work from home, while Hannah and I will alternate working the day and night shift."

"Don't forget LeAnn and Paige," Nydia reminded Jasmine. "They'll be living on the premises, and they've committed to helping with guests checking in and out."

Twelve suites in the mansion were set aside for the inn's guests, and the remaining six would have been occupied by Hannah, LeAnn, Paige, Jasmine, Tonya, and Nydia. But things changed when Hannah married St. John and moved into his house in Marigny. Tonya married Gage and lived with him in the Upper French Quarter, while Jasmine didn't plan to move into the inn once she married Cameron, and that left Nydia and the DuPont cousins to occupy three of the private suites in the historic mansion.

"I'm not going to marry Lamar, so get that out of your matchmaking head." She glanced at the clock on the dashboard. "It's time I go in and get ready to shock the hell out of these retirees."

A hush fell over the alley when Nydia walked in, carrying the bag with her ball and shoes, with Jasmine, and she ignored the stares directed at them. "Be ready," she said under her breath, "when the shit hits the fan." The words were barely off her tongue when a tall, dark-skinned man with graying dreadlocks blocked her path.

"This league is for retirees tonight."

Nydia gave him a lethal stare. "Are you discriminating against me because of my age? And how do you know that I'm not retired?"

He blinked once. "I don't."

She flashed a saccharine smile. "Then I suggest you step aside so I can pass. And for your information — good black don't crack."

Jasmine, waiting until they walked away,

said, "I didn't know you had black people in your family?"

Nydia rolled her eyes at her friend. "*Mija,* you should know that Puerto Ricans have everything in their gene pool. That's why we call ourselves the rainbow people. My great grandparents on my father's side of the family were black, and my mother's mother is half black."

"I stand corrected," Jasmine said under her breath.

Nydia did not like having to explain to people what she was, and whenever she was asked she just said Puerto Rican, and her racial makeup did not make her any less than a *puertorriqueña.* She waved to Hannah when she spied her at the far end of the alley. She and her cousins were already wearing bowling shoes and had selected their balls. She exchanged air kisses with the world-weary cousins and then Hannah.

Sitting, she opened the bag and wiped off the ball with a soft felt cloth and set it on the belt with the others. Nydia glanced up to find her bowling partners staring at her. "What's the matter?"

Hannah pointed to the colorful hand-painted ball. "I can't believe you put graffiti on your ball."

Nydia slipped her feet into her shoes. "It's

called art." She'd had her custom-made ball decorated with the New York Yankees' logo, the American and Puerto Rican flags, and street signs from East and West Harlem. "I have to rep my set," she drawled with a wide grin. "In New York when someone calls out 'BK stand up' any and everyone who lives in Brooklyn will stand up to let you know they're in the house. For me it's Harlem."

"I like the art," LeAnn said.

"Me, too," Paige agreed.

Nydia curtsied to Hannah's dark-haired, dark-eyed, petite first cousins. "Thank you very much," she said in her best Elvis Presley imitation.

Shaking her head, Hannah rolled her eyes upward. "I just hope that ball brings the Innkeepers good luck."

Nydia tied up her shoes, which were decorated similarly to the ball. "You worry too much, Hannah." A loud, nasal, buzzing reverberated throughout the alley as pins were lowered, signaling the start of the first game. "We've got this."

When it was her turn, Nydia pulled on a leather driving glove before picking up her ball. It was as if she had stepped back in time to when she'd bowled on average once a week. She threw the colorful sphere and knocked down all ten pins for a strike.

She curtsied to Hannah. "Counselor. I rest my case." Nydia executed a fist bump with Jasmine as she sat beside her. "I still got it, *mija*," she whispered.

Jasmine nodded. "No lie."

LeAnn and Paige nearly matched her prowess as they threw doubles, while Nydia managed a turkey — three strikes in a row. Hannah came in fourth bowling a 145. At the end of the night the Innkeepers were first in the standings among the ten teams.

Hannah looped her arm through Nydia's as they were leaving. "You did good, baby girl."

Nydia laughed. As she was the youngest of the innkeepers, Hannah was old enough to be her mother. "You did have your doubts."

"I must say I did, but after your first strike I became a believer."

"You didn't do too bad yourself. If we keep winning like we did tonight, then we may have to hire bodyguards to walk us to our cars."

Throwing back her head, Hannah laughed loudly before she placed a hand over her mouth. "I did see quite a few glares thrown our way."

"I prefer to call them stink-eyes," Nydia said. "They'll learn soon enough that the

404

Innkeepers will not yield to intimidation."

"You're right, Nydia. My cousins joined the Freedom Riders when they were college students, and were so militant that folks crossed over to the other side of the street when they saw them coming. I don't know if it's true, but there were rumors that they were always armed."

"That's what you call pistol-packing mamas." She stopped at Jasmine's minivan, waiting for her friend who'd lagged behind talking with Paige and LeAnn. "Will I see you and St. John Sunday at the Toussaints?"

"We wouldn't miss it. Whenever the Toussaints are cooking you can count on me being there. Are you bringing your gorgeous beau?"

"If *beau* is an equivalent to boyfriend, then yes. I invited Lamar and his daughter to come with me."

"Good. I'll see you there." Hannah waved over her shoulder as she made her way to her car.

"I'll drive back," Nydia said to Jasmine. She'd noticed her friend's attempt to smother yawns behind her hand while keeping score.

"Thanks."

Nydia slipped behind the wheel of the minivan and adjusted the seat. She programmed the hotel's address into the navigation and backed out of the parking lot. It was her first time driving in the city, and she knew it would take a while before she was familiar with the streets in the different neighborhoods.

"Honey, we're home," she intoned when maneuvering into Jasmine's reserved parking space at the Louis LaSalle.

Jasmine moaned softly as she unsnapped her belt. "I think I stayed up past my bedtime."

"What time do you usually go to bed?" Nydia asked her.

"Between nine and nine-thirty."

"Let's go, Sleeping Beauty. It's after ten."

Nydia entered her suite and stored the bowling bag in the closet off the entryway. Though Jasmine was exhausted, Nydia was energized from the excitement of bowling again. The first time she walked into a bowling alley at six years old with a group of young children whose parents were police officers, Nydia found herself mesmerized by the clashing sound of pins after they were hit by a ball hurtling down the lane. Her love of the game never waned as she grew older, and by the time she celebrated her fourteenth birthday, she had become what some people called a bowling phenom. The league was only six weeks — enough time for her to revive and hone her skills before returning to New York.

Lamar sat in the conference room with his partners, waiting for word they'd come in at the lowest bid for the Shreveport shopping mall. He glanced across the table at Omar Robinson, who was doodling and making interlocking circles on a legal pad. Omar had always been the most aggressive of the trio even when WPR Engineering was in its infancy. When Lamar first shared a class with the civil engineering major, Omar had sported distinctive dreadlocks ending midway down his back, but he decided to cut his hair when his hairline began receding. He now shaved his head, and with round, black-rimmed wire glasses he appeared quite professorial.

His gaze shifted to Kirk Wallace, who had closed his eyes and crossed his arms over his chest. Lamar thought of Kirk as the calm and collected partner. He rarely raised his voice and most times had become the voice of reason during in-house negotiations. His appearance hadn't changed much from their college days. His curly black hair was shorter and he occasionally sported a short beard. But all of their lives had changed since college. They'd married, fathered children, and their professional focus was growing their partnership.

The telephone on the table buzzed, and everyone sat up straight. Lamar tapped the intercom button. "Yes, Suzanne."

"I have Mr. King on the line."

Lamar met Omar's eyes across the table. "Put him through." He activated the speaker feature.

"Gentlemen, I wish I had good news to tell you, but you didn't come in as the lowest bid. But you were very close."

Lamar managed a wry smile. "It's encouraging to hear that." He tried not to let a thread of disappointment creep into his voice. "Let us know when the next project comes up for bid."

"I definitely will. You guys have a good one."

Omar frowned. "What the hell does he mean have a good one," he spat out within seconds of Lamar ending the call. "We just lost the fuckin' bid."

Kirk lowered his arms. "It's done, Omar. There's no need crying over spilled milk."

Pushing back his chair, Omar stood up and stalked out of the conference room. Kirk and Lamar exchanged glances. They knew he would sulk for a few days and then settle down to concentrate on their current construction projects.

Lamar looked at his watch. "I'm going out for an extended lunch." He had to get out of the office to escape what could become a toxic environment. Omar was a brilliant civil engineer, but there were times when he found it difficult to deal with his dark moods. He was aware that Omar and his wife weren't getting along; the issue was child rearing, and he wondered whether, if Valerie had survived, they would have experienced a similar problem when it came to raising Kendra.

He left the conference room and entered his office. Although he'd agreed to submit a bid on the strip mall, deep down inside Lamar felt a sense of relief that they hadn't come in lowest. He still did not feel comfortable leaving his daughter for extended periods of time. He picked up his cell phone, scrolled through the directory, and tapped the number to Cameron's private line. It was answered after the third ring.

"What's up, Pierce?"

"Can you get rid of your ball and chain to meet me for lunch at Casey's?"

Cameron's chuckle came through the earpiece. "Say no more. It's been a while since I've gone there, and I've had a bitch of a morning with clients fighting me tooth and nail about where they want to invest."

"What time, Singleton?"

"Give me twenty minutes. I'll meet you there."

"You're on."

Lamar ended the call, tightened his tie, and called Suzanne to inform her he was taking an extended lunch. He wanted *and* needed to talk to Cameron about his wife's best friend, because he was having ambivalent feelings when it came to Nydia. He liked her a lot, but part of him didn't want to, because he did not know where it would lead. Six months after losing his wife he'd begun sleeping with a woman, knowing it would never evolve beyond sex. There would be no declarations of love nor were they to be seen in public together. Once he told her of his intention and after seeing her pained expression, he decided to end it. She accused him of using her, and he had for his own selfish motives.

The next woman turned the tables on him when she proposed they have a sex-only relationship. They would meet at a motel once a week and after spending several hours together go their separate ways until the next time. Lamar's male pride was wounded, but he managed to get over it because of what he'd done to the other woman.

However, it was different with Nydia. Not only would they openly date, but he was uncertain as to where he wanted their relationship to go. He wasn't in love with her, but knew it would be so easy to love her. Everything about her appealed to him. It was as if he had been waiting for a woman like her to come into his life. He likened her to the bubbles in wine that turned it into champagne. She tickled his nose and his palate. Lamar slipped his arms into his suit jacket, walked out of his office with its views of the Mississippi River, and took a back staircase down to the street level.

Although it was late September, the heat and humidity made it feel like the height of summer. One of the many things he'd enjoyed about living in New York was the change of season. The first time he'd experienced an appreciable snowfall he took the subway to Central Park and asked a kid if he could use his sled to go sledding. The young boy gave him a strange look until he explained that he came from Louisiana, and it was a rare occasion that it snowed there. And if it did, it disappeared within hours.

Fall and winter were his favorites. Lamar became a tourist when he strolled aimlessly along broad avenues peering into department store windows gaily decorated for the holiday season. He'd been transfixed by the tiny white lights threaded through naked tree branches along a stretch of Fifth Avenue, and would occasionally stop in to St. Patrick's Cathedral to pray.

Watching the skaters in Rockefeller Center with the massive Christmas tree as a backdrop never failed to put him in a holiday mood. And now that Nydia had invited him and Kendra to join her family in New York it was something he was looking forward to, if only to relive the time when he'd been a student in a city that at first had overwhelmed him with its nonstop energy.

Lamar walked the four blocks to Casey's, waiting outside the pub for Cameron to join him. He didn't have to wait long until he spied the financial planner coming down the street. They shook hands. "Thanks for meeting me."

Cameron smiled, and attractive lines fanned out around his blue-gray eyes. "You called at the right time. I usually don't have a liquid lunch, but this is one time when I definitely need one."

Lamar seldom drank during the day, and when he did he limited it to a single beer. "Casey's is the best watering hole for a liquid lunch. I take it you had a rough morning."

"No shit," Cameron drawled as he opened the door. "It's one I'd like to forget. Should I assume yours was equally frustrating?"

"Let's say it has been better," Lamar said. "I'll tell you about it after we order." He didn't tell Cameron that losing the bid wasn't the only thing on his mind, but that would wait until after he let his friend blow off steam.

The hostess greeted Cameron by name and escorted them to a table in a corner where they did not have to shout to each other to be heard. The pub was a popular eating establishment for many of the businesspeople in the CBD. It was where they'd gather for lunch and dinner to eat and watch the many muted television screens tuned to news and sports channels.

A waiter approached the table and set down menus. "Can I get you gentlemen something from the bar?"

"I'll have a Sazerac," Cameron said.

Lamar hid a grin. His friend had ordered one of the city's signature cocktails. "I'll have a beer." If it had been later in the day he would've ordered a Rob Roy. The drink made with scotch and sweet vermouth was slightly less lethal than a Sazerac. The lunch-crowd bartender tended to be a little heavy-handed when it came to pouring bourbon.

The young man wrote down their drink order. "Do you know what you want to eat, or should I give you time to decide?"

Lamar stared at the menu. "I still have to decide."

Cameron glanced up. "Same here."

Their drinks arrived, and they touched glasses. After a long swallow Lamar felt some of his tension easing. "I take it you've had to go a couple of rounds with a client."

Cameron ran a hand over his neatly barbered graying light brown hair. Although approaching fifty, he appeared as physically fit as a man decades younger. "There are times when I ask myself if I'm crazy trying to save people from financial ruin because they want to invest in some half-baked, crazy-ass scheme their friends or relatives are concocting. And when I try and tell them it's nothing more than a hustle, they threaten to have another company monitor their investments."

Lamar gave Cameron a direct stare. "What do you tell them?"

Leaning back in his chair, the wealth manager affected a wry smile. "I always advise them that they have a choice to stay

414

or leave, but if they do, then I will *not* take them on again. My mantra is once burned, twice shy. It's just not worth the aggravation. It was the same when I dated. Once I decided not to see a young lady again, I didn't want to relive whatever problem we had with each other." Cameron paused. "Speaking of young ladies, how are you doing with Nydia?"

Lamar wanted to wait before broaching the subject of Nydia, but now that Cameron mentioned her he had to open up about how he felt about her. "Friends-wise, we're good. But it's a slow go in the romance department."

The wealth manager gave him a long, penetrating stare. "It will continue to be a slow-go until you take off that piece of jewelry you're wearing on your left hand."

Splaying his fingers on the table, Lamar looked at the ring. Valerie had placed the matching tricolor gold band on his finger at their wedding, and it had remained there to this day. His head popped up. "What's the problem?"

"The problem is no woman is going to get serious about you when you're still wearing your wedding ring. At least, no single woman who would even remotely think of considering a future with you."

A slight frown furrowed Lamar's forehead. "Is that what Nydia told Jasmine?"

Cameron shook his head. "Jasmine doesn't discuss her friends with me. The only thing I know is that if it hadn't been for Nydia I wouldn't be married to Jasmine." He told Lamar about meeting Jasmine at Hannah DuPont's wedding and asking her out. "She told me that wasn't possible because she was going back to New York. I took a chance and asked for her phone number because I go to New York every May to reconnect with my college frat buddies. And that was almost seven months away."

Lamar rested an arm on the table, completely intrigued by Cameron's story. "I take it she agreed to go out with you."

"She did, but only after she disclosed that Nydia had convinced her to answer my text and say yes."

"So, Nydia is responsible for bringing you and Jasmine together."

Cameron nodded. "And I'm eternally grateful to her." He took another sip of the Sazerac. "I can't believe I had to live nearly half a century to finally fall in love and look forward to becoming a father for the first time." He paused. "Now back to you, my friend. I know you still love Valerie, but I'm certain she wouldn't want you to spend the

416

rest of your life grieving for what was. A part of her will live on in Kendra, but what about you, Lamar?"

"What about me?" Lamar asked, answering Cameron's question with one of his own.

"You claim you're friends with Nydia, but do you want more? And the more is possibly a commitment?"

"I'm willing to commit to her, but I'm not certain whether she wants the same."

"Do you think it's because you're a single father?"

Lamar shook his head. "I don't believe so. She and Kendra get along very well together."

"So it's not about your daughter, but you. Put yourself in her place, Lamar. You're still wearing a wedding band, which says she'll have to compete with a dead woman for your love. Would you want to get involved with a woman who wasn't willing to stop talking about her dead husband or ex-lover?"

"Of course not."

Cameron pointed to his hand again. "That's what you're doing by not taking off your ring. Have you talked to her about Valerie?"

"Yes."

"Did she appear intimidated?"

Lamar smiled. "Not in the least. Nydia's not one to let anything or anyone intimidate her. She's one of the most confident women I've ever met."

"If that's the case, then you can't have it both ways, brother. You have to make a decision whether you're all in or half in. Do you want a future with Nydia?"

Cameron was asking Lamar a question he wasn't able to answer. He'd met Nydia for the first time two months ago, though it seemed so much longer. While he believed he was falling in love with her, he wasn't in love with her, but also he didn't want to lose her. Perhaps Cameron was right about him continuing to wear his wedding band. The gold circle was a silent signal to women that he wasn't available, except to those willing to engage in an affair with a married man. He wasn't married, yet he had continued to go about life as if he were.

"I can honestly say I could see her in my life."

"Does 'in your life' mean eventually proposing marriage?" Cameron asked.

A sly smile tilted the corners of Lamar's mouth. "Ask me that again in a few months."

Cameron's light brown eyebrows lifted

slightly. "What's happening in a few months?"

"Kendra and I will spend the Christmas holiday with Nydia's family in New York."

"No shit!" Cameron whispered. "You've made plans to meet the woman's family?"

Lamar held up his hand. "It's not like that," he said quickly.

Cameron shook his head. "Don't try and explain. All I know is when I met Jasmine's parents for the first time she was wearing my engagement ring. It was the same with my folks."

"That's because Jasmine was pregnant."

"Even if she wasn't carrying my baby, I knew I wanted to marry her before we slept together for the first time. There was something so different about her from the other women I'd dated, and it wasn't because she was a woman of color. Not only is she beautiful and sophisticated, she isn't afraid to speak her mind."

Lamar smiled. It was the same with Nydia. There were times when she'd say something that made it almost impossible for him to reply with a comeback. "Her best friend is definitely as outspoken."

Cameron waved a hand at the same time he shook his head. "I don't have the temperament to deal with Nydia's candor. Jasmine is forthright, but Nydia is the personification of bluntness. She's not afraid to call a spade a spade. When she came down for the wedding, she took me aside and said if I hurt her best friend, then she was going to get me good. At that point in time I was too intimidated to ask what she intended to do, so I just nodded my head like a bobblehead doll."

"Please don't tell me you were afraid of a five-foot-two woman who probably doesn't weigh more than one-ten soaking wet."

"Hell yeah! When she looked at me with those green eyes I knew she wasn't playing. So, make certain you don't get her mad before y'all go to bed together, because you may wake up not looking the same. Especially below your belly button."

Throwing back his head, Lamar laughed loudly, causing those sitting at nearby tables to glance his way. "I'll remember that if we do sleep together."

Cameron gave him a level stare. "I thought you were already sleeping together, because you two looked pretty cozy at Momma's Place."

"I want to give her time to feel comfortable taking our friendship to the next level."

"She's just getting out of a relationship?"

Lamar shook his head. "Not quite. She

broke up with some dude last November, but he's still messing with her."

"What he needs is a good ass-whooping to convince him it's over."

"I agree, but it's been settled. He's lucky her father and brother didn't get involved, because her dad is a retired cop and her brother is currently NYPD."

Cameron whistled under his breath. "That man truly likes living on the edge."

Lamar didn't want to disclose to Cameron his involvement in helping Nydia with her dilemma because his friend had admitted his wife did not discuss her friends with him. He turned his attention to the menu when he spied the waiter's approach. He ordered grilled honey Cajun shrimp with a side dish of red beans and rice, while Cameron selected a bowl of Creole-Cajun jambalaya.

"I know you didn't call me for lunch to talk about Nydia, so, my friend, what else is on your mind?"

It was a rare occasion that Lamar talked about work to someone other than his mother, but this time he needed an unbiased opinion. He told Cameron about Omar's seemingly more and more erratic behavior and how it was impacting the partnership. "We've done quite well since going into business together, but for Omar it's never enough."

"Have you thought about buying out his share in the company?" Cameron questioned.

"No, and I'm not certain whether I want to raise the idea with Kirk, who is a lot more laid back than I am, so most times Omar's outbursts don't bother him."

"If that's the case, then why don't you go into business for yourself? Of course you'll be competing with them for projects."

Lamar slowly shook his head. "That's something I can't see myself doing. We've been together too long to compete with one another. What Omar needs is a break from the business so that he can straighten out his personal life."

"Why don't you suggest that? We Singletons go through the same thing every once in a while. Right now my father is supposed to be semi-retired, but he still comes into the office four out of five days. And there are times when I have to tell him to go home and kiss his wife because he's being an annoyance. My brothers and I finally got together to institute a four-day workweek, which gives everyone a three-day weekend. Everyone returns on Monday much less stressed."

"That's something to think about," Lamar said. "We don't have that many ongoing construction projects where we have to be in the office five days a week. We can alternate covering the office every third week. And if I have to inspect a site, then I could do that during the week I don't have office duty. As for office staff we can change their hours to give them the option of taking Fridays or Mondays off."

"Are you certain you haven't been talking to Jasmine?"

"Why would you say that?"

"Because she's a human resources specialist, and it was she who gave me the idea of shortening my family's workweek."

"I can assure you," Lamar said, smiling, "that I haven't spoken to your wife. But you did make me think about a shorter workweek."

The waiter arrived with their lunch order. The topic of conversation turned to sports as he and Cameron talked about the possibility of the Saints becoming Super Bowl champs with their newly acquired young talent.

The impromptu lunch ended when Lamar paid the bill, while Cameron left a generous tip. They walked back to their respective offices with a promise to see each other

Sunday. Both had confirmed they planned to attend Gage and Tonya Toussaint's brunch gathering.

As soon as he opened the door, the receptionist told him that Omar had taken the afternoon off. He thanked her, went into his office, closed the door, and dialed the number to Omar's cell.

"Talk to me, Pierce."

He smiled when hearing the familiar greeting. It took less than two minutes to outline to his friend and partner the plan Lamar had presented to Cameron. "It's just something to think about," he added. "I haven't said anything to Kirk, but after I hang up I'll talk to him about it. What do you think?"

"I like your suggestion, Lamar. I believe we've all been pushing too hard and perhaps even overextending ourselves. I do need time off to take care of my home, which is now in crisis."

"Take as much time as you need, Omar. The company's not going to go under if you're not here. And plan to go away or do something with your wife and kids during the week of Christmas when they're out of school. Think about booking a family cruise to the Caribbean."

"I'm glad you called, because when we

hang up that's exactly what I intend to do. I'm going to research sites and then discuss it with Layla."

"Let me know what you decide."

"Will do. Thanks, buddy."

Lamar smiled. "Anytime."

He ended the call, feeling much better than he had with Omar's outburst. At least his friend and partner recognized when he had to correct a problem. Layla had assumed the role of disciplinarian while Omar had become the overindulgent father. Anything his children wanted he gave them without questioning whether it was good for them, which made his wife the bad guy.

He'd listened to Omar rant about his wife being too hard on his sons and daughters without offering commentary or an opinion. After all, he was a single father with his own set of problems with a young girl whose moods changed from one day to the other. Nydia had mentioned his daughter's fluctuating hormones, and he hoped they would soon level out so she wouldn't keep him off-balance whenever he said something to her. Lamar recalled Nydia's suggestion of giving Kendra a Halloween-themed birthday party and decided to ask her if it was something she'd want.

■ ■ ■ ■

Lamar knocked on Kendra's bedroom door and then waited for her to answer. He'd noticed she'd begun closing the door once there were noticeable changes in her body, and the last thing he wanted to do was invade her privacy.

"Yes?"

"May I come in?"

"Yes, Daddy?"

He opened the door wide enough to poke his head through. "I wanted to ask you if you want a birthday party."

Kendra glanced away from her desktop. "No thanks. I'm getting too old for kiddie birthday parties. The next party I want is a Sweet Sixteen."

"Are you sure?"

Kendra smiled, and in that instant Lamar thought he was staring at a younger Valerie. His daughter's resemblance to her late mother was uncanny. "Very sure, Daddy. Taylor and Morgan said their mother is planning a Halloween party at her house for our class that weekend, so she's probably going to call you to ask if I can go and spend the weekend."

He smiled. Now he knew why she didn't

want a party. "I'll let you go if you promise not to participate in any spin-the-bottle kissing games."

"Stop it, Daddy!"

"I'm just teasing you, sweets. Don't stay up too late."

"I won't."

Lamar closed the door and retreated to his bedroom. His daughter was enrolled in the same school he and his sister had attended. It had earned the reputation of being an elite private school with small classes that gave students the attention they needed to excel.

He lay across the bed and contemplated what Cameron had said about him continuing to wear a wedding band despite being a widower for the past four years. He wanted a relationship with Nydia, but he knew that wasn't going to happen until he let go of his past. Lamar remembered asking her to save him a dance at Cameron and Jasmine's wedding and she'd said, *I will, but only if Mrs. Pierce doesn't mind you dancing with me.* It was obvious she did not want to dance with a married man unless his wife approved.

Sitting up, he twisted the band of gold until it finally came off his finger. Lamar stared at the lighter band of skin, which hadn't been exposed to the sun. He exhaled an audible sigh as he placed the ring in a drawer in the bedside table. He sat on the bed and closed his eyes. Taking off the ring was more symbolic than he realized. He had let go of the past in order to look forward to embracing the future with a woman who made him laugh when he didn't want to laugh.

Lamar did not know why his path had crossed with Nydia Santiago's but decided to enjoy the journey as long as it lasted. But more important, he wasn't looking for a mother for his daughter, yet it was something he could not ignore. He didn't know if Nydia would be willing to assume the responsibility of caring for a preteen stepdaughter, or whether Kendra wanted to share her father with another woman. The doubts and questions assaulted him like flying missiles until he wanted to shout and tell them to stop. What he had to do was be calm and let things unfold naturally.

CHAPTER 18

Nydia peered out the side window of Jasmine's SUV as Cameron came to a stop along a tree-lined street and parked in front of a building with green-shuttered second-story windows and a fire escape leading from the second to the third story, both with decorative ironwork balconies.

Cameron unsnapped his seat belt, got out, and came around to help her and Jasmine from the car. "I'm going to let you ladies out here and go around the corner to park."

Nydia and Jasmine made their way through a set of open gates that led into the Toussaints' courtyard. She recognized the faces of many of the people she'd met a year before at St. John's family reunion. There were a few others she remembered from the wedding DVD Tonya sent her when she had been unable to attend the ceremony. She smiled when she saw Gage and his older brother, Eustace, manning grills, while folks lined up behind a portable bar where St. John had assumed the role of mixologist. A group of young children had gathered on folding chairs under a red mulberry tree to play with electronic devices while their parents were huddled together in small groups laughing and talking to one another. A DJ was spinning Motown classics.

"I deliberately didn't have a mid-morning snack because I intend to eat until I burst," Jasmine said under her breath.

Nydia gave Jasmine a sidelong glance. She was nearing the beginning of her fifth month, and her pregnancy was now obvious depending upon what she wore. "Thank goodness Cameron came with us, because he'll have to be the one to carry you out."

Jasmine rolled her eyes at Nydia. "You got fat jokes? I can't wait until Lamar swells you up and then we'll see how you look with a bowling ball–size belly."

She laughed. "That's not going to happen, because yours truly and Lamar are not sleeping together."

Jasmine caught her arm. "You're kidding, aren't you?"

Nydia met her dark eyes. "No. We're friends."

"You two didn't appeared that friendly when we were all at Momma's Place. You

430

were so close together that I thought you were sitting on his lap."

"We were talking about my teaching Kendra to make *pasteles*."

Jasmine pushed out her lower lip. "So you're really just friends?"

"Don't look so disappointed, *mija*. There's no pressure for us to sleep together. You have to know once we do we'll both be different people."

Jasmine nodded. "I know. The night, or I should say the morning Cameron and I made love for the first time I knew then I wanted to be with him. Of course we hadn't planned on my getting pregnant, but that was something beyond our control."

Nydia dropped an arm over Jasmine's shoulders. "I'm glad your daddy's condoms were defective, or I wouldn't be looking forward to becoming Titi Nydia."

"Bite your tongue, *chica*. Speaking of dads, I see Lamar talking to Evie and her husband. I'm going to get something to eat while you go and talk to your bae."

Nydia scanned the crowd and saw him. He appeared to be listening intently to something Evangeline was saying. Then as if she'd willed it, he turned in her direction. The smile on his face spoke volumes as he approached her.

Lamar reached for her hands and kissed the back of them. "I've been waiting for you to get here."

Going on tiptoe, she pressed a chaste kiss on his jaw. "How long have you been here?"

"Probably about thirty minutes. Kendra wanted to get here at the same time as her friends. You'd think they don't get to see one another at school." Attractive lines fanned out around Lamar's eyes when he smiled. "Answer one question for me."

"What's that?" Nydia asked.

"When you were their age did you and your friends all talk at the same time?"

Nydia blinked slowly. "You know that's sexist," she said accusingly.

He held up both hands. "I'm just asking."

Something caught her attention, and that's when Nydia realized Lamar wasn't wearing his wedding band. The first thoughts that flooded her mind were when and why. "You're not wearing your ring." She'd spoken her thought aloud.

Lamar stared at his left hand and nodded. "I should've taken if off a long time ago."

"Why now?"

A mysterious smile flitted over his features. "Because a beautiful young woman with the initials NSS helped me to see life as it is instead of was."

She stared at the cleft in Lamar's chin. "I want you to know I never would've asked you to take it off. That had to be your decision."

He nodded. "I know that. But I must confess I had some help making the decision. Cameron told me I had to stop living in the past or I'd lose what was right in front of me. I don't want to lose you, Nydia, because you're the best thing to come into my life . . ." His words trailed off when Kendra ran over and held onto his arm.

Nydia swallowed to relieve the tightness in her throat. She didn't want to believe Lamar had decided to express his inner feelings within earshot of anyone who could overhear him. It was the one time she would have preferred he spoke to her in Spanish. She forced a smile she did not quite feel.

Kendra flashed a wide grin, exhibiting red, white, and blue brackets on her braces. "Hello, Miss Nydia."

"Hello, Kendra. I like your hair." A chemically straightened ponytail had replaced the braids.

Kendra pulled her hair over her shoulder. "Thank you. I've been wearing braids for most of the year, and I know Miss Ramona is tired of redoing them every week." She tugged on Lamar's arm. "Daddy, can I spend the week with Morgan and Taylor so we can practice for our Fall Frolic?"

The words were barely off her tongue when Evangeline joined them. The tall, slender brunette looked very chic in a pair of slim navy stretch slacks she had paired with a blue-and-white-striped off-the-shoulder silk blouse, while many of Tonya and Gage's guests favored jeans and shorts. "It's so nice seeing you again, Nydia."

Nydia returned her friendly smile. "It's also nice seeing you, Evangeline."

"I love your dress."

In deference to the warm weather, Nydia had decided to forego slacks, instead wearing a pumpkin-orange linen sleeveless dress with large patch pockets and a slightly flaring skirt ending at her knees. She wiggled her groomed toes in a pair of strappy wedges. She'd visited a salon within walking distance of the hotel for a mani-pedi.

"Thank you."

Evangeline turned her attention to Lamar. "If you don't mind, I'd like Kendra to spend the week at my house so she and the girls can rehearse for the production of the school's Fall Frolic. My daughters just found out that I was the lead actress in the school's drama club and that their mother can sing and dance, along with playing the piano. Of course I'll make sure the girls do their homework and go to bed on time."

Lamar stared down at his daughter looking up at him. Nydia almost burst into laughter when Kendra affected a sad face. "Okay," he said after a pregnant pause. "I'll make certain Ramona packs enough clothes for the week and I'll drop them off later tonight." Kendra clapped a hand over her mouth before running away to tell her friends the good news.

Evangeline laughed. "Don't concern yourself picking her up next Sunday. After church, Daniel and I planned to take them to Momma's Place for brunch and then to a movie. My parents have changed their regular third Sunday in the month to the fourth for the family dinner."

Lamar angled his head. "Are you telling me I won't see my daughter until a week from tomorrow?"

"Yes." She patted Lamar's shoulder. "Not to worry. I'll take good care of her."

He nodded. "I have no doubt she'll be in the best care. I just don't want you to get overwhelmed."

Evangeline patted her hair. "I can't get any more overwhelmed than I am now. I keep telling my daughters that they're going to have me completely gray before I turn forty."

It was Lamar's turn to laugh. "You know I'd begun graying in high school."

Nydia held up both hands when Evangeline and Lamar stared at her. "Y'all are not going to invite me to join your gray-haired club — at least not for a few more years."

"Wait until you have a couple of kids," Evangeline teased.

"I still have time before I think of becoming a mother," Nydia said.

Lamar rested his hand at the small of Nydia's back. "Are you ready to eat?"

Her smile was as bright as the early afternoon sunshine. "I'm always ready if the Toussaints are cooking."

Nydia sat between Lamar and Hannah at one of four long picnic tables Gage and his niece's husbands had set up in the courtyard. Platters of barbecued ribs, chicken, and shrimp, pulled pork, hamburgers, hot links, and brisket were set on each table along with bowls of potato salad, coleslaw, red beans, rice, deviled eggs, and collard greens. There were alcoholic libations for the adults and fruit punch and lemonade for those under the legal drinking age. All of the children were seated at the same table.

Tonya and Gage had invited Toussaints, Singletons, and Gage's bandmates from Jazzes, and several of his former colleagues from the local high school where he once had been an artist-in-residence. And judging from the laughter and frivolity among the assembly Nydia knew the gathering was a rousing success.

She stared at Kendra smiling shyly at something Cameron's nephew whispered in her ear. Nydia estimated he was at least twelve or thirteen, and judging from the way he stared at Lamar's daughter, there was no doubt he was taken with her.

"What are you looking at?" Lamar asked her in Spanish.

"Your daughter and Evangeline's nephew," she replied in the same language. "It appears as if another generation of Singletons is intrigued by a woman of color."

"I wouldn't worry too much about that, because right now Kendra thinks boys are stupid."

Nydia bit on her lip to keep from telling Lamar that he was in denial thinking that his daughter did not like boys, but she wasn't willing to tell him because she feared he would go off on the boy. It had been the same with her and her father when she'd mentioned she liked a boy in her sixth grade class. He told her he was going to look for the hapless kid and snap his head off. Of course she didn't know her father was joking, but it was enough for her to keep her thoughts to herself.

"What are you going to do for a week now that Kendra's staying with Evangeline?"

Lamar ran a hand down her back. "Spend time with my girlfriend," he whispered in her ear, still speaking Spanish.

Turning her head slightly, she stared at him. "Can you tell me who this girlfriend is?" Nydia replied in the same language.

Lamar lowered his eyes and his voice when he said, "She's the only woman here wearing an orange dress. After I drop Kendra's clothes off at Evangeline's, I'd like to come to my girlfriend's hotel suite and hang out there for a while."

Nydia felt a wave of heat begin at her hairline and move lower and lower until she had to press her knees together to still the pulsing between her thighs. It was as if Lamar had been reading her mind. If they were to make love, then she didn't want it to be slam bam, thank you, ma'am when he had to get up and leave.

"How long do you intend to hang out with your girlfriend?" she questioned, still speaking Spanish. The gold glints in his eyes shimmered like polished amber crystals.

"I don't know. I'd like to stay at least a week, but I don't want to wear out my welcome."

"What about work, Lamar?"

"I have to go into the office, but there's always before and after work when I can give you my undivided attention."

Nydia rested her head on his shoulder. "I like the sound of that. And while you're at your office I'll be working on my projects."

Lamar kissed her hair. "That sounds like a plan. Let me know where you want to eat dinner, and I'll make the reservations."

"Okay. Speaking of reservations, I've ordered tickets for *The Lion King.* We have orchestra seats."

"How much do I owe you?"

"Nothing, Lamar. It's my Christmas gift for Kendra and my nieces."

"But I told you I'd pay for them."

"Let's not fight over money, Lamar. It's so gauche."

"I'm not fighting with you, Nydia. You're the one who's not working, while you're spending your money paying for a hotel suite."

439

Shifting on the bench, Nydia gave him a lethal stare. She wondered if she'd been a man and a CPA he would have doubted her ability to handle her own finances. "What gives you the impression I'm not working?" Her eyes gave off angry green sparks. "I do have accounts I monitor remotely." She wasn't about to tell Lamar that she didn't have to pay for her suite because Cameron had confided to her that he owned the Louis LaSalle. "And please don't concern yourself about what I pay for my suite. And furthermore, I can assure you I won't have to file for bankruptcy because I bought four tickets to a Broadway play."

Rubbing her back in a comforting gesture, Lamar winked at Nydia. "I'm sorry, sweets, for questioning your ability."

Her annoyance vanished with his apology as she blew him an air kiss. "I'll forgive you as long as you don't forget it."

His eyebrows shot up. "That tongue of yours is going to get you in trouble one of these days."

Nydia scrunched her pert nose. "How so?" she asked.

"You're going to say something that will get you in so much trouble you won't be able to extricate yourself."

"I'm not worried about that, Lamar. If I

get into trouble I can always count on you to rescue me. After all, you are my knight in shining armor. And I have a feeling that you like my sassiness, because you never know what you're going to get."

"You're so right about that," Lamar said in agreement. "And that's what I like about you. I'm never bored whenever I'm with you."

"I've been called a lot of things but never boring," Nydia said, as Lamar stood up and went over to the bar.

Hannah tapped Nydia on her bare shoulder. "I had no idea Lamar spoke Spanish."

She leaned closer to Hannah and whispered, "He's a man of many talents."

"I should say he is," Hannah whispered back. "And you've succeeded where so many women have failed. The man is totally besotted with you."

Nydia smiled. "Now that's a word I've read about in romance novels."

"That's because your life has become a romance novel, where you and Lamar are the protagonists. You're the heroine who moves from her hometown to start over after a failed relationship. She meets a handsome, devoted single father who is ready to share his life and future with her."

Nydia's smile faded as she shook her

head. "You're definitely getting ahead of yourself, Hannah. Lamar and I are just friends."

"The question is how long will you remain friends? It's as plain as the nose on your face that the man is falling in love with you."

"How do you know that? Has he said anything to you about me?"

"I don't know Lamar that well for him to confide in me. And to answer your question, he doesn't have to say anything, Nydia. The man looks at you the same way St. John looked at me once we reunited at our high school reunion. And don't forget Cameron and Jasmine."

Nydia had to agree with Hannah. St. John had come to the DuPont House to pick Hannah up for their dance lesson, and only someone visually impaired would not have noticed the way he stared at her. And she felt Cameron staring at Jasmine at Hannah and St. John's wedding reception was akin to a fixation. Nydia liked Lamar, and had admitted it to him, but she was reluctant to allow herself to fall in love with him.

When she'd fallen in love with the college instructor she was still young and impressionable. She was older, more sexually experienced when she slept with Danny, but it was for the wrong reason: loneliness. Now at thirty-three Nydia knew she was more mature, confident, and a lot more cautious than she'd been in the past, and if she did become involved with Lamar, then she knew she would have to guard her heart, because he was everything she'd wanted in a man and potential husband.

He returned with a glass filled with an amber liquid, and recaptured her attention when he rested a hand on her shoulder. "I'm sorry I didn't ask, but can I get you something from the bar?"

"Another lemonade would be nice." It was made with club soda instead of water, the carbonation adding fizz to the beverage.

She stared at Lamar as he made his way to the bar, a secret smile slightly parting her lips. *He's perfect,* she thought. The two words summed up everything she thought about the man who unknowingly had allowed her to alter her stance about not dating for a year once she ended a relationship. She'd discovered he was firm and also affectionate with his daughter while sacrificing companionship because his sole focus was taking care of Kendra.

Nydia made certain never to exhibit any indicator of affection whenever she was with the girl's father. There were no longing glances or unconscious brush of body parts.

She was her father's friend and nothing beyond that. However, she was honest enough with herself to know that her being friends with Lamar could not continue because of her rapidly changing and deepening feelings for the man.

She met his eyes when he returned to the table holding a mug of lemonade, his gaze holding and trapping her in a spell from which she was unable to escape. It was as if he were telegraphically communicating what she was feeling at that time: she wanted him to make love to her. The spell was shattered when Gage Toussaint tapped the handle of a knife against a glass bottle.

Nydia stared at the drop-dead gorgeous musician/chef as he signaled for silence. When she saw him play trumpet at Jazzes during her first visit to the city, she hadn't been able to pull her gaze away from his large gray-green eyes framed by long black lashes. A palomino-gold complexion, delicate features, and cropped straight black hair with flecks of gray, and a rich baritone voice made him the total package.

"Now that everyone has gotten a little something to eat and drink, I'd like to thank y'all for coming to the second Toussaint family reunion. The first was a few months back when I married Tonya, my beautiful bride and partner. Babe, please stand up so these good folks can see you." Tonya rose to her feet, displaying deep dimples in her flawless cheeks when she flashed a broad smile.

"For some of you," he continued, "this is your first time hanging out with the Toussaints, and hopefully it won't be your last, because those who are friends are now considered family." He pointed to LeAnn and Paige DuPont. "I don't know why y'all are looking at each other, because when Hannah married my cousin St. John you became a part of our family." Gage waited for a smattering of laughter to fade. "Tonya reminds me relentlessly that Hannah, Jasmine Singleton, and Puerto Rican princess Nydia Santiago are her sisters, so that, too, makes them family. Nydia, stand and let everyone see what a Boricua looks like."

Never in her life had Nydia felt as embarrassed as when Lamar pulled her to stand amid applause and whistling. The blood suffusing her face nearly matched the color of her dress. Recovering quickly, she made the peace sign when she wanted to put her fists to her eyes as she'd done as a child whenever she silently demonstrated payback.

Gage turned to the table with the young children. "Cameron, I see that your nephews have already acquired the Singleton swag with them trying to put the moves on my grandnieces and the other beautiful young ladies at their table." The entire courtyard erupted in laughter. "A word of caution, young fellas. You'll have to deal with their fathers if you're thinking of asking them out in the future. Dads, please stand up so these young dudes know who they have to deal with."

Placing her hand over her mouth, Nydia laughed until tears filled her eyes when Lamar and more than a half dozen men stood up and glared at the young boys sitting at the table with their daughters. A few displayed fists, which added to the rousing levity.

Lamar retook his seat. "Was that boy really coming on to my daughter?" he whispered to Nydia.

She gave him a direct stare. "If he was, then nothing is going to come out of it because you claim she thinks boys are stupid."

"Maybe she wasn't being completely truthful."

Nydia saw the frown settle onto his normally pleasant features. "Stop projecting, Lamar. You have to learn to trust your daughter."

446

He ran a hand over his face. "Raising a son is probably a lot easier than a daughter."

"Why?" she asked. "Because the only thing you have to tell him is to bag his meat in latex and he can have all the fun he wants with any man's daughter?"

"That's cold, Nydia."

Her eyebrows lifted questioningly. "Is it really, Lamar? A girl is given a litany of dos and don'ts when she goes out with a boy. Don't let him touch you places that you deem private. Always carry a phone and money so you can call if he decides to dump you somewhere if you're not willing to put out. Don't leave your drink unattended because someone may put something in it. Always leave an address or phone number where you're going in case you don't make it back home. Don't ride in cars with strange boys, and please don't be the only girl in a crowd in case they plan to run a train on you. Meanwhile, do fathers tell their sons that no means no? You can tell them to use protection, but most times it goes in one ear and out the other and they end up with more than one baby mama and on *Maury* when the results of the DNA test indicates, 'You *are* the father' of at least three or four children from different women they've slept with."

"You really watch that show?"

She nodded. "It's one of my grandmother's favorite daytime shows."

"I saw it once and I couldn't believe folks could be that silly. It has to be scripted."

"Believe me, it's not scripted. I know one girl who arranged for her boyfriend to be tested on the show because he kept denying her two kids were his."

"Were they?" Lamar asked.

"Of course they were."

"Why did he deny them?"

"Money, Lamar. His paycheck was being garnished for back child support payments from two other women."

"Why didn't he just use a condom when he slept with them?"

"You're preaching to the choir. I've heard men complain about not being able to get *their feeling,* or whatever that means if they're wearing a condom. That's the dumbest thing I've ever heard in my life, because there are condoms that are so thin they feel like skin."

"Are you speaking from experience?" Lamar asked as he stared at her from under lowered lids.

"Yes, I am," she said confidently. "I've slept with two men and there was never a time when either of them did not use a

448

condom. Having unprotected sex is not up for debate with me. The only time I'll agree to not using one is when I'm married."

"So, you're not against marriage."

"No. I've never said I was. It's just that I don't believe I'm ready for it."

"What would make you ready?"

Nydia replayed Lamar's question over and over in her mind, and had come up with a few excuses but they appeared inane even to her way of thinking. She couldn't blame lack of employment or a permanent home, because she was going to become an inn-keeper and live in a centuries-old historic mansion in New Orleans's Garden District. She didn't have children or a man in her life she had to consider.

"Falling in love with a man who would make me want to share my life with him."

"What about children?"

"What about them?" she asked.

"Do you want children?"

"Of course. I love kids."

"If that's the case, then you should make some man very, very happy."

Nydia smiled. "I'd hope I would."

She did not tell Lamar that he was in the running as a potential husband. Her mother had told her a long time ago that whenever she agreed to date a man she should think of him as a potential husband with the ability to take care of his family, and if not, then stop seeing him. Her mother's warning went out the window when she met Danny. He'd get part-time jobs waiting tables or as a deliveryman but nothing that would lead to a salary where he could live on his own. If she had a short checklist of three prerequisites for a man with whom she wanted to spend her future, then Lamar had at least two. She decided to reserve judgment on the last one.

The music changed, becoming more upbeat, which led to couples getting up and dancing in an area of the courtyard where a portable dance floor had been set up. Hannah and St. John were the first on the floor as they executed the steps they learned during their summer dance lessons.

Lamar leaned closer to Nydia when the DJ announced he was going to spin tunes for those who wanted something slower. "Please come and dance with me."

The Flamingos' "I Only Have Eyes for You" was one of his all-time romantic favorites. His father had grown up listening to doo-wop, and whenever he played his treasured vinyl disks dating back more than a half century, the house was filled with incredible harmonies. Lamar and his sister would laugh and giggle whenever their parents danced together while singing along with the tunes that were popular when they were dating.

Nydia extended her hand, placing her palm on his as he eased her to stand. Her mention that she was still recovering from surgery for a ruptured appendix was never far from his mind. Lamar led her to the dance floor and pulled her gently against his body until they were fused from chest to thigh.

Dancing with Nydia was akin to making love with her. He was able to hold her, inhale her natural feminine scent mingling with her perfume, enjoy the silken feel of her skin, and bury his face in her fragrant hair. The days she came to his house to cook with Kendra tested his so-called iron will. Whenever she stood next to him he made certain not to let their bodies touch because it would elicit erotic notions of what he wanted to share with her.

When meeting her for the first time his reaction to Nydia had been purely physical; however, over time his feelings had changed. He still wanted to sleep with her, yet that was no longer as important as getting to know who she was and what she wanted. Sex was something he could get from the woman he hadn't slept with since meeting Nydia, but he did not want it to be the foundation of the relationship he hoped to share with her.

Lamar knew he was in denial when he told himself he wasn't falling in love with Nydia because he felt as if he was being unfaithful to Valerie. As a flight attendant his late wife had talked about the possibility of losing her life during a plane crash, and had exacted a promise from him that if she did die that he would not remarry until their daughter turned eighteen.

Now that he looked back, he did not want to believe he continued to hold onto a promise he'd made to a dead woman when the very woman he wanted to share his life was in his arms. He knew the age of eighteen was important to Valerie because both her adopted parents had passed away a year after she graduated high school, and it was then she'd found herself orphaned once again.

Lamar glanced over Nydia's head to see every married couple up on the dance floor dancing to the hauntingly romantic love song. The first line of the song resonated with him, because the first time he saw Nydia and their eyes met, he only had eyes for her.

When he allowed Kendra to spend the summer vacation with his sister and mother in Baton Rouge, he'd undergone a period of separation anxiety because it was the first time they'd been apart since he'd become a widower. His initial apprehension eased when he asked whether she wanted to come back to New Orleans with him, and she said wanted to stay until it was time for the new school year. It had been a wakeup call that his daughter was not only growing up but becoming more independent. She had other interests, and there would come a time when he wouldn't be the only man in her life. Kendra staying with Evie and her daughters would allow him to spend time with Nydia and to determine where their relationship would lead.

Lamar planned to call Ramona and ask her to pack a bag with enough clothes for Kendra to last a week. All students at her school wore uniforms, which eliminated deciding what to wear every day.

He pressed his mouth to Nydia's ear. "I'm going to take a few days off next week, and if you can take a break from your work I'd like you to come with me for a few side trips beyond the city."

Leaning back, Nydia smiled up at him. "I'd like to see Cajun country."

"That's not a day trip, which means we'll have to make arrangements to stay overnight."

"What's the matter, *mijo*? Are you afraid if we share a bed I'll take advantage of you?"

Lamar winked at her. "Not if I take advantage of you first."

She returned his wink with one of her own. "We'll just have to wait and see, won't we?"

Pulling her closer, he dropped a kiss on her hair, and then spun her around and around until she admitted he was making her dizzy. What Nydia didn't know was that he was dizzy and a little crazy since she had come into his life, and he couldn't wait for the time when they went from friends to lovers.

CHAPTER 19

Nydia tapped a key on the laptop and forwarded the payroll data for her last account. She'd spent most of the day doing payroll for the three restaurants, and now that she had completed the task, the owners of the restaurants only had to print out and sign paychecks. She had also electronically filed the tax forms for the third quarter, which kept various tax bureaus from issuing penalties.

While recuperating from surgery, she'd enlisted her father to drive her to each of the restaurants, where she spent hours training the owners to submit the information on their employees' work hours on their computers, which eliminated the need for her to retrieve the data in person. They'd installed time clocks that tracked the cumulative number of work hours, which they forwarded to Nydia at the end of each payroll period. Rolling her head from side to side, she attempted to relieve the stiffness in her shoulders from sitting in the same position for hours.

Her cell phone rang and she picked it up, smiling. *"Hola."*

It had been two days since she'd last spoken to Lamar. After the Toussaint gathering she had returned to the hotel with Jasmine and Cameron. She'd thrown herself into her work to keep her mind off the man who unknowingly had her thinking of him when she didn't want to; he had invaded her sleep, and she experienced erotic dreams that left her shaken from sensations reminding her why she was born female. Nydia lost count of the number of times she'd picked up her cell to call him and invite him to spend the night with her, but in the end threw herself into her work.

"Hello to you, too," Lamar crooned, singsong. "Am I interrupting something?"

"No. In fact I just finished working and planned on ordering room service, and then turning in early to watch a movie."

"Would you like to eat out?"

Nydia smiled. Lamar was giving her the opening she wanted. "I'm too wound up to be a good dining partner. I need to stay in and relax. But I wouldn't be opposed if you'd come and eat with me."

There was a pregnant pause before Lamar said, "Do you still want to order room service, or should I bring something?"

"I'll order, Lamar. What do you want?"

"Surprise me." His velvety laugh caressed her ear.

"You may regret saying that."

"No, *mijo.* I never regret anything I say. You should know that by now."

"You're right about that. What's on your calendar for tomorrow?"

"Chillin'," she drawled.

Lamar laughed again. "How long do you plan to chill?"

"At least two days."

"I'm taking the rest of the week off, so I'm available if you want to visit Cajun country."

Nydia swiveled on her chair and stared at the rain sluicing down the windows. It had begun raining earlier that morning and was predicted to continue for the rest of the week. "I don't want to go out in the rain."

"What's the matter, brown sugar? Are you afraid of melting?"

"Yes. I'm a Leo, a cat, and we don't like water."

"What do you suggest we do?"

"Come and hang out with me and I'm certain we can come up with a few things

457

to do to keep us occupied."

There came another pause. "If I come and stay with you, you know what it means?"

"I know exactly what it means, Lamar."

"If that's the case, give me time to pack a bag and pick up a few things before I come over. Meanwhile, wait about thirty minutes before you order room service."

"What can you eat?" Nydia asked him.

"Everything but sushi. I'm allergic to raw fish."

"Okay. I'll see you later."

"Luego, mi amor."

Nydia ended the call. Lamar calling her his love lingered with her as she walked into the bathroom to shower. She knew inviting him to live with her in the suite for the next two days would definitely be a turning point in their relationship. Her attempt to hide her feelings for Lamar behind witty and what she deemed skillful repartee had failed miserably. She was in love with the single father, wanted to marry him and become the mother Kendra had lost. She knew she could never replace the girl's mother, and she wouldn't pretend to. Nydia wanted Kendra to trust her enough to confide in her, and together they would navigate the bumpy road from adolescence to adulthood.

Nydia opened the door to Lamar's knock, her smile telling him silently that she was glad to see him. A mass of damp curls framing her face had replaced the sleek hairstyle. She stepped aside, and he walked into the suite and set his overnight bag on the floor. His hands circled her waist as he lifted her effortlessly off her feet.

It had only been two days since he last saw her, but it felt as if it had been twenty-two or even longer. He still could not believe how much she had become a part of his life so that he wanted and needed to see her every day. He loved listening to the timbre of her voice, which was a sultry contralto. He also loved her catlike eyes with pinpoints of shimmering green and gold he found mesmerizing. And since meeting Nydia he had come to curse his eidetic memory, because he was able to recall everything about her down to the tiny beauty mark on her left shoulder.

He inhaled the light floral scent on her bare skin when he buried his face against the column of her neck. "I've missed you so much."

Nydia tightened her hold on his neck. "It's

only been two days since we last saw each other," she whispered in his ear.

"It wouldn't have been two days if I'd asked to come over Sunday night."

"And I would've said no because I had work to do and didn't need any distractions."

He set her on her feet. "I'm a distraction?"

Nydia cradled his face between her hands. "You would've been, because I needed to do payroll for my accounts."

Lamar kissed the end of her nose. "I stand corrected. There's nothing worse than working and not getting paid."

Walking over to the chair in the entryway, Lamar sat and unlaced his favored Doc Martens. Nydia was right about the weather. A tropical depression had stalled over the Gulf with the prediction of rain for several days. He had looked forward to touring Cajun country with Nydia; however, the weather had conspired against them. Spending time with her in her hotel suite definitely had its advantages, because it would give him the opportunity to determine whether he wanted to ask her to marry him. It was no longer about whether they were sexually compatible but whether they were like-minded and their personalities well suited to each other.

His concern whether his daughter would accept Nydia was without merit; she talked incessantly about how much she liked her and how much she enjoyed their cooking lessons.

Lamar unzipped the bag and removed a bottle each of red and white wine and a corkscrew. "I didn't know what you ordered, so I decided to bring both."

Nydia took the bottles from his out-stretched hands and placed them on the table she had set with place settings for two. She smiled at Lamar over her shoulder. "I ordered ahi tuna tartare, sushi, and sashimi."

Lamar's eyes grew wide. "I told you —"

"I got you good!" Nydia said, cutting him off. "I know you're allergic to raw fish, so I ordered roast herb chicken, smothered cabbage, sweet potatoes, and cornbread."

"That sounds delicious and . . . ." His words trailed off with a knock on the door. "I'll get it." Lamar opened the door, and a waiter pushed a cart with covered dishes into the suite. He stood off to the side while the young man placed the dishes on the dining area table.

"Please ring the kitchen when you're finished, and I'll come back and pick up everything."

Lamar nodded and slipped him a bill. "Thank you." Waiting until the man left and closing the door behind him, he turned and smiled at Nydia. She appeared so young and fresh with her bare face, tank top, drawstring cotton pants, and sock-covered feet. "I'm going to go and wash my hands."

Nydia stood at the table, waiting for Lamar to return from the bathroom. When he walked in carrying a bag, the enormity of what they would share hit her like a punch to the nose. It definitely was a wakeup call as to the turn her life had taken. She was going to share a bed and her body with a man who'd come into her life like a rising fog that cloaked her in a protective cocoon from which she had nothing to fear. He'd become her protector, her knight in shining armor, and he was so different from any other man she'd met or known.

She'd discovered him to be as candid as she was — something she admired because she never had to guess what he was thinking. He was loyal to his daughter and his business partners and always cognizant of their feelings and opinions. She had checked off two of her prerequisites: he liked women and was solvent. The remaining one was their sexual compatibility. A secret smile parted her lips when she realized she wouldn't have to wait too much longer to determine whether she could check off the last one.

Sex was important for Nydia, even though she did not think of the lack of it as the ultimate deal breaker. She knew she could continue to see Lamar without sleeping with him. She'd known some couples who had satisfying relationships where sex wasn't a paramount factor. Love and respect for each other was. Her mother had confessed that it had taken nearly two months of marriage before she learned to enjoy making love with her husband. Unlike her mother, Nydia would not come to Lamar a virgin, but a woman who knew her body and how to use it to bring herself and her partner ultimate physical satisfaction.

Her eyes caressed his tall, toned body in a black long-sleeved tee and matching jeans. "Which wine do you want?"

He neared the table and picked up the corkscrew. "The choice is yours."

"White."

Lamar reached for the bottle. "White it is."

Dinner had become a leisurely affair when Nydia had dimmed the lights in the living area and tuned a radio to a station featuring cool jazz. She kept him entertained with stories about her relatives in Puerto Rico and on the mainland. She revealed that her brother Joaquin was gay; he and his husband lived in Nebraska and had adopted two boys who'd spent most of their lives in foster homes.

"Good for him. Unfortunately there are too many children in foster care who need a forever home."

Nydia gave him a direct stare. "Would you ever consider adopting a child?"

"I would if I was a single father."

"How about if you were married?" she asked.

A dark eyebrow lifted slightly as Lamar stared at the food on his plate. "That would depend on my wife." His head popped up. "We both would have to agree; otherwise it wouldn't work." It was his turn to give Nydia a long, penetrating stare. "Would you ever think of adopting a child?"

"Of course. My mother wants more grand-children, and she has been nagging me to get married and have a baby, but I told her that I didn't have to be married to have a baby."

"Should I assume that didn't go over too well with her?"

464

"Not at all. My mother is old school when it comes to family. She believes in dating, marriage, and babies, in that order."

Leaning back in his chair, Lamar stared at something over Nydia's head. "What would she say about you dating a widower with a daughter?"

"There isn't anything she could say, because she's never told me who I could or couldn't date. Even though she wasn't too fond of my ex, she never interfered."

"Are you saying she would approve of you marrying me?"

Nydia stared at him. Nothing moved on her, not even her eyes. "Are you asking me to marry you?" The query was barely above a whisper.

Whenever he thought about Nydia the notion of marrying her was always a possibility, but now that he'd asked her he couldn't retract it. "I was just asking hypothetically."

Nydia shook her head. "There is nothing hypothetical about a marriage proposal. Either it is or it's not."

Lamar knew she had backed him into the proverbial corner. He knew he was falling in love with Nydia, but there were other factors to consider. Did she like him enough to even consider becoming his wife? Even though she and Kendra appeared fond of

465

each other, that didn't translate into her being willing to assume the responsibility of being a mother to her.

"Yes."

The single word had come from a place Lamar did not know existed. He'd never acted on impulse, but there was something about Nydia that made him do and say things that were so foreign that he had begun to doubt himself.

Nydia closed her eyes for several seconds, and when she opened them they were a deep, verdant green. "You propose marriage when we've only kissed a few times."

"That's because whenever I want to kiss you, you push me away."

"That's only when Kendra is present. What message would that send, Lamar?"

He nodded. "You're right about that."

"I know I'm right."

"Do you always have to have the last word?"

"No, but —"

Lamar held up a hand, stopping her comeback. "Can you please be quiet for a few minutes while I explain myself?" He smiled when she nodded. "I've fought my feelings for you from the very moment I saw you get out of Jasmine's minivan."

"And that's when you had your hard-on."

Lamar shook his head in exasperation. "I thought you weren't going to say anything." Nydia pantomimed zipping her lips. "I know now that I shouldn't have told you about that, but that's neither here or there. I like everything about you, Nydia. You make me feel things I've never experienced with any other woman I've known. You're always so positive despite whatever craziness that's going on in your life. You make me laugh when I don't feel like laughing, and you make it so easy for me to love you."

"You love me," Nydia said in a quiet voice.

Lamar smiled. "Yes."

She blinked once. "Why?"

His smile vanished. "You have to ask me why when I just told you why I want and need you in my life?"

"What about Kendra? Have you asked her whether she's willing to share you with me?"

"No."

"Then I suggest you do, Lamar, because I refuse to become a part of a situation with a girl who resents me because she believes I've taken her father from her."

"I'll talk to her, but only after we announce our engagement."

"There's not going to be an engagement until we work through a few things. First of all, this is happening much too quickly for

467

me, and I'm still trying to sort out my feelings for you."

"Do you think you could love me?" Lamar asked Nydia.

"Don't be silly. Of course. Do you realize we still haven't dated in the traditional sense, and you're already talking about engagements and marriage?"

Lamar knew she was right. He did not know why he was rushing her into something she wasn't quite ready for, but he did not want to lose her. "I'm sorry, *mi amor*. I have no right to put pressure on you, especially after what you've gone through with that jackass of an ex-boyfriend. I'll give you all of the time you need to either accept or reject my proposal."

Pushing back her chair, Nydia stood up and came around the table. She sat on Lamar's lap and buried her face against his neck. "You have to know that I'm falling in love with you, otherwise I wouldn't continue to see you. I haven't had the best luck when it comes to men, so if it doesn't work out with us, then I'm done with them." He listened intently as Nydia told him about the man who'd taken her innocence and then deceived her by not telling her he was married. His mouth covered hers in a healing kiss while silently communicating that she could trust him, that he would love and protect her.

Her eyes were shimmering with unshed tears, and Lamar's heart turned over when he recognized vulnerability in Nydia for the first time. The beautiful, smart, and sassy woman had just shown him another side of her bubbly personality. And as much as he wanted to make love to her he didn't want to take advantage of her when she was like this.

"Go to bed, sweets. I'll take care of all of this."

Moisture separated her long lashes. "Are you sure?"

He kissed her nose. "Of course I'm sure. Go and relax and I'll be in soon."

Nydia slipped off his lap and walked in the direction of the bedroom, his eyes following her retreat. He cursed the men who'd used her for their own selfish motives. Her college instructor and her singer-boyfriend were predators who'd exploited her generosity, and Lamar prayed it would not become a replay with him.

There were times when he wished that he'd remarried, if only to give Kendra a mother, because he did not understand all that went into raising a daughter. Nydia had run down the list that she'd been told when dating, and it had frightened him because of the dangers a young girl could be faced with when dealing with a boy. The year he turned thirteen his father had given him "the talk" about the changes going on in his body and about not having sex until he felt he was mature enough to deal with the consequences if he did get a girl pregnant. Becoming a baby daddy was never a thought for Lamar, and he always made certain to use a condom whenever he slept with a woman. There were several classmates who'd short-circuited their chances of attending college when a girl told them she was pregnant with their baby.

He recalled the time he'd broached the subject of where babies came from with Kendra, as he cleared the table, and she stopped him abruptly when she said the health teacher at school had talked to the girls about their bodies. He'd felt awkward talking to her about sex, and it was the one of the many times he wished Valerie had been alive to have the conversation with her.

Lamar recorked the bottle of wine and stored it in the mini fridge. He'd noticed Nydia's eyelids drooping before she finished her first glass, and knew it was either the wine or she hadn't gotten enough sleep.

Picking up the house phone, he dialed the

kitchen and requested someone retrieve the dishes he'd placed on the floor outside the door. Unlike some hotels, the staff at the Louis LaSalle had established and maintained a reputation for impeccable lodgings and fine dining.

Lamar glanced at the clock on the microwave. It wasn't quite eight-thirty and too early for him to go to bed, so he decided to sit up and watch television. He found a channel featuring a *Black-ish* marathon and settled down to watch the entertaining sitcom about a successful black father with a beautiful wife and five children living in an upscale California neighborhood.

After six episodes he turned off the television, retrieved his toiletry bag from the carry-on, and went into the bathroom to shower and brush his teeth. It was after eleven when he finally slipped into bed next to Nydia. She stirred slightly but did not wake up. Sharing a bed with her seemed as natural to Lamar as breathing. He lay there trying to imagine being married to her, and somehow the images weren't as clear as he'd hoped they would be. She wanted time and he would give her time, because now that she was going to live in New Orleans, distance was no longer an impediment to their relationship.

■ ■ ■ ■

Nydia opened her eyes and saw a sliver of daylight coming through the partially closed bedroom drapes. She shifted and turned over to find Lamar smiling at her. She couldn't believe she'd slept so soundly that she hadn't known he was in bed with her.

"Good morning."

He winked at her. "I was waiting for you to wake up."

She stared up at him through her lashes, unable to make out his expression in the diffused light. "How long have you been awake?"

"Long enough to know that you snore."

She clapped a hand over her mouth. "I'm sorry."

"Don't apologize, sweets. I've done my share of snoring whenever I drink too much. Where are you going?" he asked when she sat up.

"I have to go to the bathroom."

Lamar also sat up. "I'll join you."

Her jaw dropped. "You will not. You can use the other bathroom near the entryway."

He folded muscular arms under his head, bringing her gaze to linger on his toned upper body. The sheet had slipped down over

472

his midsection, and she could make out the outline of his penis under the fabric. It was obvious that Lamar slept in the nude.

"Don't take too long," he called after her when she made her way into the en suite bath.

Nydia managed to complete her morning ablution in record time, and when she returned to the bedroom she discovered Lamar wasn't there. The numbers on the bedside table read 6:50. If she were still working for Wakefield Hamilton, she would have been showered and dressed and ready to walk out the door to take the express bus down to the Financial District. She had given up riding the subway to lower Manhattan after several groping incidents. She was in bed when Lamar returned in a pair of boxers. He got in next to her and brushed a light kiss over her lips. She tasted mint on his mouth, indicating he, too, had brushed his teeth.

"Did you sleep well?" she asked.

Lamar pulled her into his arms. "Like a baby."

Nydia smiled. "Me, too."

He sniffed her hair. "What kind of shampoo do you use? Your hair always smells wonderful."

"It's made with argan oil."

She shifted to get into a more comfortable position, her arm resting over his flat belly. Nydia closed her eyes. Lying beside Lamar seemed the most natural thing to do, and she wondered what it was about this man that had changed her inside and out. She'd become a romance novel heroine and he her hero. Not only had she fallen in like with him, but she was also in love with Lamar Pierce. At that moment she experienced a sense of peace she never had before with a man with whom she had been involved, and in that instant if he had asked her to marry him again, she would have said yes.

"What are you thinking, sweets?"

"How happy I feel right now. I don't think you realize how good you are to and for me."

Lamar twirled a curl of her hair around his finger as his chest rose and fell in an even rhythm. He smiled. "I feel the same way. I'm glad I waited for someone like you to come into my life."

"Has it been lonely for you, Lamar?"

"No. If it had been, then I would've looked for a woman to fill the void. I have Kendra and my work, and that is enough to keep me occupied during my waking hours."

"How about at night? Didn't you get tired

of sleeping alone?"

"I did in the beginning. Being married to a flight attendant meant there were nights when I did go to bed alone, so I suppose I was used to it."

"Do you miss her?"

Lamar's fingers stilled. "There are times when I do, but I know I'll never forget Valerie completely because whenever I look at Kendra I'm reminded of her."

Nydia shifted again, straddled his body. "I don't want you to forget her. And what I don't want is for you to ever compare me to her, because I'll always come in second. Valerie was your first love and the mother of your firstborn, and that is something I'll never be able to duplicate." She gasped when Lamar flipped her over onto her back.

"I don't want to talk about Valerie."

She met his eyes. "What do you want to talk about?"

The corners of his strong mouth tilted as he smiled. "Us. Just you and me, and what I want to do with you."

Her smile matched his. "And what's that?"

"This."

Nydia did not have time to react when his hands searched up the top of her pajama set and with a minimum of effort pulled it over her head. She hadn't realized she was holding her breath when he lowered his head and brushed his mouth over hers. She exhaled an audible breath as he placed tender kisses at the corners of her mouth before increasing the pressure until her lips parted.

Nydia felt as if she had been drugged by Lamar's clean, masculine scent, the warmth of his lips tasting hers, and the invisible pull that made her aware of him as a man; a man she not only wanted but also needed. His hands sent tremors racing along her nerve endings when he moved lower to suckle her breasts. Desire, hot and uncontrollable, held her captive as passion thrummed between her thighs. She was ready for Lamar, ready for whatever the future held for them.

Lamar forced himself to go slowly as he opened the drawer of the bedside table on his side of the bed and removed a condom. He placed it on the pillow next to Nydia's head. He prayed there would come a time when he would be able to make love to her without a barrier of latex between them, but that would only happen if they were married.

He relieved her of the floral pajama pants, tossing them at the foot of the bed. He couldn't pull his gaze away from the perfection of her petite nude body. Lamar touched the faint scar on her right side with his forefinger. "I'll try not to hurt you," he whispered.

Lamar did not realize his hands were shaking until he attempted to put on the latex sheath over his erection. He wanted their first time together to be not only extraordinary but also memorable, and he wanted to be the last man in her life.

Cradling her face between his hands, he searched her face in the light coming into the bedroom. "I want you to know that I want you now and I'll want you tomorrow and every day thereafter, Nydia. And I want you to understand that this is not about sex."

She closed her eyes and nodded. "I know that."

His rapacious mouth charted a sensual path from her lips to her warm throat, shoulders, and breasts. He suckled her until she arched off the bed, and then continued his downward journey with the intent of tasting every inch of her silken skin. "Don't, baby," he cautioned when she reached for his head. Lamar felt her muscles tensing when his breath swept over the soft down covering her mound before he kissed her inner thighs.

■ ■ ■ ■

Nydia was filled with foreign sensations that frightened her. The pulsing between her legs increased, growing stronger, hotter, until she feared climaxing as Lamar's tongue was doing things to her body she had never experienced before. It was her first time for a man to put his face between her thighs, and she knew from the runaway beating of her heart and the soft flutters that were giving way to contractions that she was on the verge of having an orgasm.

"Lamar!" His name, torn from the back of her throat, faded as her head thrashed back and forth on the pillow. He wasn't making love but torturing her.

He moved up her body and positioned himself between her trembling legs. They moaned in unison when he entered her, her arms going around his neck. She caught her breath as her tight flesh closed around his erection, bringing another rush of moisture from her body. Nydia held onto Lamar as if her life depended on him. Tears of joy leaked from beneath her tightly closed eyes as orgasms overlapped one another, each stronger than the last. It was as if she had waited all of her life for a man to bring her

478

to heights of ecstasy where she was able to hold nothing back and surrender all of herself to him. She'd just returned from her last free-fall when Lamar buried his face against the pillow cradling her head and groaned out his own triumphant release.

He lay on her body, she feeling his strong heartbeats against her breasts. Nydia reached up and cradled his head, holding it as if she feared losing him. "I love you," she whispered.

It was a full minute before Lamar replied to the entreaty torn from the depths of her heart. "I know, because I love you, too."

She moaned in protest when he pulled out and left the bed. Turning on her side, she stared at the window as rain came down sideways. It was as if she was no different than her fellow innkeepers. They'd succumbed to the charm of New Orleans and its men. Hannah had St. John, Tonya had Gage, and Jasmine had Cameron. Now it was her turn with Lamar.

If anyone had predicted she would fall in love with a man with a child she would not have believed them. And when she married Lamar not only would she get a husband, but also a daughter. She was smiling when he returned and got into bed with her and pulled her buttocks to his groin.

"When can I expect seconds?" he whispered into her hair.

"I'll let you know. After this, I know I have to go back on the pill." Those were the last words she said before falling into a sleep reserved for sated lovers, unaware it would be a while before Lamar joined her.

Chapter 20

Nydia and Lamar had spent two full days together in her suite, loving and making love, when she got a call from Tonya. "What's up, Mrs. Toussaint?"

"Nydia, you need to come to the inn. There's been a smoke condition, and Hannah is about to lose it."

She went completely still. "What happened?"

"The guys installing the elevator claim a cable caught fire and they put it out, but there's smoke all over the house. I didn't call Jasmine because in her condition she needs to stay calm, and the smoke might harm her and the baby."

"I'm on my way." Nydia saw Lamar staring at her. "There was a fire at the DuPont House and —"

"I'll take you," he said, interrupting her.

"Thank you, *mijo.*"

Lamar reached for his keys while she

picked up her purse. "There's no need to thank me, sweets," he said, taking her hand.

Nydia tried to remain calm as they left the CBD for the Garden District. She knew how anxious Hannah was to open the inn, and the fire would set the grand opening back once again. First it had been getting various permits approved, then she had to contend with the main gate protecting the property malfunctioning. The last was to get approval for installing the elevator to accommodate the elderly and handicapped, and now Hannah had to deal with smoke after all the walls had been painted and repapered.

The rain that had been falling for three days appeared to be tapering off, and as Lamar maneuvered through the gates leading to the historic residence, pinpoints of sunlight pierced the dark clouds.

Nydia was out of the Volvo within seconds of Lamar turning off the engine. She ignored the vehicles of workmen lining the curving driveway as she raced into the house. The smell of acrid smoke burned her lungs and nostrils when she entered the great room. Hannah was sitting on a chair with her face buried in her hands. Tonya rested an arm over her shoulders in an attempt to comfort her. Several men in coveralls were standing off to the side of the elevator.

Lamar, only a few steps behind her, walked over to peer into the elevator shaft. "Who's in charge here?"

A short, slightly built man wearing a white bandana on his head stepped forward. "I'm the foreman."

"Are you aware that you used the wrong cables?"

The foreman's face darkened noticeably. "You're mistaken!"

Lamar slowly shook his head. "No, I'm not. I've inspected my share of elevators in commercial and residential buildings to see at a glance that the cables you installed aren't up to code. You're lucky it caught fire now and not when guests were here. But I doubt that because it never would've passed the city's inspection."

The foreman narrowed his eyes. "Who the hell are you?"

"You don't need to know who I am," Lamar said in a quiet voice. "But you'll find out when I tell the city inspector about how you tried to cut costs by installing cables that won't support the weight of an empty elevator car."

Hannah stood up, her hands curling into tight fists. "I want you to take your men and get off my property before I do something that may get me arrested. You're going to hear from me, because I'm going to sue the hell out of you. And when I'm finished you won't be able to get another job in the entire state."

"I'll leave, but not before you pay me for the work I've done."

Nydia shared a glance with Tonya. She knew it was going to escalate into something nasty when she saw Hannah glare at the man. "Get the fuck out of my house before I go upstairs and get my daddy's gun and blow your ass away."

"I'm not going to stand here and let some bitch talk to me like that."

"Coño!" Nydia shouted. "She just did, buddy. So I suggest you listen to her and get to stepping."

Tonya slowly shook her head. "I think he's begging for me to carve his ass up like a Thanksgiving turkey."

"What's up with these uppity bitches," he snarled, as spittle formed at the corners of his mouth.

In a move too quick for the hand to follow, Lamar grabbed the man's throat and shook him like a Rottweiler would a Chihuahua. "That's the last time you're going to call someone a bitch before I kick your

484

ass, *little man.*"

The two other workmen grabbed their boss's shirt. "Let's go. You can settle this later."

Lamar tightened his grip on the man's windpipe as gurgling sounds came from his gaping mouth. "Now apologize to these ladies."

"I'm sorry," he whispered, clawing at Lamar's hand on his throat.

Lamar shook him again. "Louder, so they can hear you."

"I'm sorry."

He released him and wiped his hand on the denim fabric covering his thigh. "That's better." He flashed a cold smile that did not reach his light brown eyes. "Gentlemen, please pack up your stuff and leave the premises. Meanwhile I'm going to call the superintendent of the city's building department and have him send out a few inspectors to check over your work. Don't be surprised if he suspends or even revokes your license. And in case you're not aware of it, Mrs. McNair is a lawyer, so make certain your business insurance is paid up, or you'll be out of business for good."

Nydia put her hands to her mouth in a prayerful gesture as she watched the three men pack up their tools and walk out. She hadn't realized how fast her heart was beating when she saw Lamar grab the man's throat. She remembered his stating that "nerds can get gangsta, too." And he'd just shown her another side of his easygoing personality that she didn't need to see, and didn't want to see again.

He walked over to Hannah and held her while she cried on his shoulder. He stroked her hair. "It's going to be all right. I know a company that can clean up the smoke damage, and once that's done I'll have my elevator people replace the cables so it can pass inspection."

Tonya came over to Nydia. "Let's go outside so Hannah can have time to pull herself together."

Nydia sat on the porch on a rocker next to Tonya. "That was some shit!"

Tonya ran a hand over her short, curly hair. "I thought it was really going to get ratchet when Lamar choked that cocky little bastard. He really fooled me, because I'd expect that type of behavior from Gage."

Nydia gave her friend a questioning look. "I can't believe you said Gage. He seems so laid back."

"Yeah, right," Tonya drawled. She recounted the time Gage went off on his ex-wife because she was abusing drugs along with his son. "If I hadn't been there, I'm certain he would've broken her arms. He was just that enraged."

Nydia remembered Tonya telling her that Wesley had been in and out of rehab for substance addiction that began in his teens, but after she married his father and he came to live with them he'd turned his life around.

"Lamar may look benign but he's anything but that." She told Tonya everything about Danny's setup engagement and Lamar coming up to New York to help her out of what had been a situation that could have ruined her reputation once her face was splashed across the pages of several tabloids.

Tonya's dimples winked at her when she smiled. "So he's a knight in shining armor rescuing damsels in distress."

She nodded. "Hannah claims he's a romance novel hero."

"I agree with her." Tonya quickly sobered. "I should call St. John and let him know his wife is going to need his support until we're able to clear up this mess."

"How long do you think it'll be before the inn will be up and running?" Nydia asked.

"I don't know. It's going to take a while before they're able to remove the soot off the walls and ceilings, and Hannah's going to have someone come in again to clean the rugs and carpets. The last time we discussed a launch date, she said she wanted to open between Thanksgiving and the end of the year. That would give us time to gear up for Mardi Gras and the tourist season."

Nydia thought about the number of times Hannah had mentioned when she wanted to open the inn for business. "She has to stop projecting an opening date, and just let everything unfold in its own time."

"You tell her that, Nydia. It seems as if you're the only one who can get through to her because you give it to her straight, no chaser, while Jasmine and I try to sugarcoat everything."

Nydia's fingers tightened around the arms of the rocker as she stared at the rows of oak trees lining the path up to the house. "I'll wait until she's not so emotional, because right now she's wound so tight she may have a breakdown. I can't believe she talked about getting her father's gun and shooting that little shit. And were you serious about cutting him?"

Tonya chuckled. "If he'd come at me I would have filleted him like a flounder."

Throwing back her head, Nydia laughed so hard tears filled her eyes. "I guess he was lucky, because he didn't know who he was messing with."

A slight frown appeared between Tonya's eyes. "I bit my tongue and took enough crap from my first husband to last a lifetime and I'll be damned if I'm going to let a man degrade me now that I'm in my fifties. Gage knows that and he walks a real fine line when it comes to making decisions with me."

Nydia sat straight. "I thought you and Gage have a wonderful marriage."

"We do, but as with most married couples we don't agree on everything. Wesley has been talking about moving out and getting his own place."

"What's wrong with that, Tonya? He's how old?"

"Twenty-one. It's not his age, but that I feel he's not ready to live on his own without supervision. Okay, he's working part-time for the restaurant, taking classes at one of the local colleges, and he's also in drug counseling. But he hasn't been clean and sober a year, and that's too soon for him to live on his own. I should know because my brother was an addict."

"You want him to stay and Gage wants him to go?"

Tonya shook her head. "Not exactly. Gage claims he can trust Wesley not to start abusing again, but I told him all Wesley has to do is run into some old junkie friends and he's bound to go down that rabbit hole." She closed her eyes. "When I agreed to marry Gage I never thought I'd become a stepmother — especially to a twenty-year-old." She opened her eyes and met Nydia's. "Don't get me wrong. I've come to love that boy as much as I do Samara, because he was given a raw deal from the day he was born. His mother was a whore turning tricks for her habit, and he never knew what it was to grow up in a so-called normal home. When he asked me what he should call me I told him I'd like Mom or Mother. You have no idea what it is to watch a young man break down and cry because he claimed he never really had a mother. But I suppose it will be different with you and Lamar because his daughter is still young."

"What are you talking about, Tonya?"

"Come on, Nydia. It's as plain as the nose on your face that you and Lamar are sleeping together, and it's just a matter of time before that man is going to put a ring on your finger. I may be new to New Orleans, but I'm privy to a lot of gossip whenever I cater a party. I become the help and the hosts believe I'm invisible when they talk about anyone and everything of note. And judging from your dance performance with Lamar at Cameron and Jasmine's wedding, you two have been the topic of several conversations."

Nydia knew it was time to trust her friend enough to tell her everything about her relationship with Lamar, including his wanting to marry her. "Everything has been moving so quickly that I'm barely able to think straight."

"Have you said yes?"

"No. I need more time to ask myself if this is really what I want. Although I've fallen in love with Lamar, right now I can't see myself as his wife. Then there's the question of his daughter. Even though we get along well together I don't know if she'll resent me sharing her father with her."

"There's only one way to find out," Tonya said. "Once you agree to marry Lamar, then he's going to have to sit down with his daughter and talk to her about it. She may or may not like it, but you have to remember Lamar is the adult and he's responsible for her and not the other way around."

Nydia shook her head. "I'm not ready for a situation where I'm going to deal with a surly and perhaps even a confrontational teenage girl, because I can assure you there will be enough fireworks in that house to light up the Fourth of July."

"It has nothing to do with becoming a stepmother, Nydia. Samara went through phases when she and I butted heads constantly until she realized her mama wasn't going to roll over and let her do whatever she wanted. Young girls have mood swings because of hormones and whatever the hell else we go through as adolescents, but somehow we've grown up to emerge from that temporary crazy cocoon as beautiful, colorful butterflies."

Nydia knew Tonya was right when she recalled some of the scenes she'd had with her mother. The back-and-forth and give-and-take until Isabel shut her down completely. Those were the times when Nydia swore if she had a daughter she would listen to her without pulling rank.

"So, what have you and Gage decided about Wesley's future?"

"We're still discussing it. I'd like for him to complete at least one or two years of counseling and earn his associate's degree before moving out on his own. He can still work for the restaurant, but I'm going to insist he take random drug tests."

"How long will he have to adhere to that?"

"For as long as I say. Don't forget, Nydia, the café and supper club are my investments, while Gage owns a portion of Chez Toussaints. And if Wesley's going to work for me, then he has to abide by my rules."

Nydia saw Tonya in a whole new light. She wasn't only a professional chef but a businesswoman looking after her investments. "I want to be tough like you by the time I'm fifty."

Tonya waved a hand. "Don't play yourself, Nydia. I wish I'd been as tough as you in my twenties. I know you had your ups and downs with your ex, but you stood your ground, because you never supported him financially. Do you realize how many women are taking care of grown-ass men nowadays? They pay their car notes, child support, buy expensive clothes and sneakers, feed their hungry asses, and still get disrespected when he goes out and cheats on them." She shook her head. "Don't sell yourself short, baby girl. You're beautiful and smart, and I don't know Lamar Pierce that well, but from what I've heard about him and just saw inside, you have yourself a winner."

"He claims nerds can get gangsta, too."

"Gangsta. The man went straight Rambo on that workman." She took her cell phone out of the pocket of her tunic. "I'm going to call St. John and let him know what happened here."

Tonya had just completed the call when Lamar joined them on the porch.

Nydia stood up. "Where's Hannah?"

Lamar rested a hand on her shoulder. "She's opening windows to let in some air. I offered to help her, but she said she needed time alone to think."

Tonya pushed off the rocker. "That's what she doesn't need. I called St. John and he says he's on his way over here."

Reaching into the pocket of his jeans, Lamar handed Nydia the fob to his SUV. "You can take the car back to the hotel."

"How will you get back?"

"I'm waiting for an inspector from the building department to come over. I'll get a ride with him."

"I can take Nydia back, Lamar," Tonya volunteered.

He turned to look at Tonya. "Are you sure?"

She smiled. "Of course I'm sure, Black Panther," she crooned, crossing her arms over her chest.

Nydia watched Lamar's expression change from bewilderment to understanding when he realized Tonya was referring to the blockbuster fantasy/science fiction movie. He inclined his head and crossed his chest. "I always wanted to be the dark knight

Batman, but I will accept being compared to the king of Wakanda."

She returned his fob. "I'll see you later." Going on tiptoe, she kissed his cheek. "Thank you for taking care of my friend."

He winked at her. "No problem. I'm just sorry I had to act crazy."

"Better you act crazy, Lamar," Tonya said, "or he was going to have to deal with three crazy women on his ass."

Lamar chuckled under his breath. "I'd rather a chokehold any day to ladies wielding knives and guns."

Tonya patted Lamar's back. "Thanks again, and here's hoping I'll see you again under more favorable conditions."

He nodded. "You bet."

Nydia rode back to the CBD with Tonya, neither attempting to break the comfortable silence. She was lost in her own thoughts about what she could expect if she married Lamar, but her imagination wouldn't allow her to think that far ahead. Unlike Jasmine, she wasn't pregnant and therefore her future wasn't inexorably entwined with Lamar's.

She had time, three months, because legally she was still a resident of New York. It wouldn't be until the end of January that the lease on the East Harlem walk-up would expire, and Tonya had given written notice that she did not intend to renew it.

A satisfied smile softened her mouth as she pressed her head against the headrest. Three months was long enough to know whether she would be ready to commit to a future with Lamar and Kendra.

Nydia turned over onto her back when she registered the light tapping on the door of the bedroom where she'd slept as a child. After spending two months in New Orleans she'd returned to New York in time to celebrate Thanksgiving with her family. Lamar had driven her to the airport, and they'd sat in his vehicle holding hands without talking until it was time for her to check in for her flight. There was no need for conversation. He knew she was going home and they wouldn't see each other again until the day before Christmas Eve.

If she had vacillated about whether she was in love with Lamar, her doubts were dashed the first time he shared her bed. He'd become her lover, hero, and knight in shining armor, and someone whom she wanted to spend her life with. Lamar hadn't mentioned marriage again and she was loath to broach the subject. She'd asked for time, and it was apparent he was willing to give it to her.

"Come in."

The door opened, and Isabel entered the room. She'd changed into one of her husband's shirts she had paired with a pair of sweatpants. "Were you sleeping?"

Nydia sat up and turned on the bedside lamp. "No. I was just waiting for my food to digest. I definitely ate too much." She patted the mattress beside her. "Come sit with me."

Isabel gave her daughter a critical stare as she folded her body next to her on the bed. "Are you certain it's only food?"

Shifting on her side, Nydia looked at her mother. "What do you mean?"

"You've been walking around with a long face ever since you came back. Even your grandmother mentioned it to me." Isabel patted her daughter's head. "Talk to me, *mija.*"

"There's nothing to talk about, Mami."

"Yes, there is, Nydia. I've been your mother long enough to know when something is bothering you. If you don't want to tell me, then I won't pry, but I'm here if you want to talk about it."

Nydia closed her eyes and sucked in a lungful of breath before slowly letting it out. "I'm in love with a man, and I don't know what to do about it."

Isabel pressed a kiss to her forehead. "Now, why is that such a bad thing? When I fell in love with your father I went around with a grin on my face."

"That's true, but the difference is Papi was never married and he didn't have kids."

"It's the man who came up to New York to stage an intervention for you." Isabel's question came out like a statement.

Nydia knew it was time for her to pour out her heart to her mother. She told her everything, from Lamar taking off his wedding band, her giving his daughter cooking lessons, to Lamar admitting that he had fallen in love and wanted to marry her.

"Do you want to marry him?" Isabel questioned.

"Yes, *pero* . . ."

"But what, *mija*? Why the hesitation?"

"Lamar and I are very careful not to exhibit any indication that we've been sleeping together whenever we're around his daughter, but it's just the way Kendra stares at me that makes me uncomfortable."

"Uncomfortable how?"

Nydia shook her head. "I can't explain it. All before she was like a giggly little girl whenever I'd come over. Now, she's more subdued and standoffish. I believe she resents seeing me with her father."

"Have you said anything to Lamar?"

"No."

"Why not, Nydia?"

"Because I'm not going to come between the man and his daughter. If he mentions it to me, then I'll say something."

"What if he doesn't?"

"Then nothing will change between us. They're coming for Christmas, and hopefully you'll be able to get a better read on her, because right now I can't be objective."

Isabel swept back curls that had fallen over her daughter's forehead. "Something tells me you're going to marry this man and make his daughter a wonderful mother."

Nydia narrowed her eyes. "Stop with the *bruja*, Mami." Over the years her mother denied having the ability of second sight, but whenever Isabella Medina-Santiago predicted something, it usually came true.

"Okay. Now that you're going to be here until the new year, what do you plan to do?"

"I'm going to start packing up my things, because Tonya's daughter found an apartment in Atlanta close to her future in-laws and she plans to move in February first."

"Are you going to be responsible for the cost of shipping everything to Georgia?"

"No. Tonya has already made arrangements with a moving company. They're going to come in and pack up everything New Year's Eve and take it to a storage unit until Samara is ready to take possession of the new apartment."

Isabel smiled. "I guess I'll get to have you a little longer before you leave for New Orleans again."

Nydia nodded. "You'll have to put up with me for the next six weeks, and then I'm leaving to become an official New Orleanian." She'd reserved a flight departing New York January sixth.

"Even though I'm happy that you're going into business for yourself, I'm going to miss seeing you."

"Don't get melodramatic on me, Mami. There's always FaceTime, so we can see and talk to each other anytime we want."

"I know, but it's not the same." Isabel slipped off the bed. "I'm going to my bedroom to relax. You're not the only one who ate too much."

"*Luego,* Mami."

She waited until her mother left the room, closing the door behind her before Nydia adjusted the pillows cradling her shoulders. Staring up at the design on the plastered ceiling, she thought about the last time she and Lamar made love with each other. It was different from their prior encounters because neither wanted to yield, to give in to the pleasurable sensations taking them beyond themselves. Both held back until the last possible moment, and then climaxed simultaneously in a shattering ecstasy where she'd struggled to breathe. It was only after her respiration returned to a normal rate that Nydia realized they were each bidding the other goodbye until they met again.

Reaching out, she turned off the lamp and closed her eyes. Within minutes she welcomed sleep, which had been more of a stranger than friend since she boarded the jet in Kenner for her flight to New York City.

CHAPTER 21

Nydia parked in the airport lot and walked to the terminal to wait for Lamar's flight to arrive. Because he was flying in on Christmas Eve, she'd recommended that he fly into Charlotte, North Carolina, and then take a connecting flight to the Westchester County Airport. The airport was only seven miles from White Plains and her brother's home.

She'd managed to keep busy since her return to New York. She assisted her mother in the salon and filled in for the receptionist and shampooer when they took their breaks.

Milagros called to ask her whether she wanted to join her bowling, but she had turned her down because she'd left her ball and shoes in New Orleans. She enjoyed bowling with the retirees, and she didn't mind the hostile stares when the victorious Innkeepers posed for photographs holding their first-place trophy. Nydia ignored the snide remarks whenever someone called her a ringer. She wanted to tell them she wasn't a ringer but someone for whom bowling had been a serious hobby.

She had set up a loop with Jasmine, Hannah, and Tonya for them to send and reply to texts. Hannah claimed she was through stressing over when the inn would open for business, and St. John had surprised her with plans to take her to an all-inclusive resort in the Caribbean for two weeks during his college's winter break.

Nydia's cell phone rang. She took it out of her pocket, a slight frown creasing her forehead when she saw Cameron's name on the display. Her heartbeat quickened and she prayed something hadn't happened to Jasmine. She still had another month before her baby was due.

"Is something wrong with Jasmine?"

"Yes and no."

"What do you mean yes and no, Cameron!" Nydia noticed people staring at her when she realized she was yelling, and she moved away from those waiting in baggage claim.

"Jasmine's in the hospital."

"What!"

"The baby's okay, but Jasmine dropped a box on her foot and broke a bone. Right now she's in a soft cast. She's going to be laid up for four to six weeks."

"What was she doing lifting boxes?"

"Please don't get me started, Nydia. I've talked to her until I'm blue in the face about doing too much in her condition. She's been complaining of backaches, and now the doctor tells me she's spotting. That's why the doctor wanted to keep her for a few days to make certain she'll be okay. And . . ."

"And what, Cameron?"

"I did something to her that I swore I'd never do."

Nydia went completely still, her hand tightening around the phone until it left an imprint on her palm. "What the hell did you do to her?"

"I yelled at her. I grew up with my father yelling at my mother, and I swore I'd never do it to my wife. Now she refuses to talk to me."

Nydia blew out a sigh of relief. Her first thought was he had hit her. "Give her a few days to get over it. I'll send her a text tomorrow asking how she's doing."

"I'd appreciate it if you would. I hate to dump on you, but I know she listens to you."

She wanted to tell her friend's husband that Tonya had said the same thing about her and Hannah. However, it was Lamar who reassured Hannah that his company would oversee the installation of the elevator once the fire marshal completed and submitted his report to the city.

"Don't worry about dumping, Cameron. Jasmine, Tonya, Hannah, and I are joined at the hip when it comes to friendship. If her foot is in a cast there's not much she can do. I'll be back in New Orleans the first week in January, so if she needs anything I'll take care of it."

"Thank you, Nydia."

"No problem, Cameron. Have a very merry Christmas and happy New Year."

"Same to you and your family."

As soon as she ended the call a text came up on her cell. A smile lit up her eyes. Lamar's flight had landed, and he would meet her at baggage claim.

It was another twenty minutes before she spied him and Kendra wearing winter jackets. Winter had come to the northeast with freezing temperatures and lightly falling snow, most of which disappeared before city officials had to authorize the use of snowplows. Meteorologists were predicting a white Christmas, much to the delight of her nieces and nephews, who were planning to sled down the hill fronting the house.

She waved to get Lamar's attention, and

he returned her greeting with a wide grin. Her smile faded when he came closer. Kendra ran ahead of him. Nydia noticed his face was thinner, and she wondered if he had been sleeping well or if he was working too hard. They spoke to each other on average of three times a week and usually before he retired for bed. He had a lot more to tell her than she did him because most of her days were uneventful. His firm had won another bid not far from the state's capital to restore a long-abandoned antebellum mansion purchased by a tech guru who wanted to use the property as a family winter retreat.

Kendra, shouldering a backpack, appeared to have grown in the few weeks since Nydia last saw her. She hugged the girl. "Welcome to New York."

Kendra smiled, and Nydia noticed the brackets on her braces were red and green in keeping with the holiday colors. "Thank you, Miss Nydia. It's snowing a little bit."

"I know. That's why I told your father to make certain you pack winter clothes, especially gloves, scarves, and hats."

"I think he packed too much," Kendra whispered in Nydia's ear when Lamar was only a few feet away.

Lamar set down his carry-on and leaned over to press a kiss to Nydia's check. "How's it going, snow bunny?"

He thought she looked absolutely adorable in a white ski cap and matching jacket. Lamar had deliberately kept himself busy so he wouldn't have to think about the woman with whom he had fallen in love. He had spent many sleepless nights fantasizing about having her in bed beside him. When he finally did fall asleep, it was time for him to get up and go to work. And work he did, seemingly around the clock to the point of exhaustion, dividing his time between overseeing the restoration of the plantation north of Baton Rouge, around the town of St. Francisville, to checking on the installation of the elevator at Hannah McNair's DuPont Inn.

Lamar had deceived himself when he'd believed he had gotten used to sleeping alone, but once he got into bed with Nydia, the moment he gazed upon her naked body, and the instant he joined their bodies he realized he'd lied to himself. And since making love with her Lamar knew he wanted to spend the rest of his life with Nydia Santiago.

"I'm good," Nydia said, smiling. "I'm going to take Kendra with me to get the car while you wait for your luggage. I'll be parked at curbside."

"Okay."

Turning, Lamar went back to the baggage claim area. He smiled. His last trip to New York had been to run interference for Nydia when she'd been hounded by the media, and now he was back this time to celebrate Christmas with her family. And he'd promised himself not to think of anything that remotely hinted of work for the next ten days.

His luggage was among the last to appear, and he grasped the handles and wheeled them out of the terminal. A blast of frigid air and lightly falling snow greeted him as he glanced up and down at the cars and taxis idling at curbside.

"Daddy, we're here."

Lamar turned and spied Kendra waving at him through the side window of a dark gray BMW. The hatch opened as he neared the SUV with New York plates and a NYPD placard in the windshield. He stored the bags in the rear, closed the hatch, and came around the vehicle to sit in the second row of seats behind his daughter.

"The heat feels good."

Nydia glanced at him over her shoulder. "It's not as cold as it is raw."

Lamar rubbed his hands together as he stared out the side window. "How far is your brother's house from here?"

Signaling, Nydia pulled out into traffic. "He lives less than fifteen minutes from here."

"How old are your nieces?" Kendra asked.

"Eleven and thirteen," Nydia answered. "I also have two nephews. They're only nine and ten."

"What are your nieces' names?" Kendra continued with her questioning.

"Noemi and Brianna, but everyone calls them Mimi and Bree."

Lamar closed his eyes, slumping down in the leather seat, and listened to the interchange between his daughter and Nydia. It was as if time and distance hadn't been a factor during their separation. Kendra wanted to know everything she could about Nydia's nieces before meeting them. There was no doubt that Kendra was her mother's child, because not only did she look like her, but both found it easy to make friends, while he had been more cautious when opening up to strangers. He never was able to bond with his college roommates the way it had been with Ignacio Gonzalez.

"Daddy, we're here!"

He opened his eyes, unaware he'd fallen asleep during the short ride from the airport to Nydia's brother's home. She had parked the SUV behind a row of vehicles lining a driveway with enough room for at least six cars parked side by side. The gleaming white, three-story colonial was set on a hill with magnificent views of the Hudson River. A towering pine tree on the front lawn was decorated with tiny winking white lights that reminded him of twinkling stars in the night sky. The property was decorated for the season with large wreaths adorning the double doors painted vibrant royal blue, and tiny electric candles were in the many windows.

Lamar got out and had unloaded the bags from the cargo area when Nydia reached for Kendra's hot-pink luggage with four wheels.

"I've got this," she said, smiling.

Lamar returned her smile. "It's heavy. My daughter thought she was staying a month, so she tried to pack everything she could find and would fit into that bag."

Nydia gave him the "you've got to be kidding" look. "It does have wheels."

"Don't say I didn't warn you," he mumbled under his breath.

The front door opened, and a tall, slender man wearing a black pullover and jeans came out of the house. He knew the man was one of Nydia's brothers because they claimed the same hazel eye color.

"Why are you guys out here in the cold?" He extended his hand to Lamar. "I'm Nelson, one of Nydia's brothers. Welcome to the Santiago insane asylum."

Lamar shook his hand. "Lamar Pierce. And this is my daughter, Kendra. Thank you for opening your home for two more patients."

Nelson laughed. "You're going to fit in quite nicely with this crazy family."

"He understands and speaks Spanish," Nydia said, "so you better warn the others when they decide to talk about him."

Nelson took the bag from Nydia. "*Coño,* what's in here?" he asked in Spanish. "I'm sorry," he apologized, when he saw Kendra staring up at him. "Does she understand Spanish, too?" he questioned.

Nydia patted her brother's shoulder. "Not yet. But I plan to teach her."

"Let's go inside before Sandra reads me the riot act for entertaining our guests outside in the cold. By the way, Lamar, do you drink coquito?"

"But, of course. It wouldn't be a Puerto Rican Christmas without it."

Nelson flashed a wide grin. *"Wepa!"*

Lamar followed Nelson, Kendra, and Nydia into the house and exhaled an inaudible sigh when the scent of burning wood and pine wafted to his nostrils. A chandelier and a real eight-foot Norwegian spruce covered with countless small red bows were the focal points in the great room. Fires roaring in twin fireplaces behind decorative screens added warmth to the space. The sound of Christmas music flowed from hidden speakers.

Lamar smiled when he saw the number of gaily wrapped gifts piled high on the brocade tree skirt. He knew his gifts were also under the tree. This year was the first time he'd done all of his Christmas shopping online after he'd asked Nydia if he could ship his purchases to her home to avoid packing them in his luggage. She'd given him her parents' address because her father would be home to accept the deliveries.

"Your home is stunning."

Nelson smiled. "I can't take credit for anything inside of this monstrosity. That honor goes to my wife."

"Did someone mention wife?"

Lamar stared at the slender woman with a complexion reminiscent of polished mahogany. She appeared doll-like with her tiny round face, delicate features, and short natural hairstyle. She wore a bibbed apron stamped with *Happy Wife, Happy Life.* Her hand went to her throat.

"Please don't tell me Don Lemon is standing in my —"

"He's not Don Lemon," Nydia said, cutting her off. "Sandra, I'd like you to meet Lamar Pierce and his daughter, Kendra. The only thing Lamar and Don Lemon have in common is that they're both from Louisiana. Lamar, this is my sister, Sandra Ruiz-Santiago."

Sandra approached Lamar, went on tiptoe, and hugged him. "It's a pleasure to meet you and your beautiful daughter. I know you must be exhausted from traveling, so Nydia will show you to your rooms, where you can change out of those heavy clothes. Kendra will be in the room with Mimi and Bree, and Nydia, you can put Lamar in one of the rooms in the attic."

Nelson hoisted the pink bag. "I suppose this one is yours, Kendra?" She nodded. "Come with me and I'll show you where you'll sleep. I say 'sleep' because most of the time the kids hang out in the basement."

Lamar followed Nydia up the circular staircase to the third story while marveling at the beauty of the grand residence. He took note of the beautiful rugs lining the landings and framed photographs on the walls. If Sandra was responsible for decorating her home, then she had exquisite taste.

"How many bedrooms are in this house?" he asked Nydia.

"There are six on the second floor, two additional ones in the attic, and the mother-in-law suite on the first floor bringing the total number to nine. Nelson had turned the attic into a playhouse for Mimi and Bree until Sandra suggested he convert them into bedrooms so they would have enough sleeping space for whenever they have the entire family over. The girls cried and pouted until he called the contractor back and had him finish the basement, where everyone hangs out twenty-four seven. There's a bathroom with a shower, vanity, and commode across the hall that you won't have to share with anyone. There's also a closet in your bedroom if you need to hang up anything."

They stopped at the top landing, and Lamar walked into the bedroom decorated in the cool colors of blue and white with floor-to-ceiling windows facing the river. A queen-size bleached pine sleigh bed positioned under an eave beckoned him to come and sleep away the hours. A bedside table with a hurricane-inspired table lamp, matching chest-on-chest and double dresser, and a rocker with plump seat and back cushions made it the perfect bedroom for guests.

Lamar set his luggage near the door. "Where are you sleeping?"

"I'm sharing a bedroom with Abuelita. As her only granddaughter she expects me to look after her."

"If you don't mind my asking, but how old is your grandmother?"

"She's a very spry and spirited eighty-five-year old. You'll have to forgive her if she begins to interrogate you about me, because she's very protective of her *nieta.*"

"Does she know about the stunt your ex fabricated?"

Nydia shook her head. "I doubt it because if she did then she definitely would've mentioned it to me. I'm going downstairs to finish helping out in the kitchen. We're going to have more folks than usual because Sandra invited a few of her coworkers to join us."

Lamar wanted to know more about Nydia's family but knew if he was going to spend a week with them, then he would

515

become more than acquainted. "Thank you, sweets."

"What for, Lamar?"

He stopped himself before taking her in his arms and kissing her with all of the passion he had repressed since seeing her again. Lamar had believed not seeing her for nearly a month was enough time for him to ask himself if it was love, loneliness, or infatuation that he felt for her, and in the end he knew it was love. For the second time in his life he had fallen in love with a woman and wanted her to share not only his life but also his future.

"For allowing me to share a little piece of your life." Lamar went completely still when he saw Nydia's eyes filled with tears. "What's the matter, sweets?"

Her eyelids fluttered as she struggled not to cry. "You don't have a little piece," she said after a pregnant silence. "You have all of it."

Turning on her heel, she ran down the staircase as if someone were chasing her, leaving Lamar staring at the spot where she had been. He stood there, unable to move for a few minutes, as he attempted to bring his tortured thoughts into focus. He loved her and there was no doubt Nydia loved him, but he wondered if it was too soon to ask her again to become his wife. They'd met for the first time in August and now it was December, and in the span of four months he'd fallen in love and made love with a woman whose mere presence had tied him into emotional knots. Sighing heavily, Lamar felt calmer than he had in a very long time. He would wait until January, when Nydia would come back to New Orleans to make it her permanent home. Closing the bedroom door, he opened the Pullman and unpacked.

Nydia opened the freezer and removed a plastic container. "How many *pasteles* do you want me to take out?"

Sandra, stirring *sofrito, alcaparrado,* salt, pepper, and cumin in a half cup of heated *achiote* oil in a five-quart pot with a wooden spoon, glanced over her shoulder. "There's going to be sixteen of us, so take out at least thirty."

"Make it forty," Isabel suggested. "Luis and Nelson never stop at two."

Nydia placed twenty parchment-wrapped vegetable and meat tamales in a large pot, covered them with cold water, and tossed in a handful of salt. She turned on the stovetop and adjusted the heat to a gentle boil.

Before driving to the airport to pick up

Lamar and Kendra, she had set the table in the dining room with place settings for sixteen. Earlier that morning her brothers had added the extra leaves in the table, doubling its length. They had also set up warmers on the buffet server where everyone would serve themselves before sitting down at the table. The menu included roast pork shoulder, *pasteles, tostones* or twice-fried green plantains with mojito, a garlic dipping sauce, *arroz con gandules,* and sliced avocado. The beverage choices were lemonade and hot chocolate for the children, and coquito and white sangria for the adults.

"Nydia, could you please go and get your *prometido* and have him taste my coquito to see if it's better than his friend's *abuela*'s."

She turned and stared at her grandmother. Although she'd informed everyone she was inviting a friend and his daughter to join them for the holiday week, her grandmother, in particular, wanted to know everything about Lamar. Nydia had told Ana Medina how he'd become fluent in Spanish and that he was fond of Puerto Rican food.

"Please don't tell me you're competing with his friend's grandmother, Abuelita," she said under her breath.

"I heard that, *nieta,*" Ana spat out. "Now,

go and get your *prometido.*"

Nydia lowered the flame under the pot. "He's not my fiancé, Abuelita."

"What else can he be if you invite him to meet your family?"

"He's my *novio.*"

Ana waved a heavily veined hand. "Boyfriend or fiancé is the same to me."

Isabel closed her eyes and shook her head. "Nydia, please go and get Lamar before my mother starts arguing with you and ruins everything," she whispered in her ear.

Ana's bright green eyes narrowed behind the lenses of her round, wire-rimmed glasses. "What did you say, Isabella?"

"I just told Nydia to go and get her boyfriend so he can sample your coquito."

Nydia left the kitchen and walked through a narrow hallway leading to the rear of the house and down a staircase to the basement. Recessed LED lights were dimmed, but there was enough illumination to see Lamar, Kendra, her brothers, and their children sprawled on reclining leather chairs and sofas watching Jim Carrey's *How the Grinch Stole Christmas.*

A long table was filled with bowls of snacks including popcorn, potato chips, guacamole, salsa, buffalo wings, deviled eggs, and pita chips to offset hunger until everyone sat down to dinner, which was scheduled to begin in an hour.

She leaned over the back of his chair. "My grandmother wants to see you upstairs," she whispered in Lamar's ear.

Nydia lingered over his head, savoring the scent of the body wash from his recent shower. He'd changed from his sweater and cords into a pair of charcoal-gray flannel slacks and a crisp white untucked shirt. Nodding, he stood and took her hand as they made their way to the staircase.

"Why does she want to see me?" he asked.

"You'll see," she said mysteriously.

Nydia watched Lamar's reaction when he took a sip of the Puerto Rican eggnog made with fresh grated coconut rather than the canned sweetened cream of coconut. "What do you think?"

"Este es el mejor coquito que he tenido."

Smiling, Ana Medina clapped her hands as a network of fine lines fanned out around her eyes. "I told you he would like it. He says it's the best he's ever had, and that means he likes it better than his friend's *abuela*'s. I got the recipe from my mother, which has been passed down through generations. She always used fresh grated coconut instead of the canned coconut milk."

Lamar nodded. "That really makes the

difference."

Isabel opened the oven to test the doneness of a pork shoulder large enough to feed at least twenty. "Lamar, Nydia told us how you learned Spanish, but I must say you speak it better than my grandchildren."

Lamar met Nydia's eyes. "Kids nowadays don't know the importance of being bilingual until they're older."

"How often do you speak it?" Isabel continued with her questioning.

"Not often enough," Lamar said as he took another sip of eggnog. "I must confess I only get to speak it with Nydia."

Sandra added rice to the smoked neck bones in the pot and stirred them until they were coated with oil. "You'll be able to speak it every day once Nydia moves to New Orleans."

Lamar gave each woman a lingering stare. "That's something I'm really looking forward to."

"So she is your *prometida*."

"Abuelita, Lamar is not my fiancé," Nydia said, as pinpoints of heat dotted her face.

Sandra turned to glare at her. "If he's not your fiancé, then what is he? Even when you were dating that bum Danny, you never invited him over for Christmas dinner."

Nydia took a deep breath to slow down

the runaway beating of her heart. "Lamar is my *novio*."

"What's going on here?" asked a deep male voice. Luis Santiago had come into the kitchen without making a sound. "Don't everyone answer at the same time."

Nydia felt with the appearance of her father she had been suddenly rescued from a pride of ravenous lionesses. She walked over to her father and looped her arm through his. "Papi, Lamar was just giving Abuelita his approval on her coquito."

Luis gave her a questioning look. "That's not what I overheard." He rested a hand on Lamar's shoulder. "You don't have to answer anything until I read you your Miranda warning, because these ladies will interrogate the hell out of you without legal counsel."

Sandra continued stirring the pot with the rice and pigeon peas. "I'm a lawyer, so I'll act as his counsel."

Luis, a retired NYPD sergeant, stroked the mustache and goatee he'd grown since losing most of his hair at fifty. "I'm sorry, Sandra, I'm not, going to let you and these other *chismosas* put my daughter's boyfriend on the spot just because you want to get into their business."

Isabel crossed her arms over the front of

her apron. "We're not gossipers, and I'm sorry if you believe we're putting you on the spot, Lamar, but it's obvious you're much more than a boyfriend to my daughter. I'm saying all of this because you know what she's been through, and I just need to make certain you'll be able to protect her."

Nydia hadn't realized she was holding her breath until she felt the constriction in her chest depriving her of oxygen that made her feel slightly lightheaded. She met Lamar's eyes, wondering what was going on behind the golden orbs.

"Not only do I love Nydia," he said in a quiet voice, "but I'm also in love with her. That means you will never have to concern yourself about whether I will protect her." That said, he turned and walked out of the kitchen.

"I like that young man," Luis said, smiling.

Nydia bit her lower lip, as she chose her words carefully. "Mami, Sandra, and Abuelita, I hope you will stop with your inquisition. When I asked Lamar to celebrate Christmas with us, I didn't think you would make him feel uncomfortable."

Sandra made a sucking sound with her tongue and teeth. "He was hardly uncomfortable. Didn't you see him give us the death stare? And I promise not to ask him any more questions."

Nydia nodded. "What about you, Mami?"

Isabel rolled her eye upward. "Okay. My lips are sealed."

"Abuelita?"

Ana narrowed the green eyes she'd passed along to her daughter and grandchildren. "The only thing I'm going to ask him is when is he going to marry my only grand-daughter?"

"Abuelita!"

"Don't Abuelita me, Nydia! You're thirty-three, practically a *vieja,* so it's time you think about getting married."

"She's not an old woman," Sandra and Isabel said in unison.

Nydia affected a graceful curtsey. "Thank you very much."

The chiming of the doorbell echoed throughout the first story. "That must be my coworkers," Sandra said. She covered the pot, wiped her hands on a dishcloth, and left the kitchen to answer the door.

CHAPTER 22

Lamar lay in bed, his head resting on folded arms, listening to the sound of sleet lashing the attic windows. He felt as if he'd become an unofficial member of Nydia's family when the younger children were instructed by their parents to call him Uncle Lamar, a title with which he was more than familiar.

And he had to admit that the Santiago women were exceptional cooks. The presentation of the dishes lining two buffet servers were worthy of a photo shoot, and proved to be as delicious as appealing. Every morsel he'd put into his mouth exceeded his expectation, and he'd watched Kendra as she concentrated on eating rather than talking to Noemi or Brianna, both of whom had kept up a nonstop dialogue with each other. Conversations were conducted in English and in Spanish for the benefit of Kendra and Joaquin's husband, who did not speak the language but had hired a Spanish-speaking nanny to care for their young sons.

Lamar sat up and flicked on the bedside lamp when he heard a soft tapping on the bedroom door. "Come in." A smile tilted the corners of his mouth when Nydia poked her head through the slight opening.

"May I come in?"

"Of course you can."

Lamar knew it was going to test whatever self-control he had left when interacting with Nydia for them to spend a week under the same roof and not be able to make love. She tiptoed across the carpet in a onesie and got into bed with him.

"Did you enjoy Christmas with the Santiagos?"

Draping an arm over Nydia's shoulders, he pulled her closer. "Yes, I did, and I hope I'll be invited back next year."

Nydia glanced up at him. "Of course you'll be invited back. Everyone loves you."

"Does that include you, too?"

"Of course it does, Lamar. You claim to have a photographic memory, yet you forget that I've told you that I love you."

He shook his head. "No, you haven't."

"I told you I love you the day we made love for the first time."

"I think I remember now. Tell me again,

sweets, because I never tire of hearing you say it."

Nydia rested her hand over the one on her shoulder. "I love you, Lamar Pierce."

Lamar buried his face in her hair, smiling when the floral-scented curls tickled his nose. "And I love you, Nydia Santiago."

Nydia closed her eyes. She loved him and he loved her, and she knew sometime in the future their relationship needed to be resolved. Would they continue as lovers or commit to a future as husband and wife? And although she was more than fond of Kendra, Nydia's intuition told her the girl did not want her to replace her mother.

She'd noticed the curious stares when Lamar's presents were distributed and the tags read: "From Lamar, Nydia, and Kendra." He'd given her parents tickets to next season's New York Mets and Yankees subway series; her nephews were the recipients of gift cards to Game Stop; her nieces were overcome with emotion when they received gift cards for an Apple product of their choice. Sandra and Nelson also received gift cards, while her grandmother was overjoyed with her luxurious cashmere throw. Joaquin and his husband were the recipients of an exquisite Baccarat vase. Kendra was nearly overcome with emotion when she opened a small box and discovered a pair of diamond stud earrings from Nydia and Lamar. The young girl had been dropping hints that she wanted her ears pierced like many of the girls, and a few boys, at her school.

Nydia had noticed everyone watching her and Lamar when they exchanged gifts. He'd given her a pink gold Cartier bracelet, and she'd presented him with a Montblanc Meisterstück fountain pen, engraved with "L. A. Pierce." "I think you spent too much money on gifts for everyone," she said.

"Are you monitoring my checkbook?"

Nydia went completely still for several seconds before relaxing again. She heard the censure in Lamar's voice. "No, I'm not. But —"

"But nothing," he said, cutting her off. "Valerie and I never argued about money, and I don't intend to begin with you."

Nydia recoiled as if struck across the face. She did not want to believe he'd compared her to his dead wife. She pulled out of his embrace, swung her legs over the side of the bed, and stood. "You're right, Lamar. Please forgive me for broaching the topic. Good night."

Lamar scrambled out of the bed, his hand going around her upper arm and stopping her retreat. "I didn't mean it like that."

"You said it, Lamar, so you had to mean it. I want you to remember one thing about me, and that is I'm not your wife, and more importantly, I don't want to compete with your dead wife. Now please let me go so both of us can get some sleep."

"Nydia, don't."

"Now, Lamar."

She left the bedroom, closing the door behind her, and went down to the first story and into the mother-in-law suite she shared with her grandmother. Nydia stared at the sleeping figure in one of the twin beds, hoping she hadn't detected her absence. She lay atop the blankets on her bed and closed her eyes. Lamar had accused her of scrutinizing his expenditures when nothing could be further from the truth. When he'd asked if he could mail his purchases to her, and she'd suggested he send them to her parents' home, Nydia was totally unaware of what he'd bought for whom because her mother had unpacked the boxes and placed the gift-wrapped packages under the tree.

When he'd mentioned he was going to give his daughter a pair of earrings, Nydia had no inkling he would indicate they would be from the both of them. Meanwhile, she'd given most family members gift cards in varying amounts for them to buy whatever they wanted, and those to whom she'd given gifts, she'd ordered them online. It had been more than seven years since she'd counted herself among the frantic shoppers waiting for stores to open to get what merchants were advertising as the best sales of the season. It stopped when a woman threatened to punch her because she'd picked up an item she wanted. Nydia gave the woman the jacket, walked out of the store, and vowed never to step foot in a store again to shop for Christmas gifts. So far, she had managed not to break that vow.

She did not want to argue with Lamar, yet she was realistic enough to know they could not agree on everything. Turning over on her side, she stared at the glow of the electric candle in the window through the fabric of the off-white, silk-lined drapes. The sound of her grandmother's light snores and the rhythmic tapping of sleet against the windows had a calming effect that lulled her asleep.

"Why the long face, Nydia? You have a gorgeous and generous boyfriend, and in a few weeks you'll be moving to a new city where you'll become a partner in your own business. So why do you look as if you've lost your best friend?"

Nydia peered over the rim of her mug at her sister-in-law. She'd gotten up early to brew a cup of coffee and was surprised to find Sandra in the kitchen cutting up ingredients for omelets. "I had words with Lamar last night. It was after midnight, so it was this morning."

Sandra gave her a sidelong glance. "What kind of words?"

She told Sandra what she'd said to Lamar and his response. "He's wrong, Sandra, if he believes I'm watching his finances."

Sandra's hands stilled. "I don't believe you, Nydia. You dated a man for years who couldn't afford to take you across the George Washington Bridge to New Jersey, and now you're involved with one who you can introduce to your family and is willing to spend his money —"

"Maybe he just wanted to impress everyone," Nydia interrupted.

"Cut the bullshit!" Sandra said angrily. "The man stood in my kitchen less than twelve hours ago and confessed in front your mother, father, and grandmother that he loves you and will always protect you, so there's no need for him to try and impress us. I'd dated your knuckleheaded brother almost a year and although he claimed he

531

adored me he would not say that he loved me until he asked me to marry him. And you've known Lamar for how long?"

"Four months."

Sandra shook her head. "You're like so many girls I grew up with. They were so used to dating no-account men that when a good one came along they didn't know how to relate to them. You have to take off your accountant's hat and focus on your own bottom line and not concern yourself with Lamar's. He's a grown-ass man taking care of his daughter, while running his own company, which means he'll continue doing that even if you decide to break up with him."

"Who said anything about breaking up with him? I have no intention of losing Lamar."

Sandra resumed dicing peppers and onions. "Are you saying if he proposed marriage you'd accept it?"

The query caught Nydia slightly off-guard. "I think it's too soon to talk about marriage proposals."

"I think not, Nydia. The man gives you a bracelet from Cartier's when he probably wanted to give you a ring. And that little circle of pink gold costs a lot more than a lot of engagement rings. I know because one of the partners at my firm gave his wife that same bracelet for their twentieth anniversary. My paralegal went to the Cartier website to look it up, and she nearly fell off her chair when she saw the price tag. I'm not going to tell you how much he paid for it, but be prepared if he does propose marriage and gives you a ring."

Nydia didn't want to talk about proposals or engagement rings. Right now she had to get beyond her questioning Lamar about spending his money. She did not have to wait long before he walked into the kitchen, casually dressed in a white waffle-weave cotton pullover, relaxed jeans, and thick white socks. He smiled and winked at her, indicating he wasn't angry.

"Buenos días." Lamar brushed a light kiss over Nydia's parted lips before he walked over and kissed Sandra's cheek.

Sandra smiled up at him. "Good morning. It looks as if you and your girlfriend are early risers."

Lamar rested a hip against the countertop. "I'm used to getting up early to share breakfast with my daughter, or to inspect a construction site. I can't believe you're cooking again after last night's feast."

Sandra brushed off mushroom caps with

533

a damp paper towel. "Once you become a part of this family you should be prepared to gain at least five pounds or more whenever we get together to celebrate an event. There's always an overabundance of food and good cheer."

"Speaking of cheer, I think I imbibed too much coquito last night."

Nydia nodded. "Abuelita was a little heavy-handed on the rum."

Sandra wiped her hands on the towel tucked under the ties of her apron. "That's because last year everyone complained that she didn't add enough rum. If you guys want to eat now, I can start making breakfast for you."

Nydia took Sandra's hand and steered her around the cooking island to sit on one of the stools. "You've done enough cooking, so I'm going to assume the responsibility of making breakfast. The only thing you'll have to take care of is making eggs."

Lamar stood straight. "Is there anything I can help you with?" He had chided himself for insinuating Valerie into their disagreement because it was something he'd vowed he would never do, and he prayed he would never do it again.

Nydia nodded. "Come with me."

He followed her across the expansive

kitchen to the pantry. The many shelves were stocked with enough food to feed a large family for several months. It was obvious the Santiagos shopped in bulk. His stared at Nydia's back as she opened a refrigerator and took out several packages of bacon, ham steaks, and a sleeve of country sausage meat.

"Can you handle this?" she said, placing them on his outstretched arms. Lamar pretended to be staggering under the weight. Nydia smiled. "That's why I gave you the meat instead of the eggs." Reaching into the fridge, she took out a carton of three dozen eggs and closed the door with her hip.

"Are you really going to cook all of this?" he asked.

"Yes. We'll serve it buffet-style like in hotels. And once it's gone, then that's it. The slow folks will have to get whatever is left."

Lamar moved closer to Nydia, blocking her attempt to reenter the kitchen. "I know it's Christmas Day, but do you have anything planned for today?"

She glanced up at him through her lashes. "What are you thinking?"

"I was hoping we could borrow someone's car and drive to Brooklyn so I can see the old neighborhood."

A smile softened her mouth. "I think that's a good idea. There probably won't be that much traffic. I'll ask Papi or Nelson because they have NYPD placards in their windshields."

"If it's all right with you, then we'll leave after breakfast." Even though he enjoyed Nydia's large and boisterous extended family, he wanted to spend some quality alone time with her, even if it was for only five or six hours.

Nydia signaled and moved over into a lane on the RFK Bridge to an exit in Harlem rather than take the FDR Drive to downtown Brooklyn. When she'd told her father she was going to take Lamar to Brooklyn, he'd told her to take his car, and if she had the time to stop by the brownstone in Harlem to pick up his mail and check to see if the tenants needed anything. He'd been away from home for several days.

"I'm going to stop at my parents' brownstone first, and then swing by my place to pick up my mail."

Lamar stared at her profile. "How long have you been away?"

"Three days. Mami and I went up to

White Plains early to shop and help Sandra cook."

"You never told me that your sister-in-law was a lawyer."

Nydia tapped lightly on the horn when the car in front of her father's Infiniti didn't move once the light changed from red to green. "Sandra has earned a reputation as a brilliant litigator who prepares most of her firm's briefs. She recently negotiated with the senior partners to work from home two days a week, because she wants to spend more time with her daughters. She keeps in touch with the office with conference calls and videoconferencing."

"Where's her office?"

"It's about four blocks from Grand Central Station. She parks in the White Plains commuter lot and takes the Metro North directly into Grand Central."

"That's really convenient. How did she and your brother meet?"

"They met during their sophomore year in college. She was just coming out of a toxic relationship with someone she'd dated for a while, and when Nelson asked her out she wanted nothing to do with him. It wasn't until later that she admitted that he wore her down because he wouldn't take no for an answer."

Nydia thought of her sister-in-a-law as a superwoman because she was pregnant during her first year in law school, delivered Brianna in June, and began her second year without missing a beat, delivered her second child during her third year, graduated number two in her class, and passed the bar on her first attempt.

Lamar rested his left hand on Nydia's knee. "I really like your family."

Nydia's tinkling laugh filled the vehicle's interior. "I think I'll keep them."

"If you don't want them, then I'll ask your parents to adopt me."

Nydia sobered. "You like them and they really like you."

"Your brother Joaquin and his husband invited Kendra and me to visit them in Omaha sometime over the summer."

"So you really did bond with my family." He removed his hand when she gave him a quick glance.

"You didn't know? While the ladies were upstairs cooking, the men were having a bromance."

"I guess that means I'll have to keep you," she teased.

"We're in this together, sweets."

Nydia wanted to tell Lamar now that they were sleeping together she also intended to

538

see where their relationship would take them. "I'm sorry about last night," she said after a comfortable silence. "I don't want you to think I'm ungrateful."

Lamar reached over and massaged the nape of her neck. "I'm the one that should be apologizing for bringing up Valerie."

"I can't pretend that she never existed."

"That's true, but I don't ever want her to come between us, Nydia. Valerie was the first woman I loved enough to want to marry, but when we exchanged vows I never could've imagined that we wouldn't grow old together."

"She may be gone, but you still have a part of her with Kendra."

"That's true," Lamar agreed, "because she's definitely her mother's child in looks and temperament."

"She's a delight. I've really grown very close to her."

"Close enough to assume the responsibility of becoming her mother?"

Nydia's fingers tightened on the steering wheel in a death grip. Her heart was pounding so hard and fast she could hear it in her ears. "What are you asking?" Her voice was barely a whisper.

"I'm asking whether you would consider marrying me. I know we haven't known each other that long and . . ."

"I don't believe you, Lamar."

"What don't you believe?"

"You wait until I'm driving to propose marriage. What happened to going on one knee, or asking my father for his permission for my hand in marriage?"

"I did that already."

Nydia's foot hit the brake, and the car came to a screeching stop, causing other drivers to look at her as they sped past. "Dammit," she swore under her breath.

"Pull over," Lamar ordered. "I'll drive."

Checking her mirrors, she signaled and maneuvered into a bus stop. It took less than a minute for her to exchange seats with Lamar. He adjusted the driver's seat to accommodate his longer legs and pulled out into traffic. "You're going the wrong way," she said when he made a left turn down a one-way street. "My parents live in West Harlem."

"We're going to your place, because we need to talk."

Nydia didn't realize her hands were shaking as she attempted to unlock her apartment door. During the ride across town she'd replayed Lamar's proposal over and over in her head until it had become a litany that made her want to scream. She pushed open the door and walked in, Lamar following. Sitting on the bench seat, she slipped out of her jacket, kicked off her booties, and walked on sock-covered feet to the living room.

She didn't want to believe he'd gone behind her back and asked her father if he could marry her, while she and Lamar had never talked about cementing their futures. Nydia wondered what was there about her that prompted men to assume just because they'd been intimate that she would automatically accept their marriage proposal without her input? She flipped a wall switch, turning on the table lamps in the living room. Boxes labeled with her name were stacked in a far corner.

Lamar bent down to unlace his Doc Martens, leaving them on the mat inside the door, and then took off his jacket. In a moment of madness he'd blurted out that he wanted Nydia to marry him without discussing the idea with her beforehand. He did not know why, but there were instances when his confidence waned and he feared losing her.

He followed Nydia into the living room and stared at her ramrod-straight back as she looked out the window. Closing the distance between them, he rested his hands at her waist. She was still, so still that she could've been a statue. "Please, come and sit so we can talk."

Nydia rounded on him, her eyes giving off green sparks. "Now you want to talk? What happened to you talking to me before you went to my father?" Her eyes filled with unshed tears. "Do you realize you're like Danny? You both blindside me with marriage proposals. The only difference is you discussed it with my father. Danny would've never approached Papi because he knew he didn't like him."

Lamar cradled her face between his palms. He hated seeing Nydia vulnerable and close to tears. Lowering his hands, he swept her up in his arms, carried her into the bedroom, and placed her on the bed, his body following hers down.

Burying his face in her curls, Lamar pressed a kiss to Nydia's scalp. "It was your father who asked me about us, and I was truthful when I told him I was in love with you and wanted to marry you. That's when he gave me his approval, but only with the proviso that I protect you."

"Why didn't we talk about this before?"

"And if I had, what would you've said?"

"I would've told you that it's too soon to talk about getting married. And I also would've asked if you'd discussed it with Kendra. Have you, Lamar?" Nydia asked when he hesitated.

"No," he answered truthfully. "I told you before, I'm not going to allow my daughter to control or monitor my life. She knows that I like you and she appears okay with that."

"That's not enough, Lamar. If I'm going to marry you, then I'll have to step into the role of her mother. It's been only the two of you for the past four years, and she may not like having to share her father."

"I promise to talk to her just before we announce our engagement. Right now I need to know if you will consider becoming my wife sometime in the future."

Nydia moved closer to him. "I'm glad you said in the future. Once I move to New Orleans and we spend more time together you just might change your mind."

"I doubt that, sweets. I knew the first time I laid eyes on you that you were special."

Nydia rubbed her nose against his cheek. "More special than those other women you were —"

Lamar placed his hand over her mouth, stopping her words. "Please don't, Nydia.

Since meeting you I haven't touched or looked at another woman." He removed his hand. "Once I commit I'm all in. Like this," he whispered, pressing a light kiss on the bridge of her nose.

Nydia smiled. "Do you know what I forgot to do?"

Lamar exhaled an inaudible sigh of relief. He had expected Nydia to go off on him. It seemed to her that he'd assumed that she'd jump at the opportunity to share his life because she'd admitted to being in love with him and because of how easily she'd bonded with his daughter.

Thankfully he had been given a reprieve, because they had been able to talk it out, and he knew if or when they did marry and live together, they would be able to discuss their problems without resorting to drama or hysterics.

His eyes caressed her face as if making love to her. "What is it, my love?" He gasped when her hand slipped under his shirt and unbuttoned the waistband on his jeans.

Springing up with the agility of a cat, Nydia straddled him. "I have to show you how much I like my Christmas present, because words would not be enough."

Lamar bit back a smile. "I take it you like your bracelet." He'd wanted to buy her a ring, but he didn't know her ring size, and at the last moment he knew it wasn't something he wanted to give her with her family as an audience. Once she accepted his proposal and ring, he wanted that to be a private moment between just them. "What are you going to do?"

"You'll see," she said, undoing his fly.

Lamar gasped. She released his penis from his boxers and going to her knees, took it into her mouth. He hardened quickly and feared ejaculating in her mouth instead of inside her. Now that she was taking an oral contraceptive he did not have to use a condom, and without the barrier of latex their lovemaking had become even more intense.

"No!" he bellowed. But Nydia did not stop. Lamar anchored his hands under her armpits and extricated her mouth from his erection. He reversed their positions and managed to undress himself and then Nydia in record time.

He was much slower in arousing her, as it was his turn to use his mouth and tongue to bring her to the point of climaxing. Her breath was coming faster as moans slipped past her compressed lips. Lamar hardened again, and both sighed in unison as he eased his erection inside her.

If Lamar had doubted his love for Nydia, he knew now what he felt for her was so good, so real, that he believed he had just entered an alternate universe where fantasy and reality merged and from which he did not want to escape.

As Nydia surrendered all she was and all she had to Lamar, she felt as if she were floating beyond herself. Making love with Lamar had stripped her bare, leaving her naked, vulnerable, and afraid he would break her heart. She loved him just that much.

Since meeting Lamar she had come to realize what true love was, and it had changed her inside and out. She was more patient and willing to listen. At first Nydia attributed it to becoming more mature, that at thirty-three she couldn't continue to conduct herself the way she had even a year ago. So many things had happened to her in a year: she'd been downsized; had gone into business for herself keeping the books for small businesses; had undergone surgery for a life-threatening infection, and she was now legally an innkeeper.

She had also unexpectedly fallen in love with a man she did not want to love because of her past track record of relationships that ended with deceit and disappointment. But somehow Lamar had wound his way under the barriers she had erected to keep men out of her life and bed with his unabashed honesty and the ease with which he was able to apologize and accept blame for his actions.

Nydia wrapped her arms around his back and legs around his hips as she arched to get even closer as the contractions in her vagina grew stronger and stronger until she gave in to the orgasms that held her captive before releasing her until another gripped her, this one even stronger than the last, until she dissolved in an ecstasy that shattered her into a million little pieces. She and Lamar returned from their simultaneous free-fall at the same time, and laughter shook them until they struggled to catch their respective breaths.

"What are you doing to me?" she whispered in his ear.

"Loving your life, babe. I can't wait until we can go to bed and wake up together."

Nydia kissed his ear. "It's going to happen," she said confidently.

"Do you want a long or short engagement?"

"I think I'd like a rather short one."

"How short, sweets?"

"Probably about six months. Anything longer would make me crazy. I want something very simple with just friends and family."

"Would you want to hold it here or in New Orleans?"

A beat passed. "New Orleans. I'd like to hold it in the garden at the DuPont Inn. Of course the Toussaints will do the catering, and we can spend our wedding night in the bridal suite at the Louis LaSalle."

Lamar breathed a kiss on her scalp. "That sounds good. What about a honeymoon?"

"Have you even been to Puerto Rico?"

"No."

"Even though it's still recovering from Hurricane Maria, we can help the economy if we honeymoon there."

"I'm willing to go along with whatever you want. I believe in the expression: happy wife, happy life."

"You may come to regret those words."

"I doubt that."

Lamar rolled off Nydia, lay beside her, and threaded their fingers together. The minutes ticked into an hour before they got up, shared a shower, and then left the apartment.

CHAPTER 23

Nydia and Lamar were forced to abandon their plan to drive to Brooklyn when it began snowing at the rate of an inch an hour. So, after picking up the mail at the West Harlem brownstone, they headed back to White Plains. Every television channel aired breaking news about the winter storm predicted to dump more than two feet of snow on the state, and many officials were warning motorists to stay off the road. It was Christmas Day, and there was light vehicular traffic, so they made it back in record time.

Nydia changed into a pair of sweats and assisted Sandra in the kitchen baking cookies, while Lamar joined the others in the basement as they watched Christmas-themed movies most had seen before.

"Did you make up with Lamar?" Sandra asked as she slipped golden brown cookies on a rack to cool.

"Yes, we did."

"So when's the big day?"

Nydia gave her sister-in-law a sidelong glance as she squeezed the lever on the cookie press to release heart-shaped dough onto a parchment-lined cookie sheet. "We haven't set a date."

"So, you will be getting married?"

She nodded. "Yes."

Sandra hugged her. "Good. I'm not going to say another thing about you and Lamar until you call and tell me you're officially engaged."

Nydia smiled. "Thank you." She finished filling the tray and handed it off to Sandra. "I can't believe you've become so domesticated. You're spending more time in the kitchen than you do in your office."

Sandra closed the door to the eye-level double oven. "It's the first time I've been able to balance career and motherhood. Working from home two days a week has made me aware of how much more energy I have to devote to Nelson and the girls. They love it when I get up and make breakfast for them, and I'm home when they get off the school bus. This is not to say they don't love their great-grandmother, but they claim they like having me home."

Sitting on a stool at the cooking island,

Nydia rested her elbows on the countertop. "Are you hinting that you want to become a stay-at-home mother?"

"I can't afford that now. Nelson and I are saving money for the girls' college education, and running a house this size isn't cheap. I usually commute into the city with a woman who lives in Mount Vernon and went to Brooklyn Law with me, and we've been talking about setting up a family law practice together."

Sandra's revelation piqued Nydia's interest. "You're really considering going into business for yourself?"

The lawyer's dark eyes twinkled when she smiled. "I'm seriously thinking about it. You and your mother are female entrepreneurs, so I want to round out the trifecta of Santiago women operating their own businesses."

"I must admit I feel a lot more secure knowing I won't come in one morning and be handed a pink slip. When do you think you'll open your own office?"

"I'm thinking about five years. By that time Bree will be in college and Mimi a junior in high school, while yours truly will be turning forty."

"That's the advantage of having your children in your early twenties."

Sandra checked on the cookies in the oven. "I really hadn't planned on having babies while I was still going to law school, but now when I look back I don't regret it. Speaking of babies, do you and Lamar plan to have any?"

"We haven't talked about it."

"Do you want children?" Sandra asked.

Nydia pondered the question for a moment. "If I marry Lamar, then I'll have a daughter."

"That's not what I'm talking about and you know it, Nydia. Do you want to have a baby with him?"

A mysterious smile softened her mouth as she stared across the kitchen at the television mounted under a row of cabinets. The crawl on the bottom of the screen indicated the governor had declared a state of emergency. "Yes. I'd like to have at least one."

Sandra glanced at the television before she removed the cookie sheet from the oven. "What's going to happen if your Broadway show is cancelled tomorrow? Will you lose your money?"

"No," Nydia replied. "When I ordered the tickets I also added cancellation insurance and gave instructions that the tickets would be picked up at the box office." She didn't tell Sandra that Lamar had reimbursed her for the cost of the tickets.

"Good for you."

The week in New York had passed all too quickly for Lamar. A snowstorm had scrapped Nydia's plan to take the girls into Manhattan for a Broadway show, but they didn't seem to mind as they huddled together watching movies, playing board games, and sledding down the hill leading from the house. He got to see another side of his daughter as she interacted with girls she'd just met, and he marveled how quickly she was able to bond with them.

Once the roads were cleared Luis and Isabel drove back to the city. Nelson's vacation was cut short when he was ordered back to work by his precinct commander. Once the airports were up and running and flights were resumed, he accompanied Nydia to drop her brother Joaquin and his family off at LaGuardia for their return trip to Omaha, Nebraska. During the drive back to White Plains they had stopped to eat at a restaurant in City Island to make up for the one he'd promised during his first visit to rescue her from the frenzied paparazzi.

It was three weeks since Lamar and Kendra left New York for New Orleans, and Lamar had taken Kendra to their favorite

Italian restaurant. The waiter had just set down their orders when his cell phone rang. Kendra peered over at the screen. "It's Miss Nydia," she said in sing-song.

"Thank you, Miss Pierce."

Kendra rolled her eyes upward. "Whatever, Daddy. You can talk to her in front of me."

Lamar glared at his daughter before he averted his eyes. "Hello."

"Surprise! I'm back!"

He went completely still. "For good."

"Yes!"

"When did you get in?"

"Yesterday morning."

Lamar didn't want to believe she'd waited more than twenty-four hours to inform him she had moved to New Orleans, even though they'd continued to call each other several times a week. "Where are you staying?"

"I'm staying with Cameron and Jasmine. They put me up in the guest wing of their beautiful new home. I suppose you would know about that because your construction company did the renovations. She just had her cast removed, so I'm helping her out for a while."

"You're a good friend."

There came a beat before Nydia's voice

came through the earpiece again. "Why do you sound so condescending?"

"I'm not being condescending, Nydia."

There came another pause. "How's Kendra?"

"She's good."

"Tell her I'll call her and we'll set up a playdate. I'm meeting with Tonya and Hannah tomorrow to plan a surprise baby shower for Jasmine. So look for an invite."

"Where are you hosting it?"

"It's going to be at Cameron's parents' house. They always have a monthly Sunday family dinner, so we're going to use that as an excuse to get her there, even though she has been complaining about not wanting to go out in public because she's so close to her due date."

"When is she due?"

"Sometime around the first week in February."

"That's only two weeks."

"That's why we have to work fast."

Lamar smiled. "There's no doubt that between you, Tonya, and Hannah you'll be able to pull it off."

"I'm praying we will. She doesn't have a baby registry so we're going to put together a layette and give her gift cards so she can buy whatever she wants. I think I hear her, so I'll talk to you later."

"Okay. I'll tell Kendra what you said." Lamar ended the call and watched his daughter staring at him. "Miss Nydia has officially moved to New Orleans, and she said she's going to call you in a few days to set up a playdate."

Kendra grinned. "I really had a lot of fun with her family in New York."

Lamar smiled. "I did, too." He pointed to her plate. "Finish your food, young lady."

Kendra picked up her fork. "When are we going back to New York, Daddy?"

He stared at her from under lowered lids. "Maybe around the spring break."

"Can we bring Taylor and Morgan? I'm certain they would like Bree and Mimi, too."

Lamar shook his head. "You're definitely getting ahead of yourself. Spring is still a few months away, and a lot of things can happen in that time."

"What, Daddy?"

He thought about his relationship with Nydia. He didn't know if they would be engaged, but he knew for certain they wouldn't be married by that time. "I don't know," Lamar answered truthfully.

Kendra kept up a running commentary about three boys in her science class who'd changed the labels on several chemicals that resulted in a small fire that caused the school to be evacuated, and ended with them being suspended for a week. "I heard they may be expelled."

"That's a lesson for everyone. If you do something that might hurt yourself or others, then your actions have consequences."

"I know, Daddy," Kendra drawled. "You tell me that all of the time."

"Just make certain you believe it."

"I do," she drawled again. "I can't eat any more. Can I take this home?"

Lamar stared at the veal Milanese and spaghetti Pomodoro on Kendra's plate. She'd barely touched her dinner. "Of course. Are you feeling okay?"

She nodded. "I'm good."

He signaled their waiter and asked that he pack up his daughter's plate. "I guess you don't want dessert."

"Not tonight."

Lamar hoped his daughter wasn't coming down with something, because she had never been a picky eater. He settled the bill and led her to his car. She was monosyllabic on the way home, and he remembered Nydia telling him that Kendra's hormones were in flux and could be responsible for her occasional mood swings.

"It's the weekend, so you should sleep in

late tomorrow," he told her once they were home.

Kendra nodded. "Okay. Good night, Daddy."

He smiled. "Good night, baby girl."

Lamar tossed his car fob in a small sweetgrass basket on the table in the entryway. Ramona had taken the weekend off, so it was just he and Kendra until Sunday night. He didn't know why, but he felt a strange restlessness that wouldn't permit him to completely relax.

He'd spent the entire day in the office, which probably added to his angst. Earlier in the week he'd visited all of the construction sites and found nothing amiss. The city inspectors had given Hannah the okay to resume work on the installation of the elevator at the inn and he'd found a company willing to do the work. As soon as they forwarded a copy of an updated insurance policy to the city, then they would be issued a work permit to begin.

It was too early to turn in for the night, and Lamar decided to go into the family room and watch reruns of a number of football games he'd missed. He hadn't realized he'd dozed off until he heard the doorbell. He walked to the door and peered through the security eye and saw Nydia staring back at him.

"What's the matter?" he asked when opening the door.

"Kendra called me."

Lamar didn't realize his heart was racing. "What for?"

Nydia pushed past him. "Female business."

"What the hell?" he whispered. Nydia was halfway up the staircase before he understood what she'd said. His hands were shaking as he closed and locked the door. It was apparent his daughter was now physically a woman.

Nydia found Lamar in the kitchen holding a glass of what appeared to be liquor. "Are you celebrating or feeling frightened that your little girl is now a woman?"

Lamar gave her what she thought of as the death stare. "Why didn't she tell me?"

Nydia filled an electric kettle with water and flicked it on. "Maybe she didn't feel comfortable talking to you about the changes going on in her body."

"And she felt comfortable with you?"

Turning slowly, she stared at Lamar as if he'd suddenly taken leave of his senses. "Of course. In case you haven't noticed, I am a woman."

"She's discussed this with you before?"

Crossing her arms over her chest, Nydia exhaled a breath. "Yes. We don't just talk about cooking. She told me the health teacher at her school discussed menstruation with the girls, so she knew what to expect. But it's not until it happens that it becomes a reality. When she called me I stopped by the drugstore to pick up the feminine products she needs because she said she misplaced the starter kit she got in school. By the way, can she take Tylenol?"

Lamar nodded. "Yes. Why?"

"She's a little headachy and she's also complaining about cramps. I'm going to make her a cup of tea, give her a Tylenol, and stay with her until she falls asleep."

Lamar ran a hand over his face. "I suppose I should've been ready for this."

"You couldn't be ready, because no one can pinpoint when a girl begins her menses. My father told me it was easier for him to accept his sons' becoming men than his daughter physically becoming a woman."

Taking three steps, Lamar pulled Nydia into the circle of his embrace. "Thank you for being here."

Leaning back, she stared up at Lamar, seeing indecision in his eyes. "You don't have to thank me, Lamar. Kendra is going to be my daughter when I marry you, and that means I'm here for the duration."

"That means both of us are very lucky."

"That makes three of us."

Not seeing Lamar for three weeks had allowed Nydia time to assess her future, and she knew unequivocally that she wanted to marry him. She'd thought Valentine's Day would be the perfect day to announce their engagement, but that was nearly a month away.

"I guess you can say we're a package deal," Lamar said, smiling.

"One for all and all for one." She laughed. Nydia pulled away from him. "The water is ready." It took her less than five minutes to add honey to a large mug and then fill it with hot water, a tea bag, and then a sliver of lemon before removing the bag. She also filled a glass of water from the indoor refrigerator and went upstairs.

Kendra was sitting up in bed, her back supported by a mound of pillows, with her eyes closed. The diamond studs her father had given her for Christmas sparkled in her pierced lobes. At that moment the girl appeared so much younger than eleven.

"Kendra, can you swallow pills?"

She opened her eyes. "Yes."

Nydia sat on the side of the bed. "I'm going to give you a Tylenol to help you with your headache." She handed the girl the glass of water and shook a gel out of the bottle and into her outstretched hand, watching and waiting for her to swallow it and follow with the water. "The tea is still a little hot, so wait until it cools before you attempt to drink it. I'm going to sit on the window seat until you fall asleep. I'll call you tomorrow to see how you're doing, so let me know if you need me."

Kendra managed a small smile. "Thank you."

Nydia kissed her forehead before she walked across the bedroom to the window seat. Reaching into her tote, she took out the magazine dedicated to southern living she'd purchased in the airport and settled down to read an article about comfort food classics. As a transplanted New Yorker she wanted to absorb as much as she could about her new home state.

She didn't have to wait long for Kendra to fall asleep. Nydia left the window seat and pulled the sheet and lightweight blanket over the girl's shoulders. She never would have imagined that at thirty-three she would claim an eleven-year-old daughter. And she didn't want Kendra to relate to her as her stepmother, but her mother. Nydia knew she would never be able to replace Valerie and would never attempt to fill the void left by the woman's death, but she wanted to be there and support Kendra until adulthood.

Nydia returned to the kitchen to find Lamar leaning against the countertop with a cup of coffee. "She's sleeping." He stood straight, his light brown eyes meeting hers. "I'd like for you to wait until Jasmine has her baby to talk to Kendra about us getting married."

A slight frown appeared between his eyes. "Why wait?"

"I don't want the news of our engagement to throw shade on Jasmine and Cameron's big event."

Lamar nodded. "When do you want to make the announcement?"

A smile parted her lips. "What do you think of Valentine's Day?"

His smile matched hers. "That's perfect. When do you want to go and look at rings?"

Nydia rested a hand on his forearm. "Easy there, sport. We have time."

"What's your ring size?"

"Five."

Lamar's smile grew wider. "I think I can remember that."

Going on tiptoe, Nydia kissed him, inhaling and tasting coffee on his lips. "Come walk me to the door." Lamar took her hand, lacing their fingers together. It was a new year, she now lived in a new state, and in the coming month she would become a fiancée.

She opened the door to Jasmine's minivan, slid in behind the wheel, and waved to Lamar as he stood on the sidewalk waiting for her to drive away. He returned her wave as Nydia checked her mirrors and pulled away from the curb. She liked driving the vehicle and knew it was only matter of time before she had to purchase a car to get around the city. And Nydia realized she couldn't live with Jasmine and Cameron, nor would she move in with Lamar before they were married, and living with Hannah or Tonya was not an option. And the inn wasn't ready for her to move in there. That meant she would check back into the Louis LaSalle until she married.

Nydia stared at the rain sluicing down the windows in the hospital's waiting room. When she'd mentioned to Cameron that she was moving out and checking into the hotel, she got to see another side of the wealth manager who always appeared so calm and in control of everything. He told her in no uncertain terms that she couldn't leave his wife now that she was so close to giving birth to her baby. He told her that Jasmine had come to emotionally depend on Nydia more than she did on him. This revelation had shocked her because she hadn't been aware of any tension between the couple, who appeared to be very much in love, but then she did not know what went on between them behind closed doors. In the end she agreed to stay, up to and including the time when they baptized the baby.

Nydia enjoyed living in the renovated warehouse designed ultimately for living and entertaining. Cameron had hired a cook and house- and groundskeepers, which meant there was little for Jasmine to do except relax and count down the days to when she would become a mother. Most mornings and afternoons found them relaxing and taking their meals in the loggia, where a man-made waterfall and tropical foliage turned the rear of the house into a jungle oasis.

The baby shower had come off without a hitch. When she and Cameron escorted Jasmine into the elder Singletons' home and she saw the expression on Jasmine's face, Nydia knew her friend was totally shocked. Jasmine, not wanting to know the sex of her baby beforehand, had decorated the nursery in green and yellow pastels.

The invitees had presented her with gift cards, car seats, crib sheets and blankets, dozens of onesies, bibs, bath products, sweaters, hats, booties, and colorful and musical crib mobiles. Everyone dissolved into hysterics when Cameron's brothers gave him a clothespin and more than ten cartons of disposable diapers in sizes ranging from newborn to toddler.

Tonya and Gage had commandeered the kitchen to prepare a buffet feast that had everyone complaining that they had eaten much too much. The children were relegated to another part of the mansion once the adults were served potent libations, and the ribald jokes flowed as freely as the lethal concoctions.

During the celebrating Nydia had watched Lamar staring at her, and she wondered if he was recalling the time when his wife was pregnant with Kendra. She was still ambivalent about giving Lamar another child, because when she married him she planned to embrace Kendra as her own. And raising a teenage girl, especially one who'd known and lost her biological mother, wasn't going to be an easy endeavor. Being an aunt was wholly different than stepping into the role as mother, confidante, consoler, and occasionally disciplinarian. Nydia regarded herself as fun-loving and easygoing. She would encourage debate, but knew unequivocally she would never entertain disrespect, especially not from a child.

"Nydia, she had a girl."

She turned and stared at Cameron. He looked as if he had been the one to go through labor; she noticed lines of tension bracketing his mouth and red, swollen eyes that indicated he'd been crying.

"How is she?"

He ran his fingers through his gray-flecked light brown hair. "She's good. The baby is beautiful."

Nydia hugged the new father. "Of course she would be. Have you decided on a name?"

"We agreed to Sabrina Maya Singleton."

"That's a name for an actress."

Taking a handkerchief from the pocket of his slacks, Cameron dabbed his eyes. "It does sound rather dramatic for a tiny six-pound, two-ounce baby."

"I know you want to spend some time with your wife and daughter, so I'm going to call a taxi and go back to the house." Cameron had given her a key and the code to the security system.

"Don't bother. I'll take you back, because

I'd like to clean up a bit before returning."

Nydia only nodded, though she wanted to tell the normally dapper new father that he did look a hot mess with a wrinkled shirt and slacks he'd hastily pulled on when Jasmine woke him to say she was experiencing labor pains. When he knocked on the door to her room to tell Nydia that he was taking Jasmine to the hospital, she told him that she was coming with him.

He'd driven like a maniac while Nydia sat in the second row of seats in the minivan with Jasmine attempting to keep her calm as the pains increased with each passing minute. She had to shout to him to slow down or they would never make it, and in the end they were able to make it to the emergency entrance to the hospital without an accident. The staff was waiting at the door to place Jasmine on a stretcher and wheel her into the labor room.

Now, after the baby had made her entrance into the world, Nydia held out her hand. "I'll drive back." Cameron dropped the fob in her hand, and together they walked out of the hospital and into the cold February rain.

CHAPTER 24

"Kendra, please give me the dishes on the table so I can finish loading the dishwasher," Ramona Griffin said softly.

"Come and get them yourself."

Lamar walked into the kitchen in time to hear his daughter's acerbic reply. "What did you say?"

Kendra glared at him. "I said she can come and get them herself. There's nothing wrong with her hands or feet."

He did not want to believe she would repeat the disrespectful remark. "Get up and put the dishes in the sink, then I want you to go to your room and stay there." Kendra popped up and stacked the dishes and dropped them in the sink, and then stalked out of the kitchen. Lamar shook his head. "I'm sorry, Ramona. I don't know what has gotten into her lately, but I intend to find out. This is the last time she will disrespect an adult in this house."

"It's all right, Lamar. She's just going through a phase and —"

"It's not all right," he countered, cutting her off. "No child of mine will act disrespectful as long as he or she resides under my roof. So consider this the last time it will happen."

Lamar left the kitchen and took the staircase to the second story and knocked on the door to Kendra's room. "Open the door."

"No!" came her reply.

He tried the knob and found the door locked. "Unlock the door, Kendra."

"No!"

Lamar raised his foot to kick the door in but changed his mind. He had no intention of damaging his property because of a surly adolescent. Retracing his steps, he went to a room where he kept a toolbox and returned with a drill. It took less than three minutes to remove the doorknob and he walked into the bedroom to find Kendra standing staring at him as if she had never seen him before. Her eyes were filled with fear.

"I want you to apologize to Miss Ramona."

"No, Daddy. She always orders me around."

He struggled to control his temper. Lamar

570

picked up the drill and removed the hinges from the door, and placed the door against a wall. "The door stays off until you come to your senses and apologize to Miss Ramona. And if I ever hear something like that coming out of your mouth again you'll be grounded until you're old enough to leave my house. I don't intend to subject Nydia to your freshness once I marry her."

"I don't want you to marry her. I hate her!"

Lamar did not intend to argue with an eleven-year-old. "The door stays off!"

He walked into his home office and closed the door, unable to understand why his daughter had gone from a sweet, affectionate girl to an angry, impudent person he did not recognize. "I don't give a *fuck* about hormones," he swore under his breath.

Once Jasmine gave birth, he and Nydia had agreed he should tell Kendra that they were planning to marry. At first his daughter seemed happy with the news, and then like quicksilver she changed, becoming more solemn each day until today's verbal barrage. Lamar knew he had to put his house in order before inviting Nydia into a hostile environment that was destined to end in divorce.

■ ■ ■ ■

Nydia parked her leased Corolla hatchback on the street in front of Lamar's house and walked through the porte cochère and into the courtyard. It had been raining off and on for more than a week and daytime temperatures were cool enough for her to wear several layers. She and Lamar had planned to shop for rings before they officially announced their engagement, and she had offered to pick him up.

The door opened before she could ring the bell, and Lamar pulled her inside. "I didn't want to tell you on the phone, but I've been going through hell with Kendra."

Nydia removed her wool jacket and hung it on a peg in the entryway. "What's going on?"

"She talked back to Ramona, and when I told her to go to her room she locked the door and wouldn't let me in. So I took the damn thing off the hinges until she apologizes."

Nydia blinked once. She did not want to believe what she'd just heard and headed for the staircase. "I hope you're kidding. How long has she been without a door?" she asked Lamar when he followed her up.

"No, I'm not kidding. I'll put it back when she apologizes and not before."

Nydia headed for Kendra's bedroom and saw the door resting on its side against the wall. "What's the hell is wrong with you, Lamar!" she shouted. "She's a young woman and you're disrespecting her right to privacy."

"Damn privacy when she disrespects my home and my rules."

She looked into the room to find Kendra sitting on the window seat, staring back at her. "Put the door back on, Lamar," she said in a quiet voice.

"I will not," he countered angrily.

Going on tiptoe, Nydia put her mouth close to his ear. "Put that fucking door back on or I'll walk out of here and never come back."

"No, Miss Nydia!" Kendra screamed. "You can't leave me!"

Nydia heard the panic in the child's voice. She had lost one mother and she suspected Kendra viewed her as a surrogate mother. "I'm not leaving, but your father is when he goes and gets the tools he needs to put up the door." She walked into the room and took the girl's hands. They were cold as ice. "Come, baby, let's get into bed so we can talk." She turned to glare at Lamar. "May we please have some privacy?" Waiting until he left, she pulled Kendra over to the bed. She removed her shoes and lay atop the quilt and patted the side of the mattress. "Get in and tell me what's bothering you."

Holding the child, Nydia listened intently as Kendra told her about the fight she'd had with her mother hours before she was killed and how she subsequently blamed herself for Valerie's death. Kendra also admitted she resented her mother going away for days at a time when other kids always had their mothers every day.

"I told Daddy I hated you but I really don't. I love you, Miss Nydia, but I'm so afraid of losing you."

Nydia kissed the girl's forehead. Kendra smelled wonderful. She'd given her a gift basket of scented body wash, lotion, and matching spray cologne to celebrate her becoming a woman. "I'm not going anywhere. You saw how old my grandmother is, and that means I'll live at least until eighty or older. By that time I hope you'll make me a grandmother or even a great-grandmother."

Kendra giggled. "Why do the kids in your family call your mother Abuela and your grandmother Abuelita?"

"That's to tell the difference between the two."

A beat passed. "Are you really going to marry my father?"

"I want to marry your father, but that's not going to happen if the three of us are fighting with one another."

"I don't want to fight with you, Miss Nydia."

"This is not all about me, Kendra. Just because you're upset with something or someone you can't say things to people — adults in particular — that put you in a bad light. I used to talk back to my mother and spent almost my entire teenage years grounded. I believed I was asserting myself when in fact I was being rude and insolent, which I'm now ashamed of.

"I know you won't agree with everything your father says, but you have to know he loves you and only wants the best for you. And when I marry him I will support whatever decision he makes for you, so don't think you'll be able to pit me against him. I only challenged him to put back the door because as a young woman you're entitled to your privacy. Now I want you to apologize to him and Miss Ramona for your behavior, because I don't want my daughter to develop a reputation for challenging authority."

"I'm your daughter?"

Nydia smiled when she saw an expression of shock cross Kendra's delicate features. "Of course you're my daughter."

Her eyes lowered. "Does this mean I can call you Mom?"

Nydia gathered her close. "Of course you can."

"Now or when you marry Daddy?"

"You can start now, so I can get used to it. Now, I want you to go and apologize to your father and Miss Ramona. I'll be here when you get back." Nydia left the bed, sat on the window seat, and stared out the window overlooking the courtyard. Somehow she had averted a major crisis that could have resulted in her walking out on the man she loved beyond description.

"What did you say to her?"

She shifted and saw Lamar standing in the doorway with a drill in one hand. "It was just girl talk."

He set the drill on the floor and closed the distance between them. "So, it's going to be like that?"

Nydia's eyes made love to his handsome face. "Yes. What goes on between me and my daughter stays between us."

Lamar sat beside her. "Will it be the same

for me and my son if we have a boy?"

Nydia laced their fingers together. "So, you want another child?"

"Of course I do," he said, giving her an incredulous look. "Did you think I'd marry you and deprive you of children?"

Her eyebrows lifted. "Children, Lamar?"

"Of course, sweets," he said. "If it's all right with you, I'd like to have at least two more."

Nydia rested her head on his shoulder. "If that's the case, then we have to start baby making on our wedding night. I'll be thirty-four in July and after we have the first one my biological clock will begin ticking."

"Not to worry, my love. Maybe you'll have twins, which means we'll have two for the price of one."

"Bite your tongue, Lamar. Can you see me carrying a couple of babies? I'll probably look like someone who swallowed a whole watermelon."

Lamar buried his face in her hair. "You'll look incredibly beautiful. You really shocked me when you came at me like a rabid lioness protecting her cub," he said after a comfortable silence. "That's when I knew you really love Kendra."

"Of course I love her, Lamar. She's my daughter."

"Once I put the door on we'll leave and look at rings. Have you decided what you want?"

"I'd like something in rose gold to match my bracelet." Nydia planned to wear Jasmine's wedding gift at Sabrina's baptism and Lamar's Christmas gift to her for their wedding.

"I want you to remember one thing, Nydia. I will try and give you whatever you want."

She smiled. "You may come to regret those words."

"Nunca, mi amor."

"Haven't you heard never to say never?" Nydia whispered as she brushed a light kiss over his mouth.

"No. Now you're going to have to let me know when you want to get married."

"May," Nydia said without hesitation.

"That's less than three months."

Nydia smiled. "I can count, Mr. Pierce. We'll just have a short engagement. Jasmine dated Cameron for the first time in May, and by August she was Mrs. Cameron Singleton."

"Don't tell me you're competing with your fellow innkeeper?"

"There's no competition between any of us. I just don't want to get married in the summer with the heat and humidity. And Hannah projects the inn will be open for business by that time. I'll let her know that I want to hold the ceremony in the garden and the reception in the ballroom. I'll also see if she can set aside most of the eighteen rooms in the inn for our out-of-town guests."

"My mother, sister, and her family can stay here."

"Who are you going to select as your best man?"

"Cameron. And I'd like my partners to be my groomsmen."

"I suppose I'll have to select two bridal attendants. I want Jasmine to be my maid of honor and my sister-in-law Sandra and Kendra will be my attendants."

Kendra reentered the bedroom, grinning from ear-to-ear. "Miss Ramona said she and I are cool."

Nydia moved over to allow Kendra to sit between her and Lamar. "Your dad and I are planning to marry in May, and I'd like you to be one of my attendants."

"Really?"

"Yes really, Kendra."

"I get to wear a gown?"

Nydia gently tugged on her ponytail. "Yes, Kendra, you'll get to wear a gown and look like a princess."

Kendra clasped her hands together in a prayerful gesture. "Thank you, Mom."

Nydia met Lamar's puzzled expression over Kendra's head. It was obvious he hadn't known she had given the girl permission to address her as if she were her mother. "Let's go downstairs and see if Miss Ramona needs help with something while Daddy fixes your door."

Hand in hand they left the bedroom, and Nydia knew the day signaled a new beginning in her. She had also selected the month of May to marry because it would commemorate two years since she'd walked into the offices of Wakefield Hamilton and was informed that she no longer had a position with them. She planned to marry Lamar and push out a couple of babies before turning forty.

So many things had happened since that momentous day, and when she looked back it wasn't with regret. She'd come to the Big Easy and fallen in love with the city and one of its native sons. She didn't know what it was about the men from New Orleans, but three Big Apple divas had been given a second chance at love in a city with nonstop music, food, and drink.

And when Hannah invited her, Tonya, and

Jasmine to become innkeepers it had changed all of their lives forever.

Three months later

Nydia rested her right hand on the sleeve of her father's suit jacket as he led her down the flower-strewn path to where Lamar stood with Cameron and his groomsmen. He looked incredibly handsome in his tuxedo with the sky blue silk vest that was an exact match to his bow tie. He and his groomsmen wore sprigs of lavender as their boutonnieres.

They'd officially announced their engagement on February fourteenth, and it began with invitations to social events where she did not know a single person. Now she knew how Jasmine felt when linked to the Singletons, who along with the DuPonts were counted as New Orleans's elite. The Pierces could trace their ancestry back nearly two hundred years as free people of color, and she found herself smiling and engaging in conversation with those who were familiar with Lamar's father.

It was early May when the DuPont Inn opened for business, and many of the city's officials attended the ribbon cutting ceremony that was followed with an invitation-only sit-down luncheon at Toussaints. The food critic had written a review of the affair in the local newspaper and predicted the restaurant would someday be listed as one of the best in the city.

The week before, Jasmine and Cameron had baptized Sabrina at the same parish where countless Singletons had been baptized, and the little baby with inky black hair and dark blue-gray eyes slept through the entire ceremony.

Nydia had felt she was on a runaway roller coaster with fittings, doing payroll for her New York clients, and maintaining the financial records for the inn, so Lamar hired a wedding planner to take care of every detail of the ceremony and the reception to follow.

The weather was perfect for a white wedding as she smiled when Lamar winked at her. As promised, they would spend their wedding night in the bridal suite at the Louis LaSalle and fly down to San Juan the following morning, and they would spend ten days island-hopping.

Luis Santiago placed his daughter's hand in Lamar's when he held it out to signal he would assume the responsibility for loving and protecting her for the rest of their lives. "Take care of my *pequeña muñeca*," he whispered to Lamar.

Lamar nodded. *"Lo haré con mi vida,"* he replied in the same language.

"Te amo, Papi," Nydia said to her father. She loved her father for asking Lamar to take care of his little doll, and Lamar had told him he would with his life. And she trusted the man who would become her husband to love, protect, and honor her all of their lives. She handed her bouquet of miniature white roses and violets to Jasmine. Her attendants were knockouts in gowns of varying blues ranging from royal to cornflower to lapis lazuli.

Nydia could not pull her eyes away from Lamar's as they repeated their vows. Every word she spoke was torn from her heart and she struggled not to cry. It all ended when the minister told Lamar he could kiss his bride.

His lips were warm and sweet on hers as he cradled her face. The intimacy of the joining made her weak in the knees as she clutched his wrists to maintain her balance.

Cameron tapped Lamar's shoulder. "Save some for tonight." The assembly burst into laughter when they overheard the best man's warning.

The minister laughed along with the others. "Ladies and gentlemen, I'm honored to introduce you to Mrs. and Mrs. Lamar

Abraham Pierce."

Nydia hugged Kendra and took her hand as she and Lamar processed over the flower petals where they would pose with the wedding party and family members for photographs before heading to the onsite restaurant for a sumptuous dinner prepared by the Toussaints.

Sunlight streaming through the branches of a towering tree fired the facets of the two-carat Asscher-cut diamond engagement ring set in rose gold on her right hand along with the Cartier bracelet on her wrist. She and Lamar had selected plain rose gold wedding bands that flattered their complexions.

She adjusted the skirt of her gown with its train of cascading ruffles on the back of the strapless silk satin sheath that added body and dimension and hinted at whimsical flirtation. She looked directly at the photographer as he snapped photos of her and her bridal attendants. Her mother had styled her hair in a mass of curls atop her head to add height to her diminutive stature and attached the waltz veil to a pearl-encrusted back piece.

"You did it, *chica*," Jasmine whispered in her ear. "*La princesa puertorriqueña* now has her prince."

Nydia smiled. "I believe all of the innkeepers have found their princes: St. John, Cameron, Gage, and now Lamar."

Hannah and Tonya joined them as they held hands and smiled from ear to ear. Hannah angled her platinum blond head. "I'd like to thank Wakefield Hamilton for having the good sense to downsize me along with my sisters and to allow us a second chance to find love and embark on a new career as innkeepers."

"Hear, hear," they agreed before dissolving into laughter.

Nydia knew when she returned from her honeymoon it would be to step into the roles of wife, mother, and innkeeper.

■ ■ ■ ■

RECIPES

■ ■ ■ ■

RECIPES

MOJITO
(GARLIC DIPPING SAUCE)

10 cloves garlic, peeled
1 teaspoon fine sea or kosher salt
1 medium Spanish onion, finely chopped
3/4 cup gently warmed olive oil
1/4 cup white vinegar
Juice of 1 each: lime, orange, and lemon
2 tablespoons cilantro (optional)

Pound the garlic and salt to a paste using a mortar and pestle. (Do not use a food processor.)

Stir in the onions, followed by the remaining ingredients.

Taste and add additional salt if needed.

You can make this up to three days in advance, and keep in the refrigerator.

Bring to room temperature 1 hour before serving.

Makes about 1 cup

SOFRITO

Sofrito is a seasoning that adds freshness and zing to dishes. You can use it to complement yellow rice, black bean soup, braised chicken, and sautéed shrimp.

2 medium Spanish onions, cut into large chunks
3 to 4 Italian frying peppers or cubanelle peppers
16 to 20 cloves garlic, peeled
1 large bunch cilantro, washed
7 to 10 ajices dulces (sweet peppers)
1 large red bell pepper, cored, seeded, and cut into large chunks

After all ingredients are rinsed and seeded, blend in small batches in either a food processor or blender.

Refrigerate in sealed container up to three days. Freeze extra in small containers.

Makes about 4 cups

TOSTONES
(TWICE FRIED GREEN
PLANTAIN CHIPS)

Green plantains
Salt
Canola Oil

Peel green plantains and slice into 1/2-inch thick rounds, and immediately soak in cold salted water. Pour enough canola oil into a skillet to fill to about 1 inch. Heat until the tip of the handle of a wooden spoon dipped in the oil gives off a faint sizzle (325° F).

Drain the plantain rounds and dry them thoroughly. Put as many of the plantain pieces into the oil as can fit without touching. Fry, turning once or twice, until fork tender, but not browned. If the plantains start to brown before they are tender, remove the pan from the heat, lower the heat, and wait a minute or two before returning the pan to the heat. Remove and drain on paper towels. Let cool 5 to 10 minutes or up to 2 hours.

Using a tostonera, or a kitchen mallet, or the broad side of a knife, whack the plantain slice so that it is smashed but still retains its shape.

To serve the plantains, reheat the oil until the tip of the handle of a wooden spoon dipped in the oil gives off a lively sizzle (360° F). Slip a batch of plantains into the hot oil and fry, turning once, until golden brown, about 4 minutes. Drain on paper towels.

Sprinkle with salt or top with mojito — garlic dipping sauce.

Each plantain yields about 20 chips

MOFONGO

1 pound salt pork
6 green plantains
6 garlic cloves, peeled
Vegetable oil
Olive oil
Salt and pepper to taste

Cut the salt pork through the skin into 1/2-inch slices. Turn the slices skin side down and cut through the fat to, but not through the skin at 1/2-inch intervals. Lay the slices on their sides in a cold skillet large enough to hold them all comfortably. Set the skillet over low heat. The salt pork will slowly render its own fat and then start to brown in the fat. The focus is to draw as much fat from the salt pork as possible, leaving behind crispy cracklings known as chicharrones. Remove the cracklings from the skillet with a slotted spoon and drain on paper towels. Chop the cracklings coarsely in a food processor. There should still be crispy-crunchy bits and more finely chopped bits. Discard the fat.

Peel the plantains and cut them into 1-inch lengths and cook them according to the recipe for twice-fried green plantain chips. Do not fry the plantains for the second time until just before you plan to serve the mofongo.

Using the vegetable oil, lightly grease twelve 4-ounce ramekins or custard cups. Working with half of the twice-fried plantains at a time, chop them coarsely in a food processor. Add half of the cracklings and garlic and enough olive oil to reach the correct consistency (similar to chewy sushi rice with a bit of crunch from the cracklings). Pulse the processor once or twice to mix. Repeat with the second batch. Taste and add salt and pepper if you like. Pack the mofongo lightly into the prepared molds. Invert onto serving plates. Serve immediately.

Makes 12 servings (Can be easily halved)

PERÑIL
(PUERTO RICAN ROAST PORK SHOULDER)

One 4-1/2–5-pound skin-on pork shoulder
Wet Rub

WET RUB — *Adobo Mojado*

12 cloves garlic, peeled
1-1/2 tablespoons fine sea or kosher salt
1 tablespoon black peppercorns
2 tablespoons dried oregano
2 tablespoons olive oil
2 tablespoons white wine vinegar

Up to 3 days before you serve the roast, set it in a bowl, skin side up. With a paring or boning knife, make several slits about 1-1/2 inches apart through the skin of the roast and into the meat. Make the slits as deep as you can. Wiggle a finger in the slits to open them up a bit and then fill each one with wet rub using a teaspoon. (Recommended: use a pair of latex gloves). Do the same on all sides. If you have rub left over, smear it all over the outside of the roast. Refrigerate, covered, at least 1 day or up to 3 days.

Preheat the oven to 450° F.

Set the roast, skin side up, on a rack in a roasting pan. Roast for 1 hour, turn the heat down to 400° F, and roast until the skin is a deep golden brown and crackly and with no trace of pink near the bone, for an additional 1-1/2 hours or until an instant-read thermometer inserted near the bone registers 160° F. Let the roast rest at least 15 minutes before carving.

To serve: Remove the crispy skin. It will pull right off in big pieces. Cut into smaller pieces with kitchen shears and pile them in the middle of the platter. Carve the meat parallel to the bones all the way down to the bone.

Makes 8 large servings plus leftovers

CUBANOS
(CUBAN SANDWICHES)

If you have a panini maker or grilled sandwich maker, this is when you should use it.

1 loaf Italian bread (about 24 inches long), or four hero rolls
Mayonnaise
Sliced leftover Roast Puerto Rican Pork Shoulder
3 fairly thick slices of boiled ham
Sliced bread and butter pickles
1/2 pound fairly thickly sliced Swiss cheese

Preheat the oven to 350° F. Split the bread lengthwise and spread the bottom of the loaf with mayonnaise. Make an even layer of the pork, then add the ham, pickles, and cheese. Top with the other piece of bread and press lightly but firmly.

Wrap the sandwich(es) securely in foil and lay between baking sheets. Set on the oven rack and weight the top sheet with a heavy ovenproof skillet. Bake until warmed through enough and the cheese has softened, about 30 minutes. Serve warm, cut into manageable pieces.

Makes 4 servings

CHICHARRONES DE POLLO
(CRISPY CHICKEN BITS)

1 1/2 pounds boneless skinless chicken
   thighs, cut into pinky-size strips
2 teaspoons Dry Rub
1 1/2 tablespoons cider or your favorite
   vinegar
Vegetable or canola oil
All-purpose flour

DRY RUB — *Adobo Seco*

6 tablespoons salt
3 tablespoons onion powder
3 tablespoons garlic powder
3 tablespoons ground black pepper
1-1/2 teaspoons ground oregano

Makes 1 cup

   Toss the chicken with the dry rub and the
vinegar until coated. Marinate, covered, at
room temperature up to 30 minutes in the

refrigerator or up to 1 day. Drain the chicken thoroughly.

Pour enough oil into a deep, heavy pot to fill to about 3 inches. Heat over medium-high heat until the tip of the handle of a wooden spoon dipped in the oil gives off a very lively sizzle (about 390° F).

While the oil is heating, dredge the chicken in the flour until coated. Tap off any excess flour. Once the oil is hot enough, carefully slip as many of the floured chicken pieces into the oil as will comfortably fit, turning them with a spoon once or twice, until deep golden brown and cooked through — about 4 minutes. Remove and drain on paper towels and repeat with the remaining chicken. Serve hot.

Makes 6 snack-size servings

ABOUT THE AUTHOR

Rochelle Alers has more than eighty titles and nearly two million copies of her novels in print. She is a regular on the bestseller lists, regularly chosen by Black Expressions Book Club, and has been the recipient of numerous awards, including the Emma Award, Vivian Stephens Award for Excellence in Romance Writing, the RT Book Reviews Career Achievement Award and the Zora Neale Hurston Literary Award. She is a member of Zeta Phi Beta Sorority, Inc., Iota Theta Zeta chapter and her interests include gourmet cooking and traveling. A full-time writer, Ms. Alers lives in a charming hamlet on Long Island.